"You are hu

"You would

"You surpris

"I am a thief, ~~~~~ ~~~ yourself."

"You are a thief, but you are nothing like me," she spat.

"Ah, yes. You must be a Guild thief," he sighed.

"Yes, and you are intruding upon Guild business, you freelance pig."

In a land filled with betrayal and sudden death, there must be some honor among thieves.

THE CROSSROADS SERIES

The Clandestine Circle
Mary H. Herbert

The Thieves' Guild
Jeff Crook

Dragons' Bluff
Mary H. Herbert
(Available July 2001)

CROSSROADS

The Thieves' Guild

JEFF CROOK

THE THIEVES' GUILD

©2000 Wizards of the Coast, Inc.

Cover art by Mark Zug
First Printing: December 2000
Library of Congress Catalog Card Number: 00-101968

9 8 7 6 5 4 3 2 1

US ISBN: 0-7869-1681-8
UK ISBN: 0-7869-2019-X
620-T21681

U.S., CANADA,   EUROPEAN HEADQUARTERS
ASIA, PACIFIC, & LATIN AMERICA   Wizards of the Coast, Belgium
Wizards of the Coast, Inc.   P.B. 2031
P.O. Box 707   2600 Berchem
Renton, WA 98057-0707   Belgium
+ 1-800-324-6496   + 32-70-23-32-77

Visit our web site at **www.wizards.com/dragonlance**

1. Theater Street
2. Horizon Road
3. New City
4. Vinus Solamnus Parkway
5. Old Temple District
6. Knights Candle Street
7. Market Street
8. Palace
9. Nobles Hill
10. Library
11. Old City Wall
12. Boulevard of Gold
13. Vingaard Road
14. Temple Road

Bay
of
Branchala

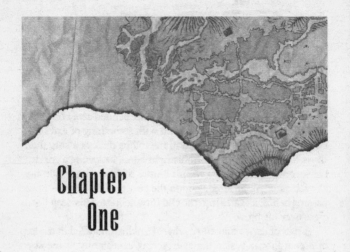

Chapter One

The citizens of the grandest of all Krynn's cities, Palanthas, City of Seven Circles, hurried along her lamp-hung streets, glancing worriedly above their heads as they rushed homeward from the markets and plazas, another day of bustling commerce at an end. Thoughts of supper and bed competed with worries about the weather and the prospects of arriving home soaked to the bone, for an ugly snarl of clouds hung over the city's rooftops, mumbling with thunder and crackling with lightning. Such violent, early-winter storms had become an all-too-common occurrence in the first years since the Chaos War, but this particular storm seemed to promise fresh surprises of fury and destruction.

The light glowing from the city's many thousands of lamps and lighted windows painted the lower tatters of the storm a leprous yellow-gray, while directly above the center of the city, almost touched by the spires of the Lord's Palace, a great

1

swirling wall of cloud had lowered threateningly from the base of the huge storm. An eerie, warm, moist wind rose from all circles of the city and began tumbling litter, dust, and sand down her centrally radiating, emptying streets. Into this rising wind stepped a lone figure, swathed in a heavy cloak despite the unseasonable warmth of the evening.

Though his back was bent and his face slanted away from the biting dust-laden breeze, he walked with something of a sailorly swagger, like a man more used to the rolling deck of a ship than the cobbles of a city street. In his right hand, he swung a gnarled black cane, marking time with it on the cobbles with a light tap at each step. As he strode across the street called Temple Row, passing before its gates into the Old City, he tugged his deep hood close over his brow.

A pair of dark-armored Knights of Takhisis huddled in the lee of a guardhouse beside the gate, gazing expectantly at the sky. With a start, they noticed his appearance, but as he simply crossed the street and entered the notoriously loathsome Smith's Alley, they let him pass without question. Instead, one rapped on the wall of the guardhouse, bringing a third Knight to the doorway. The three exchanged a few words. The third guard scratched something with a quill onto a slip of paper, and nodded.

The cloaked figure ignored them. As he entered the alley, the wind lessened somewhat. The buildings here, some of them almost as ancient the city itself, crowded close upon the narrow alleyway, shutting out all light and air. The center of the alley was worn into a deep track by two thousand years of weary treading, and down it trickled a slow noisome sump of sewage, rotting rinds of vegetables, grease, and offal. The resultant odor was stirred, albeit with some difficulty, by the rising wind, but not enough to rake the air clean of its offensive smell. No mere storm, no matter how furious, could cleanse this particular backwash of humanity. Only the sea rising in flood might hope to purge these cobbles of their ages of filth.

The man splashed across the alley with little more care than if it were a mountain brook. He muttered to himself, but not about what the alley's muck was doing to his boots, which were shoddy and heel-worn.

"A fine night," he grumbled to no one.

Smith's Alley was eerily quiet. No doubt a hundred watchful eyes, and perhaps even a few arrows, daggers, and sling stones, were trained upon his bent back. This was no place for the careless traveler. Few in the city of Palanthas, even its dreaded Knights of Takhisis, dared walked this street alone at night. Better to enter a dragon's yawning maw than turn your steps down Smith's Alley after dark. However, the man seemed to know exactly where he was going, and it was entirely possible that he belonged there. Certainly, the tattered condition of his cloak and the confidence in his stride marked him as a likely denizen of this place. As no knife winged its silent way from the shadows to quiver in his back, as had happened to so many intruders before him, the unseen watchers appeared willing to let him pass for the moment. He continued on his way as though heedless or unaware of any danger.

Perhaps the unseen watchers stayed their swift violent retribution because they thought him mad. "A fine night indeed!" he muttered again from beneath his hood.

He jerked to a stop, tilted an ear to listen, and gripped the cane tightly in his fist. Somewhere to his left, a long, low, moaning howl arose. Perhaps it was only the wind roaring through the alleyways of Palanthas, perhaps a dog crying in fright. "A bad omen," he snarled. "Nay! A good omen! A good omen for tonight's work."

As the howling rose to a quavering shriek, he continued on his way, the cane tapping out an eerie cadence in the long echoing alleyway. Somewhere behind him, a door slammed shut, while to his front a pair of ragged mongrels scurried from his path, snarling over their shoulders.

He stopped before a low, stout door set deeply into a wall of crumbling stone. He approached it, and with the gnarled cane he hammered on the door in a curious series of knocks— four, three rapid, two slow, then one as heavy as a hammer blow.

Without a sound, the door opened a crack, revealing only darkness beyond. "Who is it?" a harsh voice barked from within.

"A traveler from afar," the man said.

"Welcome, Avaril," the voice answered, this time more pleasantly. The door swung wide, and a lantern was uncovered, revealing a short figure with a long white beard poking through a green hood. "You are late. The goblin is afoot, they say."

The lantern in the dwarf's hand showed a small, low-ceilinged room half-filled with people. Many bore large heavy sacks or crates or chests, and as the dwarf stepped back to allow the man called Avaril to enter, some sighed visibly, while others returned blades to their sheaths. He surveyed the room as though looking for someone.

"Come in. Why are you standing out there?" the dwarf asked as he stepped into the alley and glanced quickly in both directions. "Strange things are moving, whispers of danger. It isn't safe. We are moving."

"Yes, I know my old friend," Avaril affirmed as the dwarf, finding the alleyway empty, turned back to the door. Perhaps some tingling premonition of danger warned the dwarf, for without even raising his eyes he ducked aside. The big man adjusted his swing and splintered the knobby cane over the dwarf's skull. Avaril snatched the lantern from the fallen dwarf's hand, spun, and flung it into through the doorway. As glass shattered and the lurid glare of flames leaped up, a kender sprang from the surprised crowd within the room and slammed the door shut before Avaril could jam it open with his broken cudgel. Shouts of anger, pain and surprise battled with the roaring of flames to fill the tiny room behind the door, while Avaril flung the cane at the door.

Seven Dark Knights rushed past Avaril. The black armored leader carried in his massive fists a huge iron hammer, which he used to smash the door to kindling. Behind him came six Knights of Takhisis with crossbows cocked and leveled. As the leader strode into the flames, the other six paused to loose their bolts into the room before drawing their swords and following.

Inside the chamber, the people dropped their bags, boxes, and crates and poured through every exit, up stairs, through windows. Archers waiting in the darkness outside murdered those who fled into the alley. The others were pursued and cut

4

down from behind. More Knights rushed in from the alley to join the chase and the slaughter, while others quickly gathered up the assorted boxes and crates and bags and carried them outside into the alley. What they couldn't move or didn't want, they smashed with hammers. The night was filled with the sounds of shattering glass and dying screams. Somewhere, an iron bell began to toll.

Meanwhile, Avaril dragged the dwarf across the alley and flung him on a heap of wet sawdust. He then settled himself onto one of the crates and watched the carnage. For a while, the screams of the dying continued. Knights rushed in and out of the building, and the pile of loot in the alley grew taller. Already, scribes and clerks of the Knights of Takhisis had gathered and begun to sort, count, and record the take, referring occasionally to Avaril about some item before adding it to their tally sheets. Teams of bearers, each heavily guarded by still more Knights, carted away the spoils as soon as each item was cleared by the clerks. Above the city, the storm had not yet broken, but every moment it promised to unleash its full fury.

* * * * *

The dwarf opened his eyes, blinking through the blood that had streamed from his cracked skull down across his face and soaked his beard. Across the alley from where he lay, weary Knights, gore up to their elbows, staggered from the blazing building that had once belonged to the Thieves' Guild of Palanthas. The upper floors were already consumed, but they had stamped out the fires on the lower floors in order to haul away the things stored there. Now, as the last two Knights exited the building, they paused at the doorway to fling their torches back into the room. Soon flames were licking around the door and windows. By the angry glow upon the clouds swirling overhead, it seemed that fires had sprung up all over the city.

By this light, the dwarf watched a peculiar conference take place near the loot pile. The bearers had already carried away most of the night's take, but a few choice selections had been left behind, carefully covered by a black tarp. Around this now lingered three men, their heads gathered close in whispered confidences.

The largest of the three was a good head taller than the smallest, but he wore a long, black cloak of the thickest wool, with a deep heavy cowl hiding his face. The next tallest of the three was a man easily recognized in any part of the city—a man with a face graven in stone, eyes like blue agates that shone even in the darkness of the alley. He was Sir Kinsaid, Knight of Takhisis and Lord Knight of the City of Palanthas. Though nominally a military advisor, he was the true ruler of the city. The third was a small man, dressed in wizard's robes of somber gray. His face was sharp, with an inquisitive nose and small eyes like chips of coal pressed into dough-colored flesh.

For a few moments the three were left alone, without their guards and clerks. The large figure knelt beside the pile of loot and, casting a surreptitious glance around, drew back one of the black coverings. The other two huddled over what he revealed. From his vantage, the dwarf couldn't see what so fascinated the three. Not that he much cared. He felt soft darkness closing in about him once again. He relaxed, and gazed at the sky above him.

The wall of the building beside him towered four stories into the Palanthian sky, and in its great age and dilapidation it seemed to lean perilously, as though about to fall. A few dark windows glowered over the alleyway, but most had long since been boarded up. However, from one of these empty windows the dwarf watched a coil of rope suddenly appear. Though dyed as black as sable, its silhouette stood out against the low, fire lit clouds. Silently, it unwound as it descended to the alley below, stretching to its full length a few inches from the dwarf's nose. He cursed in surprise, throwing up his arms to ward off the rope.

The three men spun round, startled from their gloating. A sword flashed in the mailed fist of Sir Kinsaid, while a cocked crossbow appeared in the hands of the gray-robed man. The third drew no weapon, but stared from beneath his hood.

"Who goes there?" Sir Kinsaid challenged.

The short man lowered his crossbow. "It is only the door-warden," he laughed. "He is still alive. Dwarven skulls are notoriously thick."

No one seemed to notice the black rope dangling just above the dwarf's head.

"I'll soon mend that, Sir Arach," the man in the black robes said to his small companion. "He can identify me."

At these words, the dwarf came fully and starkly awake. He struggled to move, but found that his legs would not move. He clawed desperately at the sawdust, a strangled cry of rage choking him.

"You dog!" he wept impotently into his beard. "You betrayed us!" He crawled free of the sawdust mound and dragged his frail, broken frame over the slimy cobbles, unaware of the dark figure that had slid down the rope behind him. The three ignored his cries. "You betrayed us!" the dwarf screamed.

"Captain Avaril has betrayed many in his time," snarled the figure behind him.

Again, Sir Kinsaid spun, his gleaming steel blade leaping in his hand. Sir Arach Jannon produced his crossbow. The black-robed Captain Avaril rose, his hands clenched into ham-sized fists.

A dark figure dropped from a window across the alley, a third appeared from behind a pile of empty crates, two others crawled from a sewer grate that appeared barely wide enough to admit a rat. More advanced from the shadows from either end of the alley. They wore uniforms of black cloth, loosely woven and stitched to allow full range of movement and maximum capacity for secreting tools and weapons. Their faces were hidden by swaths of a similar dark material, but above these masks dark eyes gleamed with hatred.

Soon, a black ring of death, a ring edged with gleaming steel, surrounded the three men. Like warriors long accustomed to battle, they placed themselves back to back, facing the opponents who edged closer every moment. The raging inferno behind them lit the scene in a lurid glare, which was augmented startlingly by frequent flashes of lightning. The dwarf lay within the closing circle of foes, confused, fainting with pain, burning with frustration.

"Daavyd Nelgard," Sir Kinsaid growled. "Master of the Thieves' Guild of Palanthas. Here is a prized fish your nets failed to catch, Sir Arach."

"Nay, my lord. The net draws round them even as we speak. This was not unforeseen," the gray-robed man said, a sly smile twisting his narrow face.

The dark figure that had dropped behind the dwarf stepped into the light of the fire. He jerked the mask from his face and the hood from his head, revealing an unruly mane of matted black hair surrounding a dark face made darker by his rage.

"Aye," he growled. "The net draws tight. You are caught in it." He flung back his short cloak and swept out a scimitar that caught the light of the inferno and sent it back in an arc of red fire.

"The Thieves' Guild is at an end," the Lord Knight said. "Surrender and we'll give you an execution worthy of an enemy of the Knights of Takhisis. You and your followers shall not die like criminals."

Grim laughter flowed around the circle of black-clad assassins.

"Shall we die like sheep, as did our companions whose burning flesh reeks in our nostrils even now?" the Guildmaster asked his fellows.

No one answered. They continued to close, silently, tightening the ring. They stepped over the dwarf, leaving him outside their circle.

"We may die this night, but first we shall see those who brought our Guild low ground into the dust," the Guildmaster said as he leaped, his scimitar flashing out to decapitate Captain Avaril. Sir Kinsaid's long sword met the Guildmaster's curved blade in a flash of sparks.

With a roar, the others closed, blades darting, licking, probing. Sir Arach fired his crossbow, dropping the closest of the assassins, then tossed aside his weapon and lifted a hand, palm outward. A shimmering shield of force appeared before him, stopping the dagger winging toward his heart in mid flight. It fell with a clatter to the cobbles.

"Magic user!" someone shouted. In response, Sir Arach whipped an obsidian-tipped wand from some hidden pocket in his robes. His lips moved, an arcane word crackled on the air, and a sheet of flame erupted from the wand, engulfing the thief trying to skewer him with a short sword. The man became a living pillar of fire. He staggered away, screaming among his fellows, disrupting their attacks, forcing them to dodge the flaming torches that were his flailing arms.

Meanwhile, the skill of the Dark Knight took its toll upon his attackers. His sword licked out, a man fell, his head cloven to his teeth. Another dropped, clutching the ropes of his intestines as they spilled out on the ground. A third lunged low, slashing with a dagger, and leaped back, holding the fountaining stump of his wrist.

With a crack of bone and a spray of blood and teeth, Captain Avaril sent one man sailing backwards, unconscious before he hit the cobbles. He lifted his fingers to his lips and blew a long, quavering call, like the cry of a curlew. A moment later, a deep bellowing roar some distance down the alley answered it.

At this noise, the Guildmaster urged his fellow thieves to redouble their efforts. A thunder of boots and clatter of hooves on the cobblestones echoed from both ends of the alleyway. Soldiers shouted that the Lord Knight was under attack. Officers blared orders. Sir Kinsaid staggered, clutching at a terrific gash in his mail, blood oozing between his fingers. Three thieves fell to the ground and began to snore loudly, victims of another of Sir Arach's magic spells. The knot of fighting wavered, shifted, flowed here and there. One moment, the dwarf, forgotten in the fray, had to lift his head to see the progress of the battle, the next he was in the midst of it. Someone stumbled over him, cursing, only to have his words cut short by Sir Kinsaid's sword. The dwarf tried to crawl away, only to be stomped on the fingers. Then, someone kicked him in the head. A dull pain thudded in his ears, bringing blackness and merciful oblivion.

When he awoke again, the battle had ended. Someone had rolled him over, and he lay now on his back, staring up into the sky. A steady, heavy downpour sent a plume of steam rising from the burning building. It was as though, with the work of the Knights of Takhisis completed, the rain had come to douse the fires lest they spread throughout the city. The fallen rain flowed red with blood into the gutters of Smith's Alley.

The dwarf turned his head and met, face to face, the former master of the former Thieves' Guild of Palanthas. Daavyd Nelgard's head lay next to his, lusterless eyes, lids drooping, bruised lips in a death grimace revealing teeth clamped tightly on a bloated purple tongue. Already, a rat had been chewing on his nose. The dwarf recoiled in horror, only to bump into another body. He raised himself onto his elbows and found that he had been placed in a long row of corpses that stretched into the shadows in either direction. How many had died, he could not hope to count. Of those who lived, he recognized three.

Sir Kinsaid was being tended by a healer, having the wound in his side bound with strips of cloth while two Knights stretched a tarp overhead to shield him from the rain. Sir Arach Jannon was picking through the remaining pile of loot taken from the Guild house and directing the clerks and bearers where each item, crate, or box was to be taken. Meanwhile, Captain Avaril, his face once again hidden by the heavy cowl of his cloak, sat on a crate, his elbows resting on his knees, his head in his hands, exhausted. Rain spattered on his back and hood, but he paid it no mind. Knights and guards meandered about, searching the dead, cataloguing the booty, tending their own wounds or recounting their deeds of the night.

All over Palanthas, the same scene was being played out in a hundred other alleys. Towers of smoke and oily steam rose into the storm-wracked sky, while Knights of Takhisis, their officers and servants, sorted, recorded, and carted away the collected belongings of the Thieves' Guild of Palanthas. They counted and identified the dead according to a large book that each senior officer carried under his or her arm. This book, which would in after days come to be called the Book of the Damned, bore the names and descriptions of every member of the Guild as of 27 Darkember, 34 SC. Those who had not been slain were being hounded, hunted, and smoked out of every Guild house, safe house, and sewer in the entire city. Not a single secret of the Guild, not a member, not a sympathizer, not a rat hole or bolthole, nor even the lowliest treasure hole, though it contained but a pair of thin coppers, was overlooked or missed. The jails had been emptied hours before of their least-dangerous criminals, just to make room for the sudden influx of Guild thieves this night would bring. Old dungeon cells, which had not been inspected for centuries, had their doors pried open, their hinges oiled, their locks repaired. For weeks afterward, there was a notable shortage in chain and rope throughout the city. The price went through the roof, and ropemakers and blacksmiths found themselves the unexpected benefactors. Fortunes were hurriedly invested in fresh supplies of these commodities, only to be lost when the mass executions began and all that surplus chain and rope was reintroduced into the Palanthian markets. Meanwhile, a huge mass grave, a death pit, was dug into a mountain valley five miles south of the city. Though at first the gravediggers complained of the depth of the mass grave ordered by the Dark Knights, in a few weeks it was feared that it might prove too small.

This night, as the rain sluiced Smith's Alley of some of its refuse, the dwarf lay mere feet away from his most hated enemy in all of Krynn. A short sword, broken near the tip but otherwise serviceable, lay inches from his grasp. The old door-warden of the Guild edged closer to the weapon, careful that he make no noise.

Rain and blood had made the sword's grip slick, and his hands were grown feeble, weak from pain and loss of blood. The sword slipped and scraped across the cobblestones as he lifted it. Captain Avaril glanced up but did not move. Lightning flashed, shadows leaped up, startled. One shadow in particular caught the dwarf's attention as he gripped the sword. It loomed over him like a tower. He looked up in time to see a boot lifted above his head. With a clap of thunder that shook the ground, he knew no more.

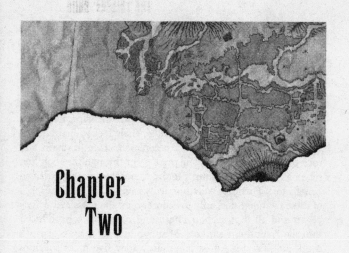

Chapter Two

A rustle in the rose bushes by the wall marked the spot where Petor and Marta had secreted themselves for the better part of an hour. A giggle and a hushed whisper preceded their stumbling appearance on the garden path just beside a white statue of a centaur aiming his marble bow at the moon. A great oak, growing in the midst of a spacious lawn, cast its moon shadow over the path, but torches set atop tall poles illuminated the garden path at regular intervals. Petor hurriedly buttoned his blue velvet coat and fluffed the white silk ascot at his neck, while Marta brushed bits of dirt and leaves from her gown. She giggled again and plucked a rose petal from Petor's hair.

"Stop that!" he hissed. "We mustn't be seen!"

"Oh, what do I care anymore?" she laughed.

"I do! Your father would kill me!" Petor cried. He was a young man of nineteen summers, his companion older than he by a mere month.

"Daddy? He's harmless," Marta said offhandedly.

"Ha! He's the seventh richest man in all Palanthas!" Petor exclaimed under his breath.

"Riches and wealth. That's all anybody ever thinks about," she sighed.

"It took my father eighteen years to be invited to one of your father's Spring Dawning parties. If I ruined it for him by being caught in the bushes with you . . ." His voice trailed off with a shudder.

He took a few moments to collect himself, making certain his fine clothes were in order, while Marta toyed with her hair and twiddled the rings on her fingers. Petor hurriedly glanced about, then grasped Marta by the hand. She gazed longingly into his eyes, her lips parted expectantly.

"I'm going in by the kitchen. Do try and not be seen returning to the party," Petor pleaded. Without another word, he dashed away, his fashionable goldbuckle shoes rutching noisily on the garden path.

"I'll do as I like!" she called after him, then turned on her heel and stomped away. Her dainty, bejeweled slippers made walking difficult on the loose gravel. She turned once more and shouted to the darkness, "I'll go in by the front door!" She spun round and stalked away. "That'll show him."

When she had gone no more than a few steps, a shadow dropped silently over the wall, landing like a cat behind the rose hedge where Petor and Marta had had their assignation. It slipped out to crouch behind the marble centaur, then flitted across the path (its footsteps making no sound on the gravel) and seemed to meld with the trunk of the massive oak on the lawn. A rustling of its long cloak, as of a breeze stirring the stems of the rose bushes, was the only sound of its passing.

Marta continued obliviously on her way, mumbling to herself, her feet crunching on the path. The shadow slipped from tree to tree, bush to bush, paralleling her course as it crossed the lawn. It seemed too swift and silent for a man, and it moved with a deadly purpose. It ran in a crouch with head eagerly thrust forward, darting across the open moonlit spaces in a flash, but when it stopped and its cloak settled about it, the normal eye could not distinguish it from wood or stone. It seemed somehow to merge with whatever shadow it crossed and to blend with the shrubbery and the trees.

Marta straightened her back and livened her step as she neared the house. The sweet sounds of a spring dance floated from the open windows. The house itself was monumental in its construction. Through only four stories tall, it loomed like a snow-clad mountain in the early spring night. Spacious lawns and luxuriant gardens surrounded the house on three sides, but on the north side a reflecting pool, fed by a canal from the Bay of Branchala, extended all the way up to the building's foundation. The estate lay in the northeast quarter of Palanthas, at the foot of the terraced slopes of an area known as the Golden Estates. It was surrounded by a tall stone wall, with an iron gate opening onto Bookbinder's Street. The wall crossed the canal by way of an arch, and there a water gate and guardhouse prevented intrusion. The canal was large enough to let small boats pass. Several guests had arrived at the party this way, for their barges stood in rows, pulled up along the shore of the reflecting pool.

Except for a narrow decorative ledge between the third and fourth stories, the walls of the house were of white marble polished to a glassy sheen and seemingly without joint or crevice, while the depth of the window embrasures showed the walls to be as thick as the bole of the oak in the garden. Every window bore stout shutters of iron-banded oak, and each was likewise protected by heavy bars of iron set directly into the stone of the walls. Though on this night many of the shutters were thrown wide, allowing light and the sound of merrymaking to spill out onto the lawn, when closed up tight and locked from within, the house of Gaeord uth Wotan stood as impregnable as a dwarven mountain stronghold.

As well it should be. Master Gaeord was one of the city's most successful merchants, with a fleet of seventeen ships sailing the seas of Krynn and bringing home their profits to fill their master's coffers. The home of Gaeord uth Wotan was known throughout the city for its collection of art, fine plate, jewels, and antiquities. Few Palanthians could boast such wealth as his.

Still, he was not a noble and his house not the home of a noble, as even the most plebeian visitor to the city could discern from a cursory glance. Compared to the elegant estates of Nobles Hill, the house of Gaeord uth Wotan was about as aesthetically pleasing as a jail. In truth, it had once been a warehouse—a huge, flat-roofed block of stone and iron. What is more, the estate did not lie within the precincts of the Old City, which fact forever doomed the Wotans to the merchant class, no matter how great their wealth might grow. The noble families of Palanthas could trace their bloodlines back to the city's founding citizens, and no amount of money could purchase a title of nobility. Gaeord uth Wotan had only gained his considerable wealth in the past thirty years, a period of time that seemed but a single drop of a water clock to the two-thousand-year histories of many Palanthian families. He was respected and honored for his contributions to the city, and not a few feared his power and influence. His Spring Dawning party was one of the premier events of the festival. An invitation to it meant prestige for the bearer, so much so that even the noble families of Palanthas found it necessary to make an appearance, however brief.

The finest minstrels in the city filled the air with their music. Marta paused as the music slowed to a waltz. She began to dance alone upon the lawn, straying nearer and nearer her silent shadow. It never moved but crouched like a boulder beside a fountain of rose quartz. Marta laughed, her gown spreading about her as she twirled, so near now that the hem of her dress actually brushed the shadow. Still, it did not move. Finally, she danced away, and as the music changed once more to a vigorous spring ring, she skipped across the lawn and rounded the corner of the house. Her shadow leapt after her silently, pausing to peer around the corner before following.

All the estate between the front door and the gate was aglow with torches burning with sweet resins. Carriages of all styles and periods covered the lawn as thick as bison on the plains of Abanasinia, while servants and coachmen tended the horses or gathered into groups to share a skin of wine or gamble with dice. Marta danced along the circle of the drive, stopping occasionally to curtsey to an imaginary suitor or admirer. Her shadow moved among the carriages, paralleling her all the way to the door.

A pair of mail-clad guards suitably attired for the occasion with ribbons of green and white wrapped like a maypole around their pikes, lounged near the front doors. At Marta's approach, they discreetly turned aside and became engrossed in a discussion of the moon, abandoning their post rather than confront their master's scandalous young daughter. Marta stuck out her tongue at their backs as she danced into the house. Her shadow slipped in almost on her heels, crossing the threshold unnoticed except for a pet owl perched on a gilded stand beside the door. The owl ruffled its feathers in an alarmed manner and swiveled its head around to watch. Her skirts swishing over the marble floor, Marta whirled down the broad entry hall toward the ball room, while her shadow ducked aside, choosing instead a wide stair spiraling up into darkness. The guards resumed their post without noticing.

At the top of the stairs, the intruder paused, freezing like one of the marble busts standing on pedestals along the balcony overlooking the grand foyer. To his right, the balcony ringed the circular foyer before disappearing beneath a marble arch. Bronze guardians stood to either side of the arch, female warriors with long slim swords at their sides. Halfway between the stairs and the arch stood a gilded mahogany door. It creaked open. The intruder instantly stepped into a niche, somehow slipping behind the pedestal filling the niche, though there didn't appear to be room enough for a cat. He steadied the rocking marble head atop the pedestal with his fingertips and merged into the shadows.

A man stepped through the door, closing and locking it behind him. He dropped an ornate brass key into his waistcoat pocket and turned toward the stairs. He was round as a bowl, but he walked with the swagger of a man long accustomed to striding the decks of a sailing ship. He wore a coat cut from the finest blue broadcloth, and several necklaces of rich gold hung about his thick, sunburned neck. A green emerald as large as a quail's egg sparkled from one of his fingers. Walking, he whistled out of tune with the music echoing from the ballroom below. As he passed the niche and started down the stair, a black-gloved hand flickered out from behind the pedestal and fingered the pocket into which the brass key had been placed. Just as quickly the hand withdrew as the portly man brushed irritably at his breast as though it were a fly and not a bold thief's fingers disturbing his pocket. He continued without stopping. The intruder stepped out from the niche and watched the master of the house, Gaeord uth Wotan, cross the foyer below him, still whistling out of tune.

With a swirl of his black cloak, he spun round and glided to the mahogany door. He paused and examined the lock, then rose and proceeded toward the arch with its bronze guardians. His footsteps slowed, his head swiveled from one guardian to another. The statues seemed ordinary enough, if rather ornate in design. The female faces were extraordinarily beautiful and as alike as twins. Each bore a slim sword gripped in a long, shapely hand, one in the left hand, the other in the right. They were naked to the waist, sublimely muscled, perfectly cast. The dim light playing over their dark metallic forms gave almost the semblance of movement, of breathing.

Suddenly, the intruder dashed forward, his cloak billowing behind him. At a movement to his left, he dove, rolling beneath the arch just as two razor-sharp bronze blades sheared a span from the hem of his cloak. He continued his roll another dozen feet before rising to his feet, already running. He glanced over his shoulder. The hall behind him was empty. He slowed his steps to listen for a moment, and hearing nothing, shrugged and continued on his way.

He hurried down the darkened hall as though he possessed full knowledge of the layout of the house. He passed without pause numerous rooms and chambers, many promising untold wealth by the stoutness of their doors and locks. But he never hesitated. Finally, he stopped at a small, nondescript door almost hidden behind a fine tapestry. Without pause, he opened it quickly and stepped through, closing it silently behind him. He found himself on a narrow landing. Plain stairs, illuminated at this landing by a pair of braziers hanging from the ceiling, rose from below and continued up into darkness. He mounted the stairs three at a time until he reached the top landing, where they ended at another door. This he opened as before and stepped out into another hall, closing the door behind him.

To his right, torches in sconces burned along an unadorned wall. The floor was laid with unpolished stone, well worn in the middle by the passing of many feet. From a door at the far end, sounds of raucous merrymaking echoed along the hall's empty length. To the left, the hall was dark as a cave. His cloak unfurled like a flag as he turned, and he vanished into the gloom, invisible in his ebon clothes, mask, and hood.

The darkness seemed not to hinder his movements. He strode quickly down the hall, right hand lightly brushing the wall as though to guide him. No obstacle arose to trouble his path, and after turning a corner, he quickly reached his destination. It was a door, no different than the score he had already passed. Removing his black gloves, he knelt beside it and produced a leather pouch from some hidden pocket in his clothes. From this, he chose a thin metal wire and slipped it into the door's weighty lock. Beside this, he inserted a second, thicker wire and began to work these back and forth inside the lock.

Minutes passed, and a sigh escaped him, the first sound he'd made since climbing over the garden wall. He chose a different wire and tried again but to no avail. He sat back on his heels and rested, tucked a stray strand of coppery hair back into his hood, chose a third wire, and tried the lock again. Still it would not turn, and he was just reaching for a fourth wire when a light appeared at the end of the hall.

A female servant of the house turned the corner, a candle in a silver holder illuminating her flushed face. She hurried along the passage while fiddling with a ring of keys in her free hand. The intruder eased away from her, moving down the hall about twenty feet before stretching himself out flat where the wall joined the floor. The servant stopped at the door he'd been trying to enter and tried several keys in the lock. The intruder tensed, noticing his pouch of lockpicks lying on the floor between her feet. Finally, she slid an iron key into the lock. It opened with a click. She hurried into the room, leaving the door open behind her. The intruder rose silently and crept to the door, retrieved his lockpicks, then slipped into the room and ducked behind a barrel. After a few moments, the servant exited, a large gold platter tucked under her arm. She closed the door, locked it, and hurried back the way she had come.

The room was dark, but not so dark as the hall. It was little more than a cupboard, long and narrow, with a small window at the far end. A little light spilled through the cracks in its shutters and gleamed off dozens of shelves of some of the finest gold and silver plate in the city. The shadow-intruder, though, ignored the riches at his fingertips and rushed to the window. He drew back its bolt and carefully opened the shutters.

The window overlooked the front lawn. He leaned out, his head passing easily between the window's thick iron bars. Directly below him stood the two guards, still at their posts by the front door, their ribbons fluttering in the breeze rising from the bay. He climbed up into the window embrasure. It was barely large enough for a kender, but somehow he managed to squeeze into it. He slipped one leg through the window's bars, then the other, then twisted and contorted himself to pass his body and shoulders through, and finally his head, until he dangled by his fingertips fifty feet above the unsuspecting guards. He looked down between his legs, took a deep breath, and let go.

The shortened hem of his cloak fluttered up around him as he fell, but before he had dropped a dozen feet, his fingers touched the tiny decorative ledge running along the wall between the third and fourth stories. He caught at it, stopping his descent in almost perfect silence. Only a slight scuffling of his boots on the polished stone wall betrayed him. He lay still, dangling by his fingertips, then glanced down. The guards had not moved.

Now, with perfect care, he slid one hand along the ledge, pulled his body and other hand after it, then repeated the action. Though people passed in and out of the party, some arriving and some leaving, others merely stepping outside for a breath of air, no one happened to look up. Not that they would have seen much of interest had they done so. A shadow perhaps, shapeless, hardly seeming to move at all. The sweet-smelling torches illuminating the grounds below blinded people. The intruder moved slowly, but without pause, along the ledge, crossing the front of the house and turning the corner, then made his careful way another dozen yards. The deepest part of the reflecting pool lay below him now.

Below the ledge but twenty feet above the water, an iron cage projected from the wall, attached by several stout bolts. The cage protected not a window but a door, like the door of a loft. Through that door, many of Gaeord's most precious cargoes were delivered at night, moving by boat up the canal without ever passing before the eyes of a Palanthian customs officer. A block and tackle could be affixed to the inside of the cage, while its bottom swung open to allow the cargo to be lifted inside. This hinged aperture was sealed by a massive lock that looked strong enough to defy even the heaviest pry bar, and the top of the cage was protected by tall iron spikes.

Having positioned himself directly above the cage, the intruder kicked out from the wall and sailed outward like an acrobat or a flying squirrel. The trajectory of his fall took him beyond the edge of the cage. A little closer to the wall and he could have landed atop the cage, and he would have been skewered by its spikes. A little farther out, and he'd have gone for a swim in the reflecting pool. As it was, his outstretched fingertips brushed the upper bars of the cage before catching hold of the bottom rung and stopping his fall with arm-wrenching abruptness. The cage held his weight with barely a shudder. He dangled from it for a few moments as though catching his breath, then swung like a monkey along the underside of the cage until he reached the lock. A fish plopped somewhere in the pool, sending long ripples across the moonlit water.

Letting go with one hand and dangling from the other, he removed from a pouch at his belt a strange device. It was a tube of dull metal, no longer than his smallest finger and not much thicker. Small square plates of steel covered both ends. This he worked carefully into place between the body of the lock and its metal loop. Once it was in place, he gingerly squeezed the center of the tube. With a sharp clang, the lock burst open. Its fragments, as well as the lock-breaking mechanism, splashed into the water below. The intruder then slid back the bolt and let the bottom of the cage swing open. He climbed up inside it, then swung across and landed in the embrasure of the door.

A pair of wooden doors confronted him now, but these were not meant to keep out thieves, only the wind and rain. A thin-bladed dagger slipped between the boards followed by a sharp upward jerk and the bar was lifted. He opened one door wide enough to slip a hand inside to catch the bar, then slowly opened the door and dropped into the room beyond.

By some instinct or uncanny intuition, he recoiled instantly. With leopardlike reflexes, he caught the hand that guided the dagger aimed at his heart. Another blinding parry trapped the fist that would have shattered his teeth, and a lifted knee foiled the boot meant for his groin. He jerked his assailant into the moonlight in front of the doorway.

The figure was dressed much like himself, except that where he wore a full mask to hide his features, his assailant wore only a strip of cloth over the lower half of her face. A pair of dark flashing eyes glared at him from beneath her hood. She struggled a moment longer, silently, then grew still, her breath hissing sharply through her mask.

"You are hurting me," she whispered venomously.

"You would have done much worse to me," he answered.

"You surprised me," she said. "Who are you?"

"I am a thief," he said, "like yourself."

"You are a thief, but you are nothing like me," she spat.

"Ah, yes. You must be a Guild thief," he sighed.

"Yes, and you are intruding upon Guild business, you free-lance pig."

He ignored the insult. Instead, he sniffed, testing the air for some elusive scent. He drew the daggered fist closer to his face. Suddenly, she jerked away, but he held her fast. He forced her wrist closer to his face until the point of the dagger tickled the thick muscular cord below his ear.

"The yellow Ergothian lotus, said to drive men mad with passion. In Palanthas, all know this perfume you wear, Lady Alynthia," he whispered.

"And your mask cannot hide the fact that you are an elf," she countered.

He stiffened as though insulted. "My name is Cael Ironstaff," he said. "Is that the name of an elf?"

"Call yourself what you will," she hissed. "After this night, the Guild will hunt you down like the dog you are. You will not escape us."

"Why should I wish to escape you, Mistress Alynthia?" he answered. "I can think of nothing so desirable as being pursued by you."

"Pig!" she almost shouted, her feet flailing at his knees and groin. He twisted her around and pinned her arms behind her back until she grew still, her chest heaving, breath hissing between clenched teeth.

"Do you have it?" he asked sternly.

"Do I have what?" she snarled over her shoulder.

"You know what I—"

He had not yet had time to take in his surroundings, and for that he was now heartily sorry. A door somewhere within the warehouselike chamber opened. A light spilled in, sending shadows leaping up the walls. He forced her down behind a crate, clapping one hand over her mouth to keep her from crying out while holding her tight with the other. For a moment, he felt her tense and struggle, but then slowly she seemed to relax against him. He felt the smooth curves of her flesh cupped into his own, and the warmth of her body sent a thrill though his limbs. The delicate perfume of the yellow Ergothian lotus began to drive him to distraction, despite the danger.

Then a whispered voice pierced the silence. "Captain Alynthia?" it inquired. "Are you here? Guards are approaching. We'd better— what the . . . ?" The lookout had just spotted the open loft door.

Alynthia wormed herself free for a moment. "Over here," she barked. "Slay me this . . ." her voice trailed off in a string of muffled curses.

He jerked her to her feet and stepped back until he stood in the loft door, keeping her between himself and the lookouts. Opposite him, a hook-nosed thief crouched half-hidden by a wooden crate, a dagger poised by his ear, ready for throwing. A second hid in the shadows by the open door, a small crossbow in his fist. Alynthia struggled and twisted until her mouth was again free.

"Slay him, you fools," she ordered the lookouts, but they hesitated, afraid lest they strike their leader by mistake.

The intruder faced no such obstacle. With a deft twist, he pried the dagger from Alynthia's grasp and sent it flying at the hook-nosed thief. Hook-nose ducked behind the crate only just in time, as the dagger whistled by his chin and buried itself in the eye of the thief by the door. He dropped like a poleaxed cow, dead before he hit the floor.

Freed from his grip, Alynthia spun around with fists clenched, but by some trick she found herself flying backwards through the air. She landed on her rear with a thump and slid across the polished floor, tumbling into Hook-nose who had just risen to launch his dagger. With a mocking laugh, the intruder stepped out of the loft and dropped from sight. Hook-nose rushed to the loft door and leaned out. He whistled in amazement.

"What is it?" Alynthia asked as she dusted herself off. "Did you get him?"

"No, Captain," the thief admitted.

"Why not?"

"He's not there."

"What do you mean? He must be there. He's in the water," she said.

"There's not a ripple, and I didn't hear no splash," the thief answered as he turned away. He sheathed his dagger with a snap. "He must be some kind of wizard."

"Perhaps," she admitted. "Well, at least he didn't get the . . ." She slapped at her pockets, a strangled howl of rage rising in her throat.

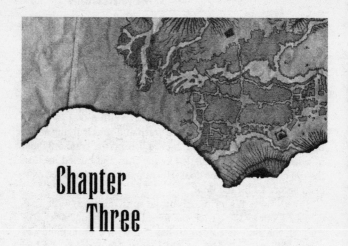

Chapter Three

"H as anyone thought to question the owl?" the man asked as he knelt on the floor. A voluminous robe the color of driftwood hid his entire body, including his head. On the floor before him lay a congealing pool of dark blood.

"The owl?" the master of the house, Gaeord uth Wotan, asked nervously. He was a man unused to being afraid of anyone or anything, and he disliked the feeling. He fidgeted with the heavy gold chain dangling below his chin, and nervously ran a hand down the front of his blue silk pajamas.

"The owl by the door," the man in the robes said. "The one given you by Amil of Sanction in exchange for certain, how shall we say, advantages in Palanthian pearl importation."

"Begging your pardon, Sir Arach," Gaeord stammered.

With a sigh, the gray-robed Knight of Takhisis pushed back his hood and stared languidly at his portly host. "The magical owl said to have the power of speech," he said with weary patience.

"Oh, that owl!" Gaeord laughed nervously. "The magical power wore off some months ago. How did you know?" he whispered.

"It is my business to know, Master Gaeord," Sir Arach Jannon said. "It is my business to know everything that passes within this city. I am its Lord High Justice, am I not? I am also the highest-ranking Thorn Knight in the city, and as such all things magical also come under my domain, especially since the unlicensed ownership of magical items is illegal in this city."

"Yes, sir," Gaeord said.

"I knew about this owl of yours, just as I know that most of these boxes and crates," he said with a gesture at the contents of the room, "have never seen the inside of a customs house, that they arrive by night from your ships, pass through the water gate into your reflecting pool, and are unloaded through that loft, the loft through which your burglar either entered or made his escape."

"Which is it?" Gaeord asked, trying desperately to change the subject. "If he entered through the door, why break the lock on the loft cage? If he entered through the loft, who entered through the door?"

"Exactly! And once here, how did he die and where is his body? If he did die here, then who was it that escaped? This case presents some interesting perplexities, Master Gaeord," Sir Arach said. "I am very glad you brought it to my attention. So glad that I may overlook certain irregularities in the way you choose to conduct your business."

"I knew of your interest in such puzzles. I am only thankful that nothing was stolen," Gaeord said quickly, with just a bit too much enthusiasm. He had not sent for Sir Arach. The man had unaccountably appeared at his door at dawn, announcing his intention to investigate the burglary of which only Gaeord and a few of his most trusted servants had known. Gaeord suspected that the Thorn Knight had spies in his household, just as it was rumored he had spies in the house of every important family in Palanthas.

"Yes. You are indeed fortunate that nothing was stolen," Sir

Arach responded, his voice tinged with irony. Droplets of sweat broke out on Gaeord's brow.

At that moment, a servant appeared at the door, clearing his throat.

"What is it?" Gaeord snapped.

"Mistress Jenna to see you, sir," the servant said nervously. "She demanded—'

Before he could finish his explanation, a woman pushed past him and entered the room. She was clad in long robes of a deep wine-colored red, bound about the waist by a belt of gold twined with what appeared to be a living vine. Her long gray hair was pulled back in a simple yet elegant braid, allowing the gold hoops in her ears the freedom to swing and glint in the light.

Though well into her sixties, Mistress Jenna was still a strikingly beautiful woman. Her steps were firm and sure, her stride vigorous. She was perhaps the most powerful mage in the city, respected, even feared. Her shop, the Three Moons, dealt in magical items, potions, scrolls, and spellbooks (though the latter were of little use since the moons of magic disappeared from the skies after the Chaos War). Strangely enough, or perhaps not so strangely, considering the position of influence that she held in the city, the Knights of Takhisis never questioned her right to deal in magic, even though the law against the sale of such items was strictly prosecuted in all other cases. Now Sir Arach rose at her entrance, and it was an indication of her position in society that he bowed slightly upon meeting her eyes.

She cast a swift, bitter glance over him, then turned to the master of the house.

"Mistress Jenna, this is an unexpected surprise," Gaeord said rather unconvincingly. He coughed, and using the excuse to cup one hand over his mouth to hide it from Sir Arach's view, mouthed the words, "Say nothing."

Mistress Jenna seemed not to notice. Her gaze had just as quickly strayed to the blood stain on the floor. "I heard there was a robbery," she said, as her eyes lighted on the open loft door, then flickered over the various boxes and crates that half filled the room.

"Nothing was taken," Gaeord quickly affirmed. How many spies did he have in his house anyway? He determined as soon as this was over to question all his servants most thoroughly.

Sir Arach merely smiled, his black eyes twinkling. "Why, Mistress Jenna!" he exclaimed with mock surprise. "I had no idea that you and Master Gaeord were such close friends. It really is too kind of you to visit him in his hour of need, but on its face, this case seems simple enough, and we certainly shouldn't need to call upon your considerable magical powers to solve it."

"You suspect who the thief is?" Gaeord asked.

"Not a clue," the Thorn Knight admitted without hesitation. "But I have every confidence that I shall discover his identity. It is a shame about that owl, though. Most strange that it should lose its magical powers, now, at this particular time."

At these last words, a strange quiet fell over the room's occupants. Gaeord wondered at its cause, looking in some confusion at his two uninvited guests, who seemed to be staring at each other. A more imaginative man might have fancied that the gray eyes of Mistress Jenna were fighting a duel with the sharp, black eyes of the Thorn Knight, each mage probing the other for some clue as to what he or she was thinking at that moment. Though no word was said, whole conversations seemed to pass between them.

Suddenly, like a wrestler who flings off his opponent to escape him, the Thorn Knight tore his gaze away from Mistress Jenna. He then spoke slowly, as though fighting to regain his composure, "Yes, we might have learned much from the owl."

Mistress Jenna turned to Gaeord. "What were the thieves after?" she asked.

"I have many things in my house that such daring thieves as these would be willing to risk their lives to obtain," Gaeord bragged. "But I assure you, they failed in their attempt to steal whatever it was they were after. See, they were interrupted and fled!"

Sir Arach clucked his tongue and shook his head. "Come, come, Master Gaeord," he said. "How can I possibly be expected to solve this crime if its victim withholds pertinent facts? I must know everything if justice is to prevail."

Despite his wealth and station in Palanthian society, Gaeord uth Wotan's face turned gray at these words. A man such as he was long accustomed to dealing with government officials while conducting his business of importation and trade. His ability to guarantee the sort of profits his partners and investors demanded depended on operating, now and then, outside of the normal confines of the law. Ways were opened and means obtained by the judicious and discreet application of coin, favors, gifts, intimidation, even violence. He was no criminal, no one would dare to call him such. It was simply how business was conducted in Palanthas.

Standing before him, however, was a man notoriously impossible to influence. Sir Arach Jannon, one of the most powerful men in all Palanthas, could not be bribed and he certainly could not be intimidated. It was he who intimidated others. Nothing could be hidden from him. He had spies throughout the city, it was said, in every household of any importance, even those of his fellow Knights of Takhisis. What was more, the man was a Thorn Knight, a magic user of the Gray Robes, and magic worried Gaeord almost as much as high taxes.

Those who opposed Sir Arach often found themselves under intense scrutiny. Those with business practices that could not bear close examination had no desire to conduct business with those under Sir Arach's eye. More than one great Palanthian family had been destroyed by this man, often without one charge ever being leveled against it.

Gaeord mopped his brow with a green silk handkerchief, then nervously tugged at the gold chain dangling around his neck. He had not shaved, having been awakened before dawn by his footman with the report of the break-in, and now his jowls itched abominably. He glanced from the Thorn Knight to Mistress Jenna, but her severe gaze only served to turn his blood to ice. She must know already, without his having said a word. His news must necessarily displease her, since what was stolen was hers. She had ordered and already paid (quite handsomely) for it the previous autumn. Then again, she might be his saving grace. The special dispensation concerning all things magical that Mistress Jenna enjoyed might shield him from Sir Arach. He could hardly be convicted of smuggling dangerous magic if he was but the carrier for someone who enjoyed immunity from the law.

He cleared his throat as he stuffed the handkerchief into the sleeve of his pajamas. "It was a quantity—mind you, a small quantity—of dragonflower pollen," he said, ending with a nervous laugh he hoped would seem nonchalant.

"Dragonflower pollen!" Sir Arach exclaimed. "I am surprised at you, Master Gaeord. I had thought you limited your activities to more mundane contraband. Little did I suspect that you were importing the most illegal substance in Palanthas. The pollen of the dragonflower grows only in the Dragon Isles, where it is death for mortals to tread. In small amounts, it prolongs life and returns the flush of youth. Greater quantities, I'm sure you know, bring madness and death."

"It was for a friend," Gaeord pleaded, staring at Mistress Jenna. The Thorn Knight followed the direction of Gaeord's gaze.

"Ah, that explains the presence of the renowned Mistress Jenna," Sir Arach said.

"Yes, it was for me," she finally admitted without apology. "I funded the expedition to the Dragon Isles, not Master Gaeord, though it was his ship and crew. I can't afford a second expedition. I want the pollen returned to me at once, and," she added to the Thorn Knight, "I expect you to see that the Thieves' Guild is punished most severely."

"Who said anything about the Thieves' Guild?" Sir Arach asked somewhat crossly. "There is no Thieves' Guild in Palanthas. This is the work of petty criminals, nothing more."

"Well, whoever they are, I want them caught. You Knights of Takhisis talk about how you maintain law and order. I want to see it in action. If you won't do it, I certainly will," Mistress Jenna angrily threatened.

"Yes, and today is Spring Dawning festival," Gaeord said, trying again to change the subject. "Might we hurry this up? The festivities begin in a couple of hours."

"I would have been finished by now, if you had been honest

with me from the beginning and if others wouldn't keep interrupting!" Sir Arach snarled. "If I might have a few moments to examine this room, I think I might be able to move forward with my investigation. Do try to stay out of my way."

With that, the Thorn Knight sank to all fours and began to crawl this way and that over the floor, pressing his nose into corners, laying his face on the flagstones, and staring for long minutes at things the others could not see. Occasionally, some exclamation of surprise or discovery escaped his lips, but only once during the course of his odd caperings did Sir Arach speak, to ask, "How often is this floor polished?"

"Daily," Gaeord answered.

Nodding, the Thorn Knight removed a pouch from a pocket of his robe and struck it against the floor. A cloud of fine white dust erupted from it and settled on the floor. He examined it for a moment, nodded again, then turned his attention to the loft door. He stood in the embrasure for some moments staring down into the reflecting pool below, then turned his attention to the inner walls, then the outside of the wall above the opening. Lastly, he lifted the doors' wooden bar and examined it in detail.

He crossed the room and carefully studied the entrance from the hallway, taking special care around the door's brass lock and running his fingers along the edges of the doorframe.

That accomplished, he finished his examination at the pool of blood where he had begun. He knelt beside it, then dipped the tip of his finger into it. He held the sample up to the light and peered at it with one eye shut, sniffed it, and popped the blood-smeared finger into his mouth.

"Gods!" Gaeord said in disgust. Mistress Jenna turned away, exasperated.

Sir Arach looked at them, still sucking his finger. Almost apologetically, he stuffed his hands into his pockets and rose to his feet. "The final test. Had to be sure," he said by way of explanation.

"Test for what?" Jenna scowled.

"Cause of death," he said.

"Whose death?"

"I think if Gaeord can have his servants drag the reflecting pool, we may discover the answer," Sir Arach said.

"So what happened?" Gaeord asked.

"Two thieves entered this chamber, one by the door from the hallway—one of them had a key. The lock has not been picked, neither has the door been jimmied. The other thief must have entered through the loft."

"Impossible!" Gaeord exclaimed. "He would need wings!"

"I am afraid it is only too probable. The bar was lifted with a knife, as evidenced by the groove at its exact center. Were the bar raised from within this room, there would be no cut in the wood."

"Perhaps he did have wings," Jenna conjectured, her brows wrinkling together suspiciously. "Perhaps he used magic to fly."

"If he had such power, he could also have lifted the bar with his magic. No, this was a common thief," Sir Arach said. "I suspect that he dropped from above."

"From the sky?" Gaeord laughed. "The roof was patrolled by my best guards, and all entrances were closely watched. What you suggest is impossible."

"The simple fact remains," Sir Arach said drily, "that two thieves, *two thieves* sir, *did* enter your house. It is pointless to argue that they couldn't have done it, for they did! If I can answer how, it might lead us to who."

"Go on," Jenna impatiently ordered.

The Thorn Knight glared at Gaeord for another moment, then continued, "Having entered the chamber, he found it occupied by another of his profession. A scuffle ensued. You can see the palm print on the floor there, where I dusted with powder, as well as a streak where one of the two slid across the floor. Having wrestled, the one killed the other with a dagger through the eye."

"How do you know that?" Jenna asked.

"By tasting the blood, I was able to detect the presence of eye fluid as well as brain fluid. I have made extensive study of bodily fluids and trained my senses to detect over three hundred different kinds. I can tell the blood of a dog from that of a man by smell alone. Mixed fluids need a more involved sampling."

"It's disgusting," Gaeord muttered involuntarily.

"It proves nothing," Jenna added.

"On the contrary, it proves that one of the two died, and since his body is not in this room, it must lie in the reflecting pool. His identity might lead us to that of his enemy, but I doubt it. In any case, having procured the dragonflower pollen . . . you have noticed, I am sure, that he stole *only* the dragonflower pollen, and left all these other valuable commodities behind him, which suggests a commissioned theft—actually, two commissioned thefts . . ." he paused, gazing from beneath his heavy lids at Mistress Jenna.

She noticed the accusation in his stare, and her face turned crimson with anger. "You dare!" she hissed.

"Who besides yourself and Master Gaeord knew of the precious stuff?" Sir Arach asked.

"Why would I steal from myself? I already purchased the dragonflower pollen!" Jenna barked.

The Thorn Knight then turned to Master Gaeord. The master of the house flushed, then began to stammer, "Yes, there were others! I . . . uh . . . the captain of my ship . . . his officers . . . the crew might have discovered . . . servants . . . enemies . . . household spies!"

"Well, it is useless to speculate at this point. I must have more data," Sir Arach said with a grim smile. It was obvious that he was enjoying his little performance. "As I was saying," he continued, "Having procured the pollen, he then made his escape . . . "

"But where did he then go?" Gaeord asked.

"An excellent question, and one that will help solve this case," Sir Arach said, as he rubbed his hands together. "Did he make his exit through the loft or the house?"

A maid appeared at the doorway and cleared her throat. As Sir Arach turned his eyes upon her, she curtsied, then said in a voice hurried by her nervousness, "M'lord said to notify him of anything out of the ordinary."

"What is it, Mira?" Gaeord asked.

"We've found something at the balcony, sir," she squeaked.

"Lead the way!" the Thorn Knight shouted in excitement. The maid fled in a swirl of cotton skirts.

Together, Sir Arach, Mistress Jenna, and Gaeord uth Wotan made their way to the balcony overlooking the main entrance to the house. The maid having long since disappeared, Gaeord led them along a circuitous route through the more fashionably decorated parts of the house, pausing occasionally to adjust the hang of a valuable painting here, running his hand lovingly along the rim a priceless vase there, using all the tricks he usually employed to impress his more frequent but less-notable visitors. However, every time his eyes met those of Mistress Jenna, he found her staring at him as though she thought him quite capable of trying to cheat her. Meanwhile, Sir Arach grew so impatient with Gaeord's diversions that he finally shoved the wealthy merchant aside and took the lead. The Thorn Knight's rapid, deliberate stride brought them quickly to their destination. Gaeord could barely suppress his astonishment that Sir Arach seemed to know the way, even taking a secret door that cut thirty steps from their journey.

They arrived at the balcony through the large gilded mahogany door. Two guards, still wearing their holiday ribbons, stood near the hall entrance flanked by the bronze statues. On the floor at the feet of one of these statues lay a palm-wide strip of black cloth about three feet long. It was to this that they directed Sir Arach's attention. He lifted it carefully by one corner and held it up to the sunlight streaming through window.

"Curious material," he noted. "I know the weaver. He shall be questioned. Hello! What's this?" He plucked something from the hem. "The thorn of a rose. Now we are getting somewhere. The material itself has been cut by a sharp instrument. The cut is not straight, which indicates that a tailor's scissors did not shear it. It looks rather more like the veil cut in twain by an expert swordsman." He eyed the statues for a moment, then nodded as though his suspicions were confirmed. He then held the cloth to his nose and sniffed deeply, while his eyes wandered over the room, taking in every detail.

Suddenly, he dropped the cloth and dashed to the head of the stairs, where one of numerous marble busts stood atop its pedestal set in a deep niche along the wall. He stared at it intensely for a moment, then turned his eyes to the floor behind the pedestal.

Seeing his interest, Gaeord remarked, "That is a bust of Vinas Solumnus. It was carved by the renowned sculptor Makennen in the year—"

"Yes, I know!" Sir Arach snarled without turning. "I find its position more of interest than its quality, which is quite poor, I assure you. It's an obvious forgery."

"A forgery!" Gaeord fairly screeched. "Why I paid over—"

Again, Sir Arach interrupted him. "Be that as it may, you have taken such great care with the perfect placement of the thirteen other busts along this wall that I find it difficult to believe you would leave this one so carelessly out of line. Why look, he faces almost a quarter turn away."

"Remarkable," Mistress Jenna said with obvious disdain. "I applaud your keen observation."

Sir Arach glared at her for a moment. "It proves that one thief, at least, entered by way of the front door."

"Impossible," Gaeord interjected.

"I was on guard at that door all night, sir," one of the guards protested. "No thief got by me, I assure you!"

"Nevertheless, he did 'get by you,' as you so eloquently put it," Sir Arach replied caustically. "He ascended these stairs, hid here for a moment behind the pedestal, then made his way under the arch protected by those two magical and highly illegal bronze guardians, who only managed to slice a few inches of cloth from his cloak. A most clever and resourceful adversary. I shall enjoy capturing him. Now, to the front door, where I am sure we shall find more of interest."

With these words, like a hound upon a scent the Thorn Knight flew down the stairs, his gray robes fluttering around him in his speed. The others followed more slowly. They found Sir Arach crawling about the grass plot near the doorway. The owl, still perched on its stand by the door, eyed him sleepily.

As the others strode out into the bright morning sunlight, Sir Arach rose slowly to his feet, wrinkling his brow. He searched the ground with his eyes while his long, spatulate fingers nervously scratched his chin.

"Why, what ever is the matter?" Mistress Jenna mockingly asked.

"Most curious. Most curious indeed," the Thorn Knight answered distractedly. "Here, as you can see, are the same footprints as those left in the dust behind the pedestal. They are quite unique, I assure you. There can be no mistake that they are identical. Observe the square toe and the curious oaken leaf pattern on the left heel."

Jenna and Gaeord leaned over the spot he indicated, but they saw nothing other than a blade or two of grass that might have been bent by a heavy tread.

Shrugging, Jenna asked, "So what is the mystery?"

"They go the wrong way. They do not enter the house, they leave it," he answered. "And there is something most strange about them. I cannot put my finger on it, something about the way . . ." His voice trailed off as he turned and walked slowly along the front of the house, his eyes scouring the ground at his feet, pausing occasionally to examine a blade of grass or touch an indentation only his eyes could see.

Jenna strolled along behind him, with Gaeord trailing the famous sorceress so that he wouldn't have to feel her eyes boring into his back. As they walked, Mistress Jenna muttered angrily to herself. Gaeord stepped closer to hear.

"Waste of time. Why doesn't he just use his magic to solve it? Over-brained fool. I could track down the thief with a spell at any time," she grumbled.

"Why don't you then?" Gaeord asked.

"What?" She spun round, and Gaeord was sorry he'd asked.

"That's *his* job!" she spat, pointing at the Thorn Knight. "I'll not waste my magic chasing . . ." She let the words die on her lips as Gaeord stared at her curiously.

Sir Arach stopped by the fountain and knelt. As Jenna and Gaeord approached, he said, "The thief paused here for a time. I wonder why, unless . . ." He crawled away, his nose almost to the ground.

"Here!" he announced. "The light tread of a lady's slippers, perhaps a girl. She was dancing."

"Dancing, you say?" Gaeord asked, the blood draining from his face.

"An accomplice?" Jenna asked.

"Not likely. Probably, she didn't even see him. I marvel, though, at his iron nerve, to stay hidden while she danced so near. In any case, her path leads toward the house, his leads, unaccountably, away." Again, the puzzle crossed his narrow brow. Rising, he continued along the trail only his eyes could see.

It led them eventually into the garden, and finally to the rose hedge beside the wall. Sir Arach stooped beneath the hedge, vanishing through a barely perceptible gap in the thick thorny screen. He returned almost immediately, something bright glimmering on his outstretched palm.

"I marvel, Master Gaeord, at the baubles you leave lying about your garden. What fruits do you expect to grow from it? This, I believe, is one of the famous Laertian Combs, renowned for their priceless rubies, which you gave to your daughter on her sixteenth Day of Life Gift. And here is an ivory button— not really ivory, whale's tooth actually, which is favored by the middle classes over the more expensive true ivory. I don't imagine you would allow your own daughter to wear such trash. Perhaps her companion lost it."

With a strangled cry, Gaeord snatched the condemning evidence from the Thorn Knight's palm. Sir Arach vanished again behind the roses. Jenna chuckled and looked away.

A burst of insane laughter erupted from the rose bushes. "What a fool I've been. It was before me all the time. There is nothing so misleading as an obvious clue," the Thorn Knight berated himself, all the while cackling hideously. The sound of it, like nails dragged across a slate board, made the others cringe,.

His head appeared through the bushes. "Come, come. You must see this. Ah, I can't have been so blind. Watch yourself. The thorns are sharp."

With obvious reluctance, Gaeord stooped through the rose bushes and found himself in a close, shadowy arbor completely hidden from any passersby in the garden. At the back of it, the outer wall of his estate rose some dozen feet above him.

Jenna remained on the path outside. "I'd rather not," she said to the Thorn Knight's entreaties.

"Suit yourself. You'll miss seeing what a fool I've been," Sir Arach said.

"I am certain other opportunities will arise," she answered coldly.

Returning to the arbor where Gaeord crouched red-faced and breathing heavily in the shadows, Sir Arach motioned to the wall. There, he pointed out the clear marks in the deep garden loam of two bootprints. Gaeord looked at them for a moment, then turned a questioning gaze on the Thorn Knight.

"Don't you see?" Sir Arach asked. Gaeord shook his head.

With a sigh, the Thorn Knight continued. "If you were to stand at the wall and leap for the edge, what sort of marks would your feet leave?"

"I haven't a clue," Gaeord answered.

"Toes indented, dirt flung away from the wall," came the shouted answer from beyond the rose bushes.

"Thank you, Mistress Jenna," Sir Arach shouted in response. Turning back to the bootprints, he continued, "As you can see, the toes here have hardly left any impression at all, while the heels are indented quite deeply, which is indicative of someone landing, not jumping."

"I see," Gaeord sighed appreciatively. "But what does it mean?"

"It means, dear Gaeord, that either your thief crossed the lawn by running backwards, or he wore his boots turned around backwards, or the boots themselves were magically altered to leave backwards impressions."

"Of course!" Mistress Jenna exclaimed from without.

"So he jumped over my wall wearing backwards shoes," Gaeord said, still confused.

"No, he dropped from the wall into your garden wearing backwards shoes." Taking the sweating merchant by the sleeve of his pajamas, Sir Arach led him back to the garden path.

"Where has Mistress Jenna gone?" Gaeord asked as they emerged from the roses.

Sir Arach looked around, equally puzzled, then shrugged and continued his explanation as he led Gaeord back to the house. The red-robed sorceress had vanished, as was her wont.

"Having gained entrance to the estate, he then followed your daughter from her assignation across the lawn and into the house, past the guards who probably thought it best to not see her entrance, in case they were questioned later. He then went up the stairs, hid for a moment in the niche, then continued down the passage after narrowly avoiding the attack of the magical bronze guardians."

"But you can't get to that chamber from that hallway," Gaeord argued.

"Yes, I know," Sir Arach said absently. He walked along, eyeing something he had drawn from a pocket of his gray robes. "Of course, I should have known at once that the boot prints were a ruse. The rose thorn stuck to the hem of his cloak proved that he had been in the garden *before* entering the house."

"What about the second thief?" Gaeord asked as they stopped at the front door. "This doesn't account for the thief you say entered through the loft. I should think he is the more talented and dangerous of the two."

"My dear Gaeord, why worry yourself needlessly? Let a professional do the thinking, for it isn't your strength. Now that I have a track to follow, I shall surely hunt down both thieves. Give me two turns of the glass on the grounds and about the house and I'll give you your men." With these words, Sir Arach turned and strode off in the direction of the reflecting pool.

* * * * *

Gaeord was just finishing a breakfast of ham and fried potatoes, a servant standing at his elbow to retrieve the empty plates, when Sir Arach returned, red faced and excited by his efforts. He slid into a seat at the table quite uninvited, and said without being asked, "Yes, thank you, I am famished. But no potatoes. I prefer eggs, poached, lightly salted if you don't mind. And do hurry, I am expected at the Spring Dawning ceremonies in little more than an hour."

The servant glanced at his master, and at Gaeord's nod, hurried away to the kitchen.

Gaeord set aside his knife and fork and dabbed at his lips with a linen napkin almost as large as a ship's flag. "So you have solved it then," he muttered through the napkin.

"Most assuredly," Sir Arach answered, as he examined the silverware. Gaeord had the uncomfortable feeling that his every possession had been carefully noted, categorized, and filed away in the enormous intellect of the Lord High Justice of Palanthas. "An interesting case, with several remarkable features. I thank you. I wouldn't have missed it for all the jewels in Ansalon."

"So who is the thief?" Gaeord asked, as a servant entered and began to clear away the other dishes and glasses.

"Thieves," corrected Sir Arach. "No, perhaps you were right—thief. I'll tell you who it is not. It is not the man who is currently at the bottom of your reflecting pool attracting sharks from the bay. Nor is it one of your household servants, nor one of your guests of the night before. They have all been accounted for. No one is missing."

So one of the thieves *was* dead! Gaeord let out a sigh of relief and wiped his brow with his napkin. Then a cold chill prickled the nape of his pomaded neck, for he realized that, during the course of an hour, Sir Arach had ascertained the current whereabouts of every guest who had visited his party, as well as all his servants. This hinted at an enormous network of informants and spies, a network more fantastic than even the most fantastic rumors circulating in Palanthas.

"Who is at the bottom of the pool, then?" Gaeord asked timidly.

"Most likely one of the servants hired for the evening—a steward, wine servant, or musician. He slipped away during a lull in the party. It is possible that he had assistance from someone else on the inside," Sir Arach said.

A servant entered with Sir Arach's breakfast, and it was some time before Gaeord could get another word out of the man. For such a small, thin fellow, the Thorn Knight polished off copious amounts of fried ham and eggs, not to mention a full pot of tarbean tea. Finally, when nothing else remained, he settled back in his chair and dabbed his lips, sucked his teeth, and eyed the plates for any crumbs he might have missed.

"Do you have any clues as to the other thief's identity?" Gaeord finally asked. He had grown anxious and wished the Thorn Knight would leave. He could recover financially from the theft, but he feared he might never shake the feeling that Sir Arach Jannon knew everything there was to know about him, from how much sugar he took with his tarbean tea, to the number of bags of untaxed steel and gold coins that lay hidden under the floor beneath his bed. Besides, the morning was getting on, and as this day was the annual Spring Dawning festival, his schedule was quite filled. He was anxious to get the awful business of the burglary behind him.

Sir Arach gazed at him for a while before answering his question, as though enjoying the tension that his continued silence created. Gaeord squirmed in his chair and toyed with his napkin, gazed out the huge windows of his breakfast room over the wide blue sweep of the Bay of Branchala—anything but look at his guest as he awaited the answer.

Finally, with a small chuckle, Sir Arach began. "I'd say we're looking for a youngish man, early twenties, with coppery hair, slim build, walks with the aid of a staff," he rattled off while he observed his host's expression.

"Really, Sir Arach. How could you—" Gaeord began, but the Knight cut him off.

"I had a man watching the estate last night. He saw just such a character pass up the street toward the University but took him for one of its students. However, the time is approximately correct, as we learned from a more careful interrogation of your guards, which established the time when your daughter returned to the party. No one else was seen in the vicinity of your southern wall at that time, though my man failed to notice anyone climbing over it."

Gaeord rose from his chair, his face flushed, and threw his napkin on the table. "Really, I—"

Sir Arach continued, "Having gained entrance to the house by following your daughter through the door while the guards looked the other way, he made his way upstairs, as I have already described. Now, you didn't mention that three weeks ago you replaced the iron bars protecting the small fourth-floor window above the front door."

"Yes. How did you—"

"The space between those bars is greater than at any other window, wide enough in fact to admit a grown man, if he is nimble enough," Sir Arach said.

"Yes, well, it would be impossible—"

"Wide enough also to allow a man to escape. That itself is a clue, as the thief probably had knowledge of the replacement and its wider bars. Probably, we shall find him in the employ of the blacksmith who wrought them, or else a close friend of said blacksmith—a dwarf named Kharzog Hammerfell, I believe."

"Yes, that's right," Gaeord croaked.

Sir Arach continued, "The thief exited through the window, then used the ledge to make his way around the house until he could drop down onto the cage protecting the loft door."

"But the spikes."

"He avoided them somehow."

"Impossible!"

"Master Gaeord, that word comes too often to your lips," Sir Arach remonstrated. "Once all other possibilities are eliminated, what remains must be true, no matter how remarkable it seems."

"I see," Gaeord said, still unconvinced.

"The rest you know. He entered and found the room already held by your inside-job thief. A scuffle ensued in which the inside thief was killed and the first made off with the loot. He then dived into the pool, swam through your water gate . . ."

Gaeord opened his mouth to make some exclamation, then clamped his teeth shut before uttering a sound.

Sir Arach continued, smiling, ". . . and made his way to shore less than a bowshot beyond the north wall. I found his boot prints in the sand, again backward as though he had entered the water there. Now it is simply a matter of following these clues to our man. The name of the thief, and his imminent capture, are only a matter of time."

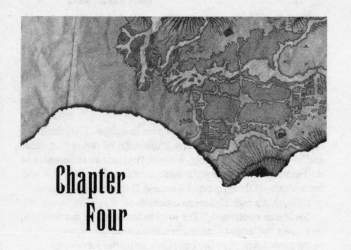

Chapter
Four

An elf hobbled out of the alchemist's shop at the corner of Trade and Truth Streets, pausing to watch as the owner, a small round man with a small round face baked brown and leathery from years of bending over his cauldrons, locked the door and propped a sign in the window that read, "Closed for the Spring Dawning Festival." The elf turned, and, smiling, he patted the coin-fat purse dangling at his belt. Long strands of fine hair the color of burnished copper framed his narrow elven face and offset by the richness of their color the brilliance of his laughing, sea-green eyes. Narrow lips smiled slightly beneath a proud nose. His cheeks showed no hint of downy hair, for no elf upon Krynn could grow a beard. He wore a white tunic, somewhat blowsy at the sleeves and breast, and a pair of loose-fitting trousers of brown homespun. A pair of hard-worn, dull black boots completed his attire. He held a gnarled staff of polished black wood gripped firmly in his left hand.

Across the street, a pair of drunken sailors stumbled from an alley and squinted in apparent surprise at the sun, already well up in the eastern sky. The elf turned right and slipped into Gravedigger Alley—a close, dusty lane lined along one side with stacks of empty caskets. Many of the city's undertakers had their shops here. The noises of hammering and sawing resounded against the walls, drowning out all other sounds, even the click of his staff against the cobblestones. The work of this alley's denizens never ceased, it seemed, not even on a day so full of hope and joy as the Spring Dawning Festival.

The elf limped along, leaning heavily on his staff. Behind him, the two drunken sailors staggered into the alley. One bumped into a stack of coffins and sent the gruesome boxes crashing to the cobbles. A man appeared in the door of Mauris and Sons Caskets and began to curse at them loudly enough to be heard even over the constant hammering and sawing.

While the elf watched them over his shoulder, someone bumped into him from in front. Instinctively, his hand grasped at the heavy coin purse at his belt, while he spun, fist clenched. A young girl staggered back from him, her basket of laundry spilling onto the dusty cobbles at her feet.

A string of shocking oaths escaped her lips as she angrily brushed a hand through her mop of long, dirty blonde hair.

"Why didn'ya look where you're going?" she swore. "Didn't see you me stannnn . . . !" Her gray eyes grew wide as they met his. Her jaw dropped.

The elf smiled, his green eyes sparkling. "What's your name?" he asked the girl.

"Claret," she whispered, her eyes still round as saucers.

"How old are you?" he asked.

"Sixteen," she answered, then started as though stung. "Nineteen!" she corrected herself with a shout. "I am nineteen."

"Almost nineteen," she amended in response to the elf's skeptical glance.

"Do you live in this place, Claret?" he asked.

"Yes. My father—" she began.

"I have lost my way. Can you tell me how to reach the Palanthas Trade Exchange?" he interrupted.

"I'll do better than that. I will show you," she said suddenly, grasping his hand.

"But your laundry," the elf said.

"It's not mine. I was only doing it as a favor." She hurriedly collected the spilled laundry and dumped it into the basket and before shoving the whole affair into an open doorway. "Come along, I'll take you there," she said. Clutching him by the hand again, she pulled him along, but he stumbled, unable to keep up.

Seeing him hobbling madly to keep pace with her, a little cry escaped her lips. "I'm so sorry," she whimpered. "Your foot."

"It's nothing," the elf consoled her. "Pay it no mind. But walk a little more slowly, if you would."

They continued on their way. She led him past more undertakers' and cabinetmakers' houses, a stonecutter's shop with finished marble headstones crowding the doorway, and an inconspicuous door that proclaimed the occupant to be a dentist and surgeon. They reached the end of the alley and stepped into the sunlight, turning right onto Horizon Road just east of the gate. The elf looked back and spotted the two sailors, still staggering along behind him.

"What's your name?" Claret asked.

"Caelthalas Elbernarian, son of Tanis Half-Elven," he answered.

"Son of who?" the girl asked over her shoulder.

"Never mind," he said with a smile. "You may call me Cael."

"I've never met an elf before, nor anyone so handsome. But handsome isn't the right word, is it? Beautiful. Yes, that's it. Beautiful. Are you married?" she asked in one long breathless string.

"You seem to have got over your shyness," Cael noted.

"I'm not really shy, you know. You surprised me, that's all. It isn't every day that you meet someone like you in that alley. How did you hurt your foot?" she rambled. "My father is missing a hand. He used to be a fine carpenter, but he accidentally cut his hand off with an axe, and now all he does is sleep and drink wine and yell at my mother."

With Cael in tow, Claret led the way down Horizon Road

toward the Great Plaza at the center of the city. Before they'd gone a stone's throw, she turned left onto Palisade Lane, so named because of the balconies shading both sides of the street. Cafe waiters were already setting out tables and iron chairs beneath the balconies or hanging clean white tablecloths along the decorative rails above in preparation for the crowds that would soon be filling the city for the celebration of the festival.

Two score paces down this lane, the girl pulled him beneath a pillared arcade and into a doorway where a flight of stairs led up into darkness. He twisted his hand free and stared at her in surprise, but found that she was looking past him. Turning, he saw the sailors stagger past, arm in arm. Neither looked his way. The girl breathed a sigh of relief.

"Were those two men following you?" she asked.

Cael paused and gazed admiringly at the girl before him. She returned his gaze unashamedly, blinking at him with her gray eyes. "No, I don't think they were," he said at last. "But I see I couldn't elude you as easily as we eluded them."

"They were probably Guild thieves," she answered proudly. "What did you do, steal something from them? Don't worry, I shan't tell. I can keep a secret better than anyone."

"I believe you," Cael said. "But it is best you don't know."

"I understand, but I'll help you just the same. If anyone asks for you, I'll tell them you're everywhere that you're not."

"Thank you for you help, Claret," he said, as he took a coin from the fat purse at his belt and pressed it into her palm.

She looked at it, then scowled at him. "I don't want this," she said, obviously hurt.

"Very well then," he countered while deftly snaking a hand around her slim waist. Her slippers scuffed across the dusty stairs as he pulled her close, her soft lips tightened in surprise as his met them, stealing a kiss, then releasing her before she had a chance to resist.

She pulled away, blushing to her ears, almost ready to bolt, her brow knotted in confusion. Cael's green eyes sparkled with mirth. "I hope that will suffice," he said.

For a moment longer, the girl stood irresolute at the bottom of the stairs, looking up at the elf. Then her face split into a grin, her gray eyes dancing. "It does for now!" she laughed, then dashed away. Cael stepped out from the stairway to watch the coltish grace of her long-legged stride as she fled, giggling, back the way they had come.

* * * * *

After he had seen her off, the elf strolled leisurely along Palisade Lane until it brought him to the Palanthas Trade Exchange. He wandered for a while among the stalls, purchasing a small tome of elven poetry from a bookseller, then a jeweled pin from a man displaying his wares atop a woolen blanket draped over a crate of live cats. A woman tried to drag him into her stall to view an alabaster figure of the god Paladine, which she assured him had been carved by Reorx himself. He managed to gracefully extract himself from her greasy fingers, only to be captured by a young boy promising to show him a pair of candlesticks carved from the eyeteeth of a black dragon. Another woman rushed up and shook a live chicken in his face, pointing out in a shrieking voice the particularly fine qualities of the hysterical fowl. He ducked aside, finding himself within a warm dark tent sharp with the odor of vinegary wine. The woman with the chicken followed, only to be chased out again by the broom-wielding wine merchant. Cael breathed a sigh of relief and slipped out the back.

This brought him into Jawbone Alley, which led away in the direction of the docks. After a few twists and turns, the alley opened onto a broad thoroughfare generally known as Bayside Road, though in truth there was little to identify it as road. Sometimes it was broad enough for three hay carts to pass side by side, sometimes two men walking in opposite directions would bump shoulders. More often than not, the widest stretches were filled with stacks of crates waiting to be loaded, making these areas as difficult to navigate as the most cunning maze. Bayside Road separated the city from the bay, running from Admiralty Street in the northwest corner of the city to Navy Point in the northeast.

This day, the docks were alive with activity. Those ships

that had wintered in Palanthas were loading and preparing to disembark. Sailors and seamen representing nearly every race on Krynn crowded the quays seeking employment aboard any ship that might take them. Other ships arrived hourly, returning from winter-long voyages that had visited nearly every port and harbor of Ansalon, bringing home to Palanthas their profits and curiosities. As far as the eye could see, masts rose high above the docks, creating the impression of a forest of tall ships. And above them all, floating and hovering and crying longingly, were the gulls of Palanthas, famous in song and tale.

Cael made his way along the cobbled waterfront, weaving among the boxes and crates and squads of city guards, customs officers, and Knights of Takhisis. Though the Dark Knights allowed the city a loose rein when it came to harbor traffic, they had very strict rules about what could and could not be imported into the city. These rules were posted at strategic points all along the docks so that no visiting ship's captain could claim ignorance as a defense. One of their most rigid laws forbade the possession or sale of any weapon. More than once, Cael was stopped and questioned, his papers checked, and his staff examined.

All the while, he felt eyes watching him, but whenever he looked around, he noticed nothing out of the ordinary. Once, he spotted a woman mending a sail who looked suspiciously like the chicken vendor who had pursued him into the wine-merchant's tent. Another time he was accosted by a beggar whom he thought resembled one of the drunken sailors.

He walked slowly, leaning heavily on his staff and stepping carefully along the slippery cobblestones. His long straight auburn hair, though not so uncommon in Palanthas as it might have been in some other cities, singled him out as did the fact that he was an elf. He received many a stare. Even in a city as metropolitan as Palanthas, it wasn't every day that a crippled elf strolled along the rough and tumble waterfront.

His cool green eyes alert and inquisitive, he seemed aware of everything that passed around him, and though obviously crippled, he had no trouble dodging the occasional netload of freight that swung too near. He handled his staff as though

47

born with it in his hand, and once, when a loose net hook careened at his face, he struck it aside without pausing in his hobbling stride.

He continued along the waterfront until he reached Fleece Street and its beggars. He passed them without a glance, ignoring their plaintive cries and miserable wails, turning at last back onto Horizon Road, having taken the circuitous route around the city wall to bypass its heavily guarded gate. At the corner of Fleece and Horizon, he passed a noblewoman dressed in a green gown, with silver bangles on her wrists. Behind her, two men struggled beneath a massive rug, bearing its rolled weight on bowed shoulders. His suspicions alerted, Cael glanced back, but they turned quickly into Washwell Alley and vanished from sight. The woman looked like the seller of alabaster figurines, while one of the male servants, though his face was hidden by the rug, was certainly the second of the drunken sailors.

As he stood staring after them, a sound behind him brought him spinning around. "Pardon me sir, could you spare—" the old man began. Cael had seen a glint of metal in the old man's hand and instinctively cracked the fellow over the head with his staff. The old man slumped to the ground at his feet, his tin cup spilling its meager bounty of thin copper coins at the elf's feet.

Quickly, Cael propped the old man up against the wall, pausing for a moment to check for the lifebeat at his throat, and sighed in relief. "Sorry, old one," he apologized. "You ought not to sneak up on me like that." He gathered up the coins, dumped them in the cup, and placed it in the beggar's limp grasp. Then, on second thought, he emptied the beggar's cup back into his palm, returned the cup, and hurried away.

After turning onto Horizon Road, the elf resumed his normal pace. The ancient cobbled way was sunk beneath the level of its curbs. Its iron sewer grates rose up to trip the unwary traveler and jolt the careless wagon driver from his seat. Where a tavern or shop stood, its doors thrown wide or darkly closed and guarded, the curbs were worn away by the passing of countless feet. Here stood a fountain spilling cool water into an ancient well, there a gate of new-wrought iron guarded a small comfortable garden where a speckled terrier yapped wildly.

As the cool morning breeze lifted, Cael felt a great longing enter his heart. All around him this great and ancient city thronged. He wondered at its multitudes, its thousands and tens of thousands of lives and loves and hates, its joys and grief. He looked at the well-ordered buildings and streets, some ancient and beautiful, some new and shabby, and a feeling for this place blossomed within him, unfolding and spilling with a thrill through all his limbs. He'd been in Palanthas, City of Seven Circles, for nearly a year, though to his elven senses it seemed but the passing of a day. After all he was an elf, and to the elves the passing of time means little. It seemed all the more strange to him that he should suddenly feel such affection for a city of humans, for nothing in the elven heart is sudden. He shook his head in wonder, his long auburn hair tousling in the freshening breeze, as he continued on his way. The breeze brought a scent of rain, and thunder rumbled in the hills to the west.

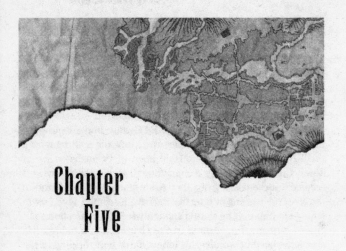

Chapter Five

"Twenty-five generations of Hammer-fells have passed since the Founder-stone was stolen from Balgard and Brimbar Hammerfell," the dwarf growled as he tugged angrily at his snowy beard. Cael smiled wearily across the table. He'd heard this tale many times before. "We were never paid for it," the dwarf finished.

"Not that they would have sold it," the elf said in his gentlest voice.

"Not that we would have sold it!" the dwarf shouted, his fist striking the table so hard that their two mugs jumped into the air. Foam leaped on high and washed across the dinted wooden surface of the table. "Never! Not for any price!"

"So tell me, Grandfather, why does the world not know this remarkable tale? Why do the minstrels not sing it at every festival?" the elf asked as he sat back in his chair and gestured at the players singing in the corner of the tavern. Outside the streets were alive with the noise of festivities, but inside the small common room of the Dwarven Spring, a group of minstrels played and sang a lively air to a nearly empty room. Other than the elf and the dwarf, the tavern's only occupants were a pair of off-duty Knights of Takhisis, a young man wearing the red robes of a mage, and an Ergothian silk merchant who snored with his head on the bar. Behind the bar, the barkeep carefully stacked a pyramid of crockery mugs. Windows set high in the walls provided the room's only illumination. These looked out at street level, presenting a fascinating view of the latest fashions in Palanthian footwear.

"Because, young Cael," the dwarf explained, "it was *forgotten*. Yes, forgotten! Having stolen from Balgard and Brimbar Hammerfell their only treasure, the citizens of Palanthas promptly forgot how they came by the stone or what it meant or why it was taken from the dwarves in the first place. You see, thieves stole it from the city treasury not long afterwards, and it was never recovered. The city forgot about it, because to remember it was to remember their failure. History was rewritten and the stone forgotten."

"Until now," Cael commented.

"We never forgot it!" the dwarf roared. "We knew where it was all along. We tried to get it back, but we failed. Meanwhile, the city gave us a pittance in return for our 'gift.' To this day, we pay no taxes, though I am sure not half the fools in the Senate know why. Nor would they question it. No, the Hammerfells have always been exempt from taxation, and so it shall remain."

"Surely, Grandfather, over the centuries your family has saved in taxes many times the value of the stone," Cael remarked.

"That is not the point, as you well know!" the dwarf growled. "You young rapscallion, you always seem to steer me to the subject of the Founderstone. Why is that? You know how it makes my blood boil."

"I enjoy the telling of the tale," Cael answered. "I am an elf, after all. I never weary of remembrances."

"Aye, that you are, my boy," the dwarf smiled. "You and I, we are as unlike as wood and stone, yet we understand one another better than we do these humans, wouldn't you say?" The elf nodded in agreement as he sipped from his mug.

The minstrels finished their song and set aside their instruments. One wandered over to the bar and eased himself atop a stool, while the rest stepped outside, rapidly ascending the stairs to the street and vanishing into the crowd. Meanwhile, the two Knights of Takhisis paid their bill and staggered to the door. Turning, they waved to the dwarf. "Good morrow to you, Mashter Hammerfell!" they shouted drunkenly.

"So long, boys. See you tomorrow." The dwarf waved and turned back to his elf companion. "They keep the rings on my fingers," he said, shrugging.

The barkeep approached the table, wiping his hands on a greasy rag. He was a slovenly man, with heavy unshaved jowls and a nap of hair clinging to his sweaty forehead. He stopped at their table and slid two coins before the dwarf. "They paid their tab in steel coin, marster," he said.

"If nothing else, the Dark Knights can be counted on for steel coin," the dwarf commented as he swept the coins from the table and into the pouch at his belt. "You can go now, if you like. The ceremonies will begin soon, I imagine."

"My boy is right keen to see them," the barkeep said, smiling with his brown teeth.

"Go on, then. I'll close up here. Just make sure you are back by dark. There'll be a crowd in here tonight, once the official festivities are over."

"Thank you, sire," the barkeep said. He left them, tossing his apron on the bar as he hurried out the door. The last minstrel finished his drink and followed him up the stairs.

"Now where was I?" the dwarf asked when they had gone.

"The Founderstone," Cael offered.

The old dwarf stroked his long white beard while he eyed the elf with some curiosity. He seemed a mere youth, a lad of no more than twenty summers but reckoned handsome as far as elves go.

"The Founderstone," the dwarf continued after a pause. "Your talk always seems to come round to that, young Cael. You've ideas better forgotten."

"I only wanted to hear the story again, since we are about to go and see the precious thing," Cael protested innocently.

"Well, you know the rest as well as I. It was stolen by the Thieves' Guild not long after Bright Horizon was renamed Palanthas, a long time ago even for dwarves. The city thought it better to forget that the stone had ever existed than admit its greatest treasure had passed beyond its grasp. The Guild, damn their greedy fingers, were untouchable. No one knew where to find them, no one knew how to stop them. Every attempt to recover the stone failed, and offers to purchase it back were ignored. So the city pretended it didn't exist, and in time it was forgotten by everyone . . . except the Hammerfells."

"And now it has reappeared," Cael said, finishing the story. "Found amongst the ruins of a Guild House when it was destroyed by the Knights of Takhisis four years ago. And the city has suddenly remembered the heritage of its greatest treasure, thanks to the researches of Bertrem, head of the Aesthetics of the Great Library. And today . . ."

"Today it sees the light of day once more, after over two thousand years of darkness," the dwarf said. "The Founderstone of Palanthas shall flower again. Though it grieves me to see it in the hands of another, I shouldn't miss this for the world. Shall we go?"

As the two rose from their chairs, the young mage in the corner dropped a couple of coins on his table. Nodding to dwarf and elf, he strolled out the door and up the stairs to the street. The old dwarf locked the door behind him, while outside, a fanfare of trumpets resounded above the city. "There's the signal," the dwarf said excitedly. "We'd better hurry."

"What about him?" Cael asked of the Ergothian silk merchant still snoring with his head on the bar.

"Let him sleep it off," the dwarf said, dismissing the fellow with a wave of his hand. "Come along. We'll go out through the smithy."

They passed through a low door behind the bar, the elderly dwarf waddling ahead, the young elf limping behind, leaning heavily on his black staff with each step. They entered a storeroom filled with barrels and burgeoning sacks. A few candles in sconces near the door provided a dim light. In the center of the room there stood a wide pool, like the walls of a well, but it was filled to the brim with crystalline water that rolled and bubbled. Set into the water was a pair of tall wooden kegs, with their taps dangling over the pool's lip. This was the Dwarven Spring, which gave the tavern its name. The water was not boiling but icy cold and rolling with a current that brought it up through one crack in the floor and out through another. The carefully joined stone walls of the pool captured the water for a brief moment on its subterranean journey and cooled the keg of beer and tun of wine set in it.

The dwarf took a bucket from a stack of others and held it under one of the taps. He filled it until suds slopped over the side and spilled on the floor. "Grab yourself a bucket," he said to the elf.

"A skin of wine would suit me better," Cael said.

"Fill her up then. Hurry. I have a place on the stage for the unveiling of the stone. You shall stand with me, my old friend."

Cael filled a large goatskin with wine and slung it over his shoulder. Then together, they ascended a stair of rough wooden planks to a door that opened into a low roofed smithy. The dwarf locked the door behind them and, taking the elf by the elbow, led him quickly through the close, hot darkness, winding amongst a wilderness of anvils and bellows, piles of scrap iron, and stacks of finished products ranging from horseshoes to delicately wrought railings destined to grace the balcony of some noblewoman's sitting room. A fire roared somewhere deep within the smithy, visible only as a wan red glow reflecting off the gently sloping ceiling. An intermittent hammer clanged out an awkward rhythm.

"Who is that?" the elf asked. "You've someone working today?"

"That's just Gimzig," the dwarf answered with annoyed scowl. "Gimzig!" he shouted. The hammer continued its weird cadence.

"Gimzig!" the dwarf roared.

The hammer ceased, and a few moments later a squat figure shuffled out of the shadows. Cael staggered back, covering his nose with his sleeve and coughing.

The figure was shorter even than the dwarf, lighter boned,

his movements quick and deerlike. The lower half of his face was covered with a thick mat of beard that was once white, as evidenced by the snowy fringe around the lips, but was now black with soot and the gods only knew what else. The upper half of his face was nearly hidden by a pair of billowing eyebrows, colored much like his beard, but tending towards gray rather than black, which hung sheepdog-like over his face. His eyes, twinkling with merriment, appeared and disappeared behind them with each movement of his head. The top of his head was quite bald, with only a thin halo of hair standing straight up from his scalp, as though he had been frightened as a baby and never recovered.

As he appeared from the shadows, he wiped his grimy hands across the breast of the filthy apron dangling around from his neck. His beard split into a wide toothy grin at the sight of the dwarf and his companion.

"Reorx's bones, Gimzig!" the dwarf exclaimed as he covered his nose with a handkerchief. "You smell like a hive of gully dwarves. Don't you ever bathe?"

"OfcourseIdowhentheneedarisesalthoughlatelythethoughthasescapedmeIadmit," the gnome answered in one breath.

Hammerfell rolled his eyes and gestured for the gnome to slow down.

"Oh. I have been working," the gnome enunciated as carefully as he could, "on some improvements to various time-saving devices. Would you like to see them?"

As a race, the gnomes of Krynn were a curious lot. First and foremost, they were inventors—of machines, devices, appliances, and bureaucracies, none of which ever worked as originally designed. They lived furiously busy lives, always planning, devising, creating, inventing, repairing, and reinventing their (more often than not) faulty first, second, third, ad infinitum, designs. Even their speech was rapid. To the unfamiliar, it sounded like a different language, but they simply spoke the common tongue at eight or nine times the rate of human speech. What was more, two or more gnomes could talk at once and understand each other perfectly. Gimzig had been a resident of Palanthas for approximately eighty-five years (like dwarves and elves, the gnomes were a long-lived race), and because of his more frequent dealings with humans, he had learned to slow his speech to a more intelligible rate. Because of this, whenever he met gnomes from his homeland of Mount Nevermind, they thought him slow and dull-witted.

The gnome continued, "Of course you are one to talk, being a dwarf after all. Dwarves are notorious for their bathing habits or lack thereof. I have often considered conducting a study to determine exactly how often . . . oh! say, Cael tell me how did the self-extending portable pocket curtain rod work?"

"Perfectly," the elf answered through his sleeve.

"I am so glad. I had some concerns about it, because the last three versions displayed some rather remarkable projectile tendencies."

"What's this?" the dwarf asked, looking from one to the other. "You've been using his gnomish contraptions? For what? Certainly not to hang your clothes."

"My inventions have multiple uses that—" the gnome began to protest.

Kharzog cut him off. "Enough! I don't want to hear it. Are you or are you not coming to the Spring Dawning festival? I have a place on the stage. I don't want to be late."

"Yesofcoursejustamomentletmegetmythings," Gimzig said as he hurried away.

"You aren't coming with me smelling like that!" the dwarf shouted after him.

The gnome's voice floated back to them from the darkness. "Of course not. Just let me step into my newest invention, a speed-washing bathtub. The water is superheated and pushed through nozzles at a high velocity in order to yeeeeooooowwwwwwwww!"

A cloud of steam boiled from the back of the smithy, carrying with it an odor of boiled meat. Cael staggered away, gorge rising in his throat. The dwarf swore a string of curses.

"Gimzig, you dolt, are you still alive?" he shouted.

After a few moments, a voice answered him from the darkness. "Yes . . . um . . . maybe you had better go without me."

"Do you need aid?"

"No I think not. Perhaps a little butter."

"I haven't got any butter, you doorknob!" the dwarf cursed. He grabbed the elf and led him through a door that brought them under a low shed. Cael ducked under the eaves and followed his companion into the narrow alley beyond.

"Why must Gimzig always smell like a dung heap?" Cael asked.

"He spends most of his time in the sewers."

"But why?"

"You're asking me?" Kharzog snorted. "Why does a gnome do anything? Whole books have been written about it, mostly by other gnomes. Hurry up. We'll miss everything."

They turned a corner, entering an alley slightly wider than the one they'd just left. A few people hurried along ahead of them, one bearing a picnic basket, another a jug of wine big enough to souse a small army.

Despite his greater stride, the elf began to fall behind his dwarven companion. "How is your limp?" Kharzog asked sarcastically of his struggling companion.

"Better. I hardly think about it now," Cael answered. His staff beat a rapid pace on the slick stones of the alley.

The dwarf scowled. "You know how I feel about that," he said.

"It keeps the fingers in my rings," the elf said with a laugh.

"And how does your *shalifi*, Master Verrochio, feel about it?" Kharzog asked angrily. Without waiting for a response, he continued, "You know how I feel about such deception, not to mention your profession. Your master would be ashamed if he were alive."

"He is alive, somewhere," Cael answered grimly. It was obvious that he had no desire to continue the conversation. Wagging his beard in frustration, the dwarf continued on his way.

They drew near the end of the alley. Revelers thronged the street beyond, some of them spilling into the alley, where they danced in small groups to the beat of a fife and drum corps. The dwarf elbowed a way through them and forced his way into the street. "By my father's black beard, this is the largest crowd I've seen in ten lustrums," he shouted above the noise.

All around them, people were dancing in the street. The air was filled with the competing sounds of bands, voices raised in song, laughter, and shouting. Noisemakers, crackers, and whistles frightened dogs and small children and sent them barking, howling, or screaming through the crowds. All the while, the people danced, huge masses of them dancing together, so that all that could be seen were their heads or hats going up and down. There was no getting through them. They filled all of Horizon Road, so that the elf and dwarf were forced to detour down sidestreets and alleys.

All along their way, people tried to pull them aside in a friendly fashion, pushing flagons of wine and foamy ale into their hands. "We want to drink with a dwarf!" they shouted stupidly.

"Out of my way, you drunken fools," the old dwarf laughed, as he pushed his way through them. He'd lived in Palanthas all his life, and he was used to the Palanthians' insensitivity to "outsiders," meaning any nonhuman, or for that matter any human not from Palanthas. It wasn't that they were mean-spirited. They just didn't know any better. "We have business in the Old City," he shouted when they plucked at his sleeves.

The elf fared no better, and perhaps worse, as curious women clung to his elbows and invited him to a quiet place for a private word. He'd gracefully dislodge them, almost reluctantly, for he knew the old dwarf, despite the smile in his beard, was impatient to get to the Great Plaza. Meanwhile, Cael resisted his natural inclination to relieve those he met of their superfluous wealth, but only to spare himself the dwarf's ire.

Palanthas was built upon a design meant to reflect the perfection of the heavenly spheres. In the center of the city lay the Great Plaza—a vast marble courtyard surrounded by the city's most important buildings, including the Lord's Palace, the Courthouse, and the barracks of the City Guard. Roads led out from the Great Plaza like the spokes of a wheel, while secondary roads were laid in concentric circles, spreading like ripples in a pool. All roads from the Great Plaza led outward.

Not long after the city was founded, a great wall was built around it, and over the years it was modified and improved until it was reckoned one of the architectural marvels of all Krynn. Where the roads passed through the wall, there stood seven mighty gates, with gate towers rising over three hundred feet above the streets of the city.

The wall was, in fact, two walls, one inside the other, with a deep muddy trench between them. It ran in a great circle, and everything within the wall was called the Old City. All the oldest and wealthiest families of Palanthas lived within the Old City, the Great Library was built here, as was the now-vanished Tower of High Sorcery. All that remained of the ancient tower was a strange pool surrounded by a small forest of magical trees—the Shoikan Grove. In the Old City also stood the Temple of Paladine, as well as the more recently constructed Shrine of Takhisis.

However, the original city planners had failed to appreciate how large and important Palanthas would grow to become. As the city outgrew its first wall and spread outward, houses and businesses began to fill up the valley between the surrounding hills and to dot their slopes. The city outside the first wall was called New City, though much of it was as old or older than many of the buildings in the Old City. In New City could be found the main markets, as well as the Old Temple District and the University. Here also lay The Dwarven Spring, the ancient public house belonging to one of the oldest families of Palanthas—the Hammerfell dwarves.

This day, the day of the Spring Dawning Festival, the streets of New City were packed with people from all over Krynn. They had come by way of the seven roads leading into the city, but most had traveled the Knight's High Road—the only overland passage through the Vingaard Mountains, an impregnable natural barrier that surrounded the city and protected it from the outside world. A great many more had arrived by ship, finding port in the calm waters of the Bay of Branchala. They filled Palanthas' inns and public houses, wine shops and streets. Those who couldn't find lodging camped in the parks and plazas, any place where a tent could be pitched or a blanket spread. Coins of steel and silver fairly rained into the merchants' pockets. Vendors packed the city's markets with their stalls like so many fishermen along a pier, casting their lines into the surf of humanity rolling along their shores. Hundreds of wagonloads of provisions flowed into the Merchandising District every morning, only to flow out again by midday to fill orders arriving from the city's inns. Only the bakers complained, for they were kept elbow deep in dough morning, noon, and night.

The Spring Dawning Festival was also one of the few times of the year when the Knights of Takhisis relaxed their control over the city's traffic. Flow into and out of the Old City was usually carefully watched at the seven gates, but on the day of the Spring Dawning Festival, when many thousands were crowding their way to the Great Plaza, not even the formidable Dark Knights could track every person passing through. Over thirty years had passed since the Dark Knights had wrested the city from the hands of the Knights of Solamnia, but the city continued to prosper. Indeed, some people thought business prospered *because* of the Knights. It seemed their greatest concern was maintaining an iron-fisted rule over the city. Though the Knights' laws were more strict than any the city had ever known, and their punishments more ruthless than civilized folk were used to seeing, there were not a few citizens who were glad of it. The level of lawlessness was at an all-time low. The city's jails were filled, and the ancient and seemingly untouchable Thieves' Guild had been destroyed. In the last ten years, the Spring Dawning Festival had grown from a civilized celebration to a veritable carnival.

Although the Knights maintained a show of force at the seven gates, this day they did more gawking than guarding. The Spring Dawning Festival was a holiday for them as well. Many looked forward to a magnificent feast to be held that evening in their barracks' mess halls, while their officers prepared for the social functions to be held throughout the night in the homes of nobles or aboard yachts anchored in the bay. All through the day, discipline was relaxed for one and all. Officers and soldiers laughed and joked among themselves as they lounged around the gates, leaning on their pikes, pointing out colorful characters in the crowd or sneaking cups of wine behind their shields. They kept only a casual watch for weapons and other contraband. The strict policy of checking identification papers was relaxed.

Cael and his dwarven companion eventually found themselves squeezed into the crush at the Horizon Road Gate. Cael's leg had tired him a bit, so his coppery hair clung damply to his pale flushed face, but the old gray-bearded dwarf fairly panted. His bucket of beer was empty, and his dwarven patience was as thin as the hairs covering his flushed pate. He cursed and shoved, trying in vain to hurry the crowd through the gate. While they waited, a tremendous boom shook the buildings, and looking up, they saw beyond the city walls a fireball hanging in the sky.

"Reorx's beard! We're late! That's the signal for the joust," the dwarf snarled. As though to reinforce his words, a fanfare of trumpets floated to them on the fine spring breeze. A second fireball exploded in the sky, shaking them to their bones, but a third, appearing as a point of light streaking up from the center of the city, sputtered and failed.

"Look at that!" someone behind them commented. Turning, they saw a small group of young men and women, all dressed in robes of red, pointing at the failed fireworks. "It is as I said," one hissed. They huddled together, whispering.

Cael looked at the old dwarf with a puzzled expression.

"Magic," the dwarf spat. "Not to be trusted, I always said, and now I'm proved right. There's a rumor that magic is failing, that magicians' spells and incantations are losing their power. And it not thirty years since the new magic was discovered after the old spells ceased to work, after Chaos stole the moons of magic. Good riddance, I say. They'd do better to use real gnomish fireworks, dangerous as they may be." He snorted, waving his hand at the failed fireball's pitiful smear of oily smoke now shredding in the breeze.

They inched their way toward the gate, passing finally beneath its massive arch into a short roofed passage between the walls. It was pleasantly cool and dark after the warm spring sun and the close air of New City's streets and alleys. However, the drums of a fife corps thundered within it, while the dancers jumped up and down like pistons in a gnomish engine. People grabbed the dwarf by the shoulders and dragged him into their dance, and in the crush Cael lost sight of his companion, though he was able to track the dwarf's progress by the occasional bellowing curse heard above the pounding of the drums. However, it was not long before he was himself caught up by the dancers and dragged into the fray. He was jostled, pummeled, pinched, pressed, elbowed, poked, and finally spun like a chip on the flood out the other end of the tunnel into the open air of the Old City. Somehow, he'd managed to keep hold of his staff. The old dwarf was nowhere to be seen.

"You there! Hey you!" a voice shouted. Looking around, Cael spotted a contingent of Knights of Takhisis standing in the shadow of the gate's southern tower. One Knight motioned for the elf to approach. Cael slowly hobbled through the streams of people. As he neared, the Knight who had hailed him winked. "Come over here," he said.

"May I be of service, Sir Garrud?" Cael asked of the winking Knight.

"I thought that was you, Cael," the Knight said. "Going to the party?"

"Eventually," the elf answered as he watched for his companion.

"Here, try a little of this, " the Knight said. He proffered a small brown bottle behind his shield. Grinning, Cael stooped, took the bottle and tilted it to his lips. Immediately, a fine silver mist erupted from his lips, filled the air with a potent odor of pure alcohol.

"Dwarf spirits," the Knight laughed. "The best."

"Indeed," Cael gasped.

"What's all this then?" shouted a voice behind them. The old dwarf appeared from the crowd. "Cael! So here you are. Confounded idiots! I thought they'd be the death of me." He stopped beside his friend and, planting his heavy dwarf boots wide apart, glared up at the Knight.

"You, what are you up to?" the dwarf demanded of Sir Garrud. "Why pick Cael out of the crowd? It's because he is an elf, isn't it? I suppose you'll be wanting to see my papers next. Do you know who I am?" he said, wagging his finger at the Knight's nose.

"We have orders to arrest someone fitting Cael's description, Master Hammerfell," the Knight said sternly. "Fortunately, his documents are in order. I'm glad of it. I wouldn't want to have to arrest an old friend. Cael and I are old friends, aren't we Cael?

"Friends we are," the elf smiled tolerantly.

"Yes, yes. That's all good and well," the dwarf growled. "If you are finished with him I'd like to go. We have a place on stage for the joust and the unveiling,"

"You're already late. The joust has begun," Sir Garrud said as he clapped Cael on the back, sending the chuckling elf and the old dwarf, sputtering with curses, on their way.

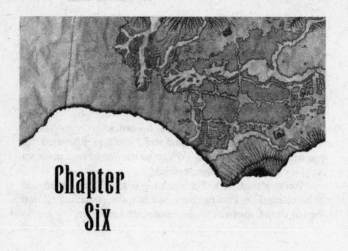

Chapter Six

In the center of the Great Plaza, a white knight lay on his back, wearily waving his hand in supplication, as a triumphant green-clad knight bowed to the raucous crowd. The Spring Dawning joust was symbolic. The white knight represented winter, while the green knight was the coming spring. Their mock battle celebrated the defeat of winter and the annual renewal of spring. Of course, the green knight always won, but the people enjoyed the event, and cheered wildly when the green knight at last overcame his white-clad adversary.

Master Hammerfell was angry at having missed the show. He and Cael made their way hastily onto the stage built upon the steps of the Lord's Palace, overlooking the Plaza. An attendant showed them where to stand, as the crowds continued to cheer. Nobody noticed their late entrance, for Master Hammerfell's place was far from the dignitaries and nobles surrounding the Lord of Palanthas, the Lord Knight of the Knights of Takhisis, and the city's senators. Among these latter personages sat

Bertrem, head of the order of Aesthetics of the Great Library of Palanthas, as well as numerous wealthy merchants, courtiers and courtesans, nobles, and prosperous captains of the city's merchant fleet. Near them, a powerful contingent of grim-faced guards huddled around a small, weasel-faced man dressed in robes of gray. He glared at anyone who approached too closely.

"Look who is here," Cael said, pointing him out.

"Arach Jannon," the dwarf snorted in disdain. "They say he knows everything that passes within Palanthas, that he sits in his chamber beneath the Lord's Palace like a great spider, controlling the web of informants and spies that he has spun across this city. No deed goes unmarked, no cargo landed, no missive dispatched by secret courier, no seditious word whispered, but that he knows about it. He is the Judge of Law of the city, a man to be feared. His is also the special duty of protecting the Founderstone and investigating its power."

"A Gray Robe, eh?" Cael noted. "Is his magic powerful?"

The dwarf shot him a suspicious glance. "I suppose. Despite his looks, he is not a man to be trifled with, I hear. He is clever and ruthless. They say it was he who brought the old Thieves' Guild low. Those warriors you see around him are his hand-picked guard. The Nine Axes they are called, very dangerous men, the best in all Solamnia. They are not Knights of Takhisis, so they are not above a knife in the back. They guard the Founderstone day and night, and are but one strand in a larger net of traps and foils. Look!"

At the center of the stage stood a man imploring the crowd to silence. He was a small, elderly fellow with a balding head and a groomed goatee protruding from his weak chin. With each pleading gesture for silence, the crowd grew less respectful, beginning to jeer.

"The Lord Mayor of Palanthas," the dwarf shouted. "Xavier uth Nostran. What a fool." Turning round, he found his elf companion gently loosening the pursestrings of their nearest neighbor—a wine importer by the name of Jevor Kannigan. Kharzog elbowed the elf in the ribs and trod on his foot with one heavy dwarven boot. Cael reluctantly left the merchant's fat purse where it hung and returned his attention to the festivities.

People were shouting good-natured obscenities at Lord Xavier, suggesting that he assume all sorts of impossible body positions. Some of the nobles and senators on the stage chuckled in embarrassment. Finally, a tall, powerfully built man wearing the black armor of the Knights of Takhisis rose pointedly to his feet. The crowd quieted somewhat, though they felt safe enough in their numbers to hurl a few curses even at the Lord Knight of the City, Sir Kinsaid. He stared ominously out at them as though memorizing their faces for future reference, and soon the jeering abated.

"People of Palanthas," the lord mayor said in a high, reedy voice. "Before the ceremonies continue, our great champion, the Lord Knight of the City of Palanthas, Sir Elstone Kinsaid, has an important announcement to make, which I am sure shall greatly benefit us all." His voice scraped an octave higher on the words "important announcement," causing many in the crowd to wince at his words. Few important announcements made by Sir Kinsaid had ever benefited anyone but the Knights of Takhisis. Lord Xavier cringingly resumed his seat.

With a final scathing glance round, Sir Kinsaid unrolled the scroll he had been clutching, and, holding it up formally, began to announce in a booming voice. "People of Ansalon and all the lands of Krynn, citizens of Palanthas, lords, ladies, and gentlemen, let it be known, by order of the Lord of the Night, Sir Morham Targonne, that from this day forward, the noble chivalric order formerly known as the Knights of Takhisis shall be known as the Knights of Neraka."

His voice echoed around the suddenly quiet plaza. People stared open-mouthed at the stage, awaiting some sort of explanation. None was forthcoming. Sir Kinsaid let the scroll snap shut, lowered his arms, and after gazing once more around the crowd, returned to his seat.

After a few moments' hesitation, Lord Xavier rose and returned to the front of the stage. He glanced back at the Lord Knight, but Sir Kinsaid simply folded his arms across his chest and set his lips in a grim line. His glacial blue eyes stared straight ahead.

"Thank . . . thank you, Sir Kinsaid," Xavier stuttered, then continued, turning back to the crowd. "And thank you citizens of Palanthas for making this the largest and most, uh, enjoyable

Spring Dawning Festival in half a century," the Lord Mayor proclaimed. The crowd applauded politely, quieting expectantly after a few moments.

"Today is perhaps more special than any day in this city's long and colorful history," the Lord Mayor continued. "For today, a great artifact has returned to us. Long have we mourned its loss . . ."

The dwarf snorted in derision.

". . . but today it shall see the light of day again, to spread its glory and blessing so that all may wonder and be proud. Today, the heart of Palanthas is returned, the stone that signified that Paladine had indeed blessed this city . . ."

The Lord Knight shifted uncomfortably, but Xavier continued unabashed ". . . and that was so rudely stolen from us after it was given to the city by the Hammerfell dwarves."

"Well, at least he mentioned us," the old dwarf muttered under his breath. Cael smiled.

"For over two thousand years it lay hidden in the bowels of the ancient and wicked Thieves' Guild, until four years ago, when the Knights of Takhisis . . . er, Knights of Neraka, led by Sir Kinsaid, crushed the accursed Guild under its heel, laying waste to their houses and lairs, jailing their members or driving them out of this city forever!"

"Are there no more thieves in Palanthas, Grandfather?" Cael asked. The dwarf loosed a loud guffaw, but said nothing.

"Even so, little did we suspect the significance of the curious stone we found among the thousands of other treasures discovered in Thieves' House," Lord Xavier continued. "To even the amateur eye, it was beautiful, and could be reckoned priceless. But its true importance remained unsuspected until one of our most respected citizens, Bertrem of the Great Library, discovered a little-known document describing the history of the Founderstone. It is a long and fascinating history . . ."

"And largely untrue," the dwarf muttered.

". . . that shall surely be put into verse by one of our talented bards before much longer," the lord of Palanthas said.

"Show us the stone!" someone in the crowd shouted. This was Xavier's big speech of the afternoon. The crowd feared he might go on forever.

"Show us the stone! Show us the stone!" Others took up the cry, until Lord Xavier's voice was lost in the noise. Finally, the lord mayor threw up his hands, smiled and nodded acquiescently. He motioned to the Thorn Knight, Sir Arach Jannon. The shouts of the crowd changed to hurrahs.

The old dwarf gripped Cael's hand as the Gray Robe came forward, fidgeting with something in his robe. Cael winced but otherwise held tightly to his friend's knobby old hand.

Sir Arach removed something from the depths of his robes, and with a ceremonial flourish held it out, cupped in his outstretched hands. A glowing, pinkish light welled forth. The crowd fell silent.

With a brilliant flash, a light like a star erupted from the Thorn Knight's hands. Shimmering cascades of sparks fell about him and spilled across the stage. A gasp of awe and wonder escaped the crowd, and even the skeptics stood spellbound by the sight. There seemed to be a quiet music in the air, like pipes and chimes heard across a sylvan valley.

"It is more beautiful than I ever imagined," the old dwarf sighed.

The Founderstone pulsed with light, as though in the warmth of the spring sun it felt its life stirring again after a long sleep. People began to laugh without knowing why. Joyous singing broke out all over the Great Plaza. The old dwarf broke into a hymn to Reorx, chanting and roaring in the terse language of his people. Tears streamed into his beard. Cael clutched his hand, his own astonished eyes wide with wonder and delight.

The Thorn Knight staggered as though under a great burden, but two of his guards came forward and held his arms aloft. No one knew how long they stood so, for the sun itself seemed to stand still. The light of the stone flowed like honey-scented mist down street and alley, through door and open window, and wherever it passed, winter-brown grass turned to lushest green and buds popped out on the naked limbs of late blooming trees.

It was not for long. The light vanished suddenly as the Thorn Knight returned the stone to a secret place in his robes. Sir Arach looked uncommonly weary and pained, staggering as he left the stage. The Nine Axes huddled around him, wary and

alert, with their hands on their weapons. The people in the
Great Plaza, thrilled beyond belief, cried for more, but Sir Arach
and the Founderstone vanished through the doors of the palace.

The people on the stage milled about as though dumbstruck.
All plans for a concluding ceremony seemed to have been forgotten. After a while, the crowd began to break up, while the
people on the stage looked around at each other and laughed
nervously at the sudden breaking of tension. There was much
slapping of backs and forced lightheartedness.

The old dwarf refused to check his feelings. "It is my heart,
my soul, in the hands of that cursed Thorn Knight," he cried.
"What I wouldn't give to hold it for a moment." He clutched
the elf's hand, weeping unashamed.

"I know, Grandfather. I know." Cael tried to console his
friend while the nobles and other dignitaries left the stage. As
they passed, they spoke in eager tones of the parties and soirees
planned for that evening. A few nodded in passing to the dwarf
and his companion, for Master Hammerfell was well known to
the denizens of the city.

Slowly, Master Hammerfell gathered control of his emotions.
The Great Plaza was beginning to empty as the revelers dispersed
to wine shops and taverns to continue the festivities. Nearby, a
party of high-ranking Dark Knights preened and strutted around
a clutch of bejeweled young noblewomen, while near the center
of the stage the elderly Aesthetic Bertrem remained, holding
forth, surrounded by a contingent of junior monks and university
students. His high, quavering voice carried through the square.
He was explaining how he had discovered the Founderstone document quite by accident while searching for information on the
background and formation of the Thieves' Guild.

As Bertrem continued his statement, a strange-looking pair
approached Master Hammerfell and Cael. One was a large man
in height and girth. Despite his huge size, his movements spoke
of hidden energy and unexpected grace. He wore grizzled side-
burns on his massive jowls, and an elegant braid of hair lay
upon one shoulder, as was once stylish among officers of the
fleets of Palanthas. His dress reinforced this impression of a
seaman, for he wore a jacket of dark blue, with brass buttons

and golden braidwork on the sleeves. His knee-length black boots were polished to a mirror sheen.

On his massive arm dangled a lovely creature draped in sheer silks of palest green. Her skin was dusky, her eyes dark and flashing. Tight ringlets of black hair clung about the perfect oval of her face, and her lips, pursed into a wry smile, were full and moist. Her body was svelte, her limbs lithe and expressive. Pointing to the dwarf and the elf, she whispered something behind her hand to her large companion. The strange pair stopped, and the man bowed slightly at the hips, clicking his heels together in a military fashion.

"Master Kharzog Hammerfell, my regards and the regards of my wife, Alynthia Krath-Mal," the man said with rigid formality.

"Thank you, Captain," the old dwarf answered. "May I present to you my long-time friend and boon companion . . ."

Cael stepped forward, planting his staff firmly on the wooden planks of the stage and bending to take the woman's hand. "Caelthalas Elbernarian, son of Tanis Half-Elven, at your service," he said as he brushed his lips across her fingertips.

"*The* Tanis Half-Elven?" the woman laughed musically.

"Truly. My mother was a sea elf. It was she who gave me these sea green eyes," Cael answered while retaining his hold on her hand.

"What did your father give you?" Alynthia asked. "Funny, I never heard that the great Hero of the Lance had any children other than Lord Gilthas, the king of the elf realm of Qualinesti. I suppose that makes you a prince. Or does it?"

"That is an interesting scent you wear, Mistress Alynthia," Cael returned smoothly, ignoring her jibe. He sniffed the air and smiled. "It reminds me of someone I met last night. Is this not the perfume of the yellow Ergothian lotus, said to have the mystical power to drive men mad with passion?"

She started, but her poise and delicate grace quickly overcame her momentary surprise. She shot the elf a knowing smile.

"How do the noble elves fare under its influence?" she asked coyly, her black eyes sparkling.

"We are, alas, completely immune to its magic," he answered as he caressed her fingertips.

"Yes, well," the captain interrupted, clearing his throat. "Master Hammerfell, there are some in this city who know the true story behind the Founderstone and how the Hammerfells have been treated by the city fathers. To you and your family we are indeed indebted. On this day, especially, it is important to remember the past."

"I thank you, Captain Oros uth Jakar, for your kind words," the dwarf said, bowing deeply.

"Come along, my dear," the captain ordered. Alynthia detached her fingers from Cael's gentle grasp and let herself be pulled away by her husband. Cael ran a pale hand through his long coppery hair and watched her descend the stairs to the plaza below. She looked back once as they crossed the plaza but made no sign nor gesture.

"Hmph!" the dwarf snorted, seeing the bewitched expression on his companion's face. "There's another treasure quite beyond your long-fingered grasp, my friend."

"I wouldn't trade her for all the jewels in Krynn," Cael answered. "A mighty prize, worthy of my skills."

The dwarf settled himself into one of the chairs left scattered haphazardly across the stage. At the farther end of the platform, attendants were beginning to sweep up and remove the chairs, while the sun lowered behind the Vingaard Mountains. A cool, pleasant twilight descended upon the plaza, and lights twinkled among the trees on Nobles Hill and the Golden Estates.

"Well, you'll never get her away from *him*. He's Captain Oros uth Jakar of Palanthas," Kharzog Hammerfell said, as he produced a brier root pipe from his jacket. "He used to be some kind of merchant captain, I hear, made a lot of money in some venture or other. Pleasant fellow, what little I know about him."

"I have heard of him. Some say he is master of the reorganized Thieves' Guild," Cael commented as a group of scholars and Aesthetics passed them.

"Pah! Don't you believe it! Mulciber is the true master of the Guild. All know that!" the dwarf exclaimed. "Captain Oros is a retired captain, wealthy from business."

At these words, a group of scholars passing on the stairs paused and looked pointedly at the dwarf and his companion. They made several signs to ward away evil. Over the past two years, the name of Mulciber had arisen like a shadow over the city. His very name invoked crime and evil. Folk were reminded of the old days, when the Tower of High Sorcery still rose like a skeletal finger above the Palanthian skyline and the name of Raistlin Majere, master of the Tower, was used to frighten wayward children.

Few had seen this mysterious figure named Mulciber, though many claimed to know someone who knew someone who had seen him. Some said he was a powerful black-robed mage, a throwback to former times. Others said the name could only refer to a famous and long-dead priestess of the evil god Hiddukel. In any case, the Thieves' Guild had indeed sprung back to life, after being nearly stamped out of existence by the Dark Knights. Those who crossed the Thieves' Guild were sometimes found hanging from the yardarms of ships in the harbor, bearing visages of such frozen horror that, it was said, they had glimpsed the true form of Mulciber in their final moments of existence. Even the scholars and the Aesthetics of the library, normally inured to such superstitious nonsense, shuddered at the merest whisper of the name Mulciber.

The old dwarf snorted and tapped his pipe against the heel of his boot. The scholars turned and hurried away. "Captain Oros is a stodgy old merchant mariner, nothing more. Lady Alynthia is another matter entirely," the dwarf said.

"Entirely!" Cael agreed.

The dwarf ignored him and launched into the history he so dearly loved to repeat. "They say her mother was a Palanthian from a wealthy merchant family. She married the third son of some noble or other, but she was wild, untamed as a tigress. She preferred to sail on her husband's ships rather than stay at home with husband and child, hearth and kitchen. On one of those voyages she met an Ergothian pirate, fell in love with him, bore him a daughter. Some say the two died when their ship was destroyed by the red dragon Pyrothraxus off the coast of the Isle of Christyne. Alynthia was but a toddler then, but her mother's husband took her in and raised her as his own. A good, noble-hearted man, he was. He died aboard the *Mary Eileen*, when she sank off the Teeth of Chaos.

"But the girl was her mother's daughter. When still but a lass, she took to voyaging with her stepfather's merchant fleet. That's where she met Captain Oros, when she was still a child and he a merchant captain in her stepfather's employ. When the man who had raised her as his own died, she dishonored his memory by taking her birth father's patronymic, in the Ergothian tradition. Oros retired from captaining, she grew up into the woman you see while off sailing the seas, and when she returned to Palanthas, she and old Oros became something of an item. They say they are married, though I won't venture to tell you the truth of it either way."

"That is why I love you, Grandfather," Cael said as he kissed the old dwarf on his bald pate. "You are a veritable living library. Is there anyone whose story you don't know?"

"As a matter of fact there is!" the dwarf barked.

"Pray tell, who?"

"Yours! Why do you go about telling folk you are the son of Tanis Half-Elven?" Kharzog demanded.

Cael hobbled to the stairs and turned. "Because I am, Grandfather. Because I am."

"Pah! You are a born liar, that's what you are. Where are you off to, elf?" the dwarf asked.

"I hear a ship bearing wondrous treasures arrived this morning from Flotsam." He waggled his fingers in farewell and descended the wooden stairs, his staff clunking with each awkward step. "Until tomorrow, Grandfather." The elf's voice floated back to Hammerfell.

The dwarf watched Cael hobble in the direction of Nobles Hill until he vanished in the shadow of the Courthouse. At his summons, an attendant brought him a candle, and with it he lit his pipe. He puffed angrily, filling the air about him with a cloud of fragrant blue smoke. "Blast that lying fool of an elf. He's going to get himself into no end of trouble. Who will get him out of it, I wonder?" he grumbled.

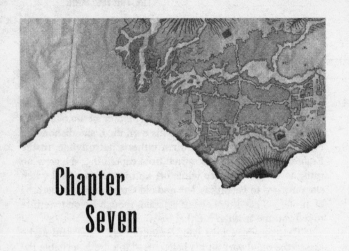

Chapter
Seven

At the corner of Knight's Candle Street and Horizon Road, Cael turned aside, ducking beneath a gleaming, hissing street lamp and entering a dark little alley called the Greenway. A slime-slick stream of water running down its center gave the alley its name. At the alley's end, a rickety wooden stair clung to the side of an old building. Cael mounted it to a door and entered a low dark hall as rain sounded on the slate roof above.

An early spring rain would do nothing to dampen the night's festivities. Indeed many in Palanthas welcomed the rain. Since the Dragon Purge, when the great blue dragon Khellendros seized the lands about Palanthas and began changing them to desert, the weather in the city had been turned on its head. In springtime little rain fell anymore, and the summers grew longer and hotter with each passing year. Yet autumn had grown unac-customedly wet, with frequent violent storms, and winter brought the occasional dusting of snow, a thing unheard of in the past. Luckily, Palanthas had never relied on agriculture for its trade, but of late those families who did farm the surrounding valleys found it more and more difficult to reap the bounty of the soil.

So a good downpour on the night of Spring Dawning seemed a welcome reprise, even a sign of hope. The streets filled with drunken revelers, splashing in the puddles and singing like lunatics.

Cael entered a narrow, dark hallway, shutting the door behind him to keep the rain from washing in. Somewhere along the hall's length, a baby wailed, while a man and a woman shouted obscenities at one another. A pair of children, naked and filthy, cowered outside an open door. Cael passed them without glancing into the room. He stopped a few doors down. As he tugged a key from his belt, a piece of crockery shattered behind him, sending fragments bounding down the hall. A woman screamed, and the children in the hall bleated as they bolted past him, their little feet slapping on the floor. Cael casually unlocked the door and entered his room.

The room was dim and small, with only a low bed beside the wall and a cheap wardrobe near the window, one door hanging crookedly ajar. Cael froze, immediately sensing that something was wrong. The wardrobe stood empty, his few possessions littering the floor before it. The thin mattress on the bed was overturned, the blankets stripped from it, and it was slashed in a dozen places. Quickly, he crossed to the window and threw open the shutters. No sign of anyone. His room had been ransacked. He swore softly to himself, but at the same time thanked his stars that he hadn't been here. That thought drove another into his head, and he stepped quickly to the door to lock it.

Too late. The knob turned, the door banged open. A man huge as an ogre shouldered into the room, followed by what was surely his twin, in size and ugliness if not in blood. They grinned broadly with their yellow teeth. Behind them strode on lithe legs a woman closely dressed in velvet green, with velvet hood and cloak. A lavender veil obscured the lower half of her face, but it did not hide her dark, angry eyes.

Cael dove for the window.

"I wouldn't do that!" the woman shouted. The note in her voice brought him up short, and he glared over his shoulder at her. ". . . if I were you," she finished. "There is a crossbowman on yonder roof who can pierce the eye of a sparrow in the dark."

"Mistress Alynthia," Cael said with a grim smile. "Quite a coincidence, running into you so often."

"Captain Alynthia, elf!" the uglier (if that were possible) of the two thugs growled.

"The same," the woman answered as she removed her veil. The second hulk closed the door behind her and put his back against it. She pushed back her cowl, freeing a mass of dark curls, which spilled onto her slim shoulders. She returned his smile, but there was no friendliness in it. Her eyes spoke daggers.

"We'll take it now," she said.

"Tea? Surely. Just let me set a kettle to boil," Cael said.

"No, you fool," Alynthia snapped. "Stop trying to delay. You've cost us enough. We want it now."

"Mistress, all I have is yours for the asking," Cael said. "Only tell me what it is, and it shall be delivered."

"You know very well, Cael Ironstaff, for you lifted it from my person last night," she spat.

"How well my unworthy hands remember the occasion," Cael answered.

Both bodyguards growled dangerously. "Let me break his head, Captain," one said as he cracked his knuckles.

Alynthia's dark eyes narrowed, her moist lips pursed. "The pollen of the dragonflower is the most valuable spice on Krynn," she said. "It grows only in the Dragon Isles. Three days past, a shipment arrived aboard the Star of Ansalon, Gaeord uth Wotan's flagship. I planned a daring theft and would have absconded with it from his private stores if you hadn't interfered. Your vile fingers lifted it from my bodice, defiling my flesh in the process."

"You speak like a novel," Cael commented.

"You speak like a man about to die!" she snapped.

"Let me break his head," the thug urged.

"My ankle pains me. May I sit?" Cael asked as he hobbled to the bed and eased himself onto it.

"Do what you like, only do not delay. I will not be trifled with."

"Of course you won't, Mistress Alynthia," Cael smiled, his green eyes flashing merrily. While one hand clasped his black staff, he gripped the rail of the bed with the other. Moving faster than imaginable, he suddenly heaved the bed onto its side and dived behind it. A quarrel thick as a man's finger thudded into the wall by his head.

With a roar of delight, the thugs rushed in. One snatched aside the bed as though it was a toy, the other sprang with clawing hands at the elf. But he was gone.

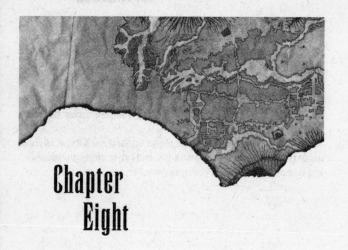

Chapter Eight

Cael listened with glee to the tumult in the room above him. A trapdoor had opened into a crawl space beneath the floor. Although there was hardly room for a cat, he managed to wriggle and writhe his way through the darkness while still gripping his staff.

Light flooded the passage as the thieves finally found the trapdoor and shoved a hastily lit candle into the hole. Dozens of rats scurried away from the light, jumping over Cael's body. One thug stuck his head through the trapdoor, looked at Cael, and got a boot in the nose for his trouble. He roared in pain and rage, but there wasn't enough room for him to follow. Cael heard Alynthia bark an order, then feet pounded out of the room and away down the hall. Cael quickened his crawl.

After knocking open another trapdoor, the elf dropped lightly to the floor of the ground floor hall. The two thugs tumbled into view from a stairwell not twenty feet away. They roared at sight of their quarry. Cael spun and dashed the other way.

No twisted foot slowed him now. He ran lightly, his feet

hardly seeming to touch the floor, his cloak fluttering behind him. He skidded around a corner, toppling a pail of rinds and garbage to foil pursuit, but the thugs came on, slamming into the wall.

The storm rumbled and poured sheets of rain. Ahead, the front door of the building stood open, filled with a wan light. A shout from one of the thugs summoned two shadowy figures from the street. They blocked the door, lead-weighted leather jacks dangling from their fists. Cael slid to a stop. As the thugs closed on him, he kicked open a small door and leaped inside, spun, slammed it shut, and shot its tiny bolt just as the first thug crashed into it. Wood splintered from the doorframe, but the bolt held.

The chamber was a privy, barely large enough for the elf to turn around. At its back stood a wooden bench, through which had been cut a hole. Pressing his black staff against the wall, Cael spoke one word in a soft voice: "Conceal." The staff shimmered, then melted into the wall, vanishing from sight. For a moment, a reddish glow marked its outline on the stone, but the glow quickly faded. The door was shaking under the onslaught. As Cael leaped atop the bench and dropped through the hole, the door burst open, and the privy filled with large sweaty cursing men and broken splinters of wood.

The fall was longer than he had expected. The metal rungs of some old ladder, rusty and corroded, flashed by, but twisting around he could only see darkness. A rushing noise grew deafening. He struck black water hard as stone, feet first, and shot quickly to the bottom. The sewer, swollen with the storm's rain, gushed and churned. Cael felt the cold current drag at his legs, pulling him under and bumping him along the bottom with the other refuse of the city. The tight bag of coins at his belt dragged along the bottom of the sewer. He kicked, fought the pull of the water while jerking at his purse. Finally, the leather cord broke. Flashing coins burst from the purse like a school of silver fish and vanished in a dark swirl of water. With an effort, Cael broke the surface, gasping for air.

A net splashed into the water beside him, then another, and then a hook at the end of a long wooden pole. Here the sewer ran long and straight like a dwarf road. Men stood along its side, crowding the access walk, with lanterns and weighted nets and gaffs in hand. "There he is!" one shouted as he cast his net. Cael ducked under the surface just as the net splashed around his head. He kicked for the far side of the fuming channel, hearing the muffled shouts and splashes as the thieves cast their weapons into the water.

He felt a sharp jerk at his leg. A gaff had caught him just behind the knee. He was dragged backward through the water. He fought, but the hook had snagged the leg of his trousers. Water gushed up his nose, choking him. He felt the hook digging into his flesh, ready to pierce and rend at his slightest resistance. He tried to undo it, but he couldn't twist around. He was yanked upward. His hands thrashed the surface.

Finally, his back bumped against stone. He grasped the pole and pulled himself up, filled his lungs with a gasp. Mocking laughter greeted him as his captors gathered on the walk above.

"Give him another dunk, Brem!" one shouted to the Ergothian thief holding the gaff.

Brem shoved the elf beneath the surface once more. Water flooded his ears. They dragged him up. He coughed, retching black sewer water, while they roared insults and urged another dunking. Down he went again, but now he was able to grab firm hold of the gaff. He dislodged the hook from his trousers, planted his feet against the stone wall of the sewer channel, and heaved. He heard a cry, followed by a tremendous splash.

Cael bobbed to the surface and watched as his captor was swept away by the storm-swollen sewer. Other thieves chased after the man, lowering poles, which he grasped, then lost. But the elf had no time to relish the sight. A net splashed around him, and before he could swim away, the weighted strands had tangled around his legs, trapping him. This time he was swiftly dragged to the shore and hauled from the water. He was dropped cruelly on the stones, and someone kicked him in the back.

Downstream, the thieves had finally caught their companion and were laughingly dragging him ashore. Between retches, the one named Brem swore revenge against the elf. Then, without warning, he vanished with a scream in a swirl of black water. A great spined tail, thick as a man's waist, thrashed the surface for a moment and was gone. One thief on the shore stood gawking at his gaff. The hook and three feet of pole had been bitten off, the end splintered into matchsticks. With a look of horror frozen on his face, he dropped the stick into the water and fled. Other thieves quickly followed him. Brem was abandoned, forgotten. They scurried up ladders, some vanishing into holes or side tunnels. Lanterns were doused or thrown hissing into the water.

A pole was quickly threaded through Cael's net and he was lifted by two men at either end of the pole and hurried away. "What was that?" he asked his captors as he jounced along. Only a few moments had passed, but already the scores of thieves participating in his capture had been reduced to a half dozen in number: the two carrying him, and two who walked in front with lanterns, two behind with daggers drawn.

"Sewer monster," the one in front snarled over his shoulder. "You're lucky we don't feed you to him. Brem was as good a mate as I ever had. But Captain Alynthia says to bring you back alive, and I daren't cross her, not for any money." Cael suddenly recognized the man as Hook-nose, whom he had bested at thievery the night before.

"Ah, all in a day's work, I suppose," Hook-nose said with an abrupt laugh. "Brem knew the risks, same as anyone. Was a time when the Guild kept the sewers clean, for its own purposes of course, and they say it was one reason the city never bent its back to heave us out. But since the Night of Black Hammers, things have begun to creep back to life in the sewers, some of them same as before, some worse."

Whatever their origin, down these subterranean avenues had swept the refuse of almost twenty-five centuries. Yet for all their wonder, few citizens of Palanthas had ever seen them or, for that matter, wanted to. The sewers were home to the dregs of humanity, and worse. Rats and gully dwarves were but the scum on the surface of a hidden world of forgotten chambers and passages, which nowadays housed, it was said, creatures born out of the nightmare of Chaos. True Palanthians believed in the sewer monsters and visited their privies in the dark of night with some reluctance, but the Dark Knights and Senate went to great lengths to discount these rumors.

Although Cael had a professional familiarity with these underground passages, his captors were taking a circuitous route and he couldn't be certain in what direction they were headed. After a long time, the thieves finally came to a halt at the end of a small passage hardly large enough for the men to stand. A trickle of water spattered through a grate above their heads, and a wan light illuminated their faces.

They set Cael under the dripping water, just for the fun of it, it seemed. All was suddenly quiet. Hook-nose enjoined the other two thieves to silence, and when one of them tried to light a pipe to pass the time, the ranking thief slapped it from his hand.

They waited now, waited while the light overhead grew stronger as the storm waned, drifting off to drench the hills and farms east of Palanthas, and the moon set behind the Vingaard Mountains. Cael's muscles ached, and he shivered violently with the cold and wet. Finally, as the light tinted to dawn's crimson, there came a noise of stone grating against stone. The thieves rose, knocking Cael around painfully as they hauled him in their net. Behind them, a section of the sewer wall slid back, and a warm yellow glow spilled out.

"Bring him in," a voice whispered.

Quickly, they stepped through the opening, dragging Cael across the threshold. They seemed to relish causing him additional pain and bruises. Every joint ached, the wets ropes rubbed his flesh raw. They dropped him in a heap just within, letting the pole fall ringingly on his skull.

A figure stood over him, a torch raised in its hand. Cael blinked in the smoky light. The door ground shut behind them.

"Where is his staff?" the figure asked angrily. As Cael's eyes adjusted to the light, he was able to make out the slim curves of the torchbearer.

"He bore no staff, Captain," Hook-nose said.

"I dropped it in the sewers, Mistress Alynthia," Cael said.

There was a hiss from the figure. "That I somehow doubt." The torch fluttered and crackled. "Free him," she growled.

The bearers extracted Cael from the net while Hook-nose voiced his concerns. "Slippery as an New Sea eel, this elf. A magician, I say he is. Tossed Brem in the water, nearly escaped, and Brem eaten by a sewer monster! Best to keep him bound, or kill him now."

"You know the law," Alynthia barked. "He must go before the Eighth Circle. Bind his arms if you like. Bind them tightly. It makes no difference to me." She turned to the captive elf. "Death lies before you as well as behind, Cael Ironstaff. There is no escape from *this* place."

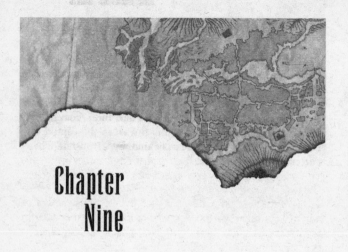

Chapter
Nine

The bearers lifted Cael to his feet and wrapped him in tight cords, binding his arms but leaving his legs free. Alynthia turned, and holding her torch aloft, stalked into the darkness. Cael followed, prodded along by Hook-nose. The two bearers vanished into the gloom, leaving the three of them alone with their charge. The echoes of their footsteps gathered around them, and rank water dripped unseen in the shadows. A deep mist hovered above the floor, obscuring the ground, but Mistress Alynthia led onward, her back erect.

They passed a heap of bones, and then from the darkness a crypt loomed. It was carved with leering faces and scenes of a tortured afterlife. A pillar of stone, marked with skulls, rose next to it. Overhead, the roof was arched and supported by numerous pillars of brick and dank stone. The party's feet kicked up objects they could not see, sending them bounding along the wet stone floor. They stepped in cold puddles, loosing a fetid stench. Rats scurried from the light of their torch only to stop just outside its circle and peer back over their brown furred backs with gleaming red eyes.

After a time, a wall rose before them and blocked their path. In its center, they found a door bound with rusty iron, with a grate and a sturdy hinge set into the stone. Alynthia rapped upon the door with the butt of her torch, showering sparks on the floor. Immediately, the grate slid back and a voice asked, "Who goes?"

"Travelers from afar," Alynthia answered.

A bang echoed through the catacomb as the door's bolt was slid back. The ancient iron portal creaked open. The door warden, an ancient man with a voice as rusty and grinding as the hinges of the door he guarded, greeted them as they entered. A loop of keys and a garrote hung from his belt. He nodded to Alynthia, cackled at Hook-nose, and shot Cael a venomous glance with his rheumy yellow eyes.

Beyond the door, a narrow stair rose into darkness. Without pause, Alynthia mounted the stair, her torch fluttering ahead of her. Hook-nose prodded Cael upward. The stair was not long, and at its top a tripod and a flaming brazier illuminated a wide landing. Alynthia opened the door into hall that stretched into darkness on either hand.

They passed many doors, most closed tight and looking as if they hadn't been opened in centuries. Others opened onto gaping darkness, filled with the echoes of their footsteps.

Cael could not restrain his curiosity. "The house is empty. Where are all the children?" he asked.

"There is no one on this level," she said levelly. "This is but one house of many. It is how we protect ourselves. No one knows every house and stronghold, so no one can betray us all."

They walked on a while longer, turning right, climbing a stair, and turning right again. Now the hall seemed less deserted. They passed a room where a candle burned atop a long table beside a book and a battered silver cup.

"Where are we heading, may I ask?" Cael ventured.

Without turning, Alynthia answered, "You are to be judged by Mulciber, our master."

"What does that mean, to be judged by Mulciber?" Cael asked.

"You will die, or you will live."

They entered a room filled with the scent of sandalwood. Incense burned on low tables that surrounded a huge silver platter set on the floor. The platter still contained the remnants of a meal. Currants and grains of white rice littered the rug surrounding it.

They passed through a larger shadowy chamber. Here columns of gray marble stood in endless ranks that vanished into darkness in all directions. However, a wide way led down their middle toward a set of tall double doors, black, bound in jeweled gold.

Alynthia led the way down the marble colonnade toward the doors. Cael noticed that Hook-nose had slipped away somewhere in the darkness. He was alone with Alynthia now. Yet even if he could escape, where would he go? With an inward shrug, he trudged after her.

"I can't believe you would prefer for me to die—"

A gloved fist struck him across his beardless jaw. He staggered into a column. The female thief threw her body against him, crushing him against the cold stone pillar. Her fingers twisted painfully in his long hair. Then a knee rose up and caught him in the midriff, driving the air from his lungs.

Cael collapsed to the floor. A little blood trickled from his lip. Alynthia scrubbed her lips with the back of her gloved hand, then twisted her fist into the collar of the elf's shirt and jerked him to his feet. "Believe it, elf. I doubt you'll survive this day, but if you do, it won't be because I prefer that you live, do you understand?"

Before an appropriate witticism could reach his bloodied lips, she threw him into the doors. They burst open, and he fell into the room beyond. Alynthia drew a poniard from her belt and followed.

He found himself sprawled on alabaster tiles in the midst of a great hall. To the left, the first light of the rising sun filtered through tall windows. To the right, the hall ended in a wide staircase descending into darkness. The walls all around were decorated with rich paneling interspersed by doors gilded with gold. Above, fine frescoes covered every inch of the ceiling. The frescoes depicted various scenes of Palanthian commerce, from city docksides to markets to religious and educational institutions. In these frescoes from another age, the Tower of High Sorcery still stood, guarded by its fearsome grove, and Astinus sat within the Great Library recording the history of Krynn in his chronicles of time. They were scenes from a past that seemed dusty and ancient.

Lining the shadowy paneled wall were eight chairs. Rich with velvet of red or forest green, polished and carved with care, they could have been the thrones of kings. One was greater than rest. Its back was wrought in the likeness of a dragon with wings outspread and head craned up at the sky. Its legs rested atop claws gripping balls of gleaming crystal. In this chair sat a massive figure dressed in darkest blue. Brass gleamed from his breast, and his cuffs were worked with gold braid. A golden bowl atop a small marble pedestal stood near his elbow, filled with cool grapes and dark succulent berries. The massive figure sat with his chin on his fist, amusement sparkling in his dark eyes. It was Captain Oros uth Jakar, who laughed aloud as Cael struggled to his feet.

To Oros's right and left, each chair was occupied by a figure cloaked in black. Each had his or her hood thrown back, revealing a group of faces representing a complex variety of the cultures and races of Krynn. A swarthy-faced man from Tarsis sat beside a woman from the plains of Abanasinia. There lounged a bearded Kalamanite and beside him a man who looked enough like the bearded Kalamanite to be his twin brother. Next to them a scowling, pale-eyed native of Sancrist. However, the chair to the guildmaster's right remained empty. To his left a dark alcove hinted at a waiting figure hidden within.

Alynthia crossed the room and took her seat in the empty chair beside Oros. Cael looked around and saw no guards but no obvious way out of the place either. He faced the gathered leaders of the Guild, acutely conscious of the blood staining his lips and the sewage drying on his tattered clothes. Any hopes for escape were drying just as fast.

When Alynthia had sunk into her seat, a bell sounded from the shadows of the hall. The room, though quiet before, grew hushed. A voice then spoke from the dark, empty alcove, "Is this the freelance thief known as Cael Ironstaff, Cael Elbernarian, the elf?"

It was a voice to chill the stoutest heart. Growling, full of menace, like the voice of a child of the elder dark before the Age of Dreams, weary as though burdened by countless ages. Whether it was that of a male or a female, human, elf, or dwarf, Cael could not discern.

As for the figure, not even his keen elven eyes could be certain of the shape within the darkened alcove, which refused to come forward into the light. He saw only suggestive shadows, ebon drapes perhaps, or something couched in black robes. The voice itself seemed to leap from empty air. His neck hairs rose in the unusual sensation of fear.

"It is, my lord Mulciber," Alynthia answered.

"Where is his staff?" the voice asked.

"Lost in the sewers," Alynthia said. "Or so he says."

"A shame. We are told it has great powers," the voice of Mulciber said.

"It is only a staff," Cael said defiantly.

"Why does he speak to us, as though he were one with us and our equal? Why is he not gagged?" Mulciber demanded.

"I thought . . ." Alynthia began, hesitating. "I thought you might expect to question him, my lord."

"You think too much, Alynthia Krath-Mal," the voice growled.

"It was I who ordered him brought before us unbound, Lord Mulciber," Captain Oros interjected.

There was a pause, then the voice answered. "Very well. It is of no consequence. What then does the elf have to say for himself? Where is the treasure he stole from us?"

"Sold," Cael answered.

"To whom? And at what price?"

"I forget his name, but the price was three hundred steel coins."

A gasp escaped the gathered leaders of the Guild.

"We know the name of the alchemist, my lord," Alynthia said. "The spice will be recovered this evening, before either Mistress Jenna or Sir Arach Jannon's agents locate it. The price was four hundred steel coins."

Mulciber ignored her. "A pittance! The dragonflower spice was worth ten times as much. Where, then, is this pittance?"

"Lost in the sewers," Cael answered. "More's the pity."

"We pity all that has been lost in the sewers," Mulciber snarled. "Does this elf know the punishment for unlicensed theft?"

"I do," Cael said. "It is a true thief who knows his punishment."

"Either he is bold or a fool. The punishment is death," Mulciber proclaimed. The other Guild captains nodded in agreement. Cael's chin sank to his breast, his long coppery hair fell about his face in apparent defeat, but he was desperately flexing his wiry arms, trying to loosen the cords binding them. They were tight, but if he had another few moments, he might free one hand. On the floor between his feet he had noticed numerous notches in the stone and a deep, brown stain. There might be hope.

A door behind him creaked open, then boomed shut. Heavy clopping footsteps approached from behind, as he continued to flex his arms, twisting ever so slightly, imperceptible, he trusted, in the gloom. The cords loosened a bit, then some more.

He glanced up and saw Alynthia stooped beside the chair of Captain Oros. With one hand shielding her lips she was whispering in his ear, while he in turn gazed thoughtfully at the doomed elf, chin propped on one massive fist. The clopping footsteps drew nearer, and Cael heard a chuffing snort, followed by the whistling swish of a blade. Cael tensed, awaiting the blow, which seemed to be falling in slow motion.

Oros shook his head and waved Alynthia back to her seat. She returned to it, obviously annoyed, but she held her tongue.

"Kolav! Stay your blade a moment," Oros suddenly ordered. The footsteps paused, but grumbling sounds indicated that the executioner was not pleased.

"What is this, Captain?" Mulciber asked. "Do you dare interrupt my order?"

Oros answered, "Never would I question your orders, my lord, but an offer has been made for this elf's life."

"One here would purchase him as slave?" Mulciber asked. The Guild captains looked from one to the other.

"Not as slave, Lord Mulciber," Oros said. "Captain Alynthia has lost two thieves of her Circle. Brem of Northern Ergoth was slain in the sewers last night, and Markom died in the house of Gaeord uth Wotan, by the hand of this very elf. Our numbers are still low, and we can ill afford to replace these two experienced thieves with apprentices. The elf has proven his talent. Captain Alynthia thinks he should be sentenced to take their place."

There was a pause during which the gathered captains of the Thieves' Guild discussed the proposition in agitated whispers. Finally, the Guild captain from Abanasinia shook her head disapprovingly and spoke aloud for the first time. Long, raven locks rippled about her sun-darkened face. "He is freelance, Captain Oros. Freelancers are notoriously independent and can rarely learn to conform to the ways of the Guild. Better to slay him and be done with it. I have a promising young pickpocket in my Circle, if Captain Alynthia has need of replacements."

"Aye, better to kill him now," growled a voice in Cael's ear. The breath was hot, and stank of raw meat and stale beer. Cael fought the heaving of his belly while continuing to work free of his bindings.

"He *is* talented, Captain Wolfheart," Oros argued. "He entered by stealth and agility the house of Gaeord uth Wotan. How many here could do such a thing? Not even Captain Alynthia, the greatest among you, dared such a feat, preferring instead to slip away during Master Gaeord's party, to which we were both invited guests."

"That is all good and well, Captain Oros," said the Guild captain from Sancrist. "But—"

Alynthia interrupted him, her voice rising to drown all arguments. "I am as opposed to this in principle as the rest of you," she almost shouted. "But even I must admit that he slyly filched the spice box from my bodice while fighting off my capable lookouts. He then escaped us, and very nearly escaped us again last night in the sewers. I would like to try and break him into the Guild but will gladly kill him myself if I fail that challenge."

The captain from Sancrist angrily pounded the arm of his chair. He was a huge man, a head taller than any other Guild Captain. "You are only trying to excuse your failure at Gaeord's by exaggerating the talents of this elf."

"Would you care to prove those accusations?" Alynthia asked as she toyed with her poniard.

The man started and gaped. "I . . . of course, not Captain Alynthia," he stuttered. The man's face paled, and he suddenly seemed more interested in the state of his manicure than the fate of the elf. The other captains once more huddled in whispers.

At that moment, one loop binding Cael's arms finally slipped off. He tore free one hand and dragged loose the other bindings. The Guild captains saw him and leaped to their feet, blades flashing from hidden sheaths. Alynthia, looking betrayed, pulled her sword, while Captain Oros merely gazed in mixed amusement and admiration.

Spinning around, Cael ran headlong into the mountainous chest of a huge creature. He staggered back and gazed up into the face of a nightmare. Though its head was like that of a bull, its eyes burned with both the fury of an animal and the intelligence of a man. Twin horns curved from its head, dark as mahogany, polished to needle points. Massive muscles swelled beneath reddish-brown fur, as laughter boomed from its thick-corded throat. It wore leather armor, barbarically studded with copper rivets and decorated with bits of semiprecious stone and bone ornaments. It stood several feet taller than the elf and in one hand held a massive tulwar, a curved sword so large the elf probably couldn't have hoped to lift it. The minotaur wielded it as though it were a toy sword.

Its other hand shot out and caught Cael by the throat before he could recover from his astonishment. Slowly, the minotaur's fingers tightened around his windpipe. Cael grasped at the hand, tore at its fingers, but it would be easier to pry loose the roots of a mighty oak. Black spots burst before his eyes.

Alynthia and the other captains of thieves sat back down nervously in their chairs. Muted laughter issued from the shadowed alcove.

"Cael Ironstaff, meet Kolav Ru-Marn of Kothas, my bodyguard, and Executioner of Justice," Captain Oros laughed from his chair. "Try not to kill him, Kolav."

The minotaur's fingers loosened around Cael's throat but held him tightly. The minotaur shook him like a rag doll. "There's no escape from me, little elf," he growled.

"Kolav here is the finest sword in all the lands of Ansalon," Oros said.

"All Krynn!" the minotaur roared.

"That's funny," Cael choked. "I always thought *I* was the finest swordsman in all Krynn." Suddenly, he found himself flying through the air. He landed squarely on his back, driving the air from his lungs and sliding to a stop against Alynthia's foot. He looked up, wincing in pain, and found Alynthia gazing down at him, her dark eyes filled with hatred and disgust.

"Give him a sword!" the minotaur roared. "You heard him. He challenged me. I'll eat his heart! By Sargonnas, I will!"

"Now is neither the time nor the place," Mulciber growled impatiently from the shadows. The room grew quiet, and even Kolav seemed cowed by the sound of that voice. He retreated to the opposite wall and glared across the gloom at Cael. At a nod from Captain Oros, Alynthia helped the elf to rise and led him to stand before the alcove.

"What will you give for the life of this elf?" the voice of Mulciber demanded.

Alynthia paused before answering, her eyes darting to Captain Oros. Unspoken words flashed between them, and all knew this episode would be debated when the two captains of thieves reached their bedchamber. Captain Oros held the upper rank, but he would feel the wrath of his lady's tongue if he didn't accede to her wishes.

"With him, we shall recover one of the stolen Guild treasures," she answered.

The other captains turned to one another and began to whisper. Captain Oros nodded approvingly to his lover.

"Which treasure? There are many," Mulciber said.

"The Eighth Circle shall name it," Alynthia said.

"Call Master Petrovius. We shall hear the list again," Mulciber ordered. Kolav opened a small door and roared the name of Petrovius into the darkness beyond. Soon, an ancient man came doddering through. His bald pate was covered with dark splotches, his eyes were milky, and when he smiled his lips parted to reveal a gaping black hole devoid of teeth. He seemed bent almost double, and he leaned upon a cane almost as gnarled as himself. He stopped beside Cael, facing the alcove, and bowed over his cane.

"Master Petrovius, eldest of all thieves, name for us again our lost treasures and tell us if you know where they are now and who has them, or whether they are lost in the mists of time," Mulciber said.

"Shall I also name our brothers and sisters murdered on the Night of Black Hammers?" the old man cawed. "The list is long and long in the telling, for only three survived— myself, and young Captain Oros, who saved my life when he stole me from the Dark Knights who had captured me. The third we do not name, for it was he who betrayed us, and though he fled we found him at last and Captain Oros strangled his protests of innocence with his own hands, as was just and right."

"I think not tonight, Master Petrovius," Oros said. "It is to hear of the Guild treasures that we desire."

The old man began to list each treasure, telling its value and when it was first won and the name of the thief who won it, where it now lay, or if it was lost. They were many and of all kinds: jewels, items of magic, famous weapons, artifacts both hideous and wonderful, but chief among them was the Founderstone of Palanthas. When it was mentioned, a great groan went up among the Guild captains, and even Cael felt a terrible temptation in his heart.

"Of course the Founderstone is beyond the reach of any thief," the old list keeper said. "Sadly, in these lesser days, there is no thief capable of stealing it back. It is lost to us, unless the world should change."

He continued on, naming now the lesser treasures, now the objects of art, now crowns and jeweled scepters stolen over the ages. Finally, his long list came to an end. Having exhausted his store of knowledge, he turned and doddered away, muttering something about his delayed breakfast. The Guild captains sat appreciatively in their chairs, as if they had just witnessed a favorite performance. During the old man's speech, servants—apprentice thieves—had entered the chamber bearing bowls of fruit and platters of bread. Now stewards brought wine in tall flagons, and cups of silver. Each Guild captain was served, although the servants passed the dark alcove of Mulciber without a glance. When all had gone and a thoughtful silence reigned, finally the Guild captain from Kalaman spoke up. "My vote is for the Reliquary," he said.

"Didn't you hear the old man?" Oros responded. "On the Night of Black Hammers, the Reliquary was taken away by the Knights of Takhisis under heavy guard. It has not been seen since, nor has any word of it reached our ears. It should be counted as lost to us."

"We could search for it. I suspect that it lies still within my Circle, the Third Circle of the city, in the Lord Knight's house. Either there, or in the old temple of Takhisis in Captain Alynthia's circle, the Seventh Circle," he said stubbornly. "Besides, the Reliquary would be a challenge worthy of this supposed thief with talent."

"Put the Reliquary out of your mind, I say," Oros said. "It is far too valuable to remain in Palanthas, where the Knights of Solamnia might somehow find it. If the Knights of Neraka know whose bones it contains, as I assure you they do, it is probably hidden away in the deepest vaults of their stronghold in Neraka, far beyond anyone's reach."

The captain of the Third Circle reluctantly acquiesced.

"What say you then, Captain Oros?" asked the captain of the Fourth Circle, the Abanasinian Captain Wolfheart. Her circle of influence was bounded by Market Street—the only road in New City that ran continuously around the full circle of the city—and included areas as widely diverse as Smith's Alley and the main Market of Palanthas, where the vast majority of the city's riches were made and exchanged.

"I suggest the Potion of Shonlay," Oros said. Surprised looks were exchanged among the other captains.

"That lies in the house of Mistress Jenna, a powerful red robe mage," the Tarsian captain of the Second Circle, whose name was Jakar Jervanian, said. "That is within my Circle of the city. As you know, her house offers many difficulties. We've tried. That is why the dragonflower pollen was to be stolen from Master Gaeord before Mistress Jenna could get her hands on it and take it beyond our reach."

"It can't be as impregnable as the Tower of High Sorcery, from whence the Potion was originally stolen, long years ago in the Age of Might," Oros answered.

"True, but those were better days," Captain Wolfheart agreed. "Our petty thefts cannot compare to the heroic deeds of those times."

"Still, it might be attempted," the Captain of the Fifth Circle countered. Her name was Kristin Ladycandle, and she hailed originally from the city of Sanction. The Fifth Circle contained mostly residences and, where it neared the bay, warehouses. A good part of her Circle also included a portion of the wealthy merchandising district, which she shared with the Fourth Circle. Her territory was bounded on the west by Knight's Candle Road, to the south by Silver Street, and to the east by New Itari Way.

"Aye, I like the idea," the Captain of the Sixth Circle agreed. "It is time we began to exert our influence over this city again. What better way than to strike where few might imagine any thief would dare to break?" The Captain of the Sixth Circle was the only dwarven member of the council of thieves. He had the usual dwarven beard and stature. However, his pale complexion and the slightly wild (some said "deranged," although not within his earshot if they valued their lives) glint in his eye marked him as one of the Daergar race. Some might call his Circle the least interesting of all the Circles of Palanthas, but Felthorn Bloodhand took pride in his turf. Under his domain lay the Old Temple District, as well as the Purple Ridge, home of the newly wealthy families of Palanthas, whom he had vowed to make "newly poor." The Sixth Circle was bounded to the west by the Boulevard of Gold, to the south by the Avenue of the Sun, and to the east by Shipwrights Lane.

"It is agreed then?" Oros asked. One by one, the other Guild captains nodded their approval.

Mulciber finally spoke. "Captain Alynthia Krath-Mal, you shall win for us the Potion of Shonlay. If you fail, you shall deliver the elf for execution of punishment. If he should escape, his punishment you alone shall bear. Both Sir Arach Jannon and Mistress Jenna are still searching for him. He must die rather than fall into their hands."

"Yes, my lord," Alynthia agreed, bowing her head.

"Captains, I leave you to conclude your business," Mulciber said. They all rose. Cael waited expectantly, but nobody emerged from the alcove. Not even the shadow of a movement marked the Guildmaster's exit. How and where had he disappeared?

At last, Oros gave a sigh and said, "Well, he is gone. And I, too, leave you to your business." He approached Cael and motioned for him to follow.

"Come with me for a while," the Guild captain said. "Alynthia has business that does not concern you."

Cael followed the Guild captain as ordered, passing through the double doors and into the hall of pillars. The minotaur fell in behind them. With a growling laugh, he grasped the elf's small wrist in his massive fist and twisted his arm behind his back.

"Gently, Kolav," Captain Oros said without turning. "He is one of us now."

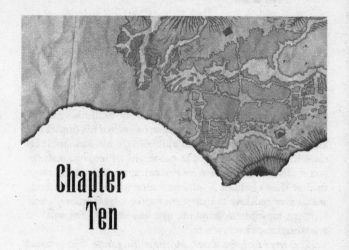

Chapter
Ten

More than anything else, Sir Elstone Kinsaid hated accountants. He hated anyone who could take a group of Knights—honorable, heroic men and women ready to sacrifice their lives for the Knighthood—and reduce them to numbers and figures in a book: a quantity of rations per day, a bill for monthly repairs to armor and equipment.

On the desk before him lay a short missive, written in a crisp, efficient hand on a half sheet of paper. It read:

> To the Lord Knight of Palanthas
> Sir Kinsaid,
>   You must reduce your monthly expenditures on supplies, rations, and payroll by eleven percent before the end of this year. The dragons in your talon stables require copious amounts of provender, and steel coins do not grow on trees. With a little imagination and ingenuity, I am confident you can do this.

Jeff Crook

Sir Morham Targonne
Lord of the Night

P.S. I am still *awaiting those reports from last month.*

With a snarl, the Lord Knight of Palanthas crumpled the letter into a tiny ball, squeezing it in his fist until his knuckles turned white. With a spasm of anger, he opened his fingers and let the note roll from his palm and fall onto his desktop. It lay there in a valley surrounded by mountains of reports, analyses, and studies that demanded his perusal, approval, and signature, so that they could be filed away somewhere where no one would ever be likely to read them for the next thousand years. Dragons may hatch, grow up, age, and die, but the work of accountants goes on forever.

The writer of the letter, Morham Targonne, had wrested control of the Knights of Takhisis from Mirielle Abrena, the Knight who had almost single-handedly held the Order together after the Chaos War. A few short months ago, around Yuletide, word had arrived by wyvern rider that Lady Mirielle had "retired" and passed the leadership of the Knights of Takhisis to Morham Targonne, a man who had entered the Knighthood as a clerk, a mere accountant, a man whose hand better fitted the grip of a pen than a sword. Everyone learned, sooner or later, what "retired" meant. She had been murdered, probably poisoned.

One of the new Lord of the Night's first orders had been to change the name of the Order to the Knights of Neraka. This was a move Sir Kinsaid opposed most vehemently ... in private. He said nothing to his officers and pretended to support the change lest they think him weak or rebellious, but within his own heart, he felt deeply offended. He had been in the Order long enough to have shared in the original Vision, the gift of their dark queen, Takhisis, to all her Knights. Thanks to the Vision each Knight knew his or her place in Her Dark Majesty's plan. Then Takhisis had abandoned Krynn, along with all the other gods, after the Chaos War, and with her went the Vision. This did not change the loyalty Sir Kinsaid felt toward his queen. The Knights of Takhisis had been founded to serve her. To change its name to the Knights of Neraka was to betray her. It bespoke of an Order whose guiding purpose had shifted from a Vision of the glory of their immortal queen to a worldly Vision, one where Knights sought the wisdom of merchants, and consulted accountants before riding off to battle.

A knock at his door brought Sir Kinsaid back to the matter at hand. At his gruff command, the door opened, and a young Knight of the Lily stepped into the room, snapping to attention as the Lord Knight of Palanthas raised his eyes from the reports on his desk. "Sir Arach Jannon to see you, sir," she said, sharply saluting with a fist to her black armored breast.

Returning her salute, he answered with a sigh. "Show him in." If there was one thing he hated almost as much as account-ants, it was mysteriously behaving wizards.

Moments later, the Thorn Knight glided into the room, his hands folded into the sleeves of his gray robe. He wore his usual smug smile, his black eyes twinkling with some inner merri-ment. Seeing him, Sir Kinsaid felt his anger at Morham Tar-gonne boil up and come rushing out, aimed like a jet of steam from a gnomish tarbean tea brewer, straight at the face of the Lord Justice.

"Remove that silly grin from your face, Sir Knight," he growled.

Sir Arach's mouth fell open at these words. He stammered, trying to regain his composure. Finally, the best he could man-age was a puzzled stare. "M'lord, I was told . . . I was told you wished to see me?"

Sir Kinsaid snatched a letter from his desk. It was not the letter he intended to grab, but it didn't matter. He shook it at the Thorn Knight. "Do you know who this letter is from?"

"No, m'Lord," Sir Arach said. By his best guess, it could be one of two dozen that had been reported to him as having arrived upon the Lord Knight's desk this day. One of these, he knew to have come from the Lord of the Night himself. He had deduced the letter had been his promotion to Lord Justice of Neraka (thus his smug grin as he entered the room). Obviously, something had gone awry.

"It's from Mistress Jenna," Sir Kinsaid barked. Actually, it was from his sister, but the wizard hadn't been invented yet that could read a letter he waved in his hands.

"Oh? What does she say?" Sir Arach asked. Strange, he hadn't known about this particular letter. A hole must exist in the circle of informants surrounding the Lord Knight.

"She demands to know the status of her case—the theft at the house of Gaeord uth Wotan. She says she has been able to get nothing from you except evasive responses and flat denials. She grows weary and demands justice or else, she says, she will take matters into her own hands."

"What does that mean, take matters into her own hands?" Arach said smugly.

"Aren't you listening to me?" the Lord Knight roared, his face red as a radish, the veins standing out along his neck like worms. "She demands! She threatens!"

"The audacity!" Arach exclaimed sympathetically.

Sir Kinsaid's face flushed a deeper shade of burgundy. "I am under strict orders from General Targonne to leave Mistress Jenna alone. Leave her alone! In other words, don't rile her up with evasions and denials!" he bellowed. Sir Arach glanced around nervously, wondering if those in the waiting area outside could hear. It would not do to have the tale of this dressing-down travel beyond the Lord Knight's castle. He noted the thickness of the door and the walls with some relief.

"Who is this thief, and why has he not been arrested?" Sir Kinsaid demanded. "Don't you think I have enough to do without having to coddle irate sorcerers and whining merchants?"

"His name is Caelthalas Elbernarian, but he goes by the alias Cael Ironstaff. He professes to be the son of Tanis Half-Elven, a Hero of the Lance, but his claim seems to have little merit," Sir Arach spouted officiously. "Probably the name is a fabrication. This Ironstaff is a notorious rogue, a liar, and braggart, by all accounts."

"You seem to know so much about him," Sir Kinsaid said, somewhat mollified. "Why haven't you captured him yet?"

"We think he has left the city," Sir Arach answered.

"How do you know that for sure?"

"We don't, but he has not been seen in three weeks, not since the day of the Spring Dawning festival, when one of your Knights let him slip through his fingers at the Horizon Road gate—he has been executed for his dereliction of duty, of course. Ironstaff's dwelling and the places he frequents—the Dwarven Spring, the alchemists' shops, the University and the Great Library—have been watched most closely. He has vanished. He has either left the city willingly, or he has been slain by another thief and his body dumped in the sewers. So, as you can see, we are working on the case but there is little I can do right now, no matter how loudly Mistress Jenna protests."

"She says in her letter that the thief is being hidden by the Thieves' Guild," Sir Kinsaid said.

"There is no Thieves' Guild in Palanthas," Sir Arach assured him.

The Thorn Knight jumped as Sir Kinsaid's fist struck the desk. An avalanche of papers and reports cascaded to the floor. "If there is one person in this city who truly believes that lie," Sir Kinsaid said in a voice tight with barely suppressed emotion, "he is a fool. I don't care where this thief is or who is hiding him. If this supposed son of Half-Elven is in Palanthas, whether he be a living thief or a bunch of bones in the belly of a sewer monster, I want him found and his theft restored. I want Mistress Jenna satisfied. Do you understand me, Sir Knight?"

"Yes m'Lord," Sir Arach responded with feigned humility, bowing his way to the door. Almost as an afterthought, he added, "If it comes to searching the sewers, it might prove expensive."

"Get out of my sight!"

Sir Arach ducked though the door as a glass paperweight shattered against the wall by his head.

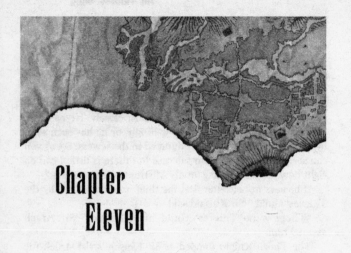

Chapter
Eleven

I t was the first time he had seen anyone other than his bunkmates and trainers in three weeks. His escort, a wavy-haired young thief from the Fifth Circle, knocked on a small, nondescript door, then stepped back to wait. The hall they stood in was low and narrow, lit at regular intervals by candles in silver sconces. Cael had never been here before. He wasn't even sure where he was. He'd not seen the light of day since that morning in the sewer, with the dawn light filtering through the grate above.

The door opened, and with a wave of his hand, Captain Oros motioned for Cael to enter and sit. The captain ordered wine, bread, and cold meats to be brought to his chamber. An apprentice thief, his eyes as wide as platters, hurried from the room, quietly closing the door behind him. Alone with the elf, Oros unbuttoned his coat with a sigh.

Cael closely watched the Guild captain. It seemed to him that the man acted a little too friendly a little too soon. Not three weeks had passed since Mulciber had sentenced the elf to death for his freelance activities, then granted his provisional pardon, and today the leader of the Eighth Circle of the Guild had summoned him and was now treating him like an honored guest, or even an old friend.

He realized of course that under the guise of casual friendliness the Guild captain was studying him. Every so often, as the man moved about the room, lighting a candle here, adjusting a chair there, pouring wine or carving the bread, he'd look up to see the elf's reactions. Though hungry and thirsty, Cael toyed with the food and drink set before him until he saw the Guild captain set to his own meal with unabashed gusto. Finally, he eased his aching throat with a cup of chilled pale wine, then devoured the meats and hearty bread brought by the servant.

Three more cups of wine carried him through the meal. Another servant arrived to remove the plates, but Cael kept a tight hold on his cup. He felt the wine, the sweet oil of conversation, loosening his tongue. He was dying to have a word with the Guild captain, but as yet the man had hardly spoken three words to him.

The chamber in which they dined was small but comfortably furnished. In one corner stood the table at which they ate their meal. Opposite the table, a pair of deep chairs huddled near a glowing brazier. A few books and curious oddments littered the shelves, but none of them attracted his curiosity. In fact, the only thing more interesting than the Guild captain himself was a sea cabinet shoved into the third corner of the room. The cabinet was banded with scrollwork iron and fastened by a silver lock. It looked large enough to hold a store of treasure.

When all the servants had gone, Captain Oros invited Cael to join him by the brazier. Cael settled into his chair, but the Guild captain remained standing, sipping thoughtfully at his wine while he eyed the elf.

Finally, the Guild captain asked, "So how have you enjoyed your little stay with us? Bogul tells me you've been coming along nicely."

"Is that so?" Cael asked, surprised. So far, he had not been able to detect much of anything in the way of training. He had been living in Thieves' House for about three weeks now, and during that time he'd done little besides rooming with a group of six other thieves, "brothers" and "sisters" of his Inner Circle (to use the Guild's terminology). Their immediate commander was old Hook-nose, whose real name was Bogul. They lived together in a small dormitory of seven beds, isolated from other thieves, playing dice and telling stories of previous thefts and jobs, eating, and drinking wine. Three hours per day they spent in a large empty room that they called the gymnasium, performing a regimen of callisthenic exercises surely meant to kill them, under the critical tutelage of a severe, ice-eyed female half-elf of the Kagonesti persuasion. If this were not enough, they spent another hour every day wrestling with a pair of dwarves, twin brothers named Gunder and Gawain, who did their very best to break every bone in the thieves' bodies. The first week of Cael's captivity and 'training' was a haze of pain broken only by bouts of extreme fatigue and excessive drinking, gambling, and telling of enormously stretched tales. By the second week, Cael could hold his own with his fellow thieves, at least in the drinking part (he'd always bested them in the telling of tales), but he still lost hugely to their dice. By the third week, they'd stopped calling him "elf" and started using his name, he'd figured out how they were cheating him at dice and had won back a good portion of his losses, and the previous day he had actually stood Gawain on his head, for which he received a hearty breath-stealing congratulatory thwack on the back from Gunder.

The brothers and sisters of his Inner Circle were not apprentice thieves, not by any measure. They were all experienced pickpockets, safecrackers, and cat burglars. The oldest of the group was Brother Mancred, an old cutpurse with some skill in magic, they said. He rarely bragged, not like the others, and spent most of his time sitting, his gaze far away. Next eldest in the group was Hoag, a dark-eyed native Palanthian who tried to assume the role of second in command to Bogul. He was the most hostile towards Cael, and never stopped calling him "elf." His particular expertise was lockpicking. He liked to tell a story of stealing the whiskers of a leopard, a story that always began the same—"I once took a bet from a gnome in Tarsis . . ."—and was always received with groans and threats.

There was Pitch, a hard-nosed ex-legionnaire from the Legion of Steel. She was more warrior than thief and wore her hair shaved close and neat. She suffered from a pathological need to win, and grew angry and violent when she lost at dice. The others seemed to suffer her without too much complaint.

A huge beefy man named Rull loved to perform feats of strength, not to intimidate or dominate his companions but simply to win their praise and applause. Still, Gunder and Gawain laid him on his back nine times out of ten during the wrestling hour. The other female of their group was Varia, an acrobat, actress, pickpocket, and con artist. Where Pitch was hard and bitter as vinegar, Varia was the very picture of womanly beauty. Surprisingly, her brother thieves never made the usual banal attempts to gain her affection. Cael learned why when he spent nearly an entire day of his first week tied up in his bed sheets after making inappropriate advances and discovering that Rull regarded her as a sister not only in name but also in blood. Before becoming a thief Varia had studied at the Citadel of Light and had learned a little of the art of mystic healing.

The sixth thief of their little band was a dark-spirited knife-in-the-back fellow named Ijus. The others said that he was a failed apprentice mage, a street magician gone terribly awry, but he rarely spoke for himself except to make some sick joke, usually at the most inappropriate times. He thought death the grandest joke of all and held a vast repertoire of macabre tales stored up in his twisted mind. However, he was a favorite lackey of Hoag's, and followed him around like a whipped dog.

Although the past three weeks had seemed tiresomely pointless to Cael, he now began to realize the reason behind his incarceration. He was building camaraderie within a group of thieves who had already been together for a while. Through shared misery (and nothing is more miserable to a thief than boredom), they had forged something resembling friendship. He was the new member in an old group, and without this bonding period, in which they got to know one another, shared wisdom and techniques, and established their social hierarchy, he posed a threat to their success in future capers. Now, he was almost one of them, and he felt it. He was accepted, even if only on a provisional basis. Their approval awaited some final test— that he understood. Perhaps this was to be it.

"I had no idea I was making any progress at all," Cael said, fishing for a hint as to the purpose of this interview.

"Your Inner Circle hasn't killed you yet," Oros commented as he poured himself another glass of wine. "I call that progress." He settled back in his chair and massaged the glass between his huge, pawlike hands, eyeing the elf curiously.

Cael returned his gaze without blinking for as long as he could stand it, but his curiosity soon got the better of him. His eyes flickered once more to the cabinet standing in the corner.

Noticing this, Captain Oros asked. "Would you like to see what is inside it?"

"If it is not too much trouble, *shaffendi*," Cael answered.

Oros laughed. "I've seen much of the world, my friend," he said. "In my travels, I learned a bit of Elvish—enough to know that you just insulted me."

Cael chuckled.

"*Shaffendi* is one of those untranslatable Elvish words, often used in reference to pompous twits," the Guild captain continued as he approached the cabinet. He removed a small key from his pocket.

"Your forgiveness, m'lord," Cael apologized, bowing his head. "It is a habit I developed in my dealings with humans. The ignorant like the sound of the word and so believe it to be a title of respect."

"That's quite all right," Oros laughed. "I know a smattering of perhaps a dozen languages. For example, if I were to address you as the Great Khashla'k, you might never know that I had called you a horse's ass."

"A hit, m'lord," Cael acknowledged. "You score on both points."

"I had hoped you might use a more respectful Elvish term when addressing me," Oros said. "One day you might call me *shalifi.*"

Cael grew serious. "That word is not lightly spoken, m'lord. Human scholars translate it as 'master' or 'teacher,' but its true meaning reaches far deeper."

"That I know all too well," Oros answered respectfully. "I only mentioned it because I like you. You have great talent, great energy and ingenuity. Many months have I watched you, Cael, tracking your career. The Vettow Ivory, that was yours, was it not?"

Cael bowed his head in assent.

"It is folk like you who are the future of the Guild—the daring, the bold. With a strong hand to guide you, there is much we could achieve."

"I don't work well with others," Cael countered. "I prefer my own company. I am a loner, an outsider. Others may walk in the light of day, but I am a dark elf, cast from the light."

Captain Oros burst out laughing. "Is that what you tell people?" he asked.

"It's true!" Cael shot back. "I am thoroughly evil. I was cast out by my mother's people for practicing the dark arts!"

"Pah! One look at you tells me that you don't have what it takes to be truly ruthless. You are dangerous, yes. All of us are dangerous in our own way. You may be twice my age, my friend, but young you are nonetheless. A shrewd judge of horses, ships, and people am I. That is how I have achieved my position."

"You know nothing," Cael said with a smile. "I love the shadows. I embrace the night."

"Be careful when you embrace the darkness that the darkness doesn't embrace you," Oros answered sharply. "Listen well to what I and others teach you. It will save your life."

"I do just fine on my own," Cael snapped. The wry smile faded from his lips. "Give me a sword and I will show you what my true *shalifi* taught me."

The Guild captain merely dismissed Cael's bluster with a wave of his hand. "I am sure you could cut me to ribbons. I am no swordsman. I am a leader of swordsmen. I get others to fight my battles for me. Kolav, for instance."

A door opened and the minotaur ducked into the room.

Cael leaped to his feet and put a chair between himself and the monster. Kolav laughed as he fingered the giant tulwar hanging at his belt. "That's twice you've challenged me, little elf," he boomed. "Be careful, or someone will make you eat your bragging words and wash them down with your own blood."

"Melodrama is not your forte," Cael said. "Why don't you go find a nice fat heifer to play with?"

"Khashla'k!" the minotaur snarled. With a speed belying his giant stature, the monster leaped across the room and snatched the heavy chair from in front of the elf. He flung it aside like a piece of doll furniture. Cael dodged aside and grabbed the wine bottle from the table.

"If I am to fight, at least give me a sword!" he shouted. Was this, then, to be his test?

"I'll give you a sword! Right between your ribs!" the minotaur returned.

"Kolav!" Captain Oros barked. The minotaur instantly halted, but a rumbling growl shook the room. Cael put the wine bottle to his lips and took a long swig, then returned it to the table.

"Leave us, now," Oros ordered the minotaur. Reluctantly, the beast obeyed. However, he paused at the door and swung his great horned head around to glare at the elf.

"You will pay for your disrespect, elf," Kolav growled. "The day of my revenge shall come. Challenge me a third time, and oath or no oath, I shall eat your liver."

With those words, Kolav slammed the door with such force that it split down its length.

"What did he mean by that?" Cael asked as he righted his chair. Despite his attempt at a casual demeanor, his heart pounded in his chest. It was all he could do to calm himself.

"Didn't you know? Elven liver is a minotaur delicacy," Oros said.

"I meant the oath. What oath?" Cael asked through gritted teeth.

"Kolav has sworn an oath to serve me without question," Oros answered.

"How did you manage that?" Cael asked. "I've always heard

minotaurs are headstrong brutes, incapable of following a human master."

"Yes, they are a great deal like freelance thieves," Oros returned. "Yet they have their own code of honor. This one, his life I saved. He swore to serve me in exchange. But his tale is woven with the contents of this cabinet," the Guild captain continued as he unlocked the sea cabinet. He threw wide the doors and stepped back to display its contents.

To Cael's great disappointment, there was no fabulous pirate-won treasure inside. Instead, the cabinet contained a finely wrought model of a three-masted Palanthian galleon. The skill and care with which it had been carved showed in the warm glow of its planks and the careful detail of its ornaments and rigging.

"This is the *Mary Eileen*," Captain Oros said, his chest swelling with pride. "She was the best command I ever had. A fast ship, a trim ship, the best ship in the Palanthian fleet, and I the youngest captain ever to earn so prestigious a command. I sailed her for five years, the best years of my life, but I drove her aground in a storm west of the Teeth of Chaos, and before I knew what was happening a pirate galley crewed by minotaurs was upon us. I lost all hands, and was myself captured by the minotaurs and chained to an oar. After a weary three months, the minotaurs were in turn rammed by a warship of the Knights of Takhisis, near Port Balifor. I was able to free myself and my bench companion from the chains and escape the sinking ship. The Knights took us captive, but my family paid my ransom, and I was released. I paid for the release of my bench companion, for we had become close mates in those three months aboard the minotaur galley. That companion was Kolav, and he has been my servant to this day."

"She's a fine ship," the elf agreed as he eyed the model.

"It broke my heart to lose her," Oros said. He grew quiet, and spent quite a long while staring thoughtfully at the model. Suddenly, he laughed, and reaching into the cabinet he pulled the model out and placed it atop the table where they had dined.

"Look here," he said as he pointed at the crow's nest at the top of the main mast. There, carefully balanced on the lip of the basket, stood a tiny gull made of carefully folded paper. The paper was old and yellowed, as though the toy gull had stood there for many years, wings poised for a flight that had never begun.

"Alynthia placed that there," Oros chuckled. "By the gods, it must have been twenty years ago. She took three voyages aboard the *Mary Eileen*, she and her father. I had a bosun's mate aboard the ship then. He used to thrill Alynthia with his little animals, which he made by folding scraps of paper. Poor old chap. He went down with the ship. I was just glad Alynthia wasn't aboard that day. I haven't been to sea since."

At these words, the door jerked open. Alynthia appeared there, a scowl darkening her face as if she suspected she was the subject of the conversation she had just interrupted. She stepped back, motioning to the elf. "Come with me!" she snapped.

Draining his glass to the lees, Cael clunked his glass to the table. He wiped his lips.

"I am ready," he said.

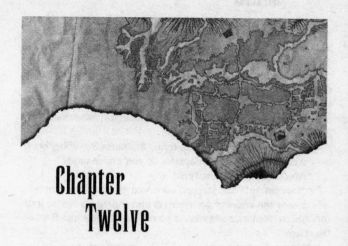

Chapter Twelve

So what did you two talk about?" Alynthia snarled as she led the way down the hall. It was the first words she had spoken to Cael since they'd left Oros's chamber. About twenty silent minutes had passed, minutes in which he could feel the tension seething within her. She walked in front of him, her back as stiff as a ramrod.

Cael began to suspect she was leading him in circles. Though the hall was bare of any identifying ornaments, a couple of doors looked familiar, as though he had passed them several times before.

"Nothing much," he responded.

"Did he tell you why you were summoned?" she asked.

"No."

"Good."

They continued on in silence for a while, passing another familiar-looking door. Cael grew impatient. He stopped. Without seeming to notice, Alynthia continued down the hall and vanished around a corner. He stood for a moment, irresolute, listening to her footsteps fading away in the distance. Finally, with an exasperated sigh, he hurried after her.

As he turned the corner, he tripped and fell sprawling to the floor. Alynthia stepped on his back and pinned him to the floor. Her lips twitched with anger. "You will follow me without question, even if I choose to lead you in circles!" she snarled as she ground her heel into his spine.

"Yes, Mistress," he groaned, trying to squirm free of her boot.

"And you will call me Captain, do you understand?"

"Aye, Captain," he answered.

"Now get up!" She stepped aside and allowed him to stand. He dusted the knees of his trousers and waited for her to lead on. She stalked away, her heels pounding on the stone flags of the floor.

"Never question my orders," she continued, turning the same corner for perhaps the fourth time. "As a freelance, individual initiative has served you well enough, but in the Guild it is a dangerous habit. There are people in this city who pay handsomely for protection."

"Meaning they pay you to not rob them," Cael said.

Alynthia ignored him. "Only the Guild captains know who they are, so we can't have you going off on a lark. You hit who I tell you to hit and no one else. Understand?"

"Aye, aye, Captain, sir," Cael barked like a theatrical pirate.

Alynthia stopped beside a low door, turned, and fixed the elf with a cold eye. "Do *try* not to be such a buffoon," she said as she opened the door. Beyond, a staircase led down into shadows.

"Where are we going?" Cael asked as he followed her down.

"Didn't I tell you not to ask questions?" she barked. "Your only concern is to follow me."

Cael reluctantly obeyed. They reached the bottom of the stair and stepped into a low, smoky, torchlit hall. By the damp, heavy stone of the walls and arched ceiling, Cael guessed it to be deep underground.

Unlike the other parts of the Guild house that he had seen, this section was alive with activity. Young men and women scurried about, tending to duties that at first glance seemed bewildering in their variety. Two burly chaps strained to carry a heavy iron door, while a girl of no more than ten summers followed them, holding a large basket of sparkling black plums. Three men bearing double jars of oil squeezed through, careful not to spill a drop. A little further down the hall, a pair of dull-eyed Kalamanites tended the torches lining the walls, replacing old, smoking torches with fresh new ones. Suddenly, a half dozen youths bolted past in hot pursuit of a young girl clutching what appeared to be a merchant's money belt, while a peg-legged instructor hopped after them, shouting to the girl that she had damn well better not let them catch her, or else she'd receive a right smart hiding. He bobbed and smiled to Alynthia as he passed, then continued on his way, loosing a string of curses at the pursuers, promising double punishment if they couldn't catch a young strip of an girl like that.

Alynthia led the way down the hall. Soon they passed doorways opening both to the right and to the left. In one room, a band of black-clad thieves were performing a series of acrobatic exercises that made even the agile-footed elf stare in amazement. In another, a meal of common but hearty food was being served to a small group of brown-robed senior apprentices. They conversed in whispers. Through a third door, Cael saw a startling variety of Palanthian citizenry, from waterbearers to sailors to bejeweled and perfume-pomaded nobles. An elder master thief stalked among them, eyeing each sweating apprentice with deliberate care, and delivering praise or correction, or, when necessary, a punishing thwack of his stick to each deserving student of the arts of disguise.

"Today you shall begin to learn the discipline of the Guild. You'll forget your independent ways and learn to appreciate the company and camaraderie of fellow thieves," Alynthia explained as she led the way.

"Surely you don't intend to place me with these," Cael said. "They are children."

"No, I have a regimen of very special training prepared for you," she said with a laugh over her shoulder. "I am sure you have heard of the tests given to apprentice wizards at the Towers of High Sorcery."

Indeed he had. Once, when the moons of magic still coursed nightly across the sky and the Towers of High Sorcery were centers of magical learning, those apprentice mages deemed worthy enough were accorded a test to see if they were prepared to assume the responsibilities that came with learning spells of power. The tests were voluntary, because failure invariably meant death.

"So I am to be tested, like some apprentice mage?" Cael asked incredulously. "I should think my besting you in the house of Gaeord is sufficient proof of my abilities."

"It is not your abilities that are to be tested," she snapped back, a little overloud. She lowered her voice, continuing, "You are still an apprentice in the ways of the Guild. You must watch how we operate, so that you may learn to anticipate the actions of your colleagues in the Inner Circle. You must learn to depend upon them for your very life, and they must be able to depend on you for the same. When you are truly a team, you will be able to act together without speaking, and live and breathe as one.

"In the days of the old Guild, few thieves trusted each other, few would work together toward a common goal. This distrust, this selfishness led to the Guild's downfall, by black betrayal. When Mulciber reformed the Guild, she used the example of the Knights of Takhisis to teach her captains how to organize and lead people who do not naturally work together. This is what you must learn. This is what you will begin to learn, tonight."

"Me, a Knight of Takhisis!" Cael laughed.

"Be quiet, you fool!" Alynthia barked.

They had reached the end of the hall, where a low, iron door stood, set deeply into the ancient stone. Few thieves were about in this area, and no one guarded this door, though it looked stout enough to be the entrance to a treasure chamber. Alynthia stopped before it and motioned for Cael to move in front of her. He stepped forward and ran an appraising eye over the door and its massive lock.

"My test is to pick this lock?" he asked.

"Of course not, you idiot!" she cried. "Haven't you been listening to me? This is not a test of your individual ability. It is a test of your integrity."

"Then I will fail, for I have none," the elf responded with a smirk.

"Then you, or one of your companions, will die," she answered coldly. "If you survive and one of your Circle dies because of your failure, rest assured, the others will gut you like a herring. And I won't stop them."

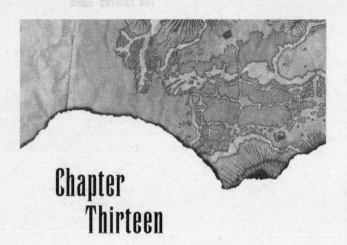

Chapter
Thirteen

ael pushed against the door. It swung open with an iron groan, revealing a stairway carved through solid rock. No torches lit the way. It descended into inky darkness. The stone walls were wet and dank and crusted with gray mold.

He turned back to Alynthia. "What's down there?" he asked.

"Yours is not to question. I am ordering you to go there, so there you must go."

"And if I refuse?"

"Then I will kill you here and now. You wouldn't be the first to die at this door," she added, as her hand strayed to the dagger strapped to her thigh. Glancing down, he noticed a number of large, brownish spots staining the stone floor.

"I'll go," he said.

"I thought so," she answered with a smile.

Cael crossed the threshold onto the first step. Immediately, his feet flew out from beneath him, and he found himself sliding down a long dark slope. Alynthia's voice seemed to follow after him, mockingly pleasant in its tones. "First lesson," she called. "Never trust only what you see with your eyes. Go ahead—I'll be watching you."

The journey down was a swift one. Someone had gone to great care to prepare this passage so that the sliding was almost fun, despite the vile odor of the substance coating the stone. But it was really too brief a journey to be able to relax and enjoy the trip. Besides, Cael worried about what he might meet at the bottom.

His eyes didn't have time to adjust to the darkness, or he might have been prepared for what awaited him. Suddenly, the slope was no longer there. His heart hammered in his throat. He was flying though empty space and total darkness. A rank stench rose up and slapped him in the face just before he landed hip deep in garbage. Luckily, the stuff broke his fall. He swore several of the more descriptive dwarven curses taught to him by Kharzog Hammerfell and struggled to climb atop the garbage heap before he sank any deeper.

A torch flared into life above him, and scornful laughter echoed around the chamber. He found himself at the bottom of a garbage pit. Twenty feet above him, a walk led along the edge of the pit. Ranged along this walk, six people stared down at him, some laughing, others working to uncoil a rope. These were people Cael knew—all members of his supposed Inner Circle. Each wore an identical uniform of loose-fitting dark gray material, with tight hoods pulled snugly around the face.

"The smell kind of reminds you of home, don't it, elf?" Hoag said with a laugh.

"Very funny," Cael returned, while biting back the gorge rising in his throat. He began to struggle across the pit, where a series of iron rings set into the stone wall served as a ladder up to the walkway.

"Cael, no!" Pitch shouted. "Don't move."

"Why in the name of the Abyss not?" he asked angrily.

"Gulguthra," she answered cryptically.

"What?"

"Gulguthra!" Ijus cackled gleefully.

"What the hell is a gulguthra?" Cael asked.

"It means 'dung eater' and you're standing on it!" the little thief answered, then clapped his hand over his mouth to stifle his laughter.

Cael looked around but saw nothing unusual beyond an assortment of rotting vegetables, well-gnawed bones, shivering masses of congealed fat, discarded bits and tatters of clothing, the odd dead rat or two, and a thing that looked like a length of pig intestine still attached to a rotting, leprous stomach. Then the thing moved, and he nearly leaped out of his shirt. A dwarven oath escaped his lips.

The thing was a tentacle of some sort, ending in a muscular, flat leaf-shaped appendage. As it inched closer to his leg, hook-shaped spines lifted along the length of the tentacle arm.

"Hurry up!" he shouted.

"I thought you were freelance," Hoag said mockingly, echoing the very words Cael had spoken to Oros earlier that evening. "You don't work well with others, remember? You prefer your own company. Mayhap you'd like to share it with the gulguthra?"

Ignoring the taunts, Cael shouted, "I'm going for the ladder!"

"You'll never make it," Pitch answered, as she and Rull continued to struggle with the rope. Varia watched their progress with a pained expression, her fingers twitching as though she wished to help but didn't want to get in the way. Mancred stood beside her, his arms folded, his face inscrutable, watching the elf as though he were watching a dog cross the street.

The tentacle inched nearer Cael's leg. It seemed to be searching him out, slowly, tauntingly.

"I'll get there quicker than you'll untangle that rope!" he answered.

"You don't know how big the monster is. It has more than one tentacle," Ijus said with a laugh.

"What is this thing?" Cael screeched. "Throw me a sword or something so I can at least fight it."

Hoag laughed and kicked a dead rat onto the garbage heap. The tentacle paused and seemed almost ready to turn towards the rat before continuing its torturous advance toward Cael's thigh.

"To hell with you!" he shouted. "I'm not going to just stand here and let this thing get me."

"Catch!"

A loop of rope unwound as it descended towards his head. He caught it, his heart in his throat lest he miss. Rull wrapped the other end around his waist and braced his massive legs. Cael clutched the rope as high as he could reach and lunged up out of the garbage. He lifted his legs and swung to the near wall, slamming into it sideways and driving the air from his lungs. Behind him, the garbage pile rose up leviathanlike, refuse and offal cascading off the huge monster like water off a breaching whale. Massive, toothy jaws snapped blindly at the place he had just been, while two tentacles whipped out, trying to encircle him.

He rose swiftly in a rapid series of jerks. Rull pulled madly at the rope, working it hand over hand while Pitch knelt at the edge and guided the elf's ascent. The tentacles slapped the wall beneath him, the hooks raked along the stone as the gulguthra searched him out. In moments, he found himself clambering at the lip of the pit, six pairs of hands clutching at his clothes and pulling him to safety. He collapsed, trembling, at their feet, while the monster champed and raged below.

"It's a good thing you're an elf," Pitch said laughing, as she pried the rope from his hands. "If you'd been as big as Rull, we'd be picking bits of you off our clothes." The others laughed too, especially Rull, but by their blanched faces, Cael knew that it had been a near thing, much nearer than they had intended.

"Was that it?" he panted. "Was that the test?"

"Get up!" Hoag snarled. "We're not even in the sewers yet."

* * * * *

They called the place a safe room. It was above the level of the flood, high enough that, even when the sewers were backed up and filled to the brim with sewage, the stuff could not reach this place. A narrow hole in the ceiling allowed fresh air to enter from the street level.

Cael stripped off his reeking, garbage-encrusted clothes and slipped into the dark gray uniform of the Thieves' Guild. His partners waited, speaking together in quiet tones. Ijus held a stub of a yellow candle while they consulted an ancient parchment map.

At first glance, the map appeared to depict the streets of Palanthas, but on closer inspection, it proved to be a map of the city's sewers. It was quite sketchy, with many areas apparently left blank, and numerous dotted lines that probably indicated connections that had never been fully explored. But even with these incomplete areas, it was easy to see how the sewers of Palanthas exactly reflected the layout of the streets above. Concentric circles spread outward from the central point beneath the Great Plaza, connected by passages following the same lines as the roads and alleys. However, in some areas, there was an obvious dearth of drainage canals. These areas were marked off, and someone had written notes into the map in a language none of the thieves could understand.

"It's dwarven," Mancred said. "Very ancient. I doubt if even a dwarf could read these runes nowadays."

"Well, we don't need to read them," Hoag said. "We know where we are going. If the elf will ever get through with his preening, he can lead the way."

"I'm ready," Cael announced as he stepped into the light of their candle. "How can I lead the way? I don't even know where we are going."

Varia stepped close and knelt beside the elf, helped him adjust the straps around his ankles so his cloth boots wouldn't rub blisters on his heels. He'd never worn clothing quite like this before. Some of the strings and straps had seemed awkward and out of place. He'd done the best he could to tie them correctly, but Varia adjusted them.

While she checked him over, she said, "We are headed to the Guild's test area. Only the very best Circles of thieves are sent there. Those who succeed receive the best assignments, the most lucrative contracts."

"What about those who fail?"

"They are lucky to escape with their lives," Hoag said.

Varia scowled at him and continued, "Mancred has failed the test twice, Hoag and I have been through it once, each without success. It's true, we've all either seen or known people who have died in the attempt."

"Seems like such a waste of life," the elf said. "To die, and for what? Bragging rights among thieves."

"Elves!" Hoag spat. "You can't understand."

"It's true," Cael said, "I don't understand. Elves revere life and hate to see it wasted, but I wasn't raised among elves. If I were going to die, I'd like it be while attempting something bold, something glorious, maybe even heroic. I wouldn't want to sacrifice myself on some ridiculous obstacle course."

"This is more than an obstacle course," Varia warned. "First of all, the operation must be conducted in total darkness. We cannot bring along any light source, and we may only use such ambient light as we come across. Your elven sight should come in handy, for the sewers are treacherous enough even when you can see where you are going,"

"So I can see in the dark," Cael remarked coldly. "I thought perhaps my *skills* were needed. What you want is a guide dog."

"Don't be such a child, Cael," Pitch scolded, as she withdrew the blade at her belt and examined its edge. "We're all in this together. We don't have to succeed, but we do have to try."

"I'd like to succeed," Mancred muttered. "Just once, before I die."

The others grew quiet at his words, and gazed reverently at the aged thief. Even Hoag showed his respect. Mancred had been in the Guild almost four years, longer than any of them. He was one of the first to be recruited by Mulciber in the days after the fall of the old Guild. He had spent his youth and middle years as a thief in cities and lands all over Krynn, from the Isle of Cristyne to the city of Flotsam. Now he was old, but his skills were not dulled. In fact, they were at their height. Though his joints had begun to creak, he knew how to mix magic with thievery to more than compensate for his age.

"Aye. If we fail, we have no one to blame but ourselves," Rull said, breaking the silence at last.

"I can think of someone to blame if we fail," said Hoag, looking at Cael.

"Well, it won't come to that, now will it?" Varia responded

angrily. "Cael is with us now. We help him, he helps us. After all, he bested Captain Alynthia."

"That was luck!" Hoag said in defense of their leader.

"Good!" Varia countered, "We'll need such luck once we reach the ruins."

"What ruins?" Cael asked, his interest growing.

"Few people know this," Varia said, her bright blue eyes twinkling conspiratorially. "The sewers of Palanthas aren't sewers at all. They are an ancient dwarven city, carved into the bedrock centuries before the first humans sailed into the Bay of Branchala, even before the wizards raised the Tower of High Sorcery with their magic. The city was abandoned long ago. Those who first arrived here found it empty and desolate. Some say it was once part of the great dwarven empire of Kal-Thax, which vanished without a trace before Thorbardin was even a dream in the mind of Reorx."

"You're more an actress than a thief," Pitch interjected as she elbowed her blonde counterpart aside. "The point is, the old Guild used to use the old road markers left by the dwarves to navigate around the sewers. When the Guild was destroyed, the Dark Knights also destroyed the ancient waymarkers, hoping to prevent any future use of what was once called the Thieves' Low Road. Now we use maps, but these are incomplete or inaccurate for the most part. The sewers are too dangerous for a complete survey."

"Dangerous how?" Cael asked. "More sewer monsters?"

"Sewer monsters are the least of your worries," Hoag said with a laugh. "The gulguthra is one of the more tame denizens of this place. When Varia said they found the ruins empty, she didn't quite tell you everything. They did find things down here, all right—things that had crept in during the centuries after the dwarves abandoned this place, things that had escaped down here from the Tower of High Sorcery."

With a scowl at her fellow thieves, Varia resumed her story. "On the Night of Black Hammers, Captain Oros escaped into the sewers with old Petrovius, the lore-master. While fleeing a band of Knights who had pursued them, the Captain stumbled across an ancient secret passageway. He followed it, and it led him to the heart of the old dwarven city, to its deepest vault. But the way was lined with cunning traps and guarded by fearsome creatures, and they had no light to see the way. Only his superb thieving skills brought the captain and Petrovius through their ordeal alive.

"What he found was beyond the dreams of dwarven avarice. The treasure of the ancient builders of the city lay before him. With this, and with the aid of Mulciber, he began to rebuild the Guild not long after the old one was destroyed," she finished.

"Now, the Guild uses the old dwarven vaults as a testing ground for its most promising thieves. Those who succeed are brought within the inner sanctum and made officers of the Guild," the ex-knight Pitch explained, as she slapped the hilt of the sword at her side. "Officers! With Circles of their own to command."

"Who is Mulciber?" Cael asked.

When none of his fellow thieves offered a response, he continued, "Have you seen him?"

"Her," Varia corrected.

"Her, then. How do you know it's a her?" he asked. "I've heard him . . . her speak, and I can't tell one way or the other."

"Captain Alynthia says Mulciber is a woman. That's good enough for us," she snapped. "Besides, I know lots of people who have seen Mulciber."

"Name one," Pitch countered.

The thin thief glared at her for a moment before answering vehemently, "Lots of people. You wouldn't know them."

"Mancred has seen her," Ijus inserted.

Mancred shrugged. "I might have. I saw someone. It doesn't matter. We have a job to do."

Cael looked to Mancred, who stood gazing at his feet. "Old one," he said. "You have been through this test twice?"

"Aye, and each time it was different," the elder thief answered. "So there's no use in counting on my experience."

"Do I have a weapon, then?" the elf asked, looking around at the weapons of his companions. Pitch wore a long sword similar to the ones favored by Knights. Ijus had his daggers, Hoag a short sword and a sling. Varia wore a short bow over her shoulder. A pair of axes were tucked into Rull's belt. Only Mancred bore no obvious weapons, though the bulges in his sleeves could very well have hidden throwing knives.

"Captain Alynthia said you favored the staff," Pitch said, pointing to a tall smooth dowel of polished ash leaning against the wall. "It's not much of a weapon for a thief."

"I prefer the sword," Cael said, shrugging as he walked over to examine the staff. He hefted it, testing its weight, and gave it a few practice twirls that hummed with speed. "But this will do."

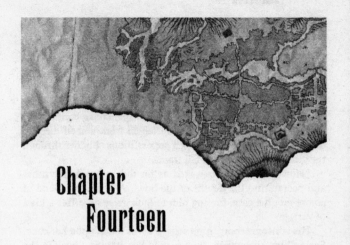

Chapter Fourteen

"Where are they?" Oros asked as he hurried into the room. The door swung shut behind him, as though of its own accord. He hardly seemed to notice it. He raced across the room to where Captain Alynthia bent over a large stone bowl set on a desk of marble. Across from her, a short man wearing robes that might once have been white but that were now a dull, dirty gray, sat on a stool, his hands held up before him with the fingers twisted into grotesque shapes, his eyes rolled back into his head to reveal only the whites staring blindly ahead. His lips quivered with whisperings that kept the magic of the enchanted bowl going, an oily suspiration that tickled the hairs and sent chills along the spines of those who heard it. Sweat streamed down his nose, and his yellow hair hung lank upon his forehead. He rocked back and forth on his stool to the rhythm of his incantation, teetering, as though any moment he might topple over.

The object of his magical casting—the enchanted bowl over

which Alynthia eagerly leaned—was filled to the brim with water. As Oros approached, he saw lights flash from the depths of the bowl, lights reflected in the glimmering of Alynthia's dark eyes, in the shadows of her dusky face. This was the only light in the room, and it starkly illuminated the surrounding shelves littered with all sorts of magical paraphernalia, from ceramic retorts for brewing potions, to spellbooks bound with animals' skin (or worse). A skull leered from a shelf directly over Alynthia's head, sending a superstitious shudder through the guildmaster's six-foot-tall frame.

"How goes it?" Oros asked as he slid in beside Alynthia and peered into the depths of the bowl. A confusing blend of colors met his gaze, forcing him to look away or suffer a kind of vertigo.

His winsome companion started at his touch upon her back. Seeing him, she smiled, then turned her attention back to the bowl.

"He almost didn't make it past the gulguthra," she said, pointing at the glowing water in the bowl.

"Where are they now?" he asked. The bowl had suddenly grown dark, black as oil. Nothing moved within it.

"They're in the sewers," Alynthia answered. As she said this, a pale shaft of light appeared in the bowl's view. Through this, the seven thieves passed, grim faced and eyes wide against the darkness. Water swirled about their knees. Cael led them, his staff probing the water ahead, with Hoag bringing up the rear. As he moved through the light, the thin thief glanced warily over his shoulder—then they were gone, vanished back into the gloom of the sewers.

Alynthia settled back and allowed Oros to run his fingers through the tight curls of her hair. She leaned against him, feeling the comfortable solidity of his massive frame. He had always been her bulwark. He pressed his lips to the crown of her head.

"Concerned?" he asked, as he gazed at the dark bowl over the top of her head. The sorcerer continued his sibilant chant, with only a slight narrowing of his brows to show their voices disturbed his concentration.

"Of course. It is dangerous, and they are not ready," Alynthia answered somewhat crossly.

"They are the best in your Circle," Oros said.

"*They* are ready, but not *him*," she amended, her voice curling into irritation on the last word. "*He* will likely get one of *them* killed. He is still too free a spirit. We'll never break him to the Guild."

"Better they fail now than at Mistress Jenna's," Oros said. "If they fail here, only a death or two is the result. If they fail there, the repercussions could reach to the core of the Guild."

"You are right, of course," Alynthia admitted. She turned to face her companion and lover. "But I rue the day I spoke up for him. There are other thieves, more worthy . . ."

"Yet none so talented. The Guild has not seen his like in a thousand years, not since Geylin Blackheart and Mirathrond Inuinen," Oros said reverently. These two famous thieves had, a thousand years ago during the Age of Might, lived side by side, sharing the rulership of the Guild as no one ever had, before or since. Though lovers, they were also bitter rivals, competing for the reputation of greatest thief in Palanthas. Their exploits were the stuff of legend, and nowadays few thieves believed even half the tales told about the duo. Some said Geylin burgled the Tower of High Sorcery itself, a tale so fantastic that few bards dared to sing it even in the company of thieves. Another version of the story claimed it was Mirathrond who accomplished the deed but that Geylin laid in wait for her outside the Tower and robbed his lover as she made her escape, thus claiming the booty and the glory for himself.

Knowing full well these legends, Alynthia was astonished by Oros's comparison. "Cael Ironstaff, the equal of them?" she asked incredulously. "I admit he is capable, but really!"

Oros shrugged, offering no further comment, and turned his attention to the magical bowl. Alynthia knew her lover well enough to realize that Oros spoke with sincerity, and she had learned to trust his judgment, even when it went against her wishes or desires. It had saved both their lives more than once, saved her from a disastrous and foolish marriage with a Knight of Takhisis three years earlier.

"You're planning to use him," she said with sudden realization.

Oros started, as though he'd just heard his innermost thoughts echoed aloud. "What do you mean?" he asked.

"You are planning to *use* him. You haven't indoctrinated him into the Guild, not in the ordinary way. You even ordered me to not waste too much time showing him our standard methods or teaching him our usual passwords. There can be only one reason for that," she surmised.

"And that is?" Oros asked. His momentary loss of composure had returned. He flashed an appreciative smile at the keenness of his companion's deductions.

"So that when he is captured or betrayed, he will not be able to reveal anything about us. What is it you are really going to send him to steal?" she probed. "It isn't the Potion of Shonlay, is it?"

"That is but a test," Oros admitted. "If this rehearsal succeeds, I will take him into my personal circle for in-depth training. If the mission fails but he survives, I will do the same, saying that he needs my special tutelage to acclimate him to the ways of the Guild. Either way, I shall have him as my student. At first, he will hate me, and then he will slowly grow to admire me. Finally, he will love me as his *shalifi*. When he is properly prepared, I shall plant the seed of something."

"You're planning to send him out alone," Alynthia guessed with undisguised awe. "If he succeeds, he brings the prize back to you. If he fails, he cannot harm the Guild because he knows nothing of its true nature."

Oros nodded appreciatively.

"What is it you covet?" the dark-eyed captain of thieves asked, her voice low.

"The Founderstone itself," Oros whispered.

The sorcerer ceased his arcane mutterings with a gasp. His eyes rolled forward to stare in wonder at the two Guild captains. Realizing that his spell had been broken, he hurriedly resumed his incantation.

It was too late. The darkness had begun to fade from the water in the bowl. Even as it faded, a line of torches hove into view. The image wavered. Oros leaned forward and pointed. "What is that?" he asked anxiously.

"Torches. Knights of Neraka!" Alynthia shouted. She turned on the sorcerer, shaking a fist at his nose. "Get it back. Get the image back!"

"I'm trying!" the poor mage squeaked.

"What are Knights of Neraka doing in the test area?" Oros asked. "Is this part of your design?"

"No, I swear it!" she answered. She stood up resolutely. "I'm going down there!" The image faded completely from the bowl. The sorcerer toppled, exhausted, from his stool.

With an exclamation of disgust, Alynthia bolted from the room.

Chapter Fifteen

"Watch your step," Cael whispered, pointing to a broken step. His gesture was useless, as the darkness of the sewers was complete. However, his elven sight allowed him to see the warm outlines of his companions' bodies, as well as the contours of the sewer tunnel they traversed. The water flowing below them was like a black river, so dark and cool that not even he could penetrate it. Still, something occasionally passed through this river of darkness, something warm and faintly outlined beneath the surface of the water, something large as a submerged canoe, with a serpentine tail that powered it through the water with silent ease. It followed them sometimes, other times swimming alongside them easily, only to vanish into the depths.

At first, Cael had pointed out their watery shadow, but as the darkness prevented his companions from seeing anything, his warnings were useless. Hoag had instructed him (as if he actually needed instruction!) to let them know if the thing loomed a threat, but otherwise to ignore it. How he was supposed to judge the level of danger was never adequately explained.

Also never explained was how other circles of thieves made their way through the sewers to the test area without the benefit of someone with night vision to lead them. His Circle followed Cael blindly, in every sense of the word. Each thief depended on him to point out the slightest danger on their most dangerous road. A misstep anywhere along the way meant a dunk in the cold, fetid water. The least deviation from their path might mean an accidental trip, a fatal stumble.

Even with his elven sight, Cael could no more read their map in the dark than the others. Instead, they relied upon Mancred's memory to direct them to the correct turnings and passages. As they made their slow, careful way through the sewers, Mancred had Cael count out the number of left- or right-hand tunnels they passed. So, it was by the count of passages and turnings that they made progress—slow, torturous progress.

"Why do we travel without light?" the elf whispered to Mancred as he helped the old thief over the broken step.

"Light shining up through the sewer grates would be noticed and investigated. We only use light where it cannot be seen from the streets," he answered.

"Who is that?" Cael asked. A distant turning of the sewer was now visible to them because of a flickering yellow light that had appeared ahead, illuminating the far wall. Human shadows danced along the walls ahead of the light, evidencing that several people bearing torches were headed toward the thieves.

In a hoarse whisper Hoag called for a halt, even though everyone was already crouched against the wall.

"Who are they?" Varia asked. "They're not thieves."

"Maybe they are. Maybe this is part of the test," Pitch said.

"We're not at the vaults yet," Rull protested. Even in a whisper, his deep voice seemed to boom against the walls of the sewer. The thieves winced at the noise. Rull shrugged in silent apology.

A jangle of armor, followed by a splash and a muttered curse, echoed through the sewer.

"They're Knights of Takhisis," Mancred said.

"Neraka," Hoag amended.

"Whatever."

The thieves sat tensely for a few moments, each with the same thought. Was this part of the test, or were these real Knights of Takhisis? Either way, they dared not attack. If they were thieves in disguise, playing a part in the test, okay. If these were real Knights, they would have to be bypassed. The thieves didn't dare match swords, daggers, and staffs against a band of well-armed, well-armored, well-trained Knights. Whatever they decided to do, they had better do it soon. The Knights were growing closer, the sounds of their awkward attempts at stealth growing louder with each passing heartbeat.

"I say we stay here," Cael said, the first to break the silence. "There are three side passages between us and them. They might turn aside at any one of them. They'll not see us here. Their torches blind them to anything outside their own light."

"Not anymore!" Mancred hissed. "Look!"

The Knights' approaching torches brightly illuminated the distant turning. From around the bend came a nightmare, bending so low that its reptilian snout almost touched the ground.

"Draconian!" Mancred affirmed, though each thief knew the creature by reputation, if not by sight. Created many years ago, before the War of the Lance, by black-robed mages and clerics of Takhisis from the eggs of the Good dragons, the draconians were the epitome of evil. They were smaller than dragons, and most were no taller than a human man. They walked upright on two legs, though there the resemblance to humans ended. They had reptilian faces and long claws for hands and feet. A pair of batlike wings sprouted from the backs of all draconians except for the kind known as auraks. They also had long, snaking, spine-crested tails.

The draconian now advancing down the sewer was of the breed known as kapaks. These draconians had long served the armies of Takhisis as assassins and spies. This one must be a scout for the party of Knights. It was slinking some thirty yards ahead of the group, far enough ahead to not be affected by their torches, far enough to espy the thieves huddled against the sewer wall if ever it bothered to lift its head and look. Instead the creature seemed intent upon some scent trail that it was following, though how it smelled anything other than garbage in this place was beyond anyone's guess.

"Back up," Hoag signaled, using the language of hand gestures known by every thief of the Guild. Cael had learned a few of the signals, not enough to follow the sometimes-remarkable silent conversations that could take place between veterans of the hand language. This signal was a simple one, though, easily deciphered.

Mancred shook his head and signaled his disagreement with a short chopping gesture. He pointed to the draconian, then lifted his hand to his ear as though listening. Obviously, he believed that if they tried to move, the draconian would hear them. If they didn't get out of sight, however, the creature would spot them in a few moments anyway.

The old thief's hands blurred as he signaled to his companions. Cael could not follow what he signed, but the others nodded in perfect understanding. Mancred then pointed with two fingers, first behind them, to a passage to their left, then ahead. Everyone nodded, except Cael, who stared from one to the other, trying to comprehend. He knew this much: Everybody was tense, ready for action, their faces set into grim lines as their hands moved to the weapons they bore.

Varia suddenly stood. Cael reached out to stop her, but Mancred held his arm and placed a silencing finger to his lips. With a fluid motion, the beautiful thief unslung her short bow, drew an arrow from the quiver strapped to her thigh, fitted the arrow to the string, and readied the bow. The draconian lifted its head, but not before the arrow was already on its way. A meaty slap echoed along the passage as the draconian clutched at its throat and collapsed to the ground with a strangled cry, its wings flapping feebly.

The Knights, hearing the monster's death rattle, rushed ahead, crying out. Around the corner came at least a dozen of them, black armored, wielding gleaming swords and black maces. Their torches sent their shadows lurching ahead of them.

Cael turned back to see Rull and Varia scurrying back the way they had come. Rull held in his fist a small iron lantern, which beamed a narrow light. Hoag and Ijus edged closer to Cael, while Pitch slipped up beside him and drew her sword.

If they didn't spot the movement, the Knights heard it and hurried their pace, shouting battle cries. Cael started to rise, but Mancred maintained his grip on the elf's arm. "Wait," the old thief whispered.

The dying draconian still lay between them and the Knights. They were close enough now to see its body in the glare of their torches. The thing's fluttering wings and thrashing tail filled the pathway. The Knights slowed their pace, with those in the lead seeming reluctant to approach any nearer.

For good reason. The wings fluttered one last time, then lay still upon the dank wet stone. A moment later, they began to dissolve, as did the rest of the draconian's body. A sickly yellow cloud rose, filling the air with a choking stench, while the dissolving fluid hissed on the stones. The Knights covered their mouths and noses and reeled away.

Mancred had drawn a scroll from the sleeve of his robe. He unrolled it and in the faint light provided by the Knight's torches began to read in a low voice. Slow and sonorously he read the language of magic, which crawled along the spine of those who heard it. He finished the spell with a snap of his fingers, and beyond the acid cloud of the dead draconian, the Knights' torches suddenly winked out like candles in the wind.

"Now!" Mancred shouted. Pitch grabbed the elf by the sleeve and, brandishing her long sword in the other, rushed straight at the reeking cloud and the darkness. Cael stumbled after her, trying to ready his weapon but knowing in his gut that these narrow, low passages were no place for staff work.

He glanced back just in time to see Mancred, Hoag, and Ijus vanish into a side passage. Then, turning ahead, he found that Pitch had disappeared as well. The acid cloud was beginning to clear. He was alone. The Knights stumbled through the cloud, coughing and gagging. One of them had a lantern lit now. He swung its beam around until it fell upon the lone elf. One of the Knights roared, "By her Dark Majesty, it's him!"

Cael skidded to a stop, turned, and raced back the way he had come, cursing his fellow thieves for abandoning him this way. Before he had gone three steps, Pitch popped out from a small side passage and pulled the elf in behind her. Crossbow bolts smashed into the walls around them or skittered about their feet.

"Where were you going?" Pitch hissed angrily.

"Following you," Cael answered.

"Come on then. Lead the way."

In a running crouch, the two fled into the low darkened passage, while the Knights cursed and swore and sent a few more bolts ricocheting harmlessly after them.

The passage coursed straight for about two hundred yards, then began to gradually bend to their left. Every forty yards or so, smaller passages joined it from the right and left. The bend continued for another two hundred yards, then ended abruptly at a wall. Iron rings set into the stone provided a ladder that led up an access shaft. Far above them, a metal grate covered the top of the shaft. Moonlight shone through it, dimly bathing their faces as they looked up.

"Now what?" Cael asked as he gripped one of the rusty iron rungs and tested its strength. "To the streets and home?"

Pitch sheathed her sword. "We wait," she said. She set her back against one of the walls and stared up into the moonlight.

"Wait? For what? For the Knights to decide to come and get us?" the elf asked. They had not heard any pursuit, but Cael doubted the Dark Knights would give up so easily, especially since one seemed to recognize him. He wondered why the Knights of Neraka were searching the sewers of Palanthas for him three weeks after he had vanished into the Thieves' Guild. What powerful enemy had he made? Certainly not Gaeord uth Wotan. Though spectacularly wealthy, not even he would dare to report the theft of an illegal substance. Cael had felt safe in that regard when he stole the dragonflower pollen.

"Mancred said to wait here," Pitch answered. She crossed her arms, as though there was nothing left to say.

"Here? Why here? What could possibly be here?" Cael asked. "Unless . . . unless this is a doorway to the vaults!" he said excitedly. He began to search the walls for any kind of catch or lever. If designed by dwarves, the mechanism wouldn't be obvious. It would more likely appear to be part of the stone itself.

"You're as bad as a kender," Pitch said, eyeing him. "You'll never find it. You have to have the key, and only Mancred . . ." Her words trailed off as a section of the wall slid grindingly back, revealing a gaping dark hole beyond.

"You were saying?" Cael asked with a smirk.

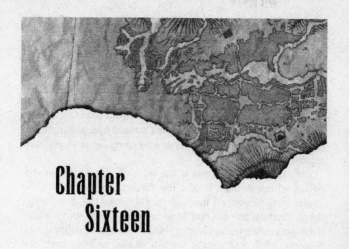

Chapter
Sixteen

A little higher," Pitch ordered as she teetered atop the elf's shoulders. Stretching out with her sword, she probed the high ceiling of the passage, trying to fit the tip of the blade into what appeared to be a niche where the mortar between the stones had fallen out.

"What do you want me to do, fly?" the elf grunted. He gripped her ankles to steady her, but his own ankles felt as though they were about to give out. "Let me try again," he said through gritted teeth.

"Almost got it," she said, for perhaps the thirteenth time.

"Gods! You're as heavy as a bull!" Cael complained.

"Can't you boost me any higher?" Pitch asked, ignoring him. "Straighten up your back and legs. What are you, a man or a boy?"

"I am an elf!" Cael groaned. With a heroic effort, born somewhat of anger at her unintended insult, he raised himself up onto his toes. He felt a jolt as Pitch's sword encountered

137

hard stone. An audible metallic click sounded through the passage, followed by a rumbling noise, as of weights and counterweights settling into new positions. The floor began to sink, and with it, Cael's knees gave out beneath him. He collapsed, and Pitch tumbled down atop him, driving her knees into his back to break her fall. His staff, which was propped against the wall, fell over and cracked her on her shaven head.

Cael laughed at her, clutching his bruised ribs, as she rubbed her stubbly pate. "A staff is no weapon for a thief," she repeated ruefully.

"It saved both our lives at the pit trap," Cael said, remembering with a shudder how, a few moments after entering the vaults from the sewer, the floor had dropped out from under them. Luckily, the pit had been narrow. Cael's staff wedged itself against the walls, stopping his fall with joint-popping suddenness. Pitch had caught his legs as she tumbled past, else she'd have dropped to the spiked floor forty feet below. They had then climbed out, and after several minutes of tugging, managed to free his staff.

The dark-eyed thief nodded grimly, but continued to look at him savagely as she rubbed her head.

The floor ground to a halt, revealing a subterranean passage. Globes of magical light hung motionless in the air at regular intervals down the passage, which curved to the right. This place was different than the passages they had encountered thus far. It looked carved from solid stone, but by what tools neither of them could guess. The walls were polished as smooth as glass, the floor was like a mirror that reflected and multiplied the light of the magical globes.

"What now?" Cael asked, as he rose and dusted himself off. He picked up his staff and thumped it against the shining floor, testing its solidity. It rang like metal, echoing loudly.

"I wouldn't do that again," Pitch said. "No telling what it might alert."

Cael nodded. Pitch checked the edge of her sword, then stepped forward, tentatively, ready to snatch her foot back if anything untoward happened, like the floor turning to molten lava, or springing sword blades. She knew to expect anything, but nothing happened. She took another step, then looked back at the elf.

"Come on," she whispered. "It's safe."

The passage took them in a large circle back to their starting point. As they approached the small section of ordinary floor where they had started, they paused and glanced up the shaft they had descended, then continued ahead for a second try. On this circuit, they were more careful to look for secret doors, hidden latches, sliding walls, anything that might indicate a way out of this circular maze. During the third trip around, Cael made it a point to touch each magical globe with the tip of his staff, hoping that one of them might be the key. But once more they came around to their starting point.

Pitch stopped and slammed her sword into its sheath. "This is pointless," she said dourly, as she gazed once more up the descending shaft. "And now we can't even get out."

Cael scratched and rubbed his chin thoughtfully. "The thing to remember," he commented, "is that this place was made by dwarves. To succeed, we must think like dwarves."

"Do you mean, think low? Perhaps the exit is at dwarven height?"

"Or maybe it is simpler than that. Maybe we are just going the wrong way," the elf said as he turned and looked back the way they had come.

"What wrong way? It is a circle," Pitch argued.

"Maybe it isn't. Maybe it is a spiral," Cael said. At his companion's skeptical look, he explained. "On the surface world we tend to think in two dimensions, this way and that. But aquatic races like the sea elves, and tunneling races like the dwarves, always think in three dimensions. Try to think of this place as a metal spring. Viewed from above it is a circle, and if you run your finger around the top, it is a circle. But turn in the other direction and go the other way, and your finger should find the spiral of the spring."

"That's nonsensical," Pitch said scornfully. "If we went round the other way, of course we would end up right back here, just like all the other times."

"It wouldn't hurt to try," Cael countered.

With a deep sigh for the foolishness of all elves, Pitch motioned for him to lead the way.

And when they had been walking for about ten minutes, her look of scorn had changed to one of obvious admiration. Cael tried not to notice it, but as he led the way, a bit of a swagger appeared in his step.

Finally, the passage began to level out, and the last magical globe came into sight. Beyond it opened a vast dark chamber. Pitch gazed longingly at the magical globe hovering teasingly just beyond her reach. Cael's earlier efforts to knock one down with his staff had proved fruitless.

Side by side, they entered the mysterious chamber. Pitch prudently drew her longsword, while Cael peered about, trying to penetrate the shadows with his elven sight. The lights from the passage winked out behind them. High overhead, at the apex of the dome-roofed chamber, another magical globe began to glow, shedding a dim illumination over the large circular chamber. They began to see . . .

Pitch gripped the elf's shoulder, her indrawn breath a hiss. He spun, ready for whatever danger she had seen, only to find her grinning like an idiot. "This is it!" she whispered excitedly. "This is the Chamber of Doors! We made it, just you and me! One more challenge, and we triumph!"

"What is the final test?" Cael asked.

"We must choose a door," she said, sweeping the circumference of the room with a gesture. Spaced regularly around the room stood seven doors, each set at one of the cardinal points. The eighth point was occupied by the passage through which they had entered. Four doors were made of stone, two of iron wrought without seam or weld. The seventh door appeared to be made of purest silver. It glistened in the dim light. "Behind one of them lies the treasure chamber of the Kal-Thax."

"And the others?"

"Death," she answered grimly, all traces of merriment vanishing from the hard lines of her face.

Slowly now, they walked the circumference of the chamber, each silently contemplating their choice. No single door held more promise than the others, at least not at face value. Each was massive, built on the grandest of dwarven scales. One of the stone doors was circular, like a great plug of rock. It was roughly hewn, made to look like it was part of the surrounding stone, but Cael quickly spotted a tiny keyhole in the very center (Hammerfell had told him many times about the doors of the dwarven city of Thorbardin, and how they were fashioned). Another door seemed but a stone etching of a towering arch. In the lines of the etching glimmered a thin vein of silver, while the door itself was covered in ancient dwarven runes. The other two stone doors faced each other across the chamber. Both were carved fantastically—one with fauns and centaurs, elves and unicorns; the other with hideous creatures leering up out of the Abyss.

The iron doors also faced each other. Neither bore any sign or device indicating its contents. One door had no visible lock at all, while the other was draped in anchor chains and mighty padlocks. Lastly was a silver door. It faced the entrance to the chamber, and was the smallest of all the doors. Upon closer inspection, it proved not to be made of silver at all, but of the scales of some silvery fish, perhaps. Yet they proved hard as granite and as difficult to mar. This door had three locks of obvious complexity. Pitch tried to examine them more closely, but the light was too dim to see anything in detail.

"You have made your decision, then?" he asked her.

"No, I was just studying the problem," she sighed as she sat back on her heels. "It isn't easy. Which door do you think a dwarf would choose?"

"The least obvious," the elf answered.

"Well, they are all rather obvious," Pitch observed.

"It must be some kind of trick."

"Except for the plug door. It took me a while to find it," she said.

"Indeed, a door that does not seem a door is the dwarven way," Cael said. "I can think of no other solution."

"Let's try it," she said.

As they approached the plug door, Pitch withdrew a set of lockpicks from a hidden pocket in her dark gray uniform. "It seems a simple enough lock," she said, as she peered at it. "That is good. Lockpicking is not my strength."

"Nor mine," the elf said.

"I think I can manage this one, though," she said. She withdrew a pair of wires and inserted them into the keyhole. "No traps, either," Pitch commented after a moment.

Cael placed his ear against the stone. "I don't hear anything beyond the door," he said hopefully, then asked, "So how did Varia, Hoag, and Mancred fail the test and yet live?"

Pitch gnawed on her lower lip as she concentrated on the work at hand. She answered distractedly, with many a lengthy pause between words, "They failed . . . because they didn't make a choice at all. Rather than open the door to let possible death rush in . . . they chose to fail and return to the Guild . . . and continue living."

He stood back from the wall and watched his companion toil at the lock, then glanced once more around the room. "This seems too easy," he commented. His eyes fell on the darkened entrance to the chamber, and a thought crossed his mind. "Wait," he said.

"Too late." With a loud click, a roughly circular section of the stone wall began to turn, like the lid of a jar. As it turned, it retreated into the wall. It made no noise at all, and it seemed impossible that something so large and obviously heavy could move without sound, but it took on a dreamlike quality. The two thieves felt as though they also had fallen into a spell. Pitch tapped her sword against the floor just to make sure she had not gone deaf. The steel rang sharply against the stone, and the silence was broken. They looked at each other and grinned, waiting for the door to roll aside.

Beyond the door no gold gleamed, no jewels sparkled. Only more darkness lay within, darkness that suddenly moved, shaking the floor like an earthquake.

Cael shoved his companion aside just as the behemoth burst into chamber. With its huge reptilian head lowered to present a pair of scimitarlike horns, the thing hurtled into the elf. Cael twisted a hairsbreadth to allow the horn to pass under his arm, but as the horn slid past, the lowered head slammed into his chest, lifting him into the air and flinging him across the room. He landed in a roll, stopping himself just before he bashed his head against the wall. The dull ache in his side told of multiple broken ribs, but at the moment, it seemed a small price to pay. He looked round for his staff and found it lying against the wall a few feet away. Then, hearing an angry curse and the ring of steel, he looked up to find a scene from hell playing out before his eyes.

Pitch was battling for her life. The thing was huge, monstrous, a great lizardlike creature with a serpentine body and twelve short muscular legs supporting its length. Each leg ended in claws that dug and gouged the floor as the beast tried to sink its teeth into the dark-eyed female thief. Only the fine edge of her sword kept those massive jaws at bay, but she could not hold out long against those snapping fangs. The creature's head was like that of a crocodile, only many times larger, and it had the cunning eyes of a dragon. It bore a pair of horns sweeping back over its long supple neck. The entire forty-foot length of its body was covered in hard blue scales that resisted the thief's sword blows better than any armor forged by man or dwarf.

No thought of flight entered Cael's mind. Gritting his teeth against the pain in his ribs, he caught up his staff and rushed at the monster. The creature spun to meet him. Its spined tail swept Pitch from her feet.

Now the elf fought desperately for his own life. He skipped backward, fending off each lunge with a ringing, hand-numbing blow of his staff. The creature was as agile as a hunting cat, its strikes as quick as a viper's, its jaws clashed like a bear trap, sending hot spittle flying everywhere in its eagerness to feed, and only a six-foot-long pole of hard mountain ash, fiendishly wielded, prevented it from biting the life from the troublesome elf.

Still, a staff was no weapon for battling such a monster, and Cael was quickly running out of space to retreat. Pitch rushed in with her sword, emitting what sounded like a Knight's battle cry as she drove her blade between two scales of the creature's thick hide. With a terrific roar that seemed likely to bring the roof down on their heads, the beast switched around. Cael leaped back, avoiding the sweep of its thrashing tail.

Pitch retreated a few steps, her sword on guard, but the creature didn't advance. Instead, it curled back its neck, sucking in air through its wide nostrils. Cael felt the hair along his arms stand on end, the air crackling and hissing. Suddenly, the great beast's head shot forward, its jaws gaping. A flash of light illuminated the chamber like an explosion, thunder shook the floor, and a blue bolt of lightning erupted from its mouth. It struck the female thief full in the chest, blasting her across the chamber like a toy swatted by a cat. She slammed into the wall and slumped to the ground, black smoke curling around her.

With a primal howl, the elf swung his staff, swatting the monster squarely. Faster than imaginable, it switched ends again. Cael swung again, this time hitting it across the snout. So mighty was the blow that his staff broke in two, one splintered end bounding across the floor. The beast blinked, the only sign that it even felt his best blow, but that thousandth of a heartbeat's hesitation bought the elf the time he needed to dive aside when the jaws came chomping down upon the space he had just vacated.

He rolled a dozen yards, scrambled to his feet, and dived aside again as wicked teeth bit the air behind him. A blinding flash of pain tore open his back. He stumbled. The tail swept his legs from beneath him. The beast was upon him, its great reeking belly crushing him down against the stone. The coils of its serpentine body looped around and began to squeeze as its claws dug into his flesh. With each breath, he felt his ribs crushed tighter. He couldn't breath, couldn't even cry out. Dark splotches appeared in his vision. He searched for help, any help, but Pitch lay against the wall, her eyes glazed, her chest a miserable charred hole. He saw no more.

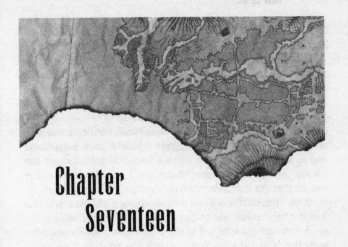

Chapter Seventeen

He vaguely remembered the scales dragging over his flesh, tearing new wounds to match the score already adding their blood to the stains on the floor. His first thought was one of amazement—that he still breathed, albeit painfully. Amazed that he hadn't woken in the belly of the beast, amazed that he wasn't reduced to small bloody chunks.

His next sensation was one of horror and revulsion, as he heard the sickening sound of rending and tearing, the crunching of bones, the splatter of gore, the slurping and catlike purring. He wondered if it wasn't his own flesh being eaten, and this thought brought him painfully to consciousness.

Still he didn't move. He opened his eyes a crack and peered through the slits, taking in his situation. The creature was no longer atop him. He was lying on his back, staring up at the glowing magical globe floating at the apex of the dome-roofed chamber. Strangely, the globe's light was tinted red, as though it were stained by blood.

He turned his head very slowly, so as to not attract the creature's attention, and looked toward the sickening noises of feeding, noticing as he did so that everything was tinted with that same blood red light. The creature faced away from him, reveling in its meal, and as he watched, it lifted its head and made a loud gulping sound. A leg vanished down its throat, forcing the elf to stifle a cry and turn away.

When he finally managed to look back, the beast was still absorbed in its feeding. The great reptilian head tugged and jerked as it tore apart poor Pitch's body and gulped down the pieces. Cael quickly realized that when it was done with her, it would turn to him. The exit lay on the opposite side of the chamber. His staff was broken in two pieces, and even whole it had not been much use except to stave off the inevitable.

A stronger glow of red at the edge of his vision caught his attention. Grinding his teeth against the pain, he rose to his elbows. There, not a half dozen feet away, lay Pitch's longsword. It glowed red with heat, and the wooden hilt and its leather bindings were flaming and crackling. The lightning bolt had struck it full force, and only its superior Solamnic craftsmanship had prevented it from being turned into a puddle of molten slag. It still held its shape, yet the edge and point were useless.

Looking at it wanly, Cael knew it was his one hope to live. He felt no pain, no anguish, no grief, no fear—only hate and the desire to avenge Pitch.

He rose silently to his feet, pushing back the blinding pain. He moved as if in a trance, as though everything was happening to someone else. When he lifted the burning sword and seared his flesh, he gazed at his hand for a moment as though it were all some wonderful joke. Then he was moving as fast as he had ever moved, flying, his lips pulled back in a deathly grimace. Before the creature was aware of the danger the sword had plunged between its ribs. Smoke erupted from the wound as Cael drove the sword deeper and deeper, calling on all his strength, the glowing blade burning through scale and hide, tendon and muscle, until it found the throbbing vitals and finally was quenched in the heart of the beast.

If a gate had been opened to the Abyss and all the fiends of that dreadful plane issued forth, no more hellish shriek could have sounded than the death cry of the beast. Cael loosed his hold on the blade and staggered away. The creature rose before him, towering, bellowing. He clutched his sensitive elven ears lest the noise drive him mad. The beast began to thrash about, filling the chamber with its violence as it coiled upon itself, biting at the sword lodged between its ribs. The floor shuddered, the walls shook, and pieces of stone rained down around the elf. He collapsed against the wall. The creature's thrashing slowed, grew feeble, and then it fell altogether still. Only its labored breathing continued. Finally, with a rattle, it breathed no more.

* * * * *

A voice nearby said, "He killed a behir." The incredulity in the voice and the murmurs of awe roused him. However, it was the touch of a cool hand on his cheek, and the soft words that followed, at which he fought off the darkness and delicious oblivion.

"Are you all right?" Alynthia asked, as she stooped over him and stroked his cheek.

Cael rose up, suddenly, to his full height, surprising everyone, including himself. Hoag was there, a look of disbelief on his face. Beside him was Ijus. Mancred was fiddling with a scroll. Rull towered protectively beside Varia, who gazed at the elf with concerned eyes.

It was their captain whom the elf now sought through the red haze of pain and hate that still colored his vision. Alynthia had staggered back, then tried to recover her dignity. With a snarl, the elf lashed out. His scorched and blackened fist caught her squarely on the chin and sent her flying into Hoag. The two tumbled to the floor, Ijus chuckling nervously as he danced nimbly out of the way.

Cael lunged for her again, but Rull was there, catching him in a bear hug, pinning his arms and lifting him completely off the ground. Despite his great strength, the thief was remarkably gentle. Cael could no more break his hold than he could have broken that of the monster.

"This is a stupid, foolish waste of life!" the elf spat at their leader. "Isn't there danger and death enough without creating it for ourselves?"

Alynthia rose slowly to her knees, all sympathy gone from her expression. Instead, danger flashed in her dark eyes. "I will forgive you for that, this time," she growled as she rubbed her chin.

"Was that . . . *thing* . . . another one of your pets?" Cael sneered.

"I warned you that this was no game," the Guild captain said. Ijus helped her to her feet, still chuckling. "Pitch knew the risks the same as you. You had to go off on your own, taking her with you, to face trials meant for a Circle of Seven, not two."

"We continued alone because we didn't know where the others had gone," the elf snapped. "We didn't want our Circle to fail the test without a chance to even try."

"Yet you failed anyway, and it cost the life of your Guild sister," Alynthia responded.

"We did not fail," the elf cried, struggling to free himself from Rull's grip. "I won't allow her to die for nothing. The guardian is dead. The way is opened."

"The way is still shut to you, apprentice thief," Alynthia scoffed. "The behir's lair is not the treasure chamber."

"I know that, but I now know the way, if you would just put me down!"

Reluctantly, the giant thief lowered Cael to the ground and released his hold. The elf, weak from his wounds, nearly collapsed, but his anger lent him strength. He stood shakily, ready to do anything to spite the beautiful, dusky-skinned Guild captain. Alynthia stepped back warily, eyeing him.

He stalked by her without even a glance and re-entered the Chamber of Doors. The others followed, hesitantly eyeing the dead behir where it lay stretched out at the center of the chamber. Cael paused just inside the room. His companions spread out around him, gaping in awe at the magnificent beast.

Varia gasped and turned aside, burying her face in Rull's massive chest. The remains of Pitch, pitiful as they were, lay scattered near the far wall. Ijus approached them, his fingers cracking and snapping in something between curiosity and nervous horror. Seeing how little of the thief remained, Alynthia turned on the elf, her dark eyes burning with anger.

"No door shall be opened to prove or disprove you," she told him. "Make your guess and be done with it."

Without a word, Cael stooped to the floor and, with his left hand, which had suffered no burns, picked up a piece of the stone that had fallen from the roof during the monster's death throes. He spun and flung the rock at the darkened entrance-way. To everyone's surprise, even Alynthia's, the stone bounced off the darkness as though it had struck a solid wall, and clattered to the floor.

"A door that does not appear to be a door," the elf said. "The room revolves." His legs began to wobble beneath him. Mancred caught his arm and helped him to stand. Cael started to thank him, then noticed that the old thief was staring at him in undisguised respect. He turned away, unable to bear such admiration.

"I am sorry," he said in a voice harsh with weariness and emotion. "I am having trouble seeing. Everything is red."

"Your eyes are filled with blood," the old man said. "Few who have been embraced by the behir survive to bear that scar."

"Pitch wanted to do it for you," Cael said. "She wanted to try."

"You succeeded. She did not die in vain," Mancred said proudly, gripping the elf in an almost fatherly embrace.

"The door is not opened, and it won't be opened, not by him," Alynthia said stubbornly. "When Pitch died, the test was ended. That is the law of Mulciber. All succeed or no one."

"Yet two accomplished what was designed to defeat seven," Mancred argued.

"You take sides with this elf?" Alynthia asked. "After what happened to Pitch?"

"She chose her way," Varia said tersely.

149

"Not since Captain Oros came here has such a thing been done. Not even you, Captain Alynthia, entered the vaults alone, not even you solved the riddle of the doors," Mancred said.

"We act as a team. A lone wolf is a liability we cannot afford, no matter how great his individual skill," she insisted. She stroked her bruised chin, thoughtfully. "You know the rules. In addition to costing you the life of one of your Circle, this elf has also ruined your careers within the Guild," Alynthia frowned. "He has shown you the secret of this Chamber, yet failed the test. Knowing the secret, you may never try again."

Mancred sighed heavily, his head bowing in dejection. Hoag's eyes flared with hatred as he looked at the elf. Even Varia looked away, unable to meet Cael's gaze. Rull set his lips into a grim line and stared at the wall. Only Ijus made a noise, and that was to giggle. He quickly stifled his laughter at a sharp glance from Hoag.

"However, what you say has some merit, and I have decided to take the six of you into my personal Circle of thieves," Alynthia concluded proudly. The others roused at these words and at the promise of adventure that they heralded.

While the others whispered excitedly, Alynthia caught a handful of the elf's long coppery hair and pulled his face near her own. She said nothing, but her threatening gaze spoke more plainly than words. He returned her stare without flinching, his teeth gritted, fighting off the darkness of weariness and pain that threatened to crush him.

"You look like a fiend from the pit," the beautiful thief said, grinning. "Varia, see what you can do for old Blood Eyes' wounds." She turned away and stalked from the chamber, Hoag dropping in obediently behind her. Cael collapsed, and soon was awash in the soothing waters of Varia's mystical healing.

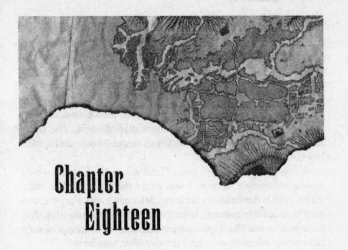

Chapter
Eighteen

The two Knights of the Lily guarding the door to the Lord's Palace glanced at each other in concern. A woman they both knew by sight and reputation was gliding across the Great Plaza below, her long red robes flowing behind her as she walked, her hands folded together and hidden by the robe's voluminous sleeves. The robe's hood was pulled up just to the crown of her head, so that rather than concealing her face, it accentuated its handsome shape. A few strands of gray hair strayed from the hood to fall luxuriously over her shoulders.

She headed for the Lord's Palace, and both Knights knew she had no scheduled appointment this morning. One glanced at his list of expected guests, just in case the name of Mistress Jenna had been added. His hopes were dashed. He looked at his companion, who returned his forlorn gaze with a sour grimace. Neither relished the thought of the approaching encounter. They gripped their swords as though these slender shafts of steel could somehow help them. Mistress Jenna, glancing up at them and seeing the resolve on their faces, did not slow her pace. She reached the foot of the stairs, where the great platform had stood for the Spring Dawning festival almost two months earlier. She mounted the stairs without breaking her stride.

The Knights stepped out from beneath the great arch of the palace entrance and met the great sorceress at the top of the stairs. She smiled patiently and moved to pass between them, but one held out a restraining, black-mailed hand. The smile faded from Jenna's face. She stopped, stepped back, and settled her robes about her.

If this were any other citizen of Palanthas, the Knights would have acted forcibly. Because it was Jenna, the female Knight made an attempt at cordiality. "I am sorry, Mistress Jenna, but you have no scheduled appointment with the lord mayor this morning. Perhaps you would like to set an appointment? The Mayor should have a free moment sometime the day after tomorrow."

"I am not here to see the lord mayor," Jenna answered coolly.

"We cannot allow you inside," the male Knight said in what he hoped was a steely voice. "Sir Kinsaid does not allow casual visitors to the Lord's Palace."

"There is nothing casual about my visits, Sir Knight," Jenna snapped. "I go where I will, when I will, and how I will. I was here before you were born and I will still be here when you are gone. You will allow me to pass or you will tell Arach Jannon to come out here and meet me. It matters little to me, either way. Now hurry up about it. You may have nothing better to do than to stand in front of doors and act important, but my time is of immense value."

"Yes, of course, Mistress," the female Knight assented. She hurried away. The male Knight remained standing before Mistress Jenna, while she returned his gaze with an implacable look. He had fought pitched battles against ogres and minotaurs, sailed a galley into the teeth of a storm on the Blood Sea of Istar, but these were nothing compared to what he now endured. Soon, he could no longer withstand her scornful scrutiny. He made a show of turning his attention to those strolling about the Great Plaza, and the clouds of pigeons rising and settling at their passing. Gulls circled overhead, crying the song of the sea.

At last, when he thought he could bear it no longer, his companion returned. Breathlessly, the female knight apologized to Mistress Jenna, ceremoniously added her name to the roll of guests, checked the name off, and ushered the elder sorceress through the doors. When she had gone, the female Knight sighed as they resumed their posts by the door. "Now what do you suppose she wants with *him?*"

"Who cares, so long as she is gone from here. Wizards! Pah, may they all rot together," the male Knight said boastingly.

The female Knight chuckled. "Brave words," she murmured.

Her companion smiled at her ruefully. "To tell you the truth, I felt as though she had stripped off my flesh and was examining my very bones."

* * * * *

Sir Arach Jannon's chambers lay deep beneath the Lord's Palace. He had chosen them ostensibly for safety's sake, as he sometimes conducted delicate magical experiments that were best performed far from sensitive view. The hallways and stairs leading to the door, and the chambers themselves, were carved from the living stone beneath Palanthas long before the Palace itself was built. For two millennia, the chambers had remained largely unoccupied, used instead for storage and, during the Chaos War, as shelter for the Lord Mayor and his family.

Jenna surmised that Arach had chosen these chambers not to protect others from his sometimes-dangerous experiments but to force his visitors to walk half a league just to see him. She would have used a spell to transport herself, but the chambers were protected against magical intrusion, and she didn't want its wards to deflect her spell and cause her harm. Her magic had grown too unstable of late to trust its use in such an inessential way.

Not that she would have admitted that her magic had grown unstable. The worst of it was, she had no idea why this was happening to her magic, and she didn't know if other mages were experiencing the same troubles. She wanted to probe her gray-robed adversary, to see if his magic might also be weakening.

She had to admit it would make her feel better if the problem was somehow rampant.

She found Sir Arach sitting cross-legged in mid-air, three feet above a fine rug from the minotaur island of Kothas. A juvenile trick! He smiled as she entered, and bowed his head in a mockery of respect. Showing off his magic like some hair-brained apprentice. How she wished the Thorn Knights, the magic-using branch of the Knights of Takhisis (Neraka!), could be forced to undergo the tests once given in the Towers of High Sorcery. She felt sure it would weed out a good many of what she considered to be spellcasting yokels.

Jenna paused just within the doorway, refusing to go further until Sir Arach came down from his magical perch. With obvious reluctance and a frown at her poor sense of humor, the Thorn Knight unfolded his legs and lowered himself onto the rug, then removed the silver ring from his finger. He held it up between his thumb and forefinger to show her.

"Ring of levitation," he explained. "It was confiscated from a kender three days ago at the Knight's High Road gate. Would you like it?" He flipped it to her.

It bounced off the front of her robe and fell to the floor at her feet. She did not move, did not even bat an eye. The ring rolled away, vanishing under a cupboard beside the wall. Arach watched it go ruefully, but he made no move to retrieve it. He turned his eyes back to his adversary and found her eyes boring holes through him.

"Mistress Jenna, it is an honor to receive you in my humble chambers. Please have a seat. I will order tea." The Thorn Knight swept behind a large, pockmarked desk and motioned Jenna to a low comfortable chair, but she remained standing at the door. Arach shrugged and settled himself into his own chair. He clapped three times, and a small bell dangling above the desk tinkled cheerfully.

"I don't want any tea," Jenna growled.

"Wine, then?" he suggested. "It is a little early in the day, but . . ."

Jenna scowled, but did not dignify his remark with a response. With an obvious show of weary patience, Sir Arach folded his hands together and placed them on the desk before him. "How may I help you, then?" he inquired.

"Why haven't you captured him?" Jenna snapped.

"Why haven't I captured who?"

"I gave you his name, told you of the magical boots I sold to him, all so that *you* could capture him. I haven't time to chase down every thief and cutpurse in Palanthas. That is your job, Lord High Justice," Jenna said with a sneer.

"When he surfaces, he shall be captured, I assure you," Arach said confidently.

"Your assurances date back approximately two months."

"Every Knight in the city knows his description, so if he shows himself on the streets, rest assured he *will* be captured. Meanwhile, his magical boots remain right where he left them. They have not been touched, and he has not returned for them. When he does, there is a glyph placed on the door of his dwelling, one that will stun him for several hours, allowing us to collect him at our leisure. Until that time, there is nothing else to be done."

"Hmmph. A glyph?"

"I placed it there myself."

"Very clever of you, I'm sure," Jenna smirked. "Still, if you really wish to capture him, I suggest that you drop by the Three Moons tonight."

"Whatever for?"

"Because the Guild plans to make an attempt on my house tonight," she said.

"There is *no* Thieves' Guild in Palanthas," Arach asserted, his voice rising slightly.

"Cael Ironstaff will be with them," Jenna continued, her eyes narrowing.

"How do you know all this?" the Thorn Knight asked suspiciously.

"Does it matter? All that matters is that it *will* happen. I strongly suggest, Sir Knight, that you be there." With these words, she spun and, pausing at the chamber door, added, "Bring your glyph if it gives you pleasure!" She stalked out, her robes sweeping behind her. The door slammed shut with a resounding boom.

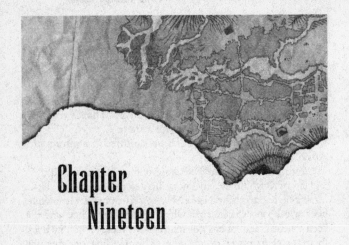

Chapter Nineteen

uckily, Cael found the privy unoccupied, though the scent of lingering pipe smoke proved that it had only recently been vacated. He pulled himself up through the hole, reentering the privy by way of a small round opening primarily meant as an exit. The privy's door had been replaced, since it was so rudely pummeled into kindling by Captain Alynthia's thugs, by a stout new one of planed pine stained a deep burgundy red. Even the doughty little bolt that allowed him time to escape had been replaced with a shining copper latch.

Cael clambered free and quickly hooked the latch to prevent anyone from barging in unexpectedly. He sat back and relaxed for a moment, pondering his next move. His clothes were in terrible shape. He'd been wearing the same outfit for the better part of two months. He could not go about much longer dressed like this, he thought with a rueful smile.

Before he left the privy, he turned to the wall and placed his hand against its stained wood. He spoke no word, but from beneath his outstretched palm there grew a bar of red light, spreading above and below, like a door opening onto a brightly lit room. Where the red bar glowed, the wall began to bulge outwards until Cael's ironwood staff, sheathed in reddish fire, burst free of the wall. Where it had been, there was neither sign nor mark upon the wall. Cael sighed and clutched it to his chest like an old friend. He unlatched the door and opened it.

The sharp end of a stiletto against his throat stopped him before he'd taken a step.

"Your arm must be long indeed to have fished that staff from the sewers," Alynthia said with a laugh from the other end of the blade.

She stood blocking the door, wearing a loose blouse of palest green silk and violet trousers bound about her hips by a wide belt and tucked into knee-high black leather boots. Swordsman's gauntlets of double-stitched leather protected her hands and completed her costume of dashing swashbuckler.

Her face grew serious. "There are agents of the Dark Knights watching this place, just as I foretold," she said. "It is good that you came by way of the sewers instead." She returned the stiletto to its sheath. "You look a mess, and you smell like a pig wallow. Phew!" Her nose wrinkled in disgust. "We have a long evening ahead, you and I, but first you need a bath! I know just the place, but first let us get you something to disguise your face and those elven ears. Your room, I seem to recall, is up those stairs?"

She stepped back to allow Cael to pass, all the while pinching her nostrils. As Cael led the way up the stairs and to his room, his staff thumped rhythmically against the floor.

"Are you limping again?" Alynthia asked in muffled tones.

"I *am* in disguise," Cael grandiloquently pronounced. "The limp allows me to smuggle an extraordinary weapon through the gates of the city. Besides, no one suspects a cripple of such deeds as I have accomplished in my career."

"Well, it's silly and altogether amateurish," Alynthia said. "You'll have to stop relying on such an outmoded weapon. We can show you ways to slip a dagger or sword past the guards."

"I will not abandon my staff," Cael said. He paused before

the door of his room and fingered his pockets for the door key. "It was given me by my *shalifi.*"

A low whistle from down the hall drew their attention. An old beggar lay in the corner under a heap of rubbish, but nothing else could account for the noise. Cael gripped his staff, but Alynthia merely smiled. "It's only Mancred," she whispered.

Slowly, the old thief rose from his resting place and shuffled toward them, taking care to not move too quickly and give away his disguise. When Cael turned back to the door, and with his staff smashed the butt against the doorknob to snap the lock, Mancred threw aside all caution and rushed at them both, wildly waving his arms.

The door creaked open as the elderly thief came running up.

"What's wrong with you?" Alynthia asked, staring around to make sure no one had seen the odd incident.

"There was a glyph of warding on that door, as sure as I am standing here," Mancred answered. "I waited here to warn you. I could not dispel it."

The three thieves entered Cael's bedroom and cautiously shut the door behind them. They found things just as they had been left. Even the bed was still lying on its side. Mancred continued to scratch his balding pate in puzzlement. "I can't understand why the glyph didn't strike him when he opened the door," he said.

"It was never a good lock," Cael said. "I've opened it that way many times."

"But this time you should have been stunned by the magical glyph. It was placed there for that purpose," Mancred answered.

"By who?" Cael asked as he righted his bed and pushed it back against the wall. He sat on the edge of his bed and pulled his tattered shirt over his head, tossing it into a corner.

"By the Dark Knights. They set a trap for you, Blood Eyes," Alynthia said with a laugh.

Several weeks had passed, but the crimson stain to the whites of the elf's eyes had only begun to fade in the past few days, allowing him to see things without having to peer through a red haze.

Though she laughed at him, Alynthia could not help but admire how finely muscled was his upper body. His sides still bore the scars of the behir's claws, though Varia's healing magic had helped speed his recovery.

Cael glanced around the room, choosing a tunic from his available clothes, and slipped it over his head.

"May I see your staff?" Mancred asked suddenly.

Cael handed it over with obvious reluctance. "I only want to examine it for a moment," the old thief said. He took it nearer the window to get a better light to see by.

Alynthia insisted, "A staff is no weapon for a thief."

"It serves me well," Cael said, refraining from any further explanation.

After a moment, Mancred handed it back, shaking his head. "It seems ordinary enough," he said, "but I sense it has unusual powers." He nodded to Alynthia, who did her best to look unimpressed.

"Anyway, the guards of the city know me as a cripple," Cael continued as he turned back to the Guild Captain. "I cannot suddenly appear on the streets healed of my injury."

"What injury?"

"I was trampled by the horse of a Solamnic Knight," Cael said, displaying his twisted ankle. He immediately straightened it, and then wiggled it around to show its flexibility. "Of course, it healed some years ago, but the Dark Knights like the story. It makes them think I am sympathetic to them."

"They don't think so anymore. Isn't it obvious that they have orders to arrest you?" Alynthia argued.

Cael shrugged and pulled his wet, torn boots from his feet. "Hand me those brown boots from the wardrobe," he said.

"Who did you offend? It must have been someone very powerful," Alynthia said thoughtfully as she retrieved his boots. Then, realizing what she was doing, she threw the boots on the floor just out of Cael's reach. "Get your own boots!" she snarled.

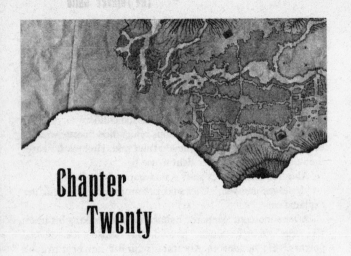

Chapter
Twenty

Alynthia knelt by the window, peering out, while Cael slipped into a black cloak and hood and drew a mask over the lower half of his face. Glancing back at him, she shook her head. "Even with the mask, anyone can tell you are an elf," she whispered.

"I cannot change who I am," he answered, his voice muffled by the mask.

"A shame. Well, it will have to do," she said, returning her attention to the window. Outside, the full moon stood poised on the peaks of the mountains to the east of Palanthas. By its light, Cael folded a small black cloth bag and tucked it into the pouch at his belt. The bag, which they had found upon entering the room a little more than an hour ago, contained the soft black outer garments, masks, and capes that he and Alynthia now wore. It also contained two broad-bladed poniards, equally suited to close fighting or throwing.

Thieves of the Second Circle of the Guild, in whose territory the building stood, had placed the bag here in preparation of the evening's work. It was the nature of the new Guild not to allow one hand to know what the other was doing, so those who left the parcel of clothing did so without knowing the reason and without questioning it. The command came from above and was authorized by the seal of Mulciber.

The room's only window commanded a crossing of two alleyways, one running east to west, the other northeast to southwest. It was partially boarded over, allowing a good view of all that passed without, while concealing those within. The moon shining down the east alley revealed anyone approaching from that direction.

"Make yourself ready. It is almost time," said Alynthia.

"It's hours yet, surely. The night is still young," Cael said.

"When the moon clears the eastern peaks, we go. That is the order."

"But wouldn't it be better to wait until the night is old and Jenna is deep into her sleep?" the elf asked.

"Mistress Jenna seals her house against all intrusion before retiring for the night, so we propose to enter while she is awake and before her wards are set."

"Sounds tricky," Cael said.

"It is. You will do nothing except under my direct order, do you understand me?"

"Aye, Captain sir," Cael answered.

They waited in silence while the moon rose behind the distant mountains. The city around them was quiet, for here, so close to the Shoikan Grove, most of the buildings were abandoned and empty. Despite the hundreds of years that had passed since the grove first appeared, these buildings remained in good repair. Rather than allow any section of Palanthas the Beautiful, City of Seven Circles, to fall into disrepair, the city paid handsomely to maintain these buildings, hiring laborers willing to brave the proximity of the magical grove in exchange for the princely sums such work commanded. A few hardy souls still lived in this neighborhood, mostly mages and folk of similar occupation, people seeking quiet and solitude away from the hubbub of the city. This situation was made all the more strange because the grove stood quite near the very center of the city, within shouting distance of some of the busiest quarters in town. For the most part, though, only the wind whistled down these alleys, and shadows played in the courtyards.

Finally, Alynthia whispered, "It is time."

Together they slipped through the window and into the alley beyond. Keeping to the shadows, Alynthia led them along a narrow path. They passed with no more sound than two cloud shadows racing along the ground. In moments, they halted beside a blank wall, and Alynthia placed her black-gloved hand against Cael's lips, enjoining him to silence. They waited again, huddling in the shadows.

A rope of black-dyed silk dropped down and dangled between them, brushing their shoulders. Alynthia steadied it with her hand and looked up, signaling to those on the roof. She pointed at Cael's staff and lifted her eyebrows as though to say, "How do you expect to climb a wall carrying a staff in your hands?"

In answer, he placed his staff against the wall and whispered, "Conceal." A reddish glow enveloped the dark wood, but the staff did not otherwise change. A puzzled expression crossed his face. "Conceal," he whispered again. The staff's crimson glow faded, then vanished.

Alynthia pulled him close and hissed into his ear, "What are you doing?"

Cael stared at the wall for a moment. "It must be protected against magical intrusion," he whispered.

"Of course it is! Now climb, before we are seen!"

Cael shrugged, still staring in bafflement at the wall. He turned away from Alynthia for a moment, and when he turned back, the staff was no larger than a cane. He slipped it under his belt.

Alynthia shook her head as though she disapproved but motioned impatiently for him to climb. He grasped the rope and started up, Alynthia following close behind.

He reached the roof's edge, three stories above the alley, and found a masked thief steadying the rope. Another extended a black-gloved hand and helped him up the last few feet. When

Alynthia appeared below, each lent a hand in lifting her to the roof and setting her on her feet. At a quick sign, they vanished into the darkness, finding ready places of concealment. Alynthia drew up the rope and left it coiled at the roof's edge.

The roof of Mistress Jenna's house was flat, unlike most of the roofs of the surrounding buildings. A short wall enclosed it, providing a sort of battlement, if it were needed. Cael scanned the roof and with his elven sight saw by the glow of their bodies' heat no less than a dozen thieves covering every possible route of escape and keeping a careful, inconspicuous watch over the city below. Not far away, the trees of the Shoikan Grove rose above the rooftops as though keeping their own watch over the thieves. The trees' shadows, looming so near, made everyone more tense and wary.

Near the center of the roof, four thieves huddled in a small group. Alynthia nudged Cael. He dropped into a crouch, running with a swift, light gait. Alynthia followed him.

Three of the four thieves turned. The fourth was busy at some task of obvious delicacy, judging by his level of concentration. He was carefully pouring something onto the roof. Acrid smoke rose up around his face, swirling up from where the liquid bubbled and hissed on the roof's surface.

"Acid," Alynthia said in a voice barely above a whisper. "Magical. All ordinary attempts to cut through this roof have failed, because of the wards placed on it by Mistress Jenna."

"What if she is below? Won't she notice the acid eating through her ceiling?" Cael asked.

"She uses the top floor for storage. Living quarters are on the second floor, shop on the first floor, laboratory in the basement. If we are lucky . . ." She ended with a shrug.

"Won't the acid eat through the next floor as well?"

"Mancred is being very careful to only use enough to dissolve a hole through the roof, aren't you Mancred?" Alynthia whispered.

The thief grunted in answer, not allowing a spoken response to break his concentration.

Meanwhile, the other three thieves busied themselves assembling a sturdy metal tripod, from the apex of which hung a small pulley. While one oiled the pulley and tested it for noise, another carefully uncoiled a thin black rope and threaded it through the pulley's wheels.

"What am I supposed to do?" Cael asked Alynthia.

"Stay close to me and keep quiet," she answered through pursed lips. "Mancred, how much longer?"

The thief grunted again, then sat back on his heels and carefully stoppered the bottle of acid before slipping it into a pouch. "A hundred slow heartbeats," the old thief estimated. "A hundred and twenty, perhaps." He coughed quietly, perhaps from the acid's fumes.

As the thieves of Cael's Inner Circle finished assembling the tripod, Mancred leaned over the hole eaten into the roof by his magical acid. A few last wisps of smoke arose from it and were shredded by the southerly wind. Without looking up, he extended one gloved hand. Varia quickly slapped a small gardening shovel into his hand. With this tool, the elder thief began to excavate, carefully removing scoops of sizzling, still-smoking debris from the hole and setting them aside, knocking gelatinous strands from the shovel with the heel of his palm. After the fourth such excavation, a thin beam of yellow light lanced up from below.

"The tripod!" Alynthia hissed. The thieves responded by placing the tripod over the hole, then covering it with a wrap of black cloth. This cloth effectively blocked the light from hole, preventing anyone from observing it from below on the street. This done, Mancred quickly dredged out a breach large enough for a man to fit through.

At a motion from Alynthia, Varia grasped the pulley rope. Ijus wrapped a loop around his waist and swung out beneath the tripod. She quickly lowered him through the hole. Hoag followed, then the old thief Mancred, who quietly grumbled of his aching joints as he slid down the rope. Next, Alynthia dropped through the hole, guiding her fall with one hand on the rope, and landing with no more sound than a cat.

Finally, Cael ducked beneath the tripod and grasped the rope. He looked into Varia's cobalt blue eyes gleaming in the moonlight over the top of her mask. "Don't worry. I won't drop you," she whispered. "Be careful not to touch the sides, or the acid will burn you."

With a nod, Cael swung out on the rope. While he dangled by one hand, he kept a tight grip on his staff with the other. Slowly, Varia lowered him through the hole.

He dropped the last few feet, landing without sound beside Alynthia. Quickly, he crouched against the wall, while their rope vanished up through the hole as noiselessly as smoke. Looking up, he saw Varia's hooded, masked face peering down at them. She signaled with a thumb's up. Alynthia nodded, then pointed down the hall. Ijus eased forward.

The hall was ordinary enough. Cael had half-expected to find it lined with all sorts of impossible traps both magical and mundane, but as far as he could tell the passage was empty. A few torches burning in iron sconces provided a thin, smoky yellow light. Nondescript doors stood open at either end of the hallway, revealing dark rooms beyond. Between the thieves and the door to their right, there opened a staircase where a little light shone from below. Ijus paused here and peered quickly around the corner. He signaled that all was clear.

Just to their left stood a large locked iron door, the last barrier to their mission. Alynthia made a motion as though opening a scroll, at which Mancred moved around her and approached the door.

The elderly thief studied the door for a moment. It was of iron plainly wrought and stoutly riveted with reinforcing bands of blued steel. Its lock, also of blue steel, looked impressively strong. At first glance, the door's metal appeared unadorned, but after a moment's study, strange patterns showed themselves in the grain. It was writing, but in a language unknown to any of them.

Mancred nodded to himself and removed a scroll from the pouch where he stored the acid. He indicated to Alynthia, but without touching the door, three places where the 'writing' seemed the most intricate. He motioned everyone except the lookout at the stairs to draw near, indicating with the scroll an imaginary circle on the floor. Alynthia grabbed Cael's hand and pulled him within the circle.

Satisfied of their positions, Mancred turned back to the door and opened his scroll. Hoag moved closer to peer over the old man's shoulder, and Cael stole the opportunity to slip a hand around Alynthia's waist. At a venomous glance from her dark eyes he quickly withdrew it and met her stare with an innocent smile. She looked away, but the twitching of her eyelid revealed her continuing annoyance.

Mancred began to read from the scroll in a voice no louder than a whisper. The air about them began to hum, not so much a sound as a buzzing feeling inside their skulls. A tremendous pressure closed over their ears and stole their breath, as though they had just been covered with deep water. Just as quickly the pressure disappeared, and the old thief let his scroll roll up with a snap.

"I have given us protection within an area of magical silence, so we can—"

A brief hiss cut him off. They started, fearing discovery, but saw only Ijus at the stairs motioning wildly. He pointed at his ear, and at them, then back at his ear.

Puzzled, Alynthia stepped outside the imaginary circle, motioning for Mancred to open his scroll. He did so, and she pointed at her ear, then at the scroll. The thief by the stairs nodded in agreement. Mancred frowned, staring at Cael's staff.

Using the language of hand signals, Alynthia asked the old thief, "What is wrong?"

"His staff disrupted the spell," Mancred silently responded.

Alynthia turned on the elf, who had not been able to follow the conversation. Her eyes flashed anger. She stabbed a finger thrice through the air, violently pointing first at Cael's staff, then at him, then at a spot on the floor outside the circle of silence. With a confused shrug, he stepped to the place she indicated.

Mancred tugged at Alynthia's sleeve and signed, "However, the staff might remove the glyphs guarding the door, as it did the door of his dwelling."

"Can you remove them with your scrolls?" she asked the old thief.

"Yes," came the answer with a quick nod.

"Better to take the sure path than the unknown," she answered.

With a final glare at Cael and his staff, Alynthia moved once more beside Mancred, who with a weary glance at the elf opened his scroll and set to work. Unfortunately, his scroll, penned by mighty wizards five hundred years before, had only one spell of silence upon it, and once cast it was erased forever from the parchment.

Now whispering, now breathing sibilant chants, the thief cast spell after spell from the ancient scroll, unweaving the threads of Mistress Jenna's protective wards. As each magical ward was broken, it expired with a release of red or blue or green light in the shape of a magical rune or sigil, which dissipated in the air like pipe smoke. Some of these signs, being similar to Elvish letters, Cael was able to interpret. One was of fire, another of ice, a third the zigzagged symbol of lightning. Had the thief not broken these wards, anyone attempting to open the door or even to touch it without first speaking the proper passwords would have been burned to ash, frozen, or blasted to smithereens before he glimpsed the wonders beyond that iron portal.

Finally, with a weary nod, Mancred indicated that all magical protections had been removed. A glance at the door showed that the mysterious patterns in the grain of its metal had vanished. The old thief stepped back, his work completed. He collapsed against the wall and mopped his sweating forehead with a black rag.

At a motion from Alynthia, and a warning finger across her mask-hidden lips enjoining silence, Hoag slipped up to the door and crouched before it. From a pouch at his belt, he removed a thick leather wallet. He placed it on the floor between his knees and opened it, then expertly eyed the massive blue steel lock. After a few moments, he chose a thin rod as long as his middle finger. He inserted it into the lock, gave it a deft twist, and a tiny silver needle appeared at the center of one of the lock's many rivets. A droplet of amber fluid glistened on its tip. Hoag carefully removed this deadly metal fang and flicked it aside, perhaps in the hope that Mistress Jenna might step on it in the dark with bare feet.

Now he set to work. First, he chose a pair of thick wires and inserted them into the lock, then pushed a narrow flat shim in beside them. Working carefully, the sounds of his tinkering muffled by the cloaked bodies around him, he jiggled, prodded, levered, wrenched, twisted, and finally with a satisfying click turned the lockpicks in the lock. He slid the lock from its stout iron staple and set it on the floor beside the door.

Alynthia stepped forward and pushed against the door. In well-oiled silence, it swung wide. The thieves grinned at each other through their masks. Cael wasn't sure whether it was because of their success or because Alynthia so trusted their abilities that she opened the door herself rather than order an underling to risk the possibility of an overlooked ward. They crowded into the doorway beside her, even old Mancred, anxious to see what fabulous treasures awaited them.

Before allowing them into the chamber, Alynthia indicated by a stern look and a raised finger that each thief might choose one item apiece, and that they must choose quickly. The thieves nodded their silent agreement, and she stepped into the room, while the others followed.

The treasure chamber looked worthy of all their efforts. Over the years since Mistress Jenna first established her Three Moons shop, she had acquired one of the strangest and rarest collections of curiosities, artifacts, relics, and magical items known on Krynn. Not even the fabled Towers of High Sorcery at the height of their power could have surpassed her treasury. Indeed, it was very likely that a great many of the items to be found here had once decorated a shelf in some tower master's library or rested upon a table in his conjuring chamber. There were wands in jeweled cases, potions in bottles of silver, porcelain, pottery, and glass. One shelf was reserved for rings, while another was stacked with what appeared to be ancient books of spells and incantations. From a bar hung a rack of wizard's robes and cloaks, some black, some red, some white. All were apparently magical, or at the very least arcane, from the runes and sigils stitched on the sleeves and hemmed in threads of silver and gold. One appeared to be sewn with something like starlight, for upon close inspection no thread was visible, but from a distance a clear silver-blue stitching was plain for all to see. A pair of rolled rugs stood in one corner, while opposite them was a wide golden brazier in which coals had been placed but not lit.

The chamber was illuminated from above by three clear glass balls that floated in the air and glowed with an inner spark. Directly below these light globes stood a number of marble pedestals atop which were placed perhaps the greatest treasures of the chamber. Some seemed quite ordinary, such as the small octagonal-framed spectacles lying atop a black velvet cloth, or the pair of plain leather gloves, somewhat tattered, that lay in a box of finely carved mahogany. Others were more fantastic, such as the great brazen horn tipped with ivory that lay on a red pillow, or the fine belt of tooled leather, gilded with gold and silver and studded with jewels that were worthy of a crown.

It was among these items that the Potion of Shonlay stood. The bottle was tall, almost as long as a man's arm, narrow as a straw near the lip. The glass was milky white. Colors swirled within it—green, red, and blue, and clouds like black ink.

As Mancred entered the chamber, his eyes settled on the octagonal rimmed spectacles. Without even a glance at the other items in the room, he walked straight towards them and lifted them lovingly in his hands. Cael followed him, detouring to inspect the gloves. Alynthia strode round the room, eyeing everything but choosing nothing, completing the full circle of the chamber in a few hurried strides. She returned to the door and turned to watch her thieves.

Hoag had already chosen his treasure—a dagger with a blade as red as fresh blood. Cael slipped the gloves onto his hands and felt them mold to his fingers, wrapping his hands in velvet softness that was both comfortably warm and pleasantly cool. His fingers felt tremblingly alive, as though he might pluck the moon from the sky if he so desired. Meanwhile, old Mancred slipped the glasses onto his face and glanced around the room. His eyes opened wide in surprise, and a smile spread beneath his mask, but he did not explain his reaction.

A warning hiss came from the hall. The thieves froze, every

ear straining, no one daring to move. They heard a noise like someone playing bowls in the hall outside. What they saw filled them with wonder and apprehension.

A huge silver ball rolled to a stop outside the door. Where it had come from, no one knew, though it might have issued from one of the open doors at the ends of the hall. The ball stood almost to Alynthia's waist. It rocked back and forth ominously. Finally, it rolled into the room. Alynthia stepped aside to let it pass, a look of horror widening her dark eyes.

The ball rolled almost to the center of the room, stopping mere inches from Cael's foot. Again, it rocked back and forth as though uncertain what to do. It shuddered to a stop and split along its equator, opening like a great silver clam. The upper hemisphere of the thing was hollow, but the lower appeared solid, its upper surface etched with spiraling lines. As they watched, the spirals began to whirl, and a great horn or funnel spun itself up out of the ball. It looked like one of the shouting devices sailors used to communicate between ships during heavy seas.

Mancred inched his way toward the door, while Cael held his breath and wondered if the thing could hear the pounding of his heart. It was close enough for him to see, by standing on tiptoe, down into the thing's funnel ear. There he saw a tiny white membrane, like the skin of a drum.

Hoag was closest to the Potion of Shonlay. Alynthia motioned for him to grab it, then move with greatest stealth to the door. Cael, however, seemed stuck. So close was the listening device that he feared even to budge. Hoag was slowly inching over to the pedestal where the potion stood. Though his eyes seemed more often on the listening ball than his destination, he crossed the half-dozen steps without incident. Breathing a silent sigh, he reached out and grasped the bottle.

Cael saw, a moment too late, the lead seal atop which the bottle rested. Without thinking, he cried out, "Stop!" but to no avail.

At the sound of Cael's voice, Hoag froze, the bottle in his hand lifted an inch above the pedestal, his head half turned toward the elf with a look of astonishment frozen on his face.

His skin, clothing, cloak, hood, and mask all faded to a dull, stony gray. He moved and breathed no more. Alynthia screamed in rage but was forced to dodge aside when the silver ball spun down its funnel ear, snapped its lid shut with a musical chime like a large silver bell, and rolled rapidly through the doorway, nearly trampling her in its haste. Mancred yanked her aside at the last moment, else she might have been crushed. The thing smashed into the wall opposite the door, sending a spiderweb of cracks radiating across the stone for several feet, then spun off toward the stair. A high, shrill voice began to shriek, "Mistress Jenna! Mistress Jenna!"

The iron door slammed shut.

"Get the potion! Now!" Alynthia shouted as she turned to the door.

"It'll break!" Cael cried, trying to pry the bottle out of Hoag's hands. "He's been turned to stone. I tried to warn him." He clawed at the petrified flesh encasing the neck of the potion bottle.

They heard the ball clanging down the stairs, all the while shrieking "Mistress Jenna! Mistress Jenna!" like some hideous parody of a parrot. Below a woman's voice answered in a language none of them knew but all understood to augur magic.

"Leave it!" Alynthia ordered. "Help me open the door." Her nimble fingers danced across the iron surface, searching for a latch, a hidden keyhole, anything that might release the door. There was no handle for her to grip and pull. She pressed against the door, throwing her body against it, but she might as well have been trying to crash through a stone wall.

"I'll break off his hand!" Cael shouted, still trying to free the potion from Hoag's grasp. He held out his staff, still cane-sized, and said aloud, "*Dinshar.*" The ironwood shaft shimmered, and suddenly it was staff-sized again. He raised it above his head and brought it ringing down on the thief's wrist. Chips of rock exploded from the blow, but the stone thief held firmly to his prize.

"Forget the potion," Alynthia shouted.

"No. If we fail, it means my life," Cael said, raising his staff for another blow.

171

"Can you open the door, Old One?" Alynthia asked Mancred.

He removed a scroll from his pouch, unrolled it, and quickly read the enchantment inscribed upon it. The door shuddered in its frame but did not move. Mancred staggered back, the scroll slipping from his grasp. "It is too powerful," he gasped.

"Trapped!" Alynthia cried, her voice almost a shriek of despair. "Trapped like gully dwarves."

"I'm no gully dwarf! Speak for yourself!" Cael exclaimed, abandoning the potion at last. The mightiest blows of his iron-wood staff had hardly marred the petrified thief's wrist. The Potion of Shonlay remained firmly in his stone grasp.

He rushed at the door, his staff a blurred wheel. His staff rang like a struck bell against the iron door. A ring of red fire spread from the point of impact, and the door opened a slight crack, revealing a lurid glow in the hall beyond.

"Good work," Alynthia shouted as she pushed past him "Do not fear," she added in a low voice, pausing to grip his arm. "All is not lost." He had no time to ponder her words.

Ijus still stood at the top of the stair, a loaded crossbow pointed into the stairwell. The stairs crackled with flames as though the entire lower floor were afire. The thief's eyes were on his captain, awaiting the order to retreat.

"What's that fire?" Alynthia asked.

"An illusion of mine," he shouted. "It won't hold her long." Even as he spoke, the flames winked out.

Cael stood beside Alynthia as Mancred scurried up the rope. He held it out for Alynthia, but she turned back, motioning Ijus to abandon his position.

Before he could move, he swore a surprised oath and fired his weapon down the stairs. There was a dull crack. He turned and shouted, "She's protected against missiles."

A single word echoed from below, and a flash of light streaked up the stairs. It exploded against the lookout's chest, flinging him against the wall like a rag. He collapsed to the floor, dead, the smell of seared flesh filling the air.

"Go!" Alynthia ordered.

Cael stared in horror at the man who had just died, the second of the Circle to sacrifice his life to save him.

"Go now! Hurry!" Alynthia shouted at him.

He turned to her. "No, you go. I will die tonight whether I flee back to the Guild or remain here, that much is certain. I might as well die in battle."

Alynthia's eyes softened. She nodded quickly, and said quietly, "Get out if you are able. I'll wait for you."

"Go," he answered her, touching her hand a moment. She pulled away from him, grasped the rope, and was lifted rapidly through the hole in the ceiling. Cael watched her feet vanish into the darkness above, to be replaced by Varia's masked face, her eyes glinting with excitement. She lowered the rope to him and hissed, "Hurry!"

A noise from behind drew him around. Mistress Jenna, her red robes flying about her like the sheets of a ghost, floated into the hall. A globe of shimmering air surrounded her.

"*Shon l'phae loch fellawathwen Tanthalas lu'ro,*" Jenna said in the Elvish tongue. "Here is the fool to whom I once sold a pair of boots enchanted to leave reversed footprints," she snarled. Her voice sounded strange through the shield of her magic, as though she spoke from the depths of a cave. "I suspected you would come. You were not hard to predict."

"Maybe not, but I was clever enough to rob two treasures from your hoard, Mistress," he responded as he gripped his staff.

"Not clever enough to escape with them," she answered. "Surrender. I do not wish to kill you."

"Neither do I want you to, but I will not surrender," the elf said.

She floated closer to him. "Were you not an elf and so inured to all charms, I would befuddle your mind and force your compliance. But I see stronger measures are needed."

With these words, she extended one hand, index finger pointed at the elf's chest. She spoke a word, and a bolt of lightning coursed down her arm and flashed from her fingertips.

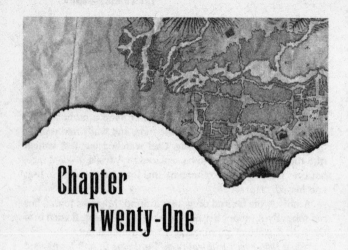

Chapter
Twenty-One

The magical attack came too swiftly for Cael to hope to dodge, and under any other circumstances, he would have died horribly. However, instead of blasting a smoking hole in his chest, Jenna's lightning bolt merely struck Cael's staff and disappeared. Such a comical look of surprise appeared on the sorceress's face that Cael actually laughed out loud before realizing his good fortune. He changed his guffaw into a shout of defiance.

"So, my staff defeats your spell, Mistress Jenna! Shall we see if it can shatter your sphere of protection as well?" He leaped at her, swinging his staff with all his might.

Jenna flew backward, avoiding his blow, and Cael's staff crashed against the wall. He recovered, preparing to strike again before Jenna could escape down the stairs.

A shout from above stopped him. Looking up, he saw Alynthia reaching a gloved hand through the hole in the roof. "Come on!" she ordered. "Now's your chance."

With one more glance at Jenna, who was busy opening a

scroll, the surprise on her face changing to indignation, Cael leaped up and caught the proffered hand. Grunting, Alynthia pulled him onto the roof.

"Shall we go?" she asked, as Varia stuffed the tripod into the hole.

"After you," Cael answered.

They sprinted for the roof's edge, Varia quickly following.

Behind them, the tripod rocketed up out of the hole into the night sky and came crashing down in the street in front of Jenna's shop. Cael and Alynthia reached the battlement wall where they had first climbed up. Their rope still lay coiled beside it. At their approach, a thief rose up from the shadow of the wall and tossed the coiled rope over the edge. He was a burly fellow, with forearms like those of a galley rower. He wrapped one end of the rope around his waist, then around his beam-thick wrist.

"Down you go, Captain," Rull said.

"Wait," she whispered. "Look, Cael!" She pointed back the way they had come.

Mistress Jenna was on the roof, her long gray hair swirling in a nimbus of power around her head. Still, the shimmering globe of air surrounded her, visible even in the darkness.

As Jenna slowly scanned the roof, searching for the fleeing intruders, her magical globe of protection was suddenly bombarded, struck by light and audible pinging noises. A second attack followed, then a third, striking from three different directions. Jenna spun quickly, trying to locate her opponents, only to suffer more blows.

"What is that?" Cael asked, amazed.

"Slingers," Alynthia answered with a smile beneath her mask. "That's our Guild for you. There are slingers on every roof. And now . . ."

She paused. A larger and louder flash, almost an explosion, burst upon Jenna's shield, spinning her around, adding to the look of frustrated rage on her face.

". . .the crossbowmen."

"Impressive, but what good are they? She is protected against both dart and slinger's stone," Cael said.

"Yes, but look how they distract her," Alynthia commented. A bolt crashed against the shield just before Jenna's face, drawing an instinctive recoil from the sorceress. "We escape while she swats flies. Follow me, Cael!"

She kicked one leg over the roof's battlement, grasped the rope, and swung over. Cael watched her rappel down the wall as expertly as any mountaineer. When she touched the ground, she shook the rope for Cael to follow.

"Wonderfully light, she is," Rull said as he held the rope's end in his iron grip. "Over you go."

Cael swung over the battlement and lowered himself hand-over-hand to the alley below. He had no skill such as Alynthia's for rappelling down ropes in the black of night. As soon as his feet touched the cobblestones, the rope came slithering down after him. He almost swore aloud, thinking the thief had tried to drop him.

But no, Alynthia quickly wound it into a remarkably small coil and stowed it in a large flat pouch at her belt. "In case we need it for further escapes," she explained. "Let's return to our safe room and stow these black clothes. We can't walk about Palanthas dressed like this."

"I should say not," a voice said behind them. They spun around, Alynthia drawing her dagger, Cael gripping his staff.

Before them stood a small man draped in heavy robes of gray. His face was thin and pale, his eyes small and black and ratlike. They seemed almost to glow red in the darkness of the alley.

Alynthia took a step toward him, but he halted her with a warning, "Ah, ah, ah! I wouldn't do that." His robe parted slightly, revealing a drawn hand crossbow. "You'd be dead before you took another step. You may drop your illegal weapon now."

Reluctantly, Alynthia let the weapon slide from her fingertips. The man's ratlike eyes then swiveled to gaze at the elf. "Cael Ironstaff of . . . Where is it you are from anyway? No matter. You and your accomplice are under arrest."

"By whose authority, and on what charge?" Cael growled.

"Why, the charge begins with burglary, though I am sure I

can conjure up a few more capital offenses if need be. As for me, I am Sir Arach Jannon, Knight of the Thorn and Judge of the Law in Palanthas. My authority here is unquestioned." So saying, he placed a pair of spidery fingers to his thin lips and sounded a piercing whistle.

"More Knights will be here shortly to take you away. In the meantime, I think a small spell to immobilize you would be in order. You thieves are notoriously slippery. Besides, it is not often that I get to try my magic against living subjects these days."

Alynthia turned quickly to face Cael, her eyes twinkling. Reading her meaning, Cael stepped toward the Thorn Knight, his staff gripped crosswise before him.

Sir Arach jumped back and held up one hand, palm forward. "Halt! I command you!" he shouted in a resounding voice. His outstretched hand glowed with silver light, and a shimmering cloud of tiny silver stars descended upon the two thieves.

Cael froze, waiting, but nothing seemed to happen. Sir Arach smiled and relaxed, turning away to see if his guards were nearing. Cael looked at Alynthia, who merely shrugged.

Cael took another step toward the Thorn Knight, who spun round at the sound of his footstep, surprise and contempt in his rodent eyes. The Knight whipped his still-cocked crossbow from his robes and held it tremblingly pointed at Cael's chest. "No closer, thief," he warned.

In a flash Cael reached out and cracked the Knight's hand with his staff. Bones crunched, and the crossbow went sailing over their heads, loosing its bolt into the night. Sir Arach staggered back, startled by the speed of the elf's attack. He sucked his broken fingers for a moment, then spun and fled down the dark alley, his gray robes flapping.

Alynthia pushed past Cael and snatched her dagger from the cobblestones. In the same movement, she reversed it with a flip and raised her arm to throw, but Cael caught her by the wrist.

"He'll raise the alarm!" she hissed.

"Kill a Lord Knight, and not even Mulciber can protect

you," Cael calmly stated. He held her wrist a moment longer, then released it. She jerked away from him, then turned and watched the Thorn Knight vanish around a corner.

"You're right," she said reluctantly. "We'd better go." Without turning to see if he followed, she stalked away. She paused at the alley's end, glanced over her shoulder, then slipped around a corner into the night.

"You're welcome," Cael called as he dashed after her.

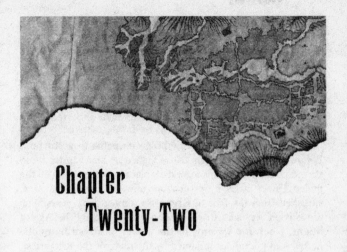

Chapter
Twenty-Two

They paused an hour later and looked behind them. A hundred feet back, the gray-robed Thorn Knight appeared from a darkened alleyway. Surrounding him were six other Knights of Neraka, their swords drawn and gleaming in the moonlight.

"Damn," Alynthia swore. "We'll never lose him. He uses magic to follow us, I'll warrant. However, I know just the place to elude him, if you have nerves of steel."

"Where you lead, I shall follow, be it even unto the gates of the Abyss, Captain," Cael said theatrically.

His chest heaved, his lungs burned. They'd been running in circles for what seemed like hours, trying to elude the patrols of Knights. They had taken to the sewers, only to be forced back into the streets and alleys to avoid being captured by a veritable legion of torch-wielding city guards.

"Follow me," Alynthia ordered, as she took his hand and tugged him along.

The dusky-skinned thief led him along a winding path,

down alleys and streets, keeping to the evening's deepening shadows. Ahead, there loomed a larger shadow, darker than the surrounding night, and as they neared it, Cael realized that it was a grove of trees. A chill wind, not born of the mountain heights but of fear and death, blew from it. Alynthia's hand in his began to tremble, her steps faltered, but her eyes dared him onward. He followed, feeling an unaccountable abhorrence and loathing fill his very soul.

Finally, they stopped, unwilling or unable to go further. Before them, the Shoikan Grove sighed as some inner wind stirred its branches. This legendary place had once guarded the fabled Tower of High Sorcery, but now the tower was gone, vanished from the face of Krynn for almost forty years. The grove itself was said to have been created during the Age of Might, when the wizards of the Tower, besieged by public hatred and prejudices inflamed by the reign of the Kingpriest, abandoned their Tower, surrendering it to the Lord of the City rather than battle the citizens of Palanthas in a war that could only end in destruction. But as the Master of the Tower placed its keys in the hands of the city's greedy lord, a black-robed mage appeared on the Tower's highest balcony. He leaped into the empty air and impaled himself on the gates below. With his dying breath, he cast a curse on the grounds, and from that curse was born the Shoikan Grove, to protect the Tower from all trespassers until the Master of Past and Present returned.

In time, the master did return and claim his own, but the grove remained, ever a watchful guardian. When, almost forty years ago, the Tower vanished, still the grove endured and even now stood guard over the empty, eerie grounds.

Now, Alynthia and Cael stood in its moon shadow. High above, the pale white moon of Krynn shone down in all its full radiance upon them, but its rays could not penetrate the shadows beneath the trees. Even Cael's elven sight failed to function in that awful place. He looked away, settling his gaze on Alynthia. Beads of sweat stood out on her quivering lip.

"You want to hide *here?*" Cael whispered.

"Are you afraid?" she asked in a voice cracking with fear.

"Not in the least," he lied.

"Neither am I. Go ahead. Lead the way."

Cael took a step forward, steeling himself for the next, and the next. His foot sank into the soft mould lying just beneath the eaves of the outer trees. It seemed he heard voices whispering, inviting and yet cold and harsh, promising both rest and torment. He summoned his courage and took another step, passing into the trees' deepest shadows.

He pulled Alynthia after him and heard her cry out in fear. Looking back, he saw her despite the darkness, visible by her body's heat. Her image was faint, as though the surrounding trees sucked the very warmth from her blood.

He saw her staring in horror at her feet, her mouth open in a silent scream. The ground about them was heaving, the trees swaying, and they drew closer, their bony branches waving and reaching, clawing at her arms, tearing back her hood, tangling themselves in the tight ringlets of her curly black hair. Behind her, ghostly faces floated among the black trunks of the trees, chill white hands beckoning, blue lips crying for warmth and blood. Below, clasping one ankle, was the shadow of a skeletal hand. Where it touched her flesh, darkness spread. Without thinking, Cael swung at it with his staff and missed, striking instead the soft leafy ground.

It was as though a pebble had been dropped in a pool. Ripples spread out from his blow throughout the grove, stilling the wind and silencing the voices. The hand clutching Alynthia's ankle withdrew into the soil, the faces of the dead fled into the darkness, their eyes glowing red with hate but shrinking in fear. Alynthia swayed, and Cael caught her in his arms. Her lips were purple, her breathing shallow. She clung to him.

Though the numbing fear did not lessen, the trees about them parted and drew back, or so it seemed, clearing a narrow lane to the grove's heart, where once the tower stood. Cael lifted Alynthia in his arms and hurried along this path, stumbling at last into the moonlight once again. He set her down in the midst of a wide glade, at the center of which lay a circular pool, a still tarn of black water or oil that reflected the moonlight like polished glass. They cast themselves beside this, though they both felt a strange reluctance to touch it.

Instead, they huddled together for warmth. Alynthia rested her head on Cael's shoulder. Cael drank in the scent of her hair. The perfume of the yellow Ergothian lotus stilled the thundering of his heart. He pulled his cloak closer around them as the full moon climbed in the sky. Her trembling reminded him of a child he'd once held in his arms, a child he had found on the beach near his home, long ago. The child was the sole survivor of a shipwreck. He'd found her clinging to the body of her mother and had been forced to pry the girl's fingers from the dead woman's hair. His warmth and his strength had gradually eased her terrors even as her body gave way to shock and exhaustion. That night, the girl child had died, and then there were no longer any survivors of the shipwreck.

With the memory of her burning pyre in his mind, he pulled Alynthia closer still.

The city beyond the magical grove had ceased even to exist. It was though they were the first children of a strange god, awakening in a strange new world. All around them, the trees watched. They formed a great black wall, lurking with an evil that had been temporarily subdued by Cael's staff. Not banished. The leaves began to stir anew, and whispers cold as death crept like a fog across the glade.

As the fresh chill began to increase, Alynthia stirred and looked into the elf's face. His green eyes glittered in the moonlight. He did not notice her watching him. His eyes were on the accursed grove, his arms wrapped protectively around her. His gaze darted here and there, as though he saw hidden things moving among the deep shadows beneath the trees.

The beautiful captain of thieves stirred, trying to wriggle free of him. "Let go," she mumbled.

Cael released her without a sarcastic remark. She rose and stepped toward the pool, then stopped suddenly. She turned back to him. "I'm sorry," she said in an odd tone. "I shouldn't have . . ."

"Shouldn't have what?" he asked.

"I am your captain," she answered firmly

Cael wearily rose to his feet. "Very well then, Captain. What now? It looks as though the Knights have no appetite to follow us here. So, how do we get out?"

She turned away again and gazed at the pool. Cael couldn't tell if she was hurt by his flippant tone or merely considering the options. She said without turning, "The same way we entered, I suppose."

Cael gazed at the weapon in his hands. Many times this day it had exhibited powers quite beyond his experience. Perhaps the proximity of so much arcane magic had triggered certain latent abilities, he speculated. Nevertheless, it seemed to wield power both against magic and the undead. It had even parted the trees of the Shoikan Grove. His master had mentioned no such powers when he gave it into his hands a little more than a year ago. Cael wondered if even his venerable *shalifi* was aware of the staff's full potential.

"Perhaps you're right," Cael said, hoisting the staff before him. He placed a hand on Alynthia's shoulder. "With this, we shall dare the trees again," he said.

She began to turn but immediately froze. A gasp of awe escaped her lips. "The pool," she whispered. "Look at the pool!"

Now close enough to see into its inky depths, Cael stared in wonder at what he saw reflected there. The Tower of High Sorcery stood once more. In the pool's shining reflection, it rose high above the treetops of the Shoikan Grove, a shape of both beauty and horror. Before it, the old gate still stood, its rusted bars twisted into phantasmagoric shapes by the power of the Black Robe's dying curse. Cael could see the remnant of the mages robe's still dangling from the spike on which he perished.

Above the image of the tower, stars wheeled in unfamiliar courses, stars arranged in constellations that shocked the elf to the core of his being. The constellations were those of the platinum dragon facing a five-headed dragon across an open book. Other figures took shape in the surrounding stars—scales, a harp, a vulture, a ram, and many others.

Chasing each other across the night sky, reflected in the pool, were three moons. Each was more beautiful and captivating than the cold white moon that shone in the real sky. One moon shone with a bright silver light, the other was a red as elven wine, the third an ebon hole evoking the tapestry of the night.

Cael knew these moons, he remembered these stars. A vision came unbidden to his mind. He remembered waking as a child and seeing through his bedroom window the red moon, Lunitari, rising from the Sirrion Sea.

Cael's staff began to glow. A nimbus of silver light spread along its length, then a red glow rose at the tips. Finally, the black ironwood of the staff itself seemed to throb with energy, not light and not an absence of light, but somehow, light's antithesis.

These moons, these stars, had vanished after the Chaos War, almost forty years ago. They could not be, and yet they were there, reflected in the mysterious pool. Both thieves looked up, only to find the familiar field of stars above them, the familiar white moon still racing among tatters of clouds.

They returned their gaze to the pool. Now, they saw on the tower's highest balcony a figure robed in darkness. He was neither an illusion nor a trick of the mind. Both Alynthia and the elf felt as though this black figure were staring fiercely at them, angry at their intrusion upon his solitude. He raised his hands, the sleeves of his ebon robes slid back, revealing milky white skin. Nimble hands scribed cabalistic symbols on the air, lips writhed. They heard a voice, filled with power yet far away, speaking not on the air but in the secrecy of their minds, as though in a dream, uttering words of magic.

Cael struck the surface of the pool with his staff. The strange liquid, thicker than water yet thinner than oil, writhed like something alive. When it finally grew still, the image was gone, the Tower was no more. The two thieves backed away until the dead grass hid the pool from their eyes.

"Let us leave this place," Cael said with a shudder.

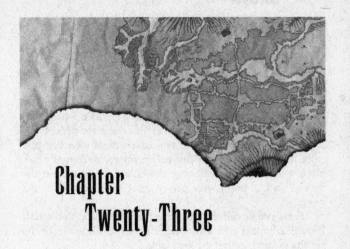

Chapter
Twenty-Three

"T his way. In here," Alynthia whispered urgently as Cael hurried up the rickety stairs. She stood at the stair's top, just beside a door and beneath a hanging sign painted with a large spreading tree. Below them, booted feet marched heavily down an alley slick with offal. Swords clanged against armored thighs, and spears clashed hollowly on shields as a patrol of Knights of Neraka passed almost beneath their feet.

"Where are we?" Cael asked as Alynthia swung open the door. A wave of light, noise, and heat, and a greasy odor of fried potatoes struck him full in the face. Just to the right of the door, a long bar stretched curvingly away into smoky shadows. Behind it stood a huge man with unshaven jowls and a great belly stretching his beer-stained apron. He looked at the two of them expectantly but said nothing as he pulled a pint and slid it down the bar to one of his customers.

"The Solace Inn," Alynthia answered. They stepped inside.

The door, hanging on titled hinges, banged shut behind them. "One of ours. We'll be safe here."

The common room of the inn was large and bean-shaped, wrapping around an irregularly curved wall painted to resemble the trunk of a massive tree. The beams of the roof were likewise made to look like tree limbs. About two-thirds of the way back into the room, a large stone fireplace crackled with flame, making the warm, early summer night even more stifling, but it proved a welcome sight to two adventurers who had just come through the Shoikan Grove. Directly across from the fireplace, a long narrow table was shoved almost up against the curved wall. It left a wide empty space in the center of the room.

"Some people call this place the Inn of the Next to the Last Home," Alynthia said with a laugh as she slid into one of the six chairs surrounding the long table.

"Why is that?" Cael asked with perfect seriousness. He dropped into the chair beside her.

"I assumed you would know."

"Why?" he asked.

"Because . . . your father . . ."

"Oh, that," he said offhandedly. "I have only once visited the village he frequented, and that long ago. Is there a waitress?" He glanced around as he pounded the table with his fist.

The inn was uncommonly empty this evening. A few customers huddled over their drinks at the bar, while a pair of dwarves sat at a table near the door and spoke in muted whispers, and an old man in a battered hat snored in one of the chairs by the fireplace. Cael again rapped his knuckles against their table and shouted for wine.

Behind the bar, a pair of doors swung open, emitting a great fat slug of a woman. She crept around the bar and slowly approached their table. Her hair, once red as a bonfire, was shot through with silvery gray locks, while her huge freckled bosom hung half out of her frowzy dress. She smiled wantonly at the elf as she neared, revealing mossy brown teeth.

"Wine for me and my friend," Alynthia said to the woman. "We'll pay with circles of steel."

"Oh, I see. Yes, madam," the woman said, bowing a hasty retreat to the kitchen.

"What was that?" Cael asked.

"They call her Big Tika. By paying with 'circles of steel,' I informed her that we are of the Guild."

"But I thought—" Cael began, before a warning glance from Alynthia silenced him. The innkeeper approached, a pair of brown crockery mugs dangling from his fist. He clapped them onto the table, then drew a bottle from his apron and filled the cups to the brim with a thick yellow fluid.

"Best of the house, Captains," he said proudly.

"I am sure," Cael said uncertainly as he eyed his cup. He raised it to his lips, sniffed, sipped, winced, and set the cup on the table. Alynthia took a long draught of hers and sighed.

"It is good, no?" the innkeeper asked.

"Very," Alynthia said. "Now leave us."

"Yes, Captain." The man bowed his way to the kitchen.

"What irks me," Alynthia said while thoughtfully staring into her cup, "is that we're still in the Old City. We can't pass the gates, not tonight, so we're stuck here, unless you care to hazard another journey through the sewers. They'll be full of Knights and city guards."

"Not particularly," Cael answered. "Where would we go? Back to the Guild so that my sentence can be executed?"

Alynthia shook her head, then took another long draught of her wine. She set the cup down with a clunk and scrubbed her lips with the back of her hand. "I take full responsibility for our failure," she said. "They cannot blame you. Oros will give us another chance."

"What of Mulciber?"

"She is not unreasonable. No, the only reason she would order your death is if you tried to escape or if you betrayed us."

"You keep calling Mulciber 'she.' Why is that?" Cael asked. "The voice I heard that morning when I was judged was neither male nor female, and I can find no one who has ever seen her. Have you?"

"Yes . . ." Alynthia said hesitantly. "At least, I have been in her presence, seen her form shrouded in robes. But it was dark.

Only Oros has actually seen her face to face, and he won't describe her except to say that she is female. He cannot speak of their first meeting without a shudder."

"All the more reason to fear for my life," Cael grumbled. "You don't even know if she is human, elf, or dwarf. She might be a monster or a creature from the Abyss."

"You have nothing to fear," Alynthia said with a smile as she placed a reassuring hand on his arm. "Trust me."

"Trust you?" Cael laughed.

Her smile faded. "I thought you might," she said indignantly.

"I am sorry," Cael chuckled. "I just keep thinking of that night at the home of Gaeord uth Wotan, when I stole the dragonflower pollen from your bodice. You wanted to kill me. Now you want me to trust you. I learned a long time ago, before you were born, to trust no one."

Slowly, her smile returned. She propped her elbow on the table and set her chin thoughtfully on her fist, eyeing the elf with something akin to curiosity. "When and where were you born?" she asked rather dreamily.

"I don't know the whole story," Cael answered evasively. "I never asked my mother and she was reluctant to talk about it. As for when I was born and how old I am, time has little meaning for me. Humans' lives burn so swiftly, it is a wonder to me how they accomplish so many great things, and so many terrible things. Elves live their lives slowly and are not in the same hurry to accomplish or destroy."

"Were you born before the Chaos War, or even the War of the Lance?" she asked.

"My first memory was of my mother standing by the sea, gazing at the horizon. A storm was blowing up, and the sea was gray as iron. She looked sad, because she had just received some news. She said to me, 'The humans are at war again.' I assume she meant the war in which Palanthas was attacked by the Blue Lady's army, about seventy-seven years ago."

Alynthia's smile widened, her dark eyes sparkled. "The things you must have seen. I would love for you to tell me about them some time."

A bang at the inn's entrance startled them. "Perhaps another time," Cael muttered as he rose from his chair.

Sir Arach Jannon stood at the bar, speaking to the innkeeper. Two of his fingers were splinted and his whole hand was swathed in a large linen mitten. He shook a finger of his good hand in the face of the innkeeper, who eyed the offending digit as if he wished to clamp his teeth upon it. Behind the gray-robed Thorn Knight, a pair of Knights of the Lily yawned and leaned on their spears.

"Is there a back way out of here?" Cael asked quickly.

"Better than just a way out. Follow me," she said as she took him by the hand and pulled him against the wall.

Behind their table, an alcove in the false tree wall created a dark niche, in which sat a chair. Alynthia pulled the chair out of the way and stepped into this hollow. "We call this 'Raistlin's Niche,' " she said. She pressed against a false knot in the wall. The back of the niche opened slightly, revealing a dark room beyond. She pulled Cael through and silently shut the entrance behind them.

They found themselves in a cozy chamber large enough to accommodate three or four people. Alynthia quickly lit a candle, and by its light Cael saw a pair of low beds pushed against the inwardly curving wall. Sacks of dried beans were stacked in the middle of the floor, atop which lay a door that served as a table. Three chairs stood around it, and a fourth was pushed against the opposite wall beneath a small shelf. A bucket beside the chair was filled with stale water, while on the shelf stood a row of bottles, some corked, others obviously empty.

"We can hide here for days, if need be," Alynthia whispered as she placed the candle in a bronze dish and set it on the table. "But we shan't need to stay so long. When that cursed Knight is gone, we can be on our way."

"How will we know?" Cael asked.

"There are peep holes in the wall, here and here," she said as she pointed out a pair of inconspicuous pinpricks in the wall. Neither hole was at eye level, probably to prevent their casual detection from the opposite side.

Cael stooped over and placed his eye to one of the holes. Through it, he saw the Thorn Knight raise his good hand as though to strike the innkeeper, who cringed and pleaded his innocence. With a wave of disgust, Arach Jannon dismissed the man and ordered his guards to spread out and search the room. One approached the pair of dwarves, who merely shook their heads and continued their conversation, ignoring further attempts to question them. The other Knight prodded those at the bar. Most answered his questions briefly, paid their bills, and quickly exited the inn.

Meanwhile, Sir Arach meandered among the inn's tables and chairs until he found himself before the long table across from the fireplace.

Cael felt a hand fumble at his sleeve, then tug on it. "I see him!" he whispered in answer to Alynthia's frantic gestures.

Sir Arach eyed their two mugs of wine, still sitting on the table where they had left them. Slowly, he approached them, then sat down at the table in the very chair that Alynthia had vacated only moments before. He placed his good hand in the seat of Cael's chair as though feeling for warmth, then returned his attention to their mugs.

"He's figuring it out!" Alynthia whispered. Cael nodded and gripped his staff.

The Thorn Knight lifted Alynthia's mug to his nose and inhaled the scent of the wine. His forehead wrinkled into a scowl, as though the smell offended him. He then took a small taste of the wine, turned his head, and spat quickly. Something there caught his attention, for he bent over for some minutes examining the scuffs and dents in the floor's ancient wooden planks.

Finally, he sat up, a puzzled expression on his face. He glanced around the room as though assuring himself of the fact that there were no other exits. One of the Knights emerged from the kitchen and shook his head at Sir Arach's inquiring glance. The Thorn Knight sat back in the chair and allowed his gaze to settle once more on the mugs before him.

"Is there a way out of this room?" Cael whispered.

"There is a trapdoor through the roof."

"You had better open it."

Sir Arach leaned forward and lifted Cael's mug from the table. He swirled the golden liquid, watching it thoughtfully. Slowly, a smile bent his thin lips. He called to his guards. They hurried to his side, one of them sheepishly wiping beer froth from his lip.

"Move this table!" the Thorn Knight ordered. His guard quickly obeyed, shoving aside the table and sending Alynthia's mug crashing to the floor. Sir Arach then stooped and quickly examined the area of the floor once covered by the table.

Satisfied that no trapdoor let through the floor here, his eyes shot to the roof above them. "Prod it with your spears!" he snapped. "Check for trapdoors. They were here, at this table, only moments ago."

The Knights stabbed at the thick-beamed ceiling, but discovered nothing. Sir Arach's gaze drifted to the wall. Cael started back, feeling as though he'd met the Thorn Knight's probing stare and been discovered. "He knows we are here!" he hissed.

As though to confirm this, the wall thundered under the blows of the Knight's mailed fists.

"Hurry!" Alynthia whispered. She stood in the chair by the wall, directly beneath a small square opening in the ceiling. "Follow me!" She leaped, caught the edge of the hole, and pulled herself through.

Cael shoved his staff up through the hole. Alynthia caught it, and Cael dragged himself onto the roof just as Raistlin's Niche burst open and the Knights shoved into the room below.

"After them!" Sir Arach screeched, pointing upwards.

Cael reached for the trapdoor to close it. A spear shot up, grazing his arm and rending his sleeve. Fingers appeared on the edge of the hole, and a head struggled upwards. Alynthia kicked the door and leaped atop it. A howl of pain from below brought a fiendish grin to her face.

"This is fun!" she growled as she jumped on the trapdoor, hearing the satisfying crack of snapping finger bones. Freed of its impediment, the door jarred shut. She slid a small bolt home, locking it. Spears hammered against it from the underside, rattling the hinges, but for the moment it would hold.

Meanwhile, Cael clambered to the roof's peak. Loosened tiles slid away behind him and shattered on the alley cobblestones below. He waited while Alynthia followed him. She was nimbler than he at rooftop acrobatics and reached his side with hardly a sound.

"Where is your precious Guild now?" Cael asked her as he looked out over the city. To his left, the old city wall curved away towards the waterfront.

Alynthia ignored his comment. "Let's get off this roof before they surround the building."

They slid together down the opposite slope of the roof until they reached a brick chimney just at the roof's edge. Alynthia quickly unwound the coil of rope from her pouch and wrapped it around the chimney. She tied it off with a fast sailor's hitch, then dropped the remaining coils over the edge.

Cael grabbed the rope in one hand, clasped his staff under the other arm, and swung out over the alley. Using his free hand and both feet, he slid down the rope. He was quickly joined by Alynthia, who was just above him.

They had not descended half the distance when a patrol of Knights appeared at the alley's end. Cael stopped to watch them, but Alynthia, unaware of the danger, continued her descent and bumped into him, nearly knocking him to the ground. He fought to maintain his grip, faltered and fell a few feet, then caught himself by one hand on the sill of an open window. Without thinking, he tossed his staff into the room, then pulled himself up and through.

He regained his footing just as a candle flared. A pair of frightened gray eyes stared at him over the edge of a blanket spread over a small, rickety bed. He began to apologize when the look of fear changed to one of recognition, then surprise.

"Cael?" said a girl's voice from beneath the blanket. "Cael Ironstaff?"

"At your service," he answered reflexively. "Do I know you?"

But the blanket flew back, and a chit of a girl, dressed only in a gauzy shift, flew from the bed and wrapped her arms around him. "How ever did you find me?" Claret cried as she squeezed the breath from him. "Oh, it is so romantic of you!"

Alynthia swung into the room and landed with a thump beside them. "Cael, what are you . . . oh, I see!" she said as she placed one fist on her hip.

Claret spun around and glared at the female intruder. "Cael, who is this person?" she asked suspiciously.

"Alynthia Krath-Mal, meet Claret. Claret, Alynthia," Cael hurriedly introduced.

"Of all the houses and all the people in Palanthas, you drop into the room of someone you know, and a girl at that! If I didn't know better, I'd say you planned this," Alynthia accused.

"It's destiny!" Claret answered, defending the elf. "I take it you're in trouble, else you'd not have intruded so boldly upon my sleep."

"Gods," Cael muttered. "Another woman who speaks like a bad romance."

"Do not fear. I can help you," Claret continued without hearing him. She gazed up at the elf with her big, soulful gray eyes.

Alynthia shot Cael a glance.

He shrugged. "Well, she did help me before," he said.

"There is a little known door out of this building. My father doesn't even know about it," Claret said. "It's *secret!* I discovered it myself. It leads to a staircase that descends to a tunnel that crosses under the city wall and comes up into a building on Smith's Alley. The secret door is in the cellar. Come on, I'll show you the way." She took Cael in one hand, her candle in the other, and pulled him from the room.

"My parents are asleep," she whispered as she led them down a narrow hall. "A dragon couldn't wake my father, but we should be careful not to disturb mother. Say!" She stopped and gazed suspiciously at the elf. "What happened to your limp?"

"I was in *disguise,*" Cael whispered conspiratorially.

Claret smiled knowingly. "Oh! How clever!" She resumed her tiptoe escort. Cael looked over his shoulder at Alynthia, a smug smile on his face.

"I hope you know what you're doing," she hissed.

"Have you any other suggestion?"

"Shhhhhh!" Claret scolded. She paused at an opening where a stair descended into darkness. "I thought you two were supposed to be stealthy thieves."

"My apologies," Cael whispered.

The stair led down two flights to a low, damp cellar. The floor was of hard-packed earth. A few barrels and numerous rotting crates lined one wall. The remainder of the room was occupied by heaps of old furniture covered with moldy sheets or moth-eaten blankets.

Claret paused near the bottom of the stair. Above her, there was a heavy beam that supported the floor of the room above. Nailed to this beam was a rusty horseshoe. Claret reached up and gave it a turn. One of the flagstones at the base of the stairs popped up. Cael helped her slide it aside, revealing a narrow stair cut into the earth. A few feet down, the clay turned to hard stone.

Claret started down the stairs, only to be stopped by the elf's hand on her shoulder. She looked up at him, her eyes steady.

"You've done enough," Cael said softly. "You should go back to bed."

"But I want to go. It's exciting," the girl answered. "I want to go with you, Cael."

"The people chasing us want to kill us," Alynthia scolded. "This isn't a game."

"Claret understands that," Cael said to Alynthia before the glowering girl could make her reply. "She is braver than her age and experience allow. Were she free to follow us, I would gladly have her in my company. But she has a family, a mother and father who would miss her, and brothers and sisters, too, I'll warrant. She has to take care of them, if danger comes."

Claret stared sulkily down into the dark stairwell. "I suppose," she finally agreed. "There wouldn't be anyone to do their laundry."

"Well, let's be going then," Alynthia snapped impatiently.

"I thank you, dearest Claret, for your aid," Cael said to the girl.

"You are most welcome, kind sir," Claret responded. With a deep curtsey, she stepped aside to let them pass. Alynthia pushed past Cael and descended into the gloom.

"Wait! If I'm not going, I must tell you something," Claret said as she gave Cael her candle. "Go down these stairs, then along the passage. Be careful, as sometimes there are rats. Then, up the stairs at the other end. They let into a cellar like this one, only it is empty. In the cellar are two stairs, one of wood and one of stone. Follow the stone stairs to a door. It opens into Smith's Alley."

"I thank you again. Now, get you back to bed, dear girl, before your parents discover your absence," Cael laughed as he started down the stairs. Claret touched his arm.

"If you escape with your life, you will return?" she softly asked.

"Most assuredly," the elf solemnly promised.

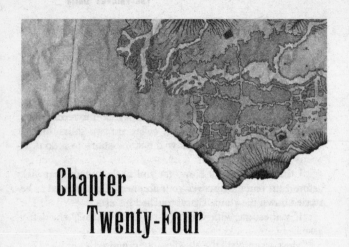

Chapter
Twenty-Four

ael and Alynthia hurried along the low passage. It ended abruptly at a steep stair. Alynthia scaled it quickly, then paused at the top to listen. Satisfied that no one was in the room above, she quietly opened a small wooden trapdoor and climbed into an empty cellar, finding things much as Claret had described them. Cael clambered up behind her, closed the trapdoor, and eyed the beautiful captain of thieves as if to say, Well, we made it!

"Unless I am much mistaken, they will have widened their search to include the whole city," she said, deflating his pride for a moment. "I am safe enough now because most people know me as the wife of Oros uth Jakar, a leading citizen of the city. But you, my friend, are in mortal danger. Mistress Jenna recognized you, as did our friend Arach Jannon. They'll not let you escape this city, if they can help it." She looked him over, then shook her head. "Do you think you can make it to the waterfront without being captured?"

Cael nodded. Obviously she expected him to obey her

unhesitatingly, and, surprising himself, he realized that was exactly what he would do. He felt proud to have earned some measure of her trust, yet also uncomfortable with the idea. He wished she would finish her speech and let him be on his way.

"My *husband,*" she said, pausing on the last word for emphasis, "has a ship moored at Blue Crab Pier. She's called the *Dark Horizon.* He'll hide you below decks until we can decide what to do with you."

"Very well, Captain," Cael said.

Alynthia smiled, her dark eyes twinkling by the light of his candle. "That's what I like to hear!" she barked happily as she gripped his arm. "Obedience! It suits you well, freelance." Her hand lingered there for a moment as the smile faded from her eyes. She quickly turned away.

They mounted the stone stair and paused at the door at its top. Outside, they heard the sounds of revelry. Smith's Alley was perhaps the seediest corner of the city of Palanthas. Few folk would want to be caught dead here after dark, even a Captain of the Thieves' Guild, for the people who inhabited this narrow, dank street were as clannish as dwarves and just as suspicious of outsiders. They protected their own and sometimes preyed on those foolish enough to venture into their domain. The people here had little to fear, even from the martial lords of the city. A contingent of Knights sent into Smith's Alley was likely to suffer a barrage of rotting vegetables if they were lucky, stones if they tried to assert their authority too strictly. When things became too hot even for the denizens of Smith's Alley, they were like rats, vanishing into a thousand holes.

"I'll go first," Alynthia whispered. "I'll head south, towards Temple Row. You head north to the dock. Don't get caught!" she finished sternly. "If you're captured . . . better you die fighting. They'll torture you for what you know."

"I'll tell them that I am a freelance," Cael boldly asserted, then finished with a shrug. "It won't be a lie either."

"Good luck to you, Cael Ironstaff," Alynthia said as she took his hand and pressed it. "I'll try to visit you tomorrow. Don't let Oros bore you with his stories."

With those words, she pushed the door open and hurried through, closing it behind her. Cael listened as her footsteps faded into the distance. He stood for a moment on the stairs, staring blankly at the light of his candle. He felt strange, as light as a wisp of smoke, yet his feet seemed heavy. It seemed as though, with each receding footstep, something was being drawn out of him.

"What am I doing?" he mumbled to himself. Then, shaking off his last uncertainties, he dashed out Claret's candle against the stone step, opened the door, and stepped boldly into Smith's Alley, trying to look as if he belonged.

The alley was dark, though not to his elven eyes. His vision adjusted to the darkness, and he scanned his surroundings. All around him, leaning through dark open windows or overhanging balconies, people silently stared down at him, like a conclave of ghosts. In one window, a soft glow swelled as a wrinkled old man drew at the pipe between his teeth. He stared at Cael without seeming to care one way or another.

To the right lay the northern way, the way to the docks and Oros uth Jakar's ship. To the left and about two bowshots away, there appeared to be some kind of party in progress. Flares were burning from the balconies and a crowd had gathered in the alley. Their shadows leaped and danced wildly, like satyrs in a drunken revel, and there was music playing, weird and high, shrill pipes and tambours thrumming. He noticed a lone, familiar figure trying to blend with the revelry.

"Alynthia," Cael said to himself. "What is she doing?"

As he watched, several figures broke away from the main group of dancers. They surrounded Alynthia. One touched her. She spun, and another grasped her from behind. Cael saw the dagger flash in her fist. Her assailant fell, grasping his belly. The music broke off and a mob swarmed around her, yelling.

Cael found himself running toward them, desperate to rescue Alynthia. They were too far away. He'd not reach them in time. Foolishly, he saw, Alynthia was facing them, brandishing her dagger.

As Cael neared, the mob suddenly began to disperse. A wild idea came into Cael's mind that they had seen him and were frightened. They bolted in all directions, flying through windows, slamming doors, up drain spouts, down cellars, and into the sewers. In ten heartbeats, the crowd vanished as though it had never been. Only the lights on the balcony, still flaring into the night, remained. Into this light strode a party of Knights of Neraka. There were five Knights, all heavily armed with cocked crossbows, swords, and heavy shields.

Cael slipped into the shadows beneath a stair, barely ten paces away. The Knights warily approached Alynthia, who still stood her ground. Her weapon had disappeared.

"Good sirs!" she called to them in a strained voice. "Glad I am that you happened this way. Surely, you have saved my life from those ruffians."

"Mistress Alynthia?" the lead Knight asked uncertainly.

"The same," she answered. "I am the wife of Oros uth Jakar, as you know. He will certainly be grateful for your timely arrival here. I am sure you will be rewarded."

The captain of the Knights remained wary, his sword drawn but dangling at his side. "What do you in this place at such an hour?" he asked. The other Knights kept careful watch over the shadows around them.

"I . . . I indulged too freely this eve and became confused on my homeward trek," she stammered. "I did not know where I had ventured until it was too late."

"May I examine your papers," the captain said.

"Why do you need to see my papers?" Alynthia asked.

"It is the law, Mistress."

"Do you know who my husband is?"

"Yes, Mistress. I still must see your papers."

Reluctantly, Alynthia withdrew a small wallet from her belt and handed it to the man. He took it and stepped back, nudging one of his fellow Knights, who casually but obviously trained his crossbow on the beautiful captain of thieves.

"We have been searching for a thief this night," the captain said as he turned so that the light of the balcony flares might fall across the identification papers in his hand. "An elf, with red hair worn quite long. A friend of yours, we are told. His name is Cael Ironstaff."

"Ah, yes, Cael! We dined together earlier tonight. Why, what has he done?" Alynthia asked.

"He may have been witness to a crime," the captain said as he thumbed through Alynthia's papers. "You dined with him, you say. What time did you part company?"

"Just before sunset."

"Where did you sup?"

"With my husband, at a place called The Portal, in the Old City. I fail to see why you are questioning me. I thank you for your rescue, but I must be on my way. My husband is expecting me."

The captain closed the leather wallet with a snap. "Forgive us, Mistress," he said. "Your papers are not in order. You must come with us."

"Not in order?" she cried.

"There is no stamp showing your exit from the Old City this evening." He took her by the arm.

"But they must have . . . I didn't . . ." she stammered.

"I am sure it will all be cleared up. Nevertheless . . ."

Cael had watched all this with a growing sense of panic. She'd be questioned, suspected. They could prove nothing, but it didn't matter. Sometimes mere suspicion was enough. Not even her husband could protect her, nor would he dare to try, for fear of exposing the Guild.

Impulsively he stepped from the shadows into the light of the flares. "Did I hear someone mention my name? Cael Ironstaff, son of Tanis Half-Elven, at your service." He bowed with sweeping arrogance to the startled Knights even as he gripped his staff.

"Grab him!" the captain of the Knights shouted as he flung Alynthia aside. Grinning, the Knights swept in a circle around the lone elf. He clutched his staff tighter, holding it awkwardly like a sheathed sword at his side.

"Mistress Alynthia, you may go," Cael said as the Knights closed around him.

"Mistress Alynthia, if you flee, you will as much as prove your complicity," the captain growled without turning. "You, elf. Surrender your weapon. You obviously have no concept of how to use it anyway. A staff is no weapon against swords."

"Mistress Alynthia, please, run!" Cael shouted.

Without thinking, she turned and started to flee. But she had not gone a dozen paces before she stopped. She whirled around to watch the drama unfold.

She was not the only one. A second pair of eyes watched from the door of the building through which they had entered the alley. A score more watched from the balconies, rooftops, and surrounding windows.

Unmindful of his observers, Cael turned his full attention to his opponents.

"A staff is no match for swords," he said. "Though my *shal-ifi* showed on more than one occasion that, properly wielded, a staff might overwhelm a good swordsman, even a vaunted Knight of Takhisis."

"Knight of Neraka! Pah, arrogant elf!" one of the Knights spat. He set aside his crossbow and drew his sword. "We'll see about that." The others followed his example.

"Then again," Cael argued, "he often told me never to match wood 'gainst steel. 'Twere better far to meet a swords-man with sword. And so he gave me this."

Cael drew from the staff a long bright sword. Indeed, it seemed almost as if the staff had transformed into a sword as his hand passed along it, for no empty scabbard remained. The hilt of the sword was wrought of the same black wood as the staff, and there was no crosspiece to protect his hands. In the pommel, a green jewel, glowed like sunlight through green waters.

"An illegal weapon, and magical to boot!" the Captain snarled. "It will make a fine trophy. Let's test its mettle."

As one, the black-armored warriors proffered the Knight's salute to an enemy. Cael stole the moment to cut down the Knight closest to him while the man was involved in foolish rit-ual. He seemed only to caress the man's belly with the edge of his sword, but the steel rings of the Knights' mail parted, and the coils of his belly flopped out onto the cobblestones. He pitched forward with a surprised cry, trying to hold in his guts.

"A thousand pardons, Sir Knight," Cael said with a smirk.

The rage-filled Knights roared and advanced as one. Cael dodged lightly over the fallen Knight, attacking the next closest. He parried the man's overhead swing, flipping the Knight's own blade back into his face. His iron helm prevented a split skull, but blood poured from a wicked gash above his eyes. He staggered back, blinded by his own blood.

Two Knights rushed Cael now, while their leader held back, shouting orders. They came at him side by side, so the elf slipped to his left, blocking the high thrust of one by placing himself opposite the other. At the same time, he lightly knocked aside the low thrust of the second Knight. Like a snake, he followed his block with a short chopping stroke that disarmed his opponent. Blood fountained from the remaining stump. The first Knight tried to shove his screaming companion aside while simultaneously delivering a high slash at the elf's neck. Cael ducked this blow, thrust his blade completely through the still-screaming Knight, and pinked his companion in the heart before he'd recovered from his failed attack. Both slumped together in death's embrace.

Now, the blood-blinded Knight staggered forward, blinking furiously. He aimed a cut at Cael's forearm, but the elf's blade caught the attack, slid round it, and quivered home. It caught the Knight in open-mouthed surprise. Steel grated against teeth as Cael withdrew his blade and let the man fall, already dead, to the cobblestones.

The elf spun, facing the captain, just in time to see the man raise a crossbow and fire. Cael dodged, while at the same time his hand leaped up, as though jerked by a string, and caught the bolt a hairsbreadth from his chest. He stared at the bolt in amazement. The hand that gripped the deadly dart glowed with a yellow light, which quickly faded. The gloves he'd taken from Jenna's vault, he suddenly realized. They must be magic!

A slow grin spread across his face as he regained his composure and tossed aside the crossbow bolt.

"Gods!" the captain swore, staring in horror at the elf. He dropped his spent crossbow and drew his blade. "Do you know the penalty . . . ?" he began. "Gods! Takhisis, my Dark Queen, help me!" he swore anew.

The elf smiled at him and waved his sword as if to say, Come on then, if you are coming.

"I cannot in honor flee you," the Knight said, "but know that you are undermatched and gain no glory in this battle."

"I seek no glory," Cael responded. "There is no reward in the death of another. So say the elves."

"Then surrender," the captain said.

"I cannot."

"Neither may you go free."

"Then attack me, for free I shall be."

Without saluting, the captain raised his sword and charged. Cael stepped into the attack and with a single lightning quick stroke of his blade unseamed the man. His still-beating heart swelled through the rent in his armor. Cael stepped back. The Knight hugged himself pathetically, and toppled to the ground. Cael looked down and watched the darkness close over the man's eyes.

Alynthia, still standing in the midst of the alley, was thunderstruck. A staff that became a glowing blade, and the freelance elf a deadly master of it.

Abruptly, she was shoved aside. "Out of the way, dog," a voice growled. She fell into a pile of garbage heaped against the city wall. Looking up angrily to see her assailant, she winced and crawled deeper into the safety of the offal. A regiment of Knights tramped past. One or two glanced at her and laughed, but no one seemed to recognize her, for which she was heartily glad.

At the head of the Knights strode gray-robed Arach Jannon, bearing his bandage-swathed hand like a standard before him. "That's the thief!" he shouted, pointing at Cael. "By the gods, he's slain our brethren!"

Cael was taken aback by the force of arms arrayed against him. So much trouble, so many deaths already, and for what? There would be more to come, his own most likely. He passed his hand over the blade of the sword, changing it back to an ordinary staff.

"I want him alive!" Sir Arach commanded. "A hundred steel coins to the one who brings me his staff."

The Knights poured forward. As they came, though, a great noise arose around them. Rocks, stones, bricks, and roof tiles rained down into the alley. A fireball erupted as a flask of burning pitch shattered in their midst. Screams, sickening thuds, and resounding clangs were heard as stone and brick struck flesh or bounded off upraised shields. From their rooftops and windows, the denizens of Smith's Alley rose up, hurling curses, and anything else that was handy, down on the invading Knights.

Cael stole that moment to duck away. He fled north, leaving the Knights to their riot-quelling.

* * * * *

A pottery jar exploded on the cobblestones near Alynthia, raking her with tiny razor-sharp fragments. She clambered from the refuse heap and fled south toward Temple Row. As she ran, a high-pitched voice shouted arcane words. A thunderous boom shook the narrow alley, and behind her a lightning bolt exploded against the side of a building. People screamed. Flames leaped up, turning the sky an angry red. She stared back for one moment longer, then slipped away into the shadows as alarm bells rang out all over the city.

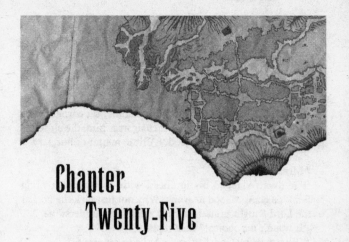

Chapter Twenty-Five

The door cracked against hewn stone old as the city itself. Cael staggered through, letting the door shudder closed behind him. He reeled down the stairs into the noisy, close familiarity of The Dwarven Spring. Kharzog Hammerfell stepped from behind the bar and greeted him harshly at the foot of the stairs.

"Where in blue blazes have you been? It's been weeks!" the old dwarf scolded.

"I'm in trouble," Cael hurriedly gasped to his old friend.

"What kind of trouble?" the dwarf asked under his breath. The bar, he indicated with a nod, was lined with drunken, off-duty Knights of Neraka.

"That kind," Cael said in a low voice.

"Reorx's beard!" the dwarf swore. At the foot of the stairs stood an old wooden hat stand and coatrack. From this, the dwarf snatched a green cloak and swung it over the shoulders of his friend. Cael pulled the hood over his head to hide his features from prying eyes.

"What have you done now?" Kharzog growled in a low voice, then louder said so that any listeners might hear, "Welcome, friend. May I show you to a table?"

He pulled Cael through the crowd to a table near the fire. A band of minstrels strummed a lively air from a corner, bowing to the two companions as they passed.

When Cael was seated at a table in another far corner of the inn and his friend had pulled up a chair near him, the elf whispered from deep inside his hood, "A little matter of burglary."

"Who?"

"Mistress Jenna."

The dwarf slapped his forehead with open palm, reeling back in his chair. "Good heavens! Why not just pick the pocket of the Lord Knight himself! Or try steal the Founderstone?"

"It wasn't *my* choice!" Cael replied.

"Whose, then? Gods! Who could be so ignorant?"

" 'Twas the Guild's decision."

"I might have known. They were using you, I'll warrant."

"I am a member now."

The dwarf tugged at his snowy beard and stared into the fire. Finally, he said, "So you probably need a way out of the city—and fast."

"No, I need to get over to the *Dark Horizon*," the elf answered.

"Oros uth Jakar's ship?"

"Aye."

"Why not leave for a time?"

"There are others to think of," Cael said.

"I smell a woman."

"Actually . . . two."

"Wonders never cease . . . Reorx's black boots, not Oros's wife!"

"I'm afraid so."

"Put her out of your mind, son! Who is the other one?"

"A girl."

"A girl?"

"Just a friend. She helped us. She helped me." Cael's head sank to the table.

"You are exhausted," the dwarf said, his voice softening.

"Hungry, too, I'll warrant. Stay here. Keep your head down. Pretend you are drunk. That shouldn't be hard—you've had some experience. I'll bring you something from the kitchen."

Kharzog hurried away, pushing a hasty path through the crowd and vanishing through the kitchen door.

Cael pulled the hood closer around his face. The warmth from the fire felt good, while its dancing red light cast soothing shadows against the green cloth of his hood. The minstrels finished a spring ring to a scattering of applause. Most put away their instruments and wandered off into the crowd for a break and a nip of food or drink. However, the harpist remained in her chair and began a soft, soothing melody, a trifle melancholy, like the winter songs of the elves. Cael felt the knots of tension in his back and shoulders loosen with the unwinding of her song. He clutched his staff to his breast, comforted by its hard, cool strength. A hearty aroma wafted from the direction of the kitchen, inciting a noisy grumble from his belly. He gaped and yawned.

He started, realizing he had fallen asleep. For how long he didn't know.

Carefully he lifted the edge of his hood and peered out at the room. A contingent of hard-eyed Knights crowded the stairs, glaring around at the crowd, which had grown quiet, if not quite silent. The harpist ended her tune in mid-strum. A minor chord hung in the air like the alarm call of some rare woodland bird.

At the head of the entranceway stood Sir Arach Jannon, his high narrow brow bearing a grisly cut from which still flowed a trickle of blood. As if he felt the eyes of everyone in the room on him, Sir Arach wiped the blood away with his bandaged hand.

"We are looking for an elf. Some of you know him, I am sure. He claims to be the son of Tanis Half-Elven and goes by the name of Cael Ironstaff," the Thorn Knight said loudly. Most of the tavern's customers shifted uncomfortably in their chairs, while the drunken Knights at the bar stared about in bleary-eyed confusion.

The kitchen door burst open and Kharzog strode out. He approached the visitors and planted himself, with iron boots set side wide apart, before them.

"What do you intend here, good sirs, ruining my custom?" he growled.

"Step aside, Master Hammerfell," Arach Jannon said. "This is a matter of law."

Cael rose from his chair and dashed toward the back door. Kharzog spun, bellowing unaccustomedly. For the drawing of one breath, Cael wondered at the dwarf's reaction. Then he discovered why.

He bowled into the waiting arms of a Knight of the Skull, the priestly order of the Knights of Neraka, who was guarding the back door. She was almost as surprised as he was and only managed to grasp the edges of his cloak before he spun free. His coppery hair flashed behind him, signaling his identity.

"That's him! Grab him!" Sir Arach shouted from the bar. His Knights gripped their clubs and rushed the elf, knocking over tables and chairs, sending the tavern's patrons sprawling and diving for cover. More Knights, many of them half drunk, poured from the curtained booths and alcoves, eager for a little fun. Cael leaped for the back door, grabbed the handle, jerked it open, and confronted an alley full of Knights. At the sight of him, they surged toward the door. He slammed it shut and turned.

A force like a wave struck him from behind, tossing him against the door, crushing the air from his lungs. He gasped in pain. Iron hands wrenched his arms behind his back, ripped the staff from his hands, then lifted his feet free from the ground. He struggled violently, kicking blindly. Harsh laughter answered his cries as they wrenched his arms in their sockets. Muscles tore, tendons creaked. He screamed in agony and ceased his resistance, knowing they would tear his arms from his body if he continued to struggle. He collapsed. Someone struck him with a mailed fist, and he tasted blood in his mouth even as his mind fought to remain conscious. The room swam.

Someone grabbed his chin and shook his head until he was awake. His eyes blinked open, and he stared about him. Sir Arach stood before him, while several other Knights crowded near. A pair held Kharzog Hammerfell by his beard and wrists, although he put up a decent struggle. Cael shook his head to clear his wits, but that only brought fresh pain, like steel rods being driven through his twisted neck.

A high-ranking Knight of the Skull stood near the Thorn

Knight, a look of bafflement on his wine-red face. Sir Arach Jannon held Cael's staff reverently, lust flaring like a green light in his eyes.

"I still don't understand, m'Lord," the Skull Knight said as he stroked his chin thoughtfully. "I know of this fellow. He's only an elf, and crippled at that. He looks harmless enough. And he carries a staff, which is ludicrous in this day and age."

"This *harmless* elf, Sir Knight, slew five of our brother Knights of Neraka in single combat," Sir Arach barked

"With what? That staff?" the Skull Knight asked incredulously. "Against trained Knights. Respectfully, sir—"

"Not with a staff, you imbecile," the Thorn Knight barked. "With this!" And so saying, he grabbed the staff by the thickest end, gripped the middle under the arm, and tried to pull the blade from its ironwood sheath. His face turned red with exertion. The sword refused to materialize. The staff remained a staff.

Muffled laughter pattered across the room like morning rain. The Thorn Knight glared around, and the room grew silent again. He approached Cael and grabbed the elf by the throat.

"Tell me how it works," he growled.

Cael spat blood in the Thorn Knight's face.

Arach released his hold, then struck Cael with a clenched fist across the nose. Blood poured from the elf's nostrils.

"Never again will you make me look like a fool!" the Thorn Knight hissed.

A dull thud just behind the right ear, a moment of blinding agony, and darkness closed over Cael's eyes.

*   *   *   *   *

"Damn you all to black hell," Kharzog roared, seeing his friend fall under the blows of the Knights. "Leave him be!" He thrashed his arms, trying to break the grip of the two Knights holding him. Sir Arach turned and eyed the dwarf with amusement.

"The dwarf is an accomplice. Arrest him," he ordered.

"Arrest me?" Kharzog shrieked. "This is your justice? This is the justice of the Knights of Neraka?" Setting his teeth into a fierce grin, the dwarf planted his iron-shod boots wide apart and clutched the arms of those holding him. Slowly the two Knights' feet left the floor. Growling like a bear, the dwarf turned and flung one into a nearby table. The other followed, crashing into his companion, and bringing howls of outrage from the patrons whose drinks were swept to the floor. Fighting erupted around the room, as years of pent-up frustration at the rulership of the Dark Knights were released. Contraband weapons appeared from nowhere, while those who had no weapons used chairs, bottles, crockery mugs, and other improvised weapons to fend off the swords and maces of the Knights, to strike blows many felt to be long overdue.

Kharzog sent a drunken Knight sprawling across the floor with one blow of his hammerlike fist. He ducked the clumsy swing of another, then stooped beside the first and dragged a hand axe from the Knight's belt. He then looked around and spotted Sir Arach, who was carrying Cael out the back of the tavern. With a roar, he waded through the melee, bellowing the Thorn Knight's name.

Sir Arach spun, his good hand outstretched with fingertips aglow. The old dwarf felt something strike him, an unseen force that slowed his steps. His arms felt as though they were weighted down with anchor chains. He could barely lift them to wield his axe. Sir Arach strode closer, knelt, and lifted a short sword from the grasp of a fallen patron.

Battling the spell that paralyzed him with all his dwarven spirit, tears streaming into his beard, Kharzog lifted his axe and aimed a clumsy blow at the Knight's knee. Sir Arach easily parried the stroke, then sent the axe spinning from the dwarf's grasp. Kharzog's jaws cracked as he ground his teeth in rage.

"Amazing," the Thorn Knight shouted over the din of battle. His eyes showed genuine admiration of the dwarf's courageous effort. "Given time, I think you might actually break free of my spell."

"Of course, I cannot allow that to happen," Sir Arach said with a grim smile as he slid the blade of his short sword between the dwarf's ribs.

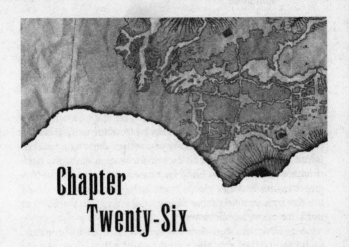

Chapter
Twenty-Six

In the next chamber a door opened, and a pair of Knights of Neraka dragged a man out into the dungeon passage. The man clawed at the doorposts, kicked, pleaded, begged, and screamed, but they lifted him bodily from the ground and carried him down the long arched shadowy hall to the iron door at the end. There they stopped, and a man wearing only a leather apron came out with a hammer and chains. While the prisoner wept, the jailer clapped irons around his legs, waist, and wrists and the Knights stripped his clothing. They dragged the man through the iron door. The jailer followed, slamming the door behind him with a resounding bang, cutting off a parting wail of despair.

Cael turned away, slumping to the floor of his tiny cell, his elbows resting on his knees, his forehead on his crossed arms. Heavy chains draped from the manacles around his wrists to the ones around his ankles, as well as to the iron collar around his neck. The collar had already begun to chafe the underside

211

of his jaw, but that pain could not be compared to the dull pounding in his head. One sea-green eye was swollen shut, the skin around it the color of a plum. He breathed through bruised lips because the blood from his broken nose had dried, clogging both nostrils. Slowly, he worked his tongue forward, wetting his parched lips and gingerly feeling for loose teeth.

He suspected several ribs were broken, because whenever he coughed up blood, he nearly fainted from the pain. His back felt as though he'd had a family of dwarves dancing on it. His joints ached as if he'd been racked for several days, his neck throbbed as if he'd been hung for twice as long. He was swiftly growing sore in other places from sitting for a night and half the day in a stone chamber neither tall enough to stand up in nor large enough to lie down.

A voice at the iron door roused the elf from his musings. Looking up, Cael saw the round face of a city clerk peering through the three-inch-square hole in the door, but the man wasn't looking at him. Instead, his eyes were lowered, as he read, "Cael Ironstaff, elf, homeland unknown, age unknown, parents unknown. You are accused of five counts of murder of her Dark Majesty's soldiers, one count of burglary, one count of breaking and entering, one count of possession of an illegal weapon, seven counts of use of an illegal weapon, one count of possession of an illegal magic item, seven counts of use of an illegal magic item, one count of disguising your person for the purposes of subterfuge, one count of traveling without proper identification, and two counts of assault with the intent to commit bodily harm. You stand before his most dread lord, Sir Arach Jannon, Knight of the Thorn, judge of the city of Palanthas. Prepare to plead your innocence or declare your guilt."

The clerk stepped aside. The tiny window remained empty for a moment, then the narrow, rat-eyed visage of Sir Arach appeared, glaring down at the thief. "Stand up before your judge," he snapped.

Slowly, Cael struggled to his feet, his chains rattling. He had to stoop, the ceiling was so low.

"So, we meet again," Sir Arach said. "This time, you do not have any friends around to help you."

"No, but you do," Cael said through his swollen lips.

"A pity we cannot meet, one to one, to see who is the better man," the Thorn Knight bragged.

"Truly, a pity. Perhaps another day," Cael said thickly.

"Alas, I fear your days are numbered."

"Where there's fear, there is also hope, as my *shalifi* used to say."

"Not much hope, considering your life is soon to end."

"Don't count your draconians before they hatch," Cael responded. "I could stand here and trade clichés with you all day, but these chains are heavy. Do what you will and be done with it."

"Very well!" Sir Arach snapped. "You have heard the accusations. How do you plead?"

"Guilty on all counts," Cael said, adding, "I'm proud to say."

"Good! I like a man who owns up to his deeds. Shame is a foolish thing. Clerk, please note that the prisoner declared his guilt of his own free will and without coercion," Sir Arach said, turning to the scribe. The pen scratched on the page.

"Of course, you realize the punishment your crimes warrant. An assault upon the Dark Queen's agent is an assault upon the Dark Queen. The usual punishment for the murder of her Dark Majesty's soldiers is death by slow torture," he said as he returned his gaze to the interior of the tiny cell. Cael stared at him.

"The slowest torture possible, mind you. I have servants steeped in the arts of exquisite pain. They can draw out the torture of a man for months, even years. I imagine that a long-lived elf such as yourself could be made to endure for several decades."

Still, Cael stared, saying nothing.

"Yes, it would be most horrible for you, rest assured. Yet, I could be persuaded to reduce the sentence to a quick, painless beheading . . ."

Cael blinked, his face as yet displaying no emotion.

"I thought that might get your attention," Arach Jannon chuckled. "All you have to do is reveal to me the secrets of your staff, and I'll see that you do not suffer."

Cael looked away.

"Think about it, my dear elf." Sir Arach said. "Unless you have a will of iron, eventually you'll tell me everything I want to know anyway. Why suffer days, nay, months of agony, when you can end your suffering in one swift moment?"

"One might think, your lordship, that the court is more concerned with my staff and the acquisition of power than with the administration of justice," Cael said blandly, not looking at him.

Sir Arach spluttered a string of oaths and curses. "Strike the prisoner's last remark from the record!" he shouted at the clerk, then turned one last time to the elf.

"I offered you mercy, elf! You will tell me every secret of the staff. Do not imagine for a moment that I cannot break your will, for I have done it many times and to stronger elves than you. Now you have made your own bed, and I have no more patience for your prattle. The sentence shall be carried out as ordered."

Cael lowered his eyes, his head sank to his chest. He slumped to the floor, exhausted.

"Death by slow torture!" Sir Arach shouted, striking the door angrily with his fist.

* * * * *

A peel of mad laughter woke Cael from a dreamless reverie. He jerked awake, rattling the chains on his wrists and ankles. The Screamer, as Cael had named the poor demented soul locked in the next cell, loosed another cry of self-induced horror that ended in a series of hyenalike twitters, warbles, and whoops. A little farther down, from yet another cell, a voice harsh with thirst shouted, "Shut up, you giggling idiot!"

He was answered by yet another series of bloodcurdling shrieks.

"Shut up! Shut yer stinkin' mouth!" the other inmate shouted. "Let me get my hands on . . . by the gods! Get me outta here! If I . . . I only . . . by the gods!"

"Rats! Rats! Oh, I ate one. There's another! Rats!" the

Screamer cried. "Oh . . . no! Not that. Not again. Not . . ." and so on, until the screams came again.

"Just shut up, will yer just shut up," the other inmate wept. "Please, for Gilean's sake, won't somebody please kill me?"

Cael kicked at a rat nosing about his feet, then adjusted his position against the wall. A little rotten straw barely softened the wet stone floor beneath him, while a tiny grate next to the floor allowed his waste, as well as the water seeping from the stone walls, to slowly escape. Very slowly. Above him, a tiny window in the iron door was the portal through which light sometimes shone and his food, when he was lucky enough to get any food, was lowered.

He had no idea how long he'd been in this cell since his "trial." The only way that he had to calculate time was by his feedings and by the regular torture sessions he endured. Tomorrow, or the next day, or perhaps the next, they would come for him again to question him with the rack or red-hot iron or something new. Again and again.

At each session Sir Arach reminded him how simple matters between them were. If Cael would only answer his questions, it would all end, quickly, painlessly. That was the one thought that kept the elf alive. The Thorn Knight couldn't kill him until he discovered the secret of the staff's powers.

Ironically, it was only in the last few days before his capture that he'd begun to suspect and experience the full extent of its magical powers. The staff had been given him by his *shalifi*, Master Verrocchio, the greatest swordsman in all Krynn, a little less than a year before. With the staff came knowledge of some of its powers, including its ability to become a sword with a magically keen edge, to merge into a solid surface so that it might be hidden, and to lengthen or shorten at will. Because it was made by sea elves, it also gave its owner the ability to breath underwater. However, its seeming power against magic and undead were new to Cael's experience. He wondered if these two new powers were somehow connected to his location, to Palanthas.

When the staff was placed in his hands and he felt the cool dark wood against his palms, he sensed what his master had told him he would feel, that the staff would serve him. He felt an instant bond to the weapon, and as he slid his hand down its length, the blade appeared effortlessly. In the year since that morning by the sea, the bond between himself and the weapon had only grown. At times he felt it was alive and if he had ears to hear, it might even speak to him. When he was away from the staff, he felt as if he were torn in two, as if he had left a part of himself. When the staff was in his hands, he felt whole, complete, and with that came a sense of peace as well as power.

He had already vowed that he would never reveal its secrets to Arach Jannon, no matter how much he was tortured. As the torture continued, he came to realize that the longer he kept such knowledge secret, the longer he would live. His elven blood would not allow him to surrender to despair. It offended his sensibilities to even consider relinquishing his staff to buy a swift end to the pain.

With these thoughts, Cael let himself slip back into the haze from which he'd been so rudely awakened only moments before. The Screamer now snored soundly, having exhausted himself. He'd wake again, no doubt, in a couple of hours, and once again give voice to the madness and horror of this place. Cael couldn't sleep, couldn't rest. Every breath he took was full of pain, as if the air itself was poison. Every breath was to gag, every sniffle of dungeon air sent his stomach heaving as surely as though he were leaning over the rail of a wave-tossed ship. He was tempted to shout for the guard, but he knew that would do no good. No, what he was really tempted to do was weep.

In the darkness of his cell he noticed a light beginning to well from the tiny sewer grate near the floor. Never had he beheld such a beautiful glow, even as he wondered at its source. The golden light danced through the sewer grate, growing in brightness until he thought he'd go blind. Even as the light grew, the malodorous air neared an extreme beyond human or even elven endurance. Cael at last identified its source, the putrid scent tickling the memory directly from his reeling brain.

"Gully dwarf!" he retched.

"For that I ought to leave you here," a shrill voice barked in reply. The silhouette of a head appeared behind the sewer grate. The head was bearded, but Cael could distinguish little else without leaning closer, something he was reluctant to do.

"Gimzig?" he inquired.

"At your service, sir," answered the figure. The gnome continued to spout a rapidfire stream of words, while fumbling with some large cumbersome object that looked like a giant spider trying to attack his bearded face. "Have you out of there in a jiffy, got a spider here in my pack that will do just the trick on these deep set bars, good thing they aren't steel. Passage is so small I didn't think I would get it in here, but where there's a will there's a thousand ways, as my grandfather Gornamop used to say. Say you look a little thin and worse for wear, haven't they been feeding you now and then? Well, we'll set that straight, just let me put this thing in place here with the legs against the stone and grasp the bars like so, did you notice the modifications? No? Well, that should do justthetricknowpresshereandlockthisintoplaceand . . . whoa! Look out!"

With an explosion of dust and splintered stone the small but stout iron grate vanished, leaving behind a ragged gaping hole slightly larger than the grate that once filled it. Fearing that the noise had been heard by his guards, Cael didn't hesitate, and despite his many injuries, immediately squeezed through the opening, nearly shredding his threadbare prison clothes in the process. When he wriggled into the tiny passage on the other side, he looked as if he had passed through a gnomish cheese grater.

The tunnel in which he found himself was barely large enough to accommodate his slender elven form. Even so, the figure that confronted him seemed little discomfited by the narrow surroundings. Only his pack, half as large again as himself, caused him any inconvenience. His grizzled white beard was now matted with dried sewage. A pair of long white eyebrows drooped over his eyes, and around Gimzig's head was a strapped a leather belt that held the two halves of an open scallop shell in which a stubby yellow candle burned and dripped with yellow wax.

Like most gnomes, Gimzig wore an odd conglomeration of

clothing replete with multiple vests of differing material, pouches, pockets, pencil bandoleers, as well as plenty of hooks and loops from which depended numerous useful tools and a good many for which the uses had been forgotten. Various scraps of paper, some covered with scrawls of ideas and design outlines and drawings, poked out from pockets all over his body (even from the cuff of one boot), giving him the appearance of a poorly stuffed toy bear. Even his grizzled beard served as a tool repository. Entangled among the matted hairs, bits of straw and metal filings, remnants of meals, and caked sludge of the gnome's sewer home was a pair of pliers hopelessly tangled beyond retrieval.

"Very good very good!" Gimzig nodded excitedly, nearly extinguishing his candle flame and flinging hot wax like a wet dog shakes off water. "The spider worked perfectly, or I should say it would have worked perfectly had I not accidentally pressed the release, but otherwise it worked very nearly just about perfectly. Of course, it almost took my head off." He took a breath, pondering for a moment. "I think I know how to fix that, in any case you are free now. My, but it's a good thing the Knights starved you or else you would never make it through this tunnel, you'd been shading a bit toward the heavy side lately and eating too much anyway, I should say it all comes of eating dwarven cooking."

All the while the gnome had been carefully folding in the legs of a large mechanical spider that he had used to rip the sewer grate from the wall. Seeing Cael's alarmed glance, he continued in an unbroken stream, "Remarkable the things you can do with springs and levers. You know my work, well, this is one of my latest creations. I call it a spider, and it was originally designed to open salt-crusted portholes on ships but it displayed an unfortunate tendency to rip great gaping holes in the hull, which of course induced advanced tendencies to sink especially in heavy seas, are you ready?"

Cael held his nose and nodded. In the meanwhile, the gnome had finished folding the spider's legs into its body, creating a remarkably compact and nondescript metal box. He dropped this over his shoulder into the pack strapped to his bent back, producing a metallic clunk, which was rapidly followed by an alarming series of sproings, poings, and pings. Gimzig paused, his mouth open to say something and waited warily, peering over his shoulder, until the noises subsided.

"Crikey! I hate it when that happens," the gnome sighed when all was quiet behind him. "There's enough in there to turn us into cabbage salad faster than you can say roto-slicerdicer. Of course everything in there is absolutely essential for the rescue of certain elves from the dungeons of Palanthas, well, come along then, follow me, are you sure you are able to, I could probably arrange for you to be pulled by a crankrope."

"I'll crawl," Cael coughed. Blood flecked his parched lips. Meanwhile, Gimzig somehow turned himself and his pack around in the narrow tunnel without setting off any of his devices. Dragging himself with his elbows, Cael struggled after his rescuer.

"The tunnel just goes a little farther before it dumps into a proper sewer," Gimzig said. "Watch that stone there, it looks ordinary enough but it's a trap."

Cael twisted himself into cramped knots to avoid the stone slightly projecting down on him from overhead.

"Someone probably placed it there to prevent just this sort of escape, I could disarm it, but that would take time, and it's just as well to leave it alone, mighty tricky those traps in the sewers and dungeons, you can always know exactly where anything important is by the number of traps you find beneath it, don't know why it took the city so long to find the Thieves' Guild in the first place, all they had to do was root around down here for a while and you get to know everything you ever wanted to know about this city, the sewers are a perfect reflection of the city above, clear as day if you know what to look for, I could have told them ages ago and I could tell you now where every Guild house lies."

The gnome suddenly vanished from sight, but his voice echoed back up the tunnel, "Watch that step there, don't fall on your head."

Cael wriggled head first down the narrow tunnel, emerging like a red-haired worm from the wall into a larger sewer passage. On the walkway below, Gimzig nervously eyed the black churning water flowing through the circle of his candle's light. "Been raining dwarves and kender up above," he commented, as Cael slid to the floor beside him.

"I am deeply in your debt, Gimzig," Cael said, rising wobbily to his feet. "How you came to find me, I haven't a clue."

"Captain Alynthia sent me of course. It was a simple enough task to track you down, all I had to do was search most of the dungeon cells, you forget that I spent forty years mapping every passage, tunnel, hole, channel, pipe drain, grate, gate lock and quoin of the vast and magnificent Palanthian sewage system that has been perfectly operational for over two thousand years!" His voice had sunk to an awestruck whisper.

He continued, "Long ago, the Civil Engineering Guild of Mount Nevermind decided the sewers should be studied to see if the gnomes ought to make any improvements, and after they placed their request before the city senate—only to be turned down, for some unaccountable reason—they commissioned me a junior Guild member only just earning his first engineer's stripe, with a worthy life quest—to make a detailed map of the sewers of Palanthas—but unfortunately it only took me forty-odd years to complete my report. Naturally by now I know these sewers like the hairs of my own beard: every nook, cranny, crevice, crack, and rat hole of it (the sewers not my beard) and so it was simplicity itself to find you and effect an escape. Say lad, are you sure you're capable of mobility, you look like you're about to faint."

"I just feel a little light-headed," Cael mumbled as he slumped to the ground.

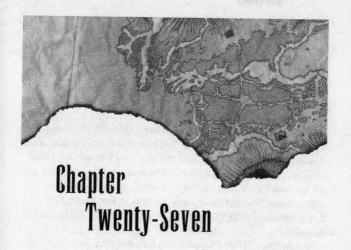

Chapter Twenty-Seven

ael awoke to the taste of water sweetened with wine being poured over his parched lips. A strong hand cradled his head, lifting him to drink. He reached out to take the proffered wine skin in his own hands and sat up, gulping to try to assuage a burning thirst, but this only made the dizziness return. He collapsed back, feeling someone catch him. The wine skin was once again placed to his lips.

"You're raging with fever," Alynthia said as he sipped.

"I've seen fevers," the gnome stated, "strike a man low in a matter of hours, it isn't a pretty sight, but it's a good sign that Cael lasted so long in that ghastly place . . ." He paused, shuddering, with a glance heavenward.

Refreshed by the water, Cael felt a modicum of strength returning. He managed to lift his head a bit and look around. He found himself lying on an access path in the sewers of Palanthas. His head was cradled in Alynthia's lap. Gimzig stood nearby, his pack on the floor before him. The gnome nervously toyed with the gadgets contained within it, sometimes casting a wary eye over his shoulder into the darkness.

"How did we get here?" Cael asked.

"Him!" She pointed at the gnome. "He smells like a garbage heap, but I wish I had him in my circle of thieves. He has the most extraordinary gadgets! It was he who found you and led me to you."

At this compliment, Gimzig smiled through his beard and bowed, sprinkling the floor with droplets of candle wax. Behind him, the sewer rushed and churned like a black river.

Cael nodded, feeling a great weariness stealing over him. He let his head sink into Alynthia's gentle embrace, feeling her warmth and hearing the steady rhythm of her heart. "Do you two know each other? How did you two meet?" he mumbled wearily.

No answer to this question was forthcoming. Instead, Alynthia and Gimzig exchanged pained glances. When no one spoke, the elf's eyes flickered open. The beautiful captain of thieves and the gnome quickly turned away, but not before he noticed their expressions of sorrow.

"What's wrong?" he demanded, trying to sit up again. The effort cost him, and he collapsed back into Alynthia's arms.

"We have to get you someplace safe," she said quickly.

"I've arranged a room, and there is a healer waiting. But we mustn't delay. Gimzig," she said, turning to the gnome, "lead us out of here."

"Always giving orders," Cael mumbled.

"Be quiet," she said. "Save your strength. I can't carry you. You are going to have to help." However harsh her words, her actions were gentle. She hooked one arm around his waist and helped him to rise. He leaned heavily upon her shoulder, his neck so weak that he could hardly lift his head.

"Now I could use a staff," he sighed. "It's gone, lost."

"Follow me!" Gimzig shouted as he led the way, his candle sending shadows leaping along the walls of the sewer. "It isn't really that far, and you needn't climb a ladder to the streets, Cael, the way I am taking is only a stair of two flights, I think you can make it with our assistance much easier than if we had to haul you up a ladder. Of course I have a remarkable pulley system, and there is always the self-extending ladder, but I doubt you have the strength to hold on to a ladder, so—"

The gnome froze, one foot lifted comically in mid-stride. His head slowly rotated until his long bulbous nose pointed at the swirling black waters racing by them.

"What is it?" Alynthia whispered.

"Shhhhhhh! Sewer monster. Big one. Right out there, watching us," the gnome whispered.

"Where? I don't see—"

"Get Cael back against the wall, and put something sharp between yourself and the water," Gimzig ordered as he slowly inched the straps of his pack from his shoulders. He set it on the ground before him and removed a pair of curious weapons, if weapons they were. Cael recognized one of them as Gimzig's mechanical spider. It was in its contracted position, all its legs stowed neatly around its body, forming a compact silver box. The other object was a short steel rod or pole, about as long as the gnome's forearm. Its use was a mystery, for it was too short to be a staff. A cudgel, perhaps? There was little time to speculate.

The gnome set these things on the ground between his feet, then eased his pack onto his shoulders again, all the while prattling on in a low voice, "Keep a close watch on the water, she'll rumble before she attacks, and you'll see a stream of bubbles, of course, by then it's too late, but if you are quick enough you can maybe get a jab in and turn her attack."

Alynthia drew her dagger and faced the water. Cael slid to the floor, helpless.

"If we move she'll attack, but if we wait here she is bound to get bored and move on to something else, it's the movement that triggers her attack instinct, anything that she perceives as trying to flee, in fact, as long as you maintain eye contact, you're probably safe—"

"But I can't see her," Alynthia broke in.

"Her eyesight isn't good enough to tell exactly where you are looking, it is the direction you are facing more than anything, but as I was saying, as long as you maintain eye contact . . ." He continued talking, as he stooped to pick up his weapons.

At that moment, the water exploded. A long, dark missile, bristling at the fore end with rows of dagger-long teeth shining in gaping jaws, shot from the water as though launched by a catapult. Gimzig only had time to stand upright and raise one small fist in defiance. He disappeared in a spray of water and flailing black-scaled hide, hooked claws, and spined tail. In a flash, the monster was gone, the water boiling, and Gimzig still stood at the brink of the water, his fist raised in defiance, his eyes closed and head turned slightly aside. Again, the monster rose up, breaching the black water, its massive jaws pried firmly apart by a man-tall rod of steel, then was gone. A few large bubbles broke the surface, their ripples swept quickly away by the current.

Gimzig opened his eyes and grinned. "Crikey! I told you she was a big one! Caw! Did you see the size of her? She was beautiful!"

"What did you . . . how did you?" Alynthia was flabbergasted.

"Self-extending weakened-timber-bracer," Gimzig explained. "I did a little work for the navy." He shrugged. "It was supposed to be useful for bracing bulkheads stressed and leaking from ramming attacks, but it had an unfortunate tendency to poke holes in the bulkheads it was supposed to brace. I also developed this," he said as he showed her the mechanical spider, "for opening salt-crusted portholes but of course it . . . look out!"

He flung the shining silver box at her head. For one horrifying moment she saw the thing's legs unfolding in flight, and then a hand grasped her tunic and pulled her down.

Just in time. The spider completed its weird transformation a spilt second before it would have reached her face. Its long bar- or porthole-gripping fangs extended and made a rapid staccato noise as it flew over her head. She glared at the gnome as though he had gone mad and reversed her dagger to aim it at his throat before Cael pulled her closer and weakly grasped her wrist and pointed.

The spider continued its strange flight, landing atop the

long, fangy snout of a second sewer monster creeping up silently on stubby legs behind the beautiful captain of thieves. As the spider's metal fangs penetrated the hide and muscle and bone of its snout and the spring-powered legs began their awful business, the monster reared up fully half again as tall as the tallest man, its nose smashing into the stone ceiling. It dropped with an agonized roar into the sewer's rushing stream, ivory-spined tail thrashing the surface into a froth.

Alynthia stared in horror at the place where it had vanished. Then she turned to the gnome. "Well, uh, thank you," she said.

"Don't mention it, my fault, really, I forgot that these beauties always travel in . . . threes," Gimzig said with a smile. They were his last words.

Behind him, the water exploded once more. A beast rose, jaws gaping, behind the distracted gnome. He instinctively leaped to avoid harm, but he was not fast enough. The awful jaws clamped down on one leg, and in the blink of an eye, he was dragged backward into the water. Cael caught a last sight of Gimzig's face twisted with terror, eyes starting out from beneath his bushy eyebrows as he was sucked beneath the current. He didn't even have time to scream. A few yards downstream, the current swept up a slick of papers covered with drawings and design ideas. They lingered on the water's surface for a moment, then swirled away.

Alynthia knelt by Cael's side and helped him to rise. He lay against her, nearly unconscious. She doubted her ability to carry him to safety, but there was no question of leaving him here to go for help now, not after what she had just witnessed. With one last terrified glance at the water, she led Cael away.

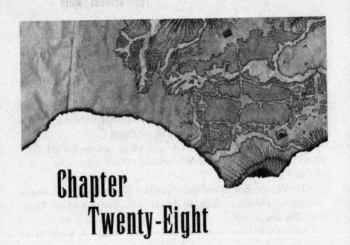

Chapter Twenty-Eight

ael awoke to the distinct sounds of someone moving about the room in the quiet fashion of someone trying not to wake a sleeper. A clink of a cup, the soft rutch of a drawer closing, a swish and rustle of long, heavy cloth across a wooden floor. The noises that propelled his mind back to his half-remembered childhood, of waking from a long illness to the patient care and heartwarming delight of his mother.

He opened his eyes and slowly turned his head. A figure stood with her back to him beside a simple dresser of pale wood, setting candles into a wooden box. She was short, dressed in a black dress that dragged the ground, hiding her feet. Over her head she wore a hood of similar material. She moved with the slow and deliberate care of the old, placing each candle in the box as though carefully counting them out.

Beside his bed stood a severe, straight-backed chair, and beside the chair a low table with a clay pitcher and battered pewter cup, and a wooden bowl over the lip of which dangled a wet rag. He lay beneath an open window, and outside the window the spreading branches of an elm were dappled with the sunlight. Opposite this was another window, also thrown wide, which, judging by the seagulls gliding in the blue empty air outside, overlooked the bay. Beside the dresser stood a door, opened a crack.

The old woman finished her task and placed the candle box into a drawer, then slowly slid it shut, making as little noise as possible. She started for the door, glancing quickly at the bed before leaving.

The face that peered out from the hood was not old but that of a girl. A few strands of dirty blonde hair spilled from the hood's depths. Her eyes opened wide with surprise and delight, seeing Cael awake.

"Hello, Claret," he said. "What are you doing here?"

In answer, she flew to the door and jerked it wide. "He's awake!" she shrieked, then dashed to his side. He feared for a moment that she would throw herself atop him, but she paused, and instead gently touched his arm beneath the coverlet. "How do you feel?" she asked softly but with excitement.

"Hungry," Cael said. "I feel thin as a wight."

"I can fix that!" Claret said, grinning. She turned to the door at the sound of a small, joyous gasp. Cael followed her gaze.

Alynthia stood in the doorway, one hand covering her lips. She wore trousers of brown homespun, a simple blouse, and her feet were bare. She had cut her hair, shorn off all her tight ringlets, leaving her with an unruly mass of short black curls.

Her hand shook as she lowered it. "It's about time you woke, you old lazybones," she said with feigned anger. The sparkle in her dark eyes revealed her happiness.

"Elves never sleep," he answered. "I was merely faint from hunger and torture."

"Well, then you fainted for a month and a day," Alynthia laughed.

"How long?" Cael cried in surprise as he rose up in bed—and found he couldn't. He fell back heavily, gasping.

"You should rest," Claret said to him as she glared at Alynthia. The captain of thieves approached the bed and laid a hand on Cael's forehead.

"Your fever only broke yesterday," she softly said to the elf. "Claret is right. I'm sorry."

"A month and a day!" Cael sighed as he let them rearrange his coverings. "What happened?"

"What do you remember?" Alynthia asked.

"Not now!" Claret barked. "Let him rest. He needs food, then more sleep."

"No, I want to know," Cael protested. "Tell me."

"Where do I begin?" Alynthia asked as she slumped wearily into the chair beside the bed.

"I'm going to heat some broth," Claret said. She left the room, her long black dress swishing over the wooden floor.

"I remember waking in the sewer. Was Gimzig there?" Cael asked.

"Yes," Alynthia answered without looking at him.

"What happened?" Cael demanded. He had the dimmest recollection.

"He was taken . . ." she began, then shook her head as though fighting to control her emotions. "Protecting us," she finished with cracking voice.

"Taken? Taken how?"

"A sewer monster, dammit! Must I relive all the horrible details?" Alynthia cried.

"No," he said. "Gods! Poor Gimzig."

"After . . . that, I brought you here. You had a fever," Alynthia continued. "You raved for a while, then you grew still as death, your eyes open, staring at nothing, lips moving. You stayed that way for weeks. I thought . . . I feared . . . but yesterday your fever broke, and you seemed to slip into a restful sleep. The healer said you would either recover or would never wake."

"Where is this place?" Cael asked, looking around.

"It's my own," she said proudly. "It isn't a palace, but no one, not even the Guild, knows of its existence. It's near the university."

"Are you hiding me from the Guild?" Cael asked.

"No, I am hiding us," Alynthia said.

"Us?"

"Oros has announced that I have been kidnapped."

"Why?"

"I rescued you, against the strict prohibition of Mulciber. She had ordered that you be allowed to die in the dungeons of Palanthas, that there was not sufficient danger of your betrayal of the Guild under torture, as you knew little of the Guild's workings."

"So why did you rescue me?" Cael asked.

Alynthia looked away and said nothing for a long while. Cael watched her, looking for any outward clue to her emotions, but her face remained rigid, her eyes staring blankly at the wall.

Finally, she spoke. "You saved my life three times that night," she said, almost choking on the words. "Risked your life to save mine. On the other hand, my dear husband has announced that your accomplices kidnapped me in order to secure their escape from the city. There have even been ransom notes. He, of course, refused to negotiate. Mulciber has, no doubt, ordered my death as well as yours. So now the Guild as well as the Knights of Neraka search for both of us."

"You shouldn't have sacrificed yourself for me," Cael said.

"There is more," Alynthia continued, ignoring his statement. Her face was grim. "You should hear it all. They killed your friend, Kharzog Hammerfell."

"Oh, gods no!" Cael groaned. He remembered what happened at the Dwarven Spring. Had Kharzog tried something foolish on his behalf?

Cael's hands wrenched at the bedsheets. "How did he die?" he asked.

"I wasn't there. They say that Arach Jannon cut him down in public, made an example out of him. There was nearly a riot over it. The dwarf was well loved."

"Aye," Cael sighed. "Aye, that he was. He was my only friend in this world. Now there is no one."

Alynthia looked away, unable to bear the sight of the elf's grief over the loss of his friend. She did not tell him of the dwarf's funeral, where fate, it seemed, had introduced her to the gnome, Gimzig and where she heard his plan for rescuing Cael. Nor did she tell him of the extraordinary turnout by the local dwarven community. Few citizens of Palanthas had ever suspected that so many dwarves lived in their fair city. Even a few gully dwarves had made an appearance, much to the dismay of everyone.

Claret opened the door and eased into the room, balancing a tray in one hand. Atop it, fragrant steam rose from a wooden bowl.

"What about her? How is she involved in this," Cael said suddenly, almost fiercely.

"Her father was imprisoned and died of fever. Her mother is in one of the labor camps, under suspicion of aiding you. Her brother is in an orphanage. They never caught dear Claret. She is too clever for them. She is too clever even for me. She found us here, and now she helps us by going in disguise to the market to purchase our supplies and gather news."

Claret smiled at these compliments while handing Alynthia the tray. She helped Cael sit up in the bed, propping him up with pillows fetched from the dresser. "I'm sorry, Claret," Cael whispered during her gentle ministrations.

"Don't be," she answered with a trembling smile. Without warning, huge tears welled out from her gray eyes. She turned and rushed through the door, pressing the hem of her dress to her face. They heard her in the other room, sobbing.

"She has not cried until now," Alynthia said.

She eased the tray with the bowl of broth onto the bed beside Cael and took up the wooden spoon. She stirred the broth.

"Are you hungry?" she asked, trying to sound cheerful.

He nodded, his eyes closed.

"Claret has made this broth for you," she said. "It smells good."

Cael turned and looked at it, then at the door. He nodded again and reached for the spoon. Alynthia held it out of his reach. "Just relax," she said. "Let me."

He lowered his hand with obvious reluctance. She held the spoon to his lips, and he noisily gulped the warm broth. "I feel like a fool," he muttered between sips.

Eventually, the sobs in the other room stilled, and Claret once more appeared at the door, stripped of her covering of heavy black wool and wearing a homespun shift. She dabbed at her red eyes with a cloth but smiled at Cael when she saw him eating.

"Is it good?" she asked.

He nodded, taking another sip. The warm broth seemed to ease the turmoil in his heart, and after a few sips he remembered how hungry he was. The simple pleasure of eating, the sating of hunger, lightened his spirit.

He finished the bowl, feeling the warm and hearty nourishment already making him feel stronger. Smiling, Alynthia started to wipe his lips with a napkin, but he took it from her.

"You can at least let me do this myself!" he said. He pressed it to his lips and chin, and as he did a strange look passed across his face.

Alynthia smiled, and Claret snickered, hiding her mouth behind her hand. Cael felt gingerly along the lower half of his face, fingering the strange nest of curling red hair that had sprouted and grown full and luxuriant from his chin and cheeks.

He looked at Alynthia with such an expression of bafflement that she laughed out loud.

"Yes," she said with a smile. "You grew a beard. Claret wanted to shave it off, but I wouldn't let her."

"I don't like it," Claret said poutingly. "It makes him look too human."

"This is impossible," Cael gasped. "Elves cannot grow beards."

"I think it makes you more handsome, not so boyish," Alynthia said, ignoring his protest. "Once you are better and have filled out those ghastly hollow cheeks, you'll have a rugged, manly look about you."

"Well, I just don't like it!" Claret protested. "He was much prettier without it."

Cael stared in horror from the girl to the woman, all the while touching the alien growth of hair on his face. "Neither of you understand, do you?"

"Understand what?" they asked in unison, gazing upon him with merry eyes.

"Oh, just leave me!" he snarled. "Leave me alone."

Slowly, laughing together, they walked to the door, Alynthia carrying the tray. "Men are so sensitive about their looks," Claret whispered loud enough for Cael to hear.

"I'll say," Alynthia agreed as she shut the door.

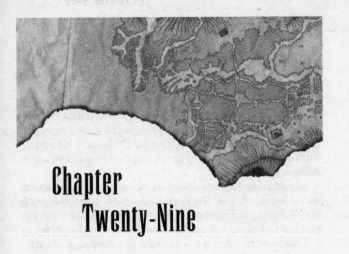

Chapter
Twenty-Nine

Amonth later, Cael stood at the foot of the bed, one gauntleted fist on his hip, the other thoughtfully tugging at the groomed red beard on his chin. Claret had trimmed it for him, since he hadn't the slightest idea how to do it himself, and he didn't dare visit a barber. He and Alynthia never left the room except after dark, and even then they avoided places like shops and taverns, instead preferring to stroll along out-of-the-way streets, alleys, and parks. Their nightly constitutionals had helped to restore Cael's health. He felt new life and a new purpose for living flowing like hot wine through his veins.

The window over the bed was thrown wide, allowing the cool breeze off the bay to waft through, rustling his hair and stirring in him the wanderlust he always felt at the first scent of autumn. A whole summer had passed during his imprisonment, illness, and recovery, and he felt its loss acutely. To his right, the window overlooking the bay was propped open, and the plaintive cries of gulls reached his ears. Toward the open sea, beyond the Bay of Branchala, the sky was the color of iron, while over Palanthas some sunlight shone through the clouds.

Behind him, the bedroom door was closed. He heard Alynthia and Claret in the next room arguing over the cut of some cloth Claret was sewing. Before him, hanging from the wall was an old polished silver mirror. He stared into it as through probing the depths of a well for some glimmer of water. He rubbed his beard, tugging his chin first to the left, then to the right, examining his profile. He pushed back his long red hair to reveal his pointed elven ears, as though checking to make sure everything was still there.

At last, he shook his head and let his hand fall to his side. It came to rest on the pommel of a long, slim rapier. Claret had managed to get the weapon for him from somewhere. He didn't know where, as unlicensed bladed weapons were illegal in Palanthas. She was indeed a neverending marvel of resourcefulness. Without her, he and Alynthia would have barely gotten by. Cael caressed the pommel of the blade. In the dungeons of Palanthas, he had been helpless to defend himself against his torturers and guards. That lingering fear left him feeling empty and afraid, even after his recovery, but the presence of the weapon, the blade at his side, gave him the confidence to face the world again.

He drew it from its sheath and, in imitation of the Knights he'd faced in the alley, saluted himself in the mirror. Lunging suddenly forward with a loud stamp of his foot, he thrust the blade ahead, parried an imaginary blade, and continued the thrust to its fullest length, hammering the tip into a spot in the wall. The blade sank into a patch of wood that looked as if it had been pecked by a hundred woodpeckers. Chips and flecks of sawdust flew as he leaped back, on guard for the next attack, his green eyes blazing.

He met his own gaze in the mirror again. He slammed the rapier home in its sheath, then resumed contemplation of his own profile, tugging his bearded chin this way and that.

"Don't even think about it. You can't shave it off," Alynthia said as she entered the room.

"Why not?" Cael asked distractedly, continuing to examine himself in the mirror.

"It's the perfect disguise," she said. "They'll never look for you, an elf, wearing a beard. Here, try this on."

Cael turned and found Alynthia holding a hooded tunic of close-woven black wool. Claret stood at the door, a sewing basket over one arm and a needle held between her lips as she gazed at the elf.

Cael stooped so Alynthia could slip the garment over his head. He worked his arms through the sleeves while she pulled it snug to his waist. She stepped back to examine him.

"Oh, here," she said, stepping towards him again. She pulled the tight-fitting hood over his head and adjusted the set of the tunic on his shoulders, pausing to briefly touch his muscles beneath the cloth. "You've filled out nicely," she commented. "Better than before."

Cael turned to Claret. "How do I look?"

"Like a thief," she said with a laugh.

"You look like a lamplighter," Alynthia disagreed. "That's how I designed it. I have another I've cut down to fit me."

Cael turned back to the mirror. His red beard spilled from the hood like a blaze. The tunic did loosely resemble the unofficial uniform of the Palanthian Lamplighters' Guild, but he did not have the perpetual squint of a lamplighter. He practiced one, evoking a guffaw from Alynthia. Claret shook her head and exited the room.

"Tell me again why we're pretending to be lamplighters tonight," Cael asked as he adjusted the fit some more.

"So we can get into the Old City," Alynthia said. "At night, lamplighters are a common enough sight. The Thieves' Guild has a secret pact with the Lamplighters' Guild. At our request, they will allow the lamps to burn out in areas we designate, to better aid our business."

"A collaboration that's not very secret, I might add," Claret noted with a scowl as she reentered the room. "Everyone knows the lamplighters and the thieves are in cahoots."

"Fine. That much I understand," Cael said. "What is our reason for entering the Old City at all and taking the risk of passing the Gates?"

"We've already discussed this," Alynthia said with an

exasperated sigh. "We are going to the Great Library to research the Night of Black Hammers. If we can find some information about the distribution of Guild treasures, we might find a clue as to the location of the Reliquary."

"Why do we want this Reliquary again?"

"With it, we can win our way back into the Guild's graces," she said.

"Why? The Guild has betrayed you. Your husband . . ." his voice trailed off at Alynthia's dark look.

"The Guild will gladly accept the Reliquary as the price of our good standing. Alone in this city, with both the Guild and the Knights hunting us, we are bound to be captured sooner or later. Don't you want to rejoin the Guild? Or do you wish to return to the dungeons of Palanthas?"

"I'll never return to the dungeons of Palanthas," Cael said gravely while fingering the sword at his side. "That's why I must recover my staff. I can defend myself with this," he said, indicating the rapier, "but I need my staff. It was given me by my *shalifi.*"

"Your what?" Alynthia asked.

"My master. Master Verrocchio. He was the finest swordsman on all Krynn. He gave me that staff in solemn ceremony, and it was given to him by the sea elves before I ever met him, to be given to the one whom the staff would serve. It is bound together with my destiny. I've told you all this before. I must get it back!" he shouted for emphasis, as he slapped a gauntleted hand against a gauntleted fist.

"Do try not to be so damned selfish for once, will you?" Alynthia snarled. "Think of all those who have suffered for you. Will you throw all away on a fool's errand? You can't get it back from Arach Jannon without risking your life—and after we have worked so hard to save it."

"I *can* get it back, with your help," Cael said.

Alynthia opened her mouth to say something, then closed it again. She blinked at the elf, who solemnly returned her gaze.

"All right," she said at last, her voice breaking. "I'll make you a deal. We go first to the Great Library. If we cannot find evidence of the Reliquary, then I will show what a soft-hearted fool I am and help you steal back your staff. But if we do find evidence, then we steal the Reliquary first."

Cael paused a moment, then said, "Agreed."

He extended one gauntleted hand. She took it, and they shook hands firmly.

Suddenly, she pulled herself to him and threw her arms around his neck. "Thank you," she said, blinking up at him with her dark sparkling eyes. "I wouldn't want to go on my next job without you."

"I wouldn't let you go alone," he said, a shadow of a smile parting his red beard.

"You've grown taller," she commented.

"No, you have shrunk. I reached my full height before you were born."

"Yes, and elves can't grow beards," she said.

"Don't let's talk about it."

"Now who's speaking like a romantic poet?"

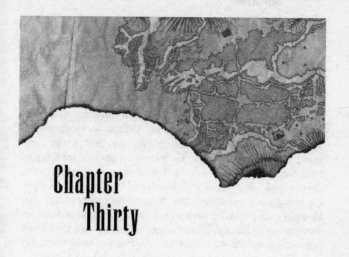

Chapter Thirty

The Great Library of Palanthas was one of the city's most famous buildings, one of the most well known buildings in all of Krynn. Here for uncounted centuries the Aesthetics of the Library had watched over and maintained the greatest repository of knowledge ever gathered, and for most of those centuries they had also attended the master of the library, the historian Astinus, who recorded the history of Krynn as it occurred. When the old master disappeared in the wake of the Chaos War, taking the contents of the library with him, the library's monks continued their duties as best they could, painfully rebuilding their vast collection of books, scrolls, documents, and artifacts. Though Krynn had lost its chronicler and they mourned the absence of their undying leader, they struggled on.

The library was ever busy collecting, cataloging, and storing every piece of information that might be gathered from the world of Krynn, from artifacts of cultures and peoples vanished before the Age of Dreams, to the binding and storing of the volumes of legal proceedings generated by Palanthas's Dark Knight overlords. Where before the Chaos War one man had recorded the history of Krynn, now a thousand Aesthetics scoured the lands and seas for history to observe and memorialize as it was happening.

Brother Gillam had long since ceased pondering the significance of the loss of Astinus. The fate of Krynn's chronicler was ancient history, so far as Brother Gillam was concerned. Tonight, Brother Gillam's primary duty was that of night roof guard of the Great Library. To that end a stout mace dangled from the belt of his brown Aesthetics' robe. Brother Bertrem, the old man who was now the leader of the Order of Aesthetics, being a prudent fellow, had declared several years ago that all night roof guards be drawn from the Astronomical Sciences division of the library. Thus, they could both guard the library (a pointless task, as no one dared desecrate this sacred building by breaking into it) and also study the new stars of Krynn.

At the end of the Chaos War, when the Graygem shattered, all the old stars and constellations had disappeared and were replaced in the night sky by the myriad fragments of the Graygem. Astronomy, as a science, was reborn, and Brother Gillam was one of its foremost scholars. In his career, he had already named over a hundred stars, from the dim red New Forge in the northern sky, to the hazy cluster near the south polar star, a cluster he had named the Dwarf's Beard.

The first breath of autumn was in the air this night, and it promised to be a fine evening for viewing the stars. Brother Gillam settled himself atop a stool beside a broad wooden desk, quite near the edge of the southern wall of the housing wing of the library, the darkest corner of the roof and thus the best place to observe the sky. This wing was also the only one whose roof was flat. The roofs of the library's other wings were all steeply pitched, but the roof of the housing wing had been constructed flat to serve as a rooftop garden on one end as well as an observatory. This meant, of course, that his guard duties only required him to patrol a small area, leaving him plenty of time for study.

In the rooms below him, most of the Aesthetics were fast

asleep, but Gillam's work was just beginning. At his left hand stood a dark lantern, smelling of hot metal, and on the desk before him was spread a star map, beside it a bottle of ink, and a quill. The mace hanging from his belt proved to be as bothersome as ever, so as he always did, he unclipped it and dropped it into one of the desk drawers. He leaned over the map, flashed the light of the dark lantern over it for a moment, lifted the quill, and turned his gaze to the sky.

The stars of Krynn wheeled slowly overhead. His breath catching in his throat, Brother Gillam spotted a dim twinkle of blue rising in the east, one he didn't immediately recognize. His hand already reaching out to flip open the dark lantern, he turned his attention away from the sky in time to see the desk, the lantern and ink bottle atop it, slide across the roof and come to a thudding halt against one of the library's many chimneys, very near the edge of the roof. It was not this, though, that caused the Aesthetic to cry out. It was the breeze that lifted the map from the desk and sent it fluttering in the air. Brother Gillam leaped from his stool and dashed after it just in time to watch the map rise and disappear into the dark Palanthian night.

A dagger was already at his throat, while the second thief was still scrambling onto the roof. The means of their ascent, as well as the cause of the desk's movement, became all too apparent as the second thief quickly wound up a black rope and stowed it into some deep, hidden pocket in his dark outfit, but only after dislodging the small grappling hook that had caught one of the desk's sturdy legs and sent it hurtling across the library roof.

It was a good thing his mace was safely stowed in the desk drawer, Brother Gillam thought with a sigh of relief. Now he wouldn't be obligated to try to use it. The thief holding the dagger was somewhat smaller than himself, but he had no doubt that he or she—perhaps a she, judging from the eyes glittering darkly over her mask—would kill him at the slightest move. Brother Gillam needn't be tempted to resist. He only hoped he wouldn't faint, something he was prone to do when excited.

"Take us to Bertrem," the female thief hissed, slapping the monk for emphasis. "We're not here to steal anything or hurt anyone, but if you give us trouble or raise the alarm . . ." Her voice trailed off as she waggled the dagger at the Aesthetic's nose. He quickly nodded his silent assent, especially after the grim look her accomplice gave him.

Among the many chimneys and ventilation shafts that sprouted forestlike from this section of the roof of the Great Library, there were also several small wooden sheds. One was used for storage, partly for garden equipment but mostly for the paraphernalia of the astrological sciences division. Another served as a shelter for those whose job it was to patrol the rooftop. There were even a few pigeon coops, used to house the carrier pigeons with which the Aesthetics sometimes maintained contact with their far-traveling scholars. One, however, covered a staircase that led down to the living quarters of the Aesthetics. It was a testament to the reverence most people held for the Great Library that no lock barred this door. Prodded from behind by the thief's dagger, Gillam opened it quickly and led the two thieves down the dark staircase within.

* * * * *

"Bertem, wake up!" a stern, familiar voice ordered.

"Yes, master!" The elderly Aesthetic sat bolt upright in his bed, nervous sweat popping out on his brow. Instinctively, he moved to rise from the bed, but the aching in his bones and the slowness of his joints slowly brought him back to reality. His room was dark, and he could tell by the faint sound of snoring come from other rooms that the night was not far progressed.

"A dream," he sighed, dabbing at his brow with the corner of a bedsheet. He felt along the table beside the bed for his spectacles, found them, and slipped them onto his nose. He glanced around the room as though to assure himself of his own words, peering nervously at the deeper shadows.

Nothing seemed out of the ordinary. His room was spartan, with few furnishings beyond those absolutely essential for his needs: a bed and night table, a desk and chair, a wardrobe, a washstand, hearth and coal shuttle, and the inevitable bookshelves. A little light shone under his door, dimly illuminating a plain square of rug.

He was about to remove his spectacles and return to his slumber when the sound of the door's knob made his eyes pop. To his horror, the door began to swing open, pushed by a pale white hand. The elderly Aesthetic trembled, clutched his blankets almost up to his eyes, and sought for his voice in a throat strangled by fear.

"Astinus?" he finally managed to croak.

"Master Bertrem?" the intruder responded in a voice tight with its own fear.

Bertrem relaxed, realizing with a profound sigh that it was just one of the Aesthetics. He wondered what terrible thing had caused the young scholar to disturb his sleep. Fire? Flood? Rats devouring the books? Kender?

His answer came as two darkly clad figures stole in behind the young Aesthetic. They rushed at the old man in his bed, and despite his advanced age (rumored to be closer to a hundred than to ninety), he nearly climbed the wall trying to get away from them. Brother Gillam spun, dashed out into the hall to call for help, and fainted before the first cry had passed his lips.

Alynthia wrestled the old Aesthetic back down on his bed and clapped a gloved hand over his mouth before he could find his voice and raise an alarm. She turned to Cael and hissed, "Drag that other one back in here, and shut the door." The elf complied, unceremoniously dumping the brown-robed scholar on the square rug beside the bed.

"Bind him and gag his mouth," she said.

Cael made quick work of him, tying his wrists behind his back with the black cord they had used to scale the library's wall, then stuffed one of Bertrem's dirty socks into the Aesthetic's mouth and took up a position beside the door.

Alynthia turned back to Brother Bertrem. The old man trembled like a reed. His spectacles had slipped off his nose and hung comically from one ear. His feet were hopelessly tangled in his own bedsheets.

"I'm going to remove my hand now, old man," she said gently. "We're not here to hurt you or to steal anything. We simply want some information, to look at a book or two for a few hours in peace and without any warning raised. Do you understand?"

For a moment, Brother Bertrem hesitated, but as his assailant's dark eyes hardened, he nodded. Alynthia lifted her hand, but left it hovering over him, ready to clap down again. Bertrem kept his lips pressed firmly together, though few other parts of his body remained as still.

"We are looking for information about the items taken from the Thieves' Guild on the Night of Black Hammers," the female thief quietly informed him. "Do you know of this?"

"I compiled the information myself," Bertrem whispered.

"Will you take us to it?" she asked.

He nodded.

Warily, Alynthia removed herself from atop the Aesthetic and helped him untangle his feet from the bedclothes. Throwing a robe around his frail old shoulders, she guided him towards the door, which Cael stood ready to open. Brother Bertrem paused and settled his spectacles back atop the bridge of his nose. Then he nodded. Cael opened the door.

The hallway beyond led past a long row of doors to their right, beyond which lay the private chambers of the Aesthetics of the Library, while to their left the wall was lined with tall, narrow, stained-glass windows that looked north toward the city's center. Brother Bertrem led them quietly along the hall, his long robe swishing around his slippered feet. Behind some doors, they heard rattling snores, behind others, the scratches of pens across parchment or the rattles of turning pages.

This hallway eventually left the Aesthetics' quarters behind and, passing beneath an arch, continued until it ended at a large ornate door. Halfway down this hall, another door opened to the right. Bertrem stopped here, opened the door, and entered the library's Research Wing.

This wing was actually one cavernous room, the great arched roof lost in shadows high overhead. Down the center of the chamber ran row after row of desks, tables, and cubicles, with here and there a lamp or candle burning for any who might come late to study. All around the outer walls of the room, rows of bookshelves towered up into darkness. Wheeled ladders, attached to rails above and below, provided access to these shelves. Some of the ladders reached four stories high, so great had been the collection of books, tomes, and scrolls in the library's heyday. Now, sadly, many of the shelves were empty.

Above the ladders ran a narrow iron-railed balcony, adding yet another level of shelves. This room was but one chamber of the Great Library. There were others, many far larger.

Alynthia stared about her in awe. Even Cael, who had frequented the public sections of the Library before his capture and induction into the Guild, was nearly overcome by the sense of grandeur this chamber instilled in those who first entered it. There was a templelike quiet here, a feeling of presence, almost a watchfulness. This place was one of the private sections of the library, reserved for the Aesthetics, entered by the uninitiated only by invitation and under close supervision.

Had they come here without a guide, probably they could have spent years searching for the books they sought, but Brother Bertrem led them unerringly to their goal. Up a twisting stair of wrought iron to the high balcony above, he climbed, puffing with the exertion. Alynthia followed on his heels, and Cael came behind, bearing a lamp taken from one of the tables. Along the balcony for half its eastern length they went to a shelf as similar to all the others as a tree is to other trees in a forest. But with hardly a scan of the bindings, he quickly withdrew three large tomes, turned, and dropped them into Alynthia's waiting arms.

* * * * *

Brother Bertrem yawned like a cave. He missed his sleep, but he didn't dare leave the two thieves alone with his precious books. Not that he could have stopped them if they decided to steal the books, but he knew that as long as they were here, he wouldn't be able to close his eyes.

Alynthia slammed a book shut, sending a boom echoing through the cavernous chamber, disturbing the reverent silence. "Nothing," she snarled. "There's nothing here either."

Blinking back sleep himself, Cael shook his head sympathetically, then scratched at the prickling beneath his mask for perhaps the thousandth time that night. Without thinking, he tugged the mask aside to better scratch the unaccustomed facial hair.

Brother Bertrem gasped, and, looking up, Cael found the old man staring at him in horror. Quickly, his face shading to scarlet at his careless mistake, he jerked the mask back over his face.

Alynthia looked up from the book she had just opened. A half dozen others were stacked beside this one on the table around which they sat. "What is it?" she asked.

"N-nothing," Brother Bertrem stammered. "I thought I saw a ghost, was all. A ghost of an old hero."

The elf's eyes narrowed at these strange words, but Cael said nothing.

Brother Bertrem continued, "There *are* ghosts here, of course. One meets them sometimes at night among the stacks, ghosts of old scholars still trying to solve the mysteries that consumed their lives, ghosts of historians. . . ." His voice trailed off as his gaze wandered to a small, nondescript door in the northwester corner of the chamber.

Alynthia shrugged and returned her attention to the book. Cael watched the Aesthetic closely now, and found the old man's gaze riveted upon him.

An hour later, the book slammed shut, booming noisily. Alynthia picked it up and shook it as though she would tear it in half. Brother Bertrem half-rose from his seat, reaching out in his concern for the book, his fingers twitching. He grabbed it away from her before she could harm it and clutched it to his chest.

"This is impossible," Alynthia complained.

"What exactly is it that you seek?" Brother Bertrem asked wearily. He had already asked this same question a dozen times in the hopes of speeding the departure of the thieves, but every time he asked it, Alynthia snarled to mind his own business.

"Information on one of the items found in the Guild treasuries after the Thieves' Guild was destroyed," Cael said quickly before Alynthia could repeat her customary answer. "They call it the Reliquary. I suppose it holds some old bones or something."

Alynthia fumed at her red-bearded companion but said nothing.

"I don't recall anything by that name," Brother Bertrem said, while thoughtfully stroking his beard. "I created a complete inventory for the city senate, researching those items about which nothing was known. The Founderstone, for instance."

"This item was said to be a small silver dragon," Alynthia reluctantly admitted. "It is hollow, and inside, on a cushion of velvet, sits an old brown skull."

The old Aesthetic pondered for a few moments, searching the ceiling with his dim eyes. "No," he said at last. "I don't recall anything by that description. Although it is entirely possible that some private looting took place among members of the raiding parties. Such allegations have been made in the past."

"It would have been coveted by the Dark Knights," Alynthia said, her voice lowered with disappointment. "Perhaps it was taken by the Lord Knight, Sir Kinsaid, before you had a chance to inventory it?"

"As far as I know, Sir Kinsaid took nothing from the scene that was not shown to me first, for historical purposes. In fact, Sir Kinsaid himself went to great pains to see that every item was carefully catalogued and recorded for posterity. I doubt he would have taken anything without my knowledge. There are many things about Sir Kinsaid that are questionable, but I believe he is sincere about preserving history."

Alynthia stared in mute appeal at the elf, but he merely shook his head as if to say, You knew this was hopeless from the start. She turned back to Brother Bertrem.

"We thank you for your assistance, old man," she said with a disappointed sigh.

"You are welcome. What use is all this knowledge if it is not shared?" he asked.

"We should have asked you earlier," Cael said.

Brother Bertrem rose, eager for the thieves to be gone, eager to get back to his bed. "Shall I show you the way out?"

"We know the way," Alynthia said.

"You may use the front door. I will let you out," Brother Bertrem said. "After all, you seek knowledge, the same as other visitors to the Great Library."

With a weary shrug, the two thieves rose and followed the elderly Aesthetic as he led them from the room.

* * * * *

Alynthia paused on the steps of the Great Library and looked back at the door as it closed behind them. "We could continue to search. It is possible he overlooked something," she said.

"Not likely," Cael answered. "He seems honest and wise to a fault."

"What are we going to do, then?"

"Retrieve my staff. That's the bargain, isn't it? Afterwards, we'll leave this city once and for all. Krynn is a wide world. Palanthas isn't the center of it." Cael's words felt hollow. He felt no more real desire to leave Palanthas than to leave Alynthia.

Alynthia gasped, appalled by the idea, "Leave Palanthas! Leave the Guild?"

"The Guild has already abandoned you," Cael retorted. "Even your own husband betrayed you. Why do you cling to it so?"

"My husband and the Guild are all I have, Cael," she cried. "The Guild is my family. My husband has his faults, but he is wily, and maybe he has some plan in mind. The men and women under his command have been brothers and sisters to me. Do you know how it would feel to forfeit all that?"

"I suppose not," Cael bitterly commented. "Seeing as how I've never had a family to lose."

Alynthia took his hand and pulled it close. "All the more reason to rejoin the Guild. The Guild will protect us, give us a home. The Guild is family, kith and kin, people we can depend on, even for the protection of our lives."

"They want to kill us!" Cael snapped.

"Please, Cael," Alynthia cried.

He looked in her dark eyes. Facing innumerable dangers did not frighten the beautiful captain of thieves, but the thought of losing the Guild terrified her beyond description.

"Very well," he sighed.

She smiled, pulling him close.

"First, my staff," he finished.

At her dark look, he said, "You promised. The Reliquary is a hopeless quest. Now we get my staff. After that, I will stop at nothing to help you regain your place in your precious Guild."

"*Our* precious Guild," she corrected, taking his hand and leading him down the stairs to the street below. They turned toward the rising sun and hurried away.

A pair of eyes followed their progress until they were out of sight. Then the owner of those eyes, a red-robed sorceress, stepped from an alley across the street and turned west, toward the Shoikan Grove and the Three Moons shop.

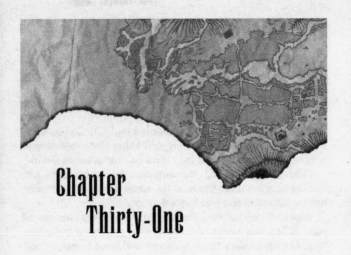

Chapter
Thirty-One

Footsteps receded down the hall, leaving the passage in quiet shadows. Alynthia peered out from a curtained alcove, making certain that everyone had gone, before stepping out from the hiding place where she and Cael had just spent the better part of five hours waiting for Arach Jannon to leave his study. The door leading to the Thorn Knight's chambers was visible from the alcove, and Sir Arach had just hurried down the hall, called away to some important late night meeting by a palace page. Alynthia and Cael had wondered if he would ever leave, and they were becoming concerned that the mage might sleep in his underground study and laboratory, deep beneath the lord mayor's palace, rather than in the upper chambers indicated on Alynthia's detailed floor plan as the bedchamber of the lord high justice.

Their acquisition of the map had neither come easily nor quickly. They had spent an interminable eight days waiting while Claret scoured the markets of Palanthas, finally finding a copy in a bibliophile's shop on Windsong Street. During those eight days, Cael had nearly climbed the walls with impatience.

Sir Arach's laboratory lay deep beneath the Lord's Palace. The chambers and passages leading to them were discovered during the construction of the first Lord's Palace. As the passages connected directly to the sewers, the lord at that time ordered these entrances blocked. Not long afterward, the Thieves' Guild had cleared it, replacing the wall with one of their own devising, one with a door only they could find. Their entrance into this hallway came by way of that ancient, not-so-blocked-up passage connecting to the sewers. Alynthia knew about the door, of course, and she knew how to spot it and open it. She had been taught this by her husband, Oros uth Jakar, but she had never actually been here. Still, after only a half dozen attempts, she had managed to open the door.

Now, as she stepped out from the alcove and motioned for Cael to follow, she once more removed the parchment document from her pouch and, by the light of a nearby torch, examined the layout of the lord's palace. The level of detail of the document was impressive, for it showed not only the visible rooms, but the hidden ones as well. In addition, all exits and doorways, both mundane and secret were also described.

Cael stepped out from the alcove and joined her in studying the floor plan. "Here is Sir Arach's laboratory," she said, indicating it first on the map and then by pointing to a door a short distance down the hall.

"Let's go then," Cael said.

"Wait! We dare not try the door. It's probably warded. Remember what happened at Mistress Jenna's? We have no magic to dispel the wards," Alynthia said.

"How will we get in?"

"There is a secret door here," she said, tracing the symbol on the paper with her finger. "I doubt even *he* knows about it. If we are lucky, it won't even be locked. But if it is . . ." She smiled beneath her mask and patted the pouch at her belt.

She continued. "From there, a short hall and another secret door. This lets directly into the laboratory. Let's hope it isn't blocked by a stone table or fixed cabinet."

"Or guarded," Cael added.

Alynthia pouched her map and then slipped down the passage, moving by habit from torch's shadow to torch's shadow, while the elf paced noiselessly behind her. They passed one door that stood ajar, open onto empty darkness, a storeroom perhaps. Next they passed the door through which Sir Arach had exited moments before. Now Alynthia slowed and allowed her fingertips to gently brush the stone wall. This passage was deep underground, one of the many secret vaults and treasuries beneath the lord's palace. The wall was cut from the limestone bedrock that underlay the entire city, carved by patient dwarven hands more than twenty-five centuries ago. Here and there a crack marred the otherwise polished surface, evidence of the destruction of the first Cataclysm, when the gods hurled a fiery mountain upon Krynn, destroying the gleaming city of Istar, creating new seas and draining old ones. Not even Palanthas, beloved of Paladine, City of Seven Circles, was left unmarred, though it faired better than most. The dwarves have a saying—heroes live and die, trees grow tall and wither, and all are soon enough forgotten, but stone never forgets. Palanthas the fair might forget the Cataclysm, her bards might no longer sing of its horror and tragedy, but the stone on which she was built still bore the scars of that day.

Cael paused to look at the marred stone, wondering at its age. Once more, as on that morning of the Spring Dawning festival, he felt a great love for this city surge through him, and he found himself loath to leave it despite the dangers. Palanthas the Ancient was perhaps the city's best epithet, he thought. Few other works of human hands had endured so long or so gloriously.

Alynthia tugged at his sleeve. "What are you doing?" she asked. "The secret door is over here!"

"I forgot about the secret door," he answered dreamily.

"What is wrong with you?" she hissed.

"Nothing," he answered, pulling himself together. "Have you found it?"

"Yes. Now come on."

He allowed himself to be drawn another ten yards down the hall, to a place where the wall was breached by a small portal hardly tall enough for a kender to pass.

Alynthia ducked through without explaining how she had found the door. By the look of it, when closed it was probably indistinguishable from the wall. Such was often the case with dwarven construction. Cael followed her into the low passage beyond, pausing only to close the secret door behind him.

The passage was filled with such darkness as is only known in the deep places of the earth. The walls of the tunnel felt close, the air stale as though it had not been stirred in a thousand years. A little dust of the ages, raised by their shuffling passage, made them cough. Before long, the passage turned right, and after a dozen feet ended. Alynthia felt along the wall until she found the release. With a quiet snap, the tunnel's end opened a crack. Alynthia pushed against it, and it swung open with hardly a sound. They crept into the room beyond.

Not even the treasure chamber of Mistress Jenna could compare to the magical laboratory and study of Arach Jannon, Knight of the Thorn. Along the further wall and flanking an iron door that looked heavy enough to defy the stoutest battering ram, stood bookshelves sagging under the weight of magical tomes, encyclopedias, and spellbooks. No doubt, the Thorn Knight had been confiscating them from travelers and visitors to Palanthas for years. In their presence, one felt a strange uneasiness, for although magic was gone from Krynn, many of the books still contained hidden power.

Along the wall to the left stood a complete alchemical laboratory, replete with beakers, jars, urns, crocks, braziers, kettles, chafing dishes, retorts, crucibles, and alembics, all atop a large flat marble table whose entire surface was scored by acids of varying strengths. On a smaller table behind it stood a rack of mortars, pestles, probes, tubes, straws, spoons, spatulas, droppers, sifters, grinders, and various other implements for the measuring and preparing of reagents. Beside the marble table, a large, black rendering caldron dangled from a chain that was suspended over a fire-blackened pit in the floor. In this pot stood Cael's staff, its lower third soaking in a roiling, viscous liquid that glowed a sickly shade of green and boiled even though no fire heated it.

With a little cry of dismay, Cael leaped across the room and snatched his staff from the caldron. Droplets of the weird green fluid fell hissing on the floor, but the staff appeared undamaged. Cael carefully wiped it clean with a rag he found on the conjuring table, then tossed the rag into a corner. It began to smoke, and a strange stink filled the air.

"I wonder what that stuff is!" Alynthia pondered aloud as she peered into the caldron. The green liquid had ceased boiling. Now only an occasional large slow bubble burst to the surface.

"I wonder what was on that rag," Cael coughed. "Gods, what a smell! Let's get out of here."

As they ducked through the secret door and closed it behind them, the smoldering rag erupted into purplish flame.

* * * * *

Alynthia and Cael hurried silently along the passageway, back toward the sewer entrance. As they neared the doorway, Cael grabbed his companion and pulled her back down the hall. The ancient door was ajar. They ducked into the curtained alcove just as the door swung wide. They dared not even look out to see who approached.

They had no need. The voice that echoed down the passage was one both thieves knew well. It was a voice neither masculine nor feminine, a voice as harsh and cold as the black void between the stars.

"Wait here for my return," Mulciber growled.

A pair of voices assented in whispers. The door closed with a muffled click. Brisk footsteps quickly approached, passing outside the curtain behind which the two thieves hid, and continued down the passage in the direction Sir Arach had taken.

Slapping back Alynthia's attempts to stop him, Cael parted the curtain and peered out. What he saw made him start, and brought a soft gasp from his companion as she, unable to resist, ducked in front of the elf to have a look for herself.

This was no wizened archmage creeping along bent over a cane and with breath rattling like someone dragging a coffin from a tomb. The person beneath those long black robes and hood was huge, a veritable bear, with a brisk stride and vigorous swing of the arms. It wasn't a "she," it was a "he" who disappeared into the darkness of distance, his footsteps echoing.

"Mulciber is no more a woman than I am a dwarf," Cael whispered.

"I think you are right," Alynthia agreed, with frowning eyes. "Let's follow her . . . him," she said.

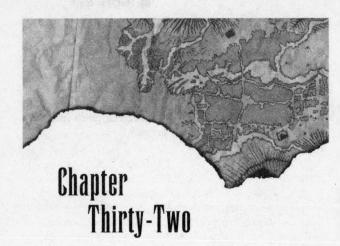

Chapter
Thirty-Two

Let's have another look at your map," Cael whispered. They had followed the sound of Mulciber's footsteps for some time, and the passage had gone on straight as a swordblade through the solid rock for many more steps than either thief remembered seeing on the map. A quick glance at the floor plan confirmed their suspicions. They were now in some new construction, one that probably began at that staircase they had passed a minute ago, one that wasn't covered on the map. Mulciber's footsteps led this way, and they were determined to follow.

As Alynthia folded up the map and stowed it in a pouch, Cael asked, "What would Mulciber be doing here?"

His beautiful companion shrugged, her dark eyes filled with worry, but she did not voice her thoughts. Instead, she hurried onward, her soft boots making little sound as she walked. Cael followed.

Eventually, the passage brought them to a crossroads. Directly ahead, the passage sloped upward, illuminated at regular intervals by torches set into the walls. To the left, a stairway descended steeply into darkness. To the right, another passage joined this one. They paused, listening, but were unable to determine the direction of the echoing footsteps. Alynthia swore softly in indecision.

"I don't like the feel of those stairs," Cael said as he peered into the darkness. "There's a lion's den smell about them."

"Straight ahead, then," Alynthia said. "That way, at least, is lit by torches."

They hurried up the slope. Cael, the taller of the two and likely to be the first to spot anything ahead, now took the lead. The slope only took them a short distance, no more than a bowshot, before it leveled out again. In the distance, a brighter light shone between thick pillars. They slowed their steps, cautiously approaching the end of the passage and entering a cavernous chamber brightly lit from above.

They found themselves on a pillared balcony overlooking a wide circular arena. The floor was scattered with straw, and beside some of the pillars stood barrels of tools: long brooms and brushes, mops, and rakes. Numerous cedar buckets, most of them filled with water, were stacked near the balcony's edge. Also near the edge stood a pair of fine, tooled-leather dragon-saddles.

Clearly, they were still underground, but this place could well have served as a coliseum, had there been seats for the spectators. Instead, there was only the one balcony, six pillars deep around its entire circumference. Twenty feet below the balcony was a sawdust floor ringed by a stone wall. Into the wall had been cut numerous tall archways, which, by their darkness, spoke of cavernous chambers beyond. Above, the stone arched in a great dome, the top of which was covered by a peaked wooden roof. Magical globes of light floated and hovered about the massive chamber, some meandering among the pillars of the balcony, others gliding mere inches from the floor. One or two bumped about the wooden roof as though trying to find an escape.

The air here had a peculiar reek to it. It was a stable-smell: hay and sawdust, leather and grease, saddle soap. There was, however, no odor of horses. Rather, something more pungent pierced the air, sharper in the nostrils, an ozone smell, and the coppery smell of fear. The two thieves paused for a moment, nodding to one another in silent realization of where they were. This was the Dark Knights' dragon stable. The place was nothing more than a rumor on the streets of Palanthas, but those rumors spoke of a place where blue dragons were housed, ready to fly to war at a moment's notice. Rumors also said that wyverns, the small vicious cousins of true dragons, were kept here to fly as couriers to any region of Ansalon.

Warily now, realizing the true extent of their danger, Cael crept up to the edge of the balcony. At first, the room had appeared empty, but as he gazed over the ledge, he saw that the black-robed master of the Thieves' Guild was standing directly below him, his arms folded across his massive chest. Alynthia slid up beside Cael to view their great leader. Her dark eyes burned as she gazed down at Mulciber.

She recoiled, pulling the elf away from the edge of the balcony. From beneath a darkened arch opposite the chamber where Mulciber stood, two Dark Knights appeared. One wore the black armor of a Knight of the Lily, the other the gray robes of a Thorn Knight. The two stopped just beneath the arch, one resting a gauntleted hand on the pommel of his long sword, the other folding his hands into his robes.

Even from this distance, Alynthia and Cael recognized the Knights. Sir Kinsaid's eyes gleamed like agates as he stared across the chamber at the dark-robed figure of Mulciber, while Arach Jannon's narrow visage peered out from the depths of his gray hood.

Alynthia trembled as her fingers dug painfully into the elf's shoulder. "Will there be a fight?" she whispered in his pointed ear. "Should we help Mulciber?"

From below came Sir Kinsaid's thundering voice. "It has been a long time since last we met, Avaril," the Lord Knight said.

Alynthia stiffened at these words, all the illusion draining from her eyes.

"Aye," came the answer, a deep voice, no longer the harsh, vaguely feminine croak of Mulciber.

"Oros!" Cael hissed. He pried himself from Alynthia's frozen grasp and crawled to the edge of the balcony, but he feared to draw too near lest the Dark Knights spot him. He backed away until he reached the shadows of the columns, leaving Alynthia huddled on the floor, staring dumbly at her own hands.

As he ghosted among the columns, circling the huge chamber, the conversation continued below.

"The same deal as before, old friend?" asked Sir Arach. "You turn over everyone, and in exchange, you take your pick of the treasures."

"Aye," the dark-robed figure answered grimly. "It's a cycle of nature."

"Everyone," the Thorn Knight reaffirmed. "Including the elf and his accomplice."

Cael crept through the shadowy columns to the edge of the balcony.

The dark-robed figure pulled back his cowl, revealing the ashen face of the Captain of the Eighth Circle of the Guild. He swallowed, then nodded his assent. "What must be must be," Oros said. "I have never been one to shrink from the hard realities."

"What will you offer to assure your cooperation?" Sir Kinsaid growled. Possibly, he was as disgusted by the thief's betrayal as was Cael. "This time I will brook no return of the Guild. This time, it ends."

Oros opened his robe and swung a heavy bag forward, dropping it with a metallic thud on the floor. Cael crept closer to the edge of the balcony.

"Coins?" the Lord Knight of Palanthas laughed without mirth. "Is that the limit of your imagination? With all the treasures in your hoard, you bring coins. You underestimate me, *Captain Oros,*" he ended sarcastically.

"I do apologize, my Lord," said the black-hooded figure.

An angry Cael looked back along the curve of the balcony and saw Alynthia staring at him, silent tears soaking her mask. As quickly as it had come, now, his anger cooled. He knew his place was beside her. He began to edge away to safety.

At the same time, the staff in his hand began to vibrate. The vibration rose to a barely heard hum and then to an audible buzz.

"What is that noise?" Sir Arach asked sharply.

What indeed? Cael wondered. The buzzing grew steadily louder while he crept back to the columns as rapidly and stealthily as his elven feet could hustle.

"I know that noise," a voice thundered from beneath his feet. "All my kind know that sound. We hear it in our darkest nightmares. It is the sound of a sword of power!"

Numbing fear swept over the elf. Looking round in horror, he saw Oros stagger back, throwing up his arms as though to ward off a blow. Sir Kinsaid and Sir Arach backed away from something emerging from the archway below Cael. The Thorn Knight scoured the room for the source of the buzzing noise even as the dragon emerged from its stable.

"The elf!" Sir Arach shouted as he caught sight of his quarry, frozen with dragonfear atop the balcony.

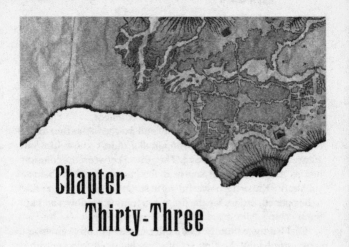

Chapter
Thirty-Three

The staff leaped in Cael's hands as the dragon's head came into view. Great curving ivory horns guarded a noble, evil brow. Azure scales glittering in the magical light of the globes overhead, the creature crept into the arena, its claws scrabbling at the sawdust covered stone floor.

At the movement of the staff, Cael felt the dragonfear drop from him like a cloak. Clutching the head of the staff in one hand, he ran the other down the length of the staff. Where his hand passed, a gleaming steel blade replaced black wood. The blade was straight and double-edged and gleamed with a green light, as though lit by an inner source.

A deep rumbling shook the castle to its foundations. Every window in the palace above shattered. Throughout its hundreds of rooms and hallways vases tumbled from their pedestals, framed paintings fell from walls, and crockery tumbled from shelves. Those in the chamber were thrown to the floor, but Cael managed to keep his feet. The Knights cried out in fright, and the voice of the blue dragon boiled over the noise.

"Are we under attack?" The terrible voice of the blue dragon rose above the din.

Two guards stumbled through an archway. "My lords, fire in the cellars, a great explosion!"

"My laboratory!" Sir Arach shrieked as he forgot everything else and leaped up and raced from the chamber.

Cael dashed across the balcony and dragged Alynthia to her feet. She stared at him as though she didn't know him but allowed him to pull her along. They dived between the columns just as a lightning bolt smashed the balcony behind them to rubble. Sir Kinsaid's powerful voice shouted orders for the roof to be opened, orders for the dragon to hunt them down and kill them.

Cael led them blindly. The explosion had cut off their escape route, so he took the first set of stairs he could find and raced up them, Alynthia in his wake. They entered the main levels of the lord's palace as chaos swept the corridors. Servants dashed here and there, screaming conflicting directions to either save the palace treasures or fight the fire. Most chose instead to save themselves and ran heedless of the pleading of their fellows through any door or window they could find. It was a simple enough matter for the elf and his companion to blend into this confusion, except for the sword gleaming in his fist. Wherever they ran, whomever they encountered screamed and fled in the opposite direction.

Cael spotted a door leading out into a garden. He turned in that direction, where many servants were pressed into the doorway, trying to escape the palace. With a shout, he charged into them, brandishing his weirdly glowing blade high above his head. In less than a heartbeat, the way was cleared as the servants dispersed, screaming. Cael pulled Alynthia through the door, then shoved her aside as a sword whistled between them and crashed in sparks against the stone floor. Cael parried a second slash with his blade, then reversed the attack with a thrust that sent a guard staggering back, his breath gurgling through the hole in his chest. At a cry from Alynthia, Cael spun, barely knocking aside the attack of a second guard. The guard continued his onslaught with an overhand swing, which Cael caught but seemed unlikely to hold. The guard laughed cruelly as he pressed down. The two blades scraped against each other as the guard tried to overpower the elf, forcing him to his knees.

Cael disengaged his blade and lunged aside. With a deft twist, he sent the guard's sword spinning away to land with a rustle among a clump of bushes, thirty yards away.

A third guard charged from the shadows. Cael turned, letting a poorly aimed thrust slip past his chest. He brought his own blade up, cutting through mail and flesh to grate against the man's spine. The guard fell with a groan against the wall.

The elf spun, finding the second guard with a dagger in his raised fist. The man collapsed toward him, dropping his dagger, clawing at the one sprouting from his back. Alynthia had finally come to her senses. Now she rushed to Cael's side and dragged her blade from the man's body.

"Let's get out of here," she snarled to the elf.

They flew off through the night-darkened gardens of the lord's palace.

At this late hour, there ought to have been few people about. Though at first they saw no attackers, Cael and Alynthia did hear arrows and crossbow bolts whistling and smashing through the trees above and around them. Pandemonium reigned. In the palace behind them, many of the windows glowed with light. Bells rang out stridently from various quarters of the city. Shouts could be heard and torches seen within the garden itself.

The two thieves halted under the shadow of a leaning oak near the edge of the gardens, at the corner of Horizon Road and Lord's Way. Through the trees ahead, they could see the gleaming lights of the Temple of Paladine, the grounds of which occupied the opposite corner of this usually busy intersection. However, at this time of night, the streets were deserted and dark.

"What happened back there?" Alynthia asked as she stripped off her cloak and dark trousers, revealing the street clothes beneath.

"Which do you mean? With me or the sword?" Cael asked. He passed his hand down the length of the blade, returning it to its ordinary staff form, then leaned it against the trunk of the tree.

"Both!" she snapped. "Are you really that stupid, or were you just trying to get us killed? That was a dragon!"

"Yes I know."

"So, what happened?"

"I never really believed it. My *shalifi* told me that when the sea elves gave him this staff, they said that it was made at the same time as the sword once owned by Tanis Half-Elven, that it was made in Silvanost during the second Dragon War, and that of the three great swords of that time, this one was the most powerful."

"What do legends have to do with anything?" Alynthia asked.

"Have you never listened to the songs of the bards?" Cael said in dismay. "The tale of the Sla-Mori and the rescue of Pax Tharkas?"

"What about it?"

Cael sighed. "In the Sla-Mori, it is said, Tanis either found or was given by the dead hand of the great elf king, Kith-Kanan, the sword known as Wyrmslayer. It was the buzzing of this sword when it was brought too close that awoke the dragon Flamestrike."

"So?" Alynthia queried.

"My sword buzzed!" Cael almost shouted. "In the presence of a dragon." He tossed aside his mask and ran his fingers through his beard, brushing it out.

Alynthia shook her head. "There is only one way out of the Old City now—the docks. We cannot pass the gates at this hour, especially not with the alarm raised."

"We could use Claret's tunnel," Cael suggested.

"They blocked it up after your capture."

"To the docks then."

A deep rumble shook the ground, setting the trees to swaying. "Another explosion," Cael said. They looked back through the trees, half-expecting to see the towers of the palace crumbling, flames leaping into the night sky. Instead, they saw a gargantuan shadow rise above the palace. Great leathern wings spread wide to gather the air as it soared upward from some hidden place beyond the trees.

"Gods, what a dragon!" Cael sighed in awe.

Alynthia tugged madly at his sleeve, but the elf seemed rooted to the spot, spellbound.

"So terrible. So beautiful," he muttered.

With a grace that belied its massive size, the dragon's massive wings beat once, twice, lifting it slowly higher. The wind from those wings struck them seconds later with a force like a gale. Trees around them cracked and crashed. Cael sidestepped a falling branch that would have crushed him like a fly. He turned and found Alynthia lying on the ground, blood pouring from a cut above her eye. She stared around in a daze. He helped her to rise.

"What happened?" she asked thickly.

"Can you run?" he asked.

"I think so," she responded.

He grabbed his staff, and together they lurched from the trees and into the street. Above and behind them, thunder growled in the cloudless sky as a shadow rose above Palanthas.

They hurried across the street and into the dark safety of an alley, Cael running, Alynthia stumbling behind him, pulled along by his hand on her elbow. Because he did not know the way, he followed no planned course. Instead, he tried to steer them north according to his best guess. Alynthia said nothing. Whenever they paused, she shook her head as though trying to clear the fog in her mind.

Far overhead the shadow followed them ominously. The city, raised in alarm by the explosions at the palace, now cowered in fear. Screams of terror pierced the night. As Cael and Alynthia scurried through alley, court, and garden, people looked out in terror from their windows, their eyes searching the dark starry skies. Lightning arced across the heavens, thunder boomed, and the ground shook. Fierce winds ripped down street and alley, carrying with it a tide of trash and leaves, dust and sand, stinging the eye and cutting the flesh with its ferocity. Ever and again, a shadow passed between them and the stars above, blotting out the waning moon, a shadow that bellowed and roared like a whirlwind.

Still, somehow, Cael got them to the waterfront. With the northern way now blocked by the sea, Cael turned west. They raced along the docksides where captains bellowed orders to their frightened crews and dockmasters were racing about, battening down cargoes or staring in terror at the sky.

Alynthia jerked Cael to a stop. "This way," she shouted. To their right, a long pier jutted out into the bay. Along it, ships hailing from the farthest corners of Krynn were docked. "Blue Crab Pier. My husband's ship. We'll hide there," she said.

"We can't go there," Cael argued. "He's already betrayed us once."

"We've nowhere else to turn," she said, pointing to the sky above. "If he is a traitor, the dragon will not hasten to burn his ship down. Think of it as a temporary measure," she countered.

With a shrug, the elf leaped up the steps and raced along the pier.

"Which one?" he asked as they ran. To their right and left, the hulls of ships rose up, their masts and beams towering like the trees of a forest. At regular intervals along the pier stood lamp poles, and as the two thieves raced along the pier, the lamps began to toss madly in a rising wind, sending shadows chasing each other crazily up and down the hulls of the ships.

Alynthia stumbled to a halt and stared around. Then, pointing over at another pier, she shouted, "There, where those crates are piled! *Dark Horizon!* They must have shifted anchor. It looks as if they're loading her for a voyage! We'll circle back."

"Too late!" Cael cried.

Glancing over her shoulder, Alynthia saw the dragon starting to glide down. Though it was still far away, they had only moments left. The dragon's malevolent gaze turned their bones to water as the great beast banked round and leveled off. Now it tucked up its wings and dropped.

"Run!" Cael shouted as he pulled her after him.

Slowly at first, and then faster, her feet began to fly. She ran faster than she'd ever run before, but still it was difficult to keep pace with the elf. It was speed born of terror.

Terror became horror. She saw the end of the pier ahead. "Trapped" she shrieked.

"Into the sea!" Cael shouted in answer. "Grab my staff. Don't let go."

Without slowing they reached the pier's end and leaped. Cael sailed out ahead of her and struck the water. Alynthia crashed after him, feet first. She struggled to the surface and gasped for air. The water was black and cold as the grave.

Hands grasped her ankles and dragged her under. She struggled, fighting to kick free. She drew her dagger and lashed out, but still the hands pulled. Down, down she sank, the golden light from the pier's lamps fading. Replacing it was a greenish glow. Something cold and hard touched her face. She clutched at it, and then she saw in the weird glow the face of the elf, his long hair floating about his head like the fronds of a sea plant. His jaws gaped and closed, as though he were breathing the water. He held her, and held the staff in her hands.

The need for air grew too great. Blood pounded in her ears, her chest began to heave for want of breath. He shook his head and gripped her tighter to hold her under, but she struggled free of him, her fear of drowning lending her the strength of an ogre. She thrust for the surface, seeing the golden light growing stronger.

A light like a thousand suns burst before her eyes. The water around her exploded, the air was driven from her lungs in an agonized scream. She was propelled backward, downward.

The sea closed round her with its dark, cold, deadly embrace.

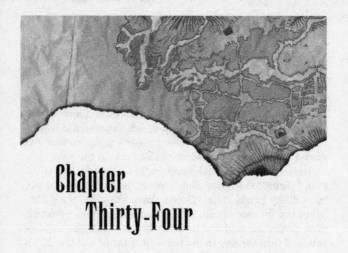

Chapter Thirty-Four

Cael dragged Alynthia's limp body ashore beneath Blue Crab Pier, down amongst the piles and the scurrying blue crabs. He laid her gently on the pebbly shore, kneeling beside her as he lowered her head to the ground. He bent over, opened his mouth, and exhaled enough seawater to fill a bucket, retching it out in one long groan. The first thing that his master taught him about the ironstaff was that it gave him the ability to breath water as readily as air, but the transition was always a painful one, something he avoided when he could.

At last, he threw his head back, his lank, wet red hair whipping across his back, and filled his lungs with air. Again. Again, drinking in the salty air, until finally he began to cough, clearing his lungs of the last remnants of the sea.

He turned his attention to his companion. She lay before him, her flesh chill, her lips blue, eyelids parted to reveal her dark eyes, now dull, staring blankly at nothing. He felt no lifebeat when his fingers touched her neck. His coughs turned to sobs. His hair fell across his face, hiding his features from her unblinking stare.

When the blue dragon breathed its lightning breath into the water, the blast had stunned Alynthia. Cael had felt the staff absorb much of the energy just as it had done with Mistress Jenna's spell. Now, he berated himself, blamed himself for letting go of Alynthia, for not holding her beneath the water while the dragon attacked. By the time he had reached her, she had already filled her lungs with water

Now, as he looked at her, he saw in his mind the faces of all the others who had been killed on his account. He saw Pitch's charred remains heaped against the wall of the Chamber of Doors. He saw Hoag turned to stone and Ijus blasted by Mistress Jenna's magic, Kharzog with a sword through his old dwarven bellows, Gimzig gripped in the jaws of a sewer monster, and Claret's entire family pulled apart and destroyed. Now, one more life was added to this score, one more innocent victim of his games, and this one, he realized, grieved him more than all the others, even more than Kharzog. If only he had stayed by Alynthia's side while in the dragon stables of the Lord's Palace, if only he had not let her struggle free of the staff, if only the dragon hadn't blasted the depths of the sea with its lightning breath.

With a scream of rage, he unleashed his sword. He stormed about beneath the pier, sending blue crabs scurrying in every direction, slashing heedlessly at everything around him. His magical blade passed through braces, supports, ropes, and even through a wooden pile supporting the pier. Only when the pier began to creak ominously, after many of its supports lay in chunks along the shore or bobbed in the surf, did his anger begin to subside. Still the pain remained.

He returned to Alynthia's side, tossing his sword on the ground beside her. "She will not die," her growled. He knelt at her side again, placing one hand beneath her neck and lifting it slightly, tilted back her head, which caused her lips to part. He'd seen his mother do this a dozen times. A dozen times she'd saved the lives of shipwrecked sailors in this manner. He wasn't even sure if he knew how to do it properly. But he had to try.

"You will not die, Alynthia Krath-Mal," he whispered as his placed his lips over her cold blue ones. He covered her eyes with his hand, at the same time pinching together her nostrils, then breathed forcibly into her mouth, puffing out her cheeks.

He lifted, inhaling, and listened to the air escape her lips in a sad parody of breathing. "Come back to me," he whispered again, returning his lips to hers. Again her cheeks puffed.

"Come back to me." Again. Again.

He continued, continued on past the moment when hope failed, grimly past the moment when it began to seem a sacrilege, when his conscience told him to leave her body in peace. He continued, with each breath whispering, "Come back to me, my love."

As he bent to her lips yet one more time, she blinked. He paused, waiting, hope renewing, searching her dull eyes for a flicker of life. It came, dimly, but it came. He blew into her mouth again, felt her twitch, and when his breath escaped her lips this time, with it came a bubble of seawater. She coughed. He rolled her on her side, letting her retch the fluid from her lungs, gently patting her back, and holding her in his arms until she had finished.

* * * * *

The place was called The Bone and Four, which was short for the Bone and Four Skulls. Above the door hung a battered wooden sign painted with these symbols. Cael kicked open the door and lurched into the room, carrying over his shoulders what appeared to be a large wet bundle, and leaning heavily on his staff.

"We're closed, mate," said a man behind the bar. "After curfew." Another man rose from the end of the bar, his head bumping among the low rafters. He was fully seven feet tall, and his sallow yellowish skin identified him as having ogrish parentage. He clenched a pair of warty, ham-sized fists and growled.

"Plus, the dragon's about," the first man added.

Cael merely stared at the two for a moment, then shut the

door with his staff. The common room was small, having only a few tables and booths, but at most of these sat wretched-looking men in various stages of debauchery. Not a few snored with heads sunk onto folded arms. The place was remarkably quiet. It seemed most of the patrons were content to wallow in their private miseries.

"Closed. Right," the elf snorted, but there was no mirth in his laugh. He struggled to an empty corner booth and, leaning his staff against the wall, lowered his bundle onto one of the benches and shoved it into the corner. He then squeezed in beside the bundle and gently pushed aside the wet blankets in which it was wrapped. A face, dusky but drawn, with sunken cheeks and a bluish tinge about the lips, appeared from the folds.

The innkeeper shrugged, and the ogre resumed his seat.

A barmaid approached Cael's booth. "Brandy," he barked, as he chafed Alynthia's cold hands between his own. "And a dry blanket, if you have one."

Soon, the brandy was brought, and a new blanket was wrapped around Alynthia's shoulders. The barmaid stood by, watching him try to warm his companion.

"She's pretty. What happened to her?" the girl asked. "Did she fall overboard?"

"That's right," Cael said, while pouring a little of the warm liquor between Alynthia's lips. She coughed and stirred, blinked, then grasped the cup held to her lips and tilted it back. Brandy flowed in runnels down her cheeks as she gulped the fierce liquid.

"Are you a sailor?" the barmaid asked.

"I've sailed the sea, if that's what you mean."

Alynthia set the cup down and leaned over the table. Her back heaved as she wretched up more seawater. Cael hovered over her tenderly.

"Is she your woman?" the barmaid asked.

"You ask too many questions, girl," Cael said.

"Because if she isn't . . ."

"How old are you?" Cael asked.

"I've seen nineteen summers," the girl boasted.

"I am old enough to be your grandfather," he said as he pushed back the wet tangle of his hair, revealing one pointed elven ear. The girl gasped.

"Go and fetch some more brandy and hot food if you have it," he commanded.

"I couldn't eat," Alynthia groaned.

The girl squeaked a quick "Yes sir!" and dashed away.

"How do you feel?" Cael asked as Alynthia sat up, somewhat recovered. Her lips still bore a bluish tinge. She shivered with cold.

"Like a netted codfish," she joked feebly. Her teeth chattered.

"More brandy will fix that," Cael said as he turned to look for the barmaid. The girl hurried from the kitchen, bearing a jug and two steaming bowls. She slid these onto the table and turned to go. Cael grabbed the hem of her dress.

"Thank you," he said to the girl.

She blushed and performed a small curtsey, then hurried away.

Alynthia shook her head bemusedly, then turned to the food. She sniffed at it, then groaned and leaned back. "I really don't think I could," she complained.

Cael poured them each a brimming cup of warm brandy. "Drink this," he said, pushing it into her hands. She drank it down in quick sips, and by the time the cup was empty, her chattering and shivering had ceased. She set the cup on the table for Cael to pour more, then sniffed at the stew.

Cael lifted the heavy crockery jug, then set it down with a gasp of pain. He clutched his right shoulder.

"What's wrong?" Alynthia asked.

"It's nothing," he said through clenched teeth.

"Nothing, my eye. Let me see." She pushed his hands aside and peeled back his wet tunic to expose his shoulder. What she found there made her start back and gasp.

"It's only a scratch," the elf said as he eyed the gash in his shoulder. A little blood trickled between the ragged white edges of the wound.

"A scratch!" she exclaimed as she gingerly examined it.

"Why, it goes right down to the bone. You are lucky it didn't slice the artery. How did it happen?"

"An Ergothian she-shark, I'd say," Cael said.

"I . . . I did this?" Alynthia asked incredulously.

"Aye, my captain," the elf answered. "When you thought I was a lacedon dragging you to your watery grave."

"Oh, Cael, I'm sorry," she cried. "And you saved me after that!"

"I thought it was your corpse I was hauling ashore," the elf whispered. "I'm sure we're both taken for dead. The dragon breathed a bolt of lightning into the water above us. You should have seen all the dead fish. There'll be a glut in the market tomorrow morning."

"This wound needs stitching," Alynthia said, trying to change the subject.

"We'll not find a sawbones at this hour," Cael said. "Best wait until morning. Then we'll find Claret and leave the city."

"Leave the city?" Alynthia asked.

"There's nothing else to be done. Your husband is in league with the Knights. He plans to betray the Guild to them, just as he must have done four years ago."

"I don't believe it," Alynthia muttered. "It seems like a dream, a horrible dream."

"Believe it, young lady," said a gravely voice from the next booth. A wizened head, wrinkled as a dried apricot and of nearly the same hue, appeared over the top of the partition. A surly gray beard grew in patches along his sunken cheeks, and one eye was covered in a milky white sheath that oozed a thick tear. But the other eyed glittered at them.

"You believe your young friend, Alynthia Krath-Mal. He sees your husband for what he is!" the old man cackled.

"Do I know you?" Alynthia haughtily asked, but there was a note of uncertainty in her voice. A troubled shadow darkened her eyes.

"Aye, you know me," the old man said as his head ducked away. A moment later, a lathe-thin old sea dog, dressed in an oiled otterskin coat and bending over a cane carved from a whale's bone, slid onto the bench opposite them. He smiled a huge toothless grin that set his good eye sparkling with mirth. He then pointed at Cael's cup. The elf slid the brandy across to the old man, a curious expression on his face.

"I'm sorry, but I can't seem to recall . . ." Alynthia slowly said, her words trailing off as the old man reached across the table and set something in front of her. When he pulled his hand away, Alynthia's lips began to tremble.

A tiny dragon made of intricately folded paper stood on the dinted table before her.

"Knodsen?" she cried.

"Aye, my pretty. It's Old Knodsen," the ancient sailor said, a tear springing out from his good eye.

Suddenly, Alynthia was across the table, embracing the old man and sobbing pitifully. A few people lifted their heads and stared, but most ignored them. Cael shifted uncomfortably, unsure of how to react.

Slowly, the old man extricated himself from her arms and pushed her back to her seat. Cael wrapped the blanket close around her shoulders and pressed a brandy into her hands. She gulped at it, not looking at the elf. The old man sipped his, then eyed the bowls of stew. Cael nodded and pushed one of the bowls closer.

"I'm sorry, but I see you two are old friends," Cael began as he rose to leave. Alynthia grabbed his arm and pulled him down again.

Without looking at him, she said, "When I was a little girl, voyaging on my stepfather's ships, Old Knodsen here was the dearest friend a girl ever had." She picked up the little paper dragon and clutched it to her chest. "He used to make these paper animals and leave them all over the ship for me to find. It was a wonderful game. He watched over me. Old Knodsen was father, brother, and playmate to me."

"Aye, that I was," the old man said with a grin.

"But you went down with the *Mary Eileen*," she said accusingly. "Oros . . . er, Captain Avaril told me all hands were lost. Only he survived."

"I was lost," the old man said, his voice far away and his eye staring into the stew. "Lost for years." He shook his head as though refusing to remember. He looked up, a tear in his eye.

"I was taken aboard the minotaur galley, as were others from the *Mary Eileen,* as your Avaril well knows. I was chained to an oar three benches away from him. It grated him to be a galley slave, no better than the men he once commanded, though even then we looked to him to lead us to freedom. He was our captain still.

"He seemed to believe his responsibilities to us ended when the *Mary Eileen* foundered. He made a private deal with the minotaur captain—Kolav was his name—and got himself released from the oar chain. What he traded, I do not know. Likely it was information. We began to raid the northern coast of Solamnia, striking unprotected villages. They had great success, seeming always to hit just after a patrol of Knights of Solamnia had left the villages."

"But then their luck eventually ran out. They were surprised by a fleet of the Knights of Takhisis. The galley was rammed and sunk. Your future husband surrendered, and because he was once a Knight, they didn't execute him."

"Avaril was never a Knight!" Alynthia exclaimed.

"Aye, he was a Knight of the Rose at one time, my dear," the old man said. "That's something very few people know. He was shamed for some reason or other, probably cowardice or betrayal, if I know him at all. If not for his family's influence, he'd probably have been hunted down and executed with his own sword.

"He let his men die aboard that pirate galley, while he saved himself. I'd been working for months on loosening my chain's staple, and when the ship began to sink, her hull staved in by the Knights' ram, I escaped. Fear lent me strength. I couldn't save the others. I couldn't free the others," he cried. "They called my name, begging me to rescue them, but they cursed the name of Avaril. But I was not strong enough to free them, and he abandoned us all.

"When the battle was over, I found myself adrift atop a bit of flotsam, while the Knight's fleet sailed away. Eventually, I washed up on an island in the Blood Sea, and there I lived a haunted life, always in fear, always running. The island was home to shadow wights. Finally, I was rescued, and from there I was able to follow Avaril's career by talking with sailors, pirates, smugglers and the like. They say he purchased his and the minotaur captain's lives by revealing the locations of the treasures they had buried during the months of raiding the coast.

"The Knights put them off in Palanthas, penniless and destitute. He was disgraced as a merchant captain, and no ship's master would trust him. For a while, he made a living as a street illusionist, pulling coins from people's ears and throwing his voice to amaze the ignorant, all the while hating the people he entertained. Eventually, Avaril joined the Thieves' Guild, it is said, and his minotaur companion served as his loyal bodyguard. What keeps the two together I'll never understand. I think Avaril never purchased the minotaur's freedom. I think the Knights of Takhisis released the brute to be a constant reminder of his treachery. 'Tisn't loyalty that drives Captain Kolav Ru-Marn. Because of Avaril, he survived the sinking of his ship and disgraced himself. He can never return to the minotaur homeland."

Alynthia stared blankly at the table, slowly shaking her head. "It can't be true," she muttered. "It's too much to believe."

"Think about it Alynthia," Cael said. "Because you helped me, he has declared you kidnapped. He has betrayed you as well."

"I would have done the same thing to him to protect the Guild. It was I who betrayed him by failing," she argued.

"No, you wouldn't have betrayed him," Cael said. "You haven't betrayed the Guild. You would have done whatever it took to free your husband. Even now, you protect him."

"It was Mulciber's decision," Alynthia said. "Oros is only following Mulciber's orders."

Slowly, Cael nodded. "Yes, I see that now," he said.

"What do you mean?" Alynthia sharply demanded.

"He was only following Mulciber's orders. He isn't the Guildmaster. Mulciber is," he said.

"That's right," Alynthia said. "We all follow Mulciber's orders."

"Who *is* Mulciber?" Cael asked.

"She is the true leader of the Guild."

"From where did she come?"

"No one knows. She first appeared and reformed the Guild after the Night of Black Hammers, recruiting first my husband and then the others to her cause."

"I see," Cael said.

"What do you see?" Alynthia barked.

"The truth," he answered.

"Good. So now you see Oros can't have betrayed me. If he really wanted to kill us, don't you think we'd be dead by now? No, he has only been giving us time to redeem ourselves," she declared. "The gods only know what risks he has taken protecting us."

"Alynthia, my dear sweet Alynthia," Old Knodsen said in a husky voice. "Do you believe that Old Knodsen would lie to you?"

She stared at the old sailor as though he had struck her across the face. Fresh tears trickled down her cheeks. "No," she whispered.

"Listen to your friend," the old man encouraged. "Oros betrayed the crew of the *Mary Eileen*, as he will betray you now."

She looked at Cael. Slowly, her head sank to her chest. "Very well," she sobbed.

"If I were you," the old man said, "I'd leave the city. I am ship's cook aboard the *Albatross*. She sails with tomorrow evening's tide for Kalaman. My captain is a goodly woman. She'll take the both of you upon my word."

"I thank you," Cael said. "We'll be there. Can you take a third, a young girl—"

"No!" Alynthia snapped. "Before I go, I must hear all this from his lips. He owes me that much."

"It is too risky," Cael said. "We dare not confront him. If we are captured—"

"I must do it," she said. "With or without your help. I know his habits like no other. Every night after he dines, he spends several hours in his private library. We'll lie in wait for him

275

there, and question him without his lackeys about. If what you say is true, dear Knodsen, then we can use that information against him to clear our names and regain our places in the Guild."

"Don't be a fool, Alynthia. After what we have heard this night, Oros will try to have us and your friend Knodsen here killed at the first opportunity. As long as we live, we are a threat to him," Cael admonished. "Better he never knows what we have learned about him."

"I will hear the truth from him, come what may!" Alynthia declared. "If it is true that he intends to betray the Guild, we must stop him."

Cael opened his mouth to protest, but the old sailor cut him off. "It's no use arguing with her once she's made up her mind. I should know," he said with a laugh, turning to Alynthia. "Once you've had your say, my dear, come with all speed to the Merchant Harbor, where my ship is waiting. Bring your other young friend, if she is also in danger."

"Dear old Knodsen," she smiled. "Beyond hope I've found you again. Thank you."

"You can thank me best by sailing away with me," he said.

"If there is no other way," Alynthia said, rising, "I promise." She pushed Cael from the booth. "We will be there."

The elf pulled a few wet coins from his pocket and tossed them on the table to pay for the brandy and the stew no one had even tasted.

"Come on," Alynthia said to the elf. "It's late. We must enter his library before Oros retires for the night." Together, they bowed once to the old sailor and exited the inn.

Old Knodsen bent over the no longer steaming bowl of stew and shoveled a spoonful into his toothless mouth. He contentedly gummed the meal, chuckling occasionally to himself, while from one of the other tables rose a squat figure cloaked in black, his back bent and bearing a large misshapen hump beneath his filthy robes. Limping grotesquely, he followed Cael and Alynthia through the door and into the dark streets of Palanthas.

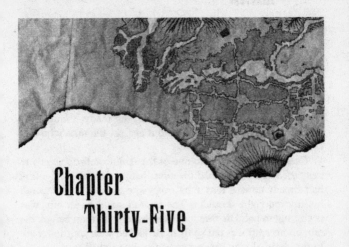

Chapter
Thirty-Five

ael lit a yellow candle from the coals still burning on the hearth, while Alynthia opened the library door a crack and peered out into the hall. The house was dark and silent, for everyone had long ago retired for the night, but there was a watchful feeling in the air. The master of the house was gone, and the servants lay abed listening for his return. It was a feeling Alynthia knew well, for often she had lain awake in this very house, listening for her husband's return. Besides, both thieves had burgled enough places to know when the house was sleeping and when its occupants lay nervously awake, listening to the creaking darkness.

In the distance came the rumble of thunder. The library window looked out over the rooftops of the city district known as Purple Ridge, out across the length and breadth of the city, toward the Bay of Branchala, where a storm brewed over the iron-dark sea. Slowly the stars along the northern horizon winked out, eclipsed by the boiling clouds.

Cael silently closed the window's shutters. Since he had broken the shutters gaining entry to the library, he used a strip of golden cloth torn from the curtain to tie them firm. Alynthia eased the library door shut, satisfied that none of the servants were up and about. She didn't sheath her dagger. Her husband had not survived so long nor become so powerful by walking blindly into traps. She wanted a dagger ready, though she wasn't yet sure if she could wield it against the man who had shared her bed.

Cael eased himself into one of the large comfortable chairs near the fire and warmed his boots before the coals. Alynthia had already noticed that in his every movement, the elf favored his injured right shoulder. The wound she'd given him was beginning to tell. His face looked a shade paler than before, his grip on his staff was not so firm. He looked weary, sitting there in the chair. Slowly his eyes closed and he sighed.

Alynthia was no better for her experiences earlier in the evening. She'd already nearly been drowned and exploded into bits by dragon breath, but the event that drained her the worst was learning of her husband's treachery. Her stomach was twisted into knots, her anger burned like hot coals in her heart. She paced the floor restlessly, her booted feet swishing across the thick carpet that covered the library floor.

Cael opened one eye to observe her. The knuckles of her hand, clenched round her dagger, were pale and bloodless, her jaw muscles stood out, quivering. Her eyes seemed sunken into her dusky face, giving her a haunted look, and the bluish tinge had returned to her lips. He started to rise to go to her, but the moment of relaxation he'd allowed himself had given his shoulder time to stiffen. Instead, he stumbled as he tried to rise and caught himself painfully and noisily against the library's mahogany desk. Both thieves froze at the sound, listening for any reaction from below. For the moment, the house remained silent.

"What are you trying to do, you fool!" Alynthia hissed. She shook her dagger at him like a long admonishing finger.

"I thought I would search his desk," Cael responded lamely.

"Well, try to be more quiet about it. The servants are not the typical spineless, witless peasants so often found in servile positions. Many are retired thieves and adventurers. Our butler is a fiend with a short bow."

The elf glared at her for a moment, until she spun on her heel and resumed her worried pacing. Cael turned his attention to the desk.

First and foremost, the desk was heavy and compact, marvelously compartmentalized. More than likely, it had once been the desk of the captain of a ship, for there was no wasted space either atop or beneath it. Deep wells in the corners held ink bottles and long quills. Other troughs on the desk's surface originally must have served the purpose of holding navigational compasses and rules to keep them from sliding around in heavy seas. Now they contained an assortment of sugar candies. Cael popped a chewy orange one in his mouth and savored the flavor. Alynthia shot an annoyed look at him at the smacking noises he was making but said nothing.

Down one side of the desk were an assortment of cubbyholes, where rolled maps detailing every shore and major river of Krynn were still stowed. It was a kender's delight. Cael turned his attention to the drawers. They were, of course, locked.

He felt along all the desk's edges for a release, and, finding none, turned to an examination of the bottom of the desk. There he found a small throwing dagger in a leather sheath tacked to the underside, nicely placed within easy reach of anyone sitting behind the desk. He tucked the dagger into his belt and continued his search.

He couldn't find the drawer key anywhere. Probably, Oros kept the key on his person, so Cael settled down to trying to break into the lock instead. It was a simple lock, with a simple enough poison needle trap, which made him extremely suspicious as to what he hadn't detected. As a rather famous thief once said, "Why even bother putting such a simple lock on a door"—or a desk? He bent closer, trying to spot the real trap, but if there was one, it was beyond him to find out. He stood up, frustrated, glowering at the desk.

"What's the matter?" Alynthia asked.

"Nothing," the elf said.

The only other thing of interest on the desk was a fist-sized river stone onto which a simple childish picture had been painted in crude red lines. The picture was of a ship at sea. At the sterncastle wheel stood a large man, while at the prow danced what appeared to be a girl. Cael picked it up and turned it over. There, scrawled in awkward letters, were the words,

> *The Mary Eileen*
> *For Captain Avaril*
> *on his day of life-gift*
> *from Alynthia*

Cael smiled, hefting the stone and judging its weight. He was of a mind to use it to bash open the drawers, but then he noticed the scrap of yellow paper atop which the stone had rested. It was a bill of transport from the Carters' Guild, dated this very day.

"This is curious," Cael whispered.

Alynthia turned. "Leave that alone," she snapped. "I made it for him when I was nine."

"Not this," Cael said, setting aside the stone. He lifted the bill. "This."

"What is it?" Alynthia asked.

"A bill of transport, for stonecutting tools to be delivered to *Dark Horizon* tonight at Darkwatch. What use has your husband for stonecutting tools?" he asked.

Alynthia did not immediately respond. Her face grew thoughtful, and she paused in her pacing. Suddenly, she sheathed her dagger. "None," she said. "But 'stonecutting tools' is an old Guild codeword for treasures. Treasures, mind you, not ordinary loot or the proceeds of everyday Guild business. Oros must be putting Guild treasures aboard his ship."

"I think we know why," Cael said, grimly reminded of the Guild captain's treachery.

"I wonder which treasures," Alynthia mused.

"Perhaps we should go see," the elf offered with a smile.

"Perhaps we should. Perhaps that's where he is now."

Alynthia hurried to the window and tore aside the loose strip of curtain that Cael had used to tie the shutters. A cold gust of wind from the approaching storm blew the shutters open with a loud bang. Alynthia leaped though, the elf closely following her.

Behind them, a moment later, the library door swung open. Oros uth Jakar stood there, glowering. Behind him stood an elderly man in his nightshirt, a short bow clenched in his fist. Oros glanced quickly around the room, eyeing first the open window, then spotting the missing bill of transport. The breeze blowing through the window stirred his hair, but it also seemed to stoke the fires of anger burning in his eyes. At the same time, it snuffed out the yellow candle on the desk and sent sparks crackling up the chimney.

Oros turned to his butler. "Wake Kolav," he growled. The man nodded and hurried away.

Behind him, a distant flash of lightning briefly illuminated a short, hunchbacked figure lurking at the window. As though sensing eyes upon him, Oros spun. The next lightning flash came soon after and showed the window empty, the shutters flapping in the rising wind.

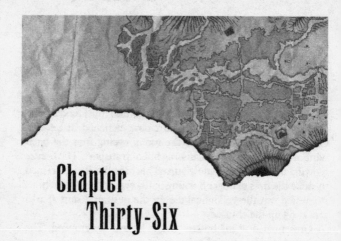

Chapter Thirty-Six

For the second time this night, a pier stretched before them, walled on either side by the hulls of ships, while overhead swayed naked masts. Ropes sang, lashed by wind and spray. A single lantern at the far end of the pier provided an eerie, wavering illumination; all the other lanterns along the pier had failed to survive the first gusts of the storm. By the light of that one distant lantern, the two thieves saw that the crates that were once piled beside *Dark Horizon* had been loaded. The ship now rode the rising swells, lashed securely to the pier by stout ropes.

Cael and Alynthia crept warily along the pier. The night seemed short. Though storm clouds now hid and further darkened the sky, both felt that morning was nigh. With it would come unwelcome activity and watchful eyes. They hurried while trying to appear leisurely. As they neared the ship, Alynthia could no longer contain herself. She rushed along the pier, leaped up, and caught the ship's railing, timing her leap to meet the descent of a swell. She pulled herself onto the deck, then peered over the rail at the elf.

"I can't do that, Alynthia," Cael said. "My shoulder."

She nodded once, then stooped to look for something. A moment later, a rope ladder uncurled down the side of the hull. Cael caught it. After passing his staff up to Alynthia, he pulled himself by one arm up the heavily swaying side of the ship.

They picked their way across the heaving middeck as the first heavy drops of rain splattered around them. The ship was battened down against the storm, showing that the night watch was aboard somewhere. Alynthia led the way among coiled ropes and stowed rigging to the sterncastle, where a narrow ornate door signified the entrance to the captain's cabin. She paused before it and drew her dagger. Cael looked around to make sure no one had spotted them. It seemed the watchman was safely below decks. Alynthia opened the door and slipped into the cabin. The small, orderly chamber was dark, lit in somber gold by lightning flashes through the horn-paned starboard windows. She quickly lit a whale oil lamp fastened to the wall above the bed. Cael stepped inside and closed the door as a storm wave lifted the ship, sending him staggering painfully into the wall.

On the floor beside the bed stood several large sea chests, one made of rich teak bound with silver and iron, the other two of thick leather with bronze fittings. Alynthia nodded at Cael. He looked at her wearily, then moved to the door to keep watch.

Alynthia knelt by the largest of the three chests and fingered its heavy lock, then took from a pouch at her belt a leather wallet of lockpicking tools. She unrolled it on the floor and chose a braided wire and an octagonal probe. While the deck lurched beneath her, she worked the tools into the lock, prying, probing, turning. Her lips compressed in concentration, all else fading from her notice. Not even the growing roar of the storm intruded upon her. She listened closely for the satisfying click that would announce success.

Her skill told at last, and the lock parted. She tore it free and cast it aside, and with a victorious glance at the elf, opened the chest's hinged lid.

A cloud of hissing yellow gas boiled into her face. She coughed once and reeled away, toppling onto the floor.

Hearing the warning hiss, Cael had torn open the door before he even saw the danger. A violent wind swirled through the chamber, dashing out the lamp, as the sickly yellow gas rose up wraithlike and was dispersed by the wind. The elf lunged to Althynia's side and lifted her under one arm.

Cael dragged her onto the rain-lashed deck. He rolled her over, pressed two fingers to her neck. A weak pulse struggled there but one which grew stronger with each breath of clean sea air. A flash of lightning revealed her eyelids flickering as she fought to regain consciousness.

Probably only her natural quickness had saved her life, Cael guessed. Oros had set a deadly trap on that chest. Finally satisfied that she would recover, he returned to the door. By the storm's glare, he saw that the chest was still open. He lurched into the room, reached a hand into the chest, and stumbled back to the deck clutching something metal and gleaming.

He collapsed beside Alynthia and examined the object. It was a dragon, not much larger than a cat, expertly wrought in gleaming silver. The figure reared on its hind legs, wings spread, head thrown back to scream at the sky. Tiny sapphire eyes burned beneath hooded lids, talons of carved yellow ivory clawed at the air. In the belly of the creature, he noticed, there was a latched and hinged door. Cael opened it gingerly.

A flash of lightning illuminated a grinning brown skull seated on black velvet in the hollow belly of the artifact. Beside the skull lay a Solamnic rose, red as the day it was cut.

"That's it," Alynthia lifted her head to say.

"What is it?" Cael asked, suppressing for the moment his delight at seeing her alive and alert.

"The Reliquary," she said as she pawed weakly at the treasure.

"What is it? Why is this so special?" Cael asked.

"It is our greatest achievement, our greatest theft, said to be stolen from the gods themselves during the Age of Might." She sighed, falling back weakly against the rain slick deck. "The bones are the bones of—"

"Alynthia!" a voice roared behind them.

Cael spun, clutching the Reliquary beneath his robe.

Oros uth Jakar stood before them, legs braced against the surging of the ship. The storm increased suddenly, sheets of rain pounding from prow to stern. Looming behind the Guild captain, the huge, monstrous form of the minotaur, Kolav Ru-Marn, leaned against the larboard rail. He shook his heavy horned head, water spraying from his ears and thick reddish-brown fur.

"Alynthia, what have you done?" Oros cried furiously.

"What have *you* done, my husband?" she gasped.

"Your treachery is revealed, Captain," the elf snarled.

The color faded from the Guildmaster's face. His eyes shifted from the elf to his wife. She glared at him, contempt burning in her dark eyes. The strength seemed to drain from his limbs, his head sank, and Oros turned away.

"Kill them," he said heavily to the minotaur. "Kill them both." He staggered to the rail and leaned against it.

"I've been longing for this day," Kolav growled, as he drew his massive gleaming tulwar, the giant curved blade of the minotaur-wrought sword screaming from its sheath. Long used to battle at sea, Kolav moved with ease across the storm-tossed deck of the ship, his steps thundering louder than the storm itself.

The elf remained half in a crouch, for it was the only way he could be sure of his footing. He pulled his staff close against his body and, running his free left hand down its length, revealed his magic blade.

Kolav roared with laughter. "Magic blades will do you little good. I am the finest sword in all of Krynn."

"I tell you again that, no, I am the finest," Cael countered, but he knew his boast was hollow. The wound in his shoulder had stiffened his right arm to the point where he could barely move it. He could fight left-handed—he'd been trained thoroughly by his *shalifi*—but against the mighty minotaur he stood little chance in his present condition.

The beast shook his huge bull's head, water spraying from his ears and fur and streaming from his gleaming black horns. Cael gripped the silver dragon closer against his body and rose onto one knee, his sword held on guard.

Alynthia cried out, "Oros, don't do this."

Oros uth Jakar merely shook his head, never even turning to glance at his doomed wife.

Kolav leaped at Cael, horns flashing. The elf managed to roll aside. Kolav lunged after him, stepping over the prone form of the female captain of thieves. With a cry, Alynthia rose up and sank her dagger into the monster's thigh.

Kolav bellowed in pain and turned. Cael's blade flashed before his black snout, then raked down, shearing though leather armor and reddish fur to shave the belly of the brute. Another inch and his bowels would have run across the deck. The elf swore and barely ducked the minotaur's return swipe.

Now the minotaur roared in rage and came leaping after him. Cael parried with every ounce of strength, striking aside the minotaur's heavy curved blade at the last instant, time and time again. Each movement weakened him, while the minotaur seemed to grow stronger, seeing his opponent stumble and stagger under the rain of blows.

The battle raged around the mainmast fore and aft. Kolav's sword took chip after chip from the mast's hard timber as Cael used it as both shield and foil. Brute strength battled unrivaled training in the sword and its tactics, but even the elf could do nothing more than forestall his doom.

The minotaur began to limp more acutely from the wound in his leg. His attacks grew more savage. His tulwar flashed and stabbed relentlessly. The minotaur handled it as easily as a fencing foil. His leg wound, though, stopped him from lunging. The elf took advantage of this, staying just out of reach, and by attacking the minotaur on the side of his wound. Alynthia's thrust had bought him that little advantage. He only hoped he had the strength left to capitalize on it.

The storm mounted in fury. The ship began to slam against the pier. Again and again, just when the minotaur seemed to have cornered the elf, the ship lurched, forcing him to pause and allowing the elf to dodge. Finally, Kolav could bear no more injury to his pride. With a bellowing roar, he rushed across the deck, timing his charge to a mounting wave. In his weariness, Cael didn't move in time. The ship's deck rose up behind the beast. His charge became more of an onrushing fall, and Cael staggered back against the rail, unable to avoid the inevitable collision.

With a triple report the ship's moorings broke. The ship righted itself suddenly, sending the minotaur sprawling and flipping Cael backward over the rail and onto the pier. Alynthia had crawled across the slick deck and was poised to follow, but her husband caught her by the wrist and dragged her back.

Kolav regained his footing and vaulted after the elf. Cael was nowhere to be seen. The minotaur peered between the dock and the ship but saw nothing other than broken bits of wood. All along the pier now men shouted from the decks of ships, while sailors worked to secure moorings, and ropes snapped and went writhing into the air like aroused serpents. And at the shore end of the pier, a cloaked figure was running, a gleaming sword in his fist. The minotaur bellowed a battle cry and limped after him.

Captain Oros glared at his wife, but she returned his gaze with a black accusing stare.

"Now you will have to kill me yourself, my husband," she spat.

"No, I won't. The Guild will do it for me," he returned. He dragged her across the deck to his cabin door. The contents of the room had been tossed about when the ship's moorings broke. The sea chest lay open on its side. "You are a traitor to the Guild and you will suffer the punishment you richly deserve," he snarled as he heaved her inside.

She fell on the floor. Pain twisted her face, but anger fought for control. She jerked the empty chest upright. "It is not I who betrayed the Guild!" she cried. "Cael has the Reliquary as proof!"

Oros staggered back, clutching at the door. He slammed it shut, locked it quickly, then rushed forward shouting orders to the frightened, sleepy-eyed crew of the *Dark Horizon* as they stumbled from their forecastle quarters, at last aroused by the commotion.

The storm was tearing the ship and the pier apart.

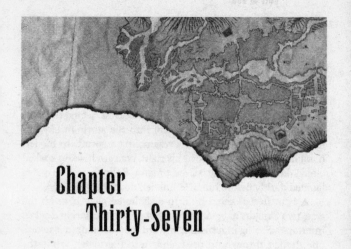

Chapter
Thirty-Seven

Leaning into the wind against the lashing rain, Cael scuttled across the wide empty cobbles between two towering warehouses. His cloak rippled out behind him, and lightning streaked across the sky, arcing explosively over rooftops, spires, and trees.

He crossed Fishmonger's Street and paused at the entrance to Palisade Lane, looking back. The constant lightning flashes showed him the jerky progress of his limping pursuer. Cael was weary down to his bones, but a grim determination drove him onward.

He dashed under the relative protection of Palisade Lane's balconies. For a moment, he considered hiding in the shadows here, in the mad hope that the minotaur might pass him by, but he knew better than to trust his luck. He hurried along, reaching the street's end where it met Horizon Road. There he heard the minotaur bellow and, glancing back, he saw to his dismay that the distance between them had been halved.

Cael's one thought was to somehow circle back the *Dark Horizon*, while at the same time losing the minotaur in the twisting streets of night-darkened Palanthas. He knew that the best place to lose him was Smith's Alley. He turned onto Horizon Road, headed for the gate there, beyond which lay the northern entrance to that noisome lane.

Now for the last leg of this race, he thought, seeing the massive gate towers rising before him into the storm-lit sky. He forced himself into something resembling a sprint. In his left hand he carried his sword, in his right, beneath his rain-soaked cloak, he clutched the silver dragon Reliquary. The gates loomed darkly before him. He hurried down the road.

A light flared before him. In a sheltered glow beneath the gate, two Knights of Neraka warily observed the darkly cloaked interloper. Seeing him rushing toward them with drawn sword, one dashed through an open door into the tower, while the other drew his blade and prepared to meet the elf's charge. A bell clanged somewhere above. Down the short gate tunnel, more torches flared as Knights poured from the guardhouse built on the New City side of the gate.

Cael slowed, but upon hearing the familiar roar behind him, he renewed his pace. The young guard performed a Knight's salute, and in that foolish moment, Cael veered through the open tower door.

His dash surprised the guard. The man fumbled at his sword, gaping at the elf, who vaulted up the tower stairs. The Knight started after him, but a cry of pain brought him around. Before the young man could raise his sword in defense, Kolav burst into the chamber and in one slash of his massive sword cut him down.

Cael reached the first landing of the stair and paused. He glanced quickly around, seeing that the stair continued upward, vanishing in the shadows above. To his left was a stout wooden door, barred from the inside. He knocked the bar free, kicked open the door, and dived through.

Once through the doorway, Cael found himself atop the city wall. There was nowhere else to run. To his left he was offered a plunge of thirty feet or more to the nearest rooftops, to his right a crenellated battlement overlooked the trench between the inner and outer wall. The trench was filled with soft dirt turned to deep mud by the violent autumn storm. Ahead, the wall curved gently to the south in the direction of the Temple Row gate, where more Knights of Neraka waited. Behind him, the tower door burst open. Kolav ducked through and strode out onto the rain-lashed parapet. Lightning illuminated his monstrous form. His tulwar dripped with the blood of the man he'd just slain.

"I barred the door below so that we should receive no more interruptions," the beast growled as he limped toward the elf. From somewhere below, Cael heard the Knights pounding on the tower door and yelling angrily. He backed along the wall, keeping his naked blade at guard while carefully watching his footing.

"It is time we settled this, you and I," Kolav continued. His tulwar whistled through the air above his head.

"Indeed," Cael agreed. Everything depended on one perfectly timed, perfectly placed lunge. He released his hold on the Reliquary, letting it fall from his cloak. It landed at his feet.

A deep growl rumbled from the minotaur. "A thief to the last, I see," he said.

Cael readied himself. Kolav limped closer. Another wary step, another.

"No longer can you hide behind that beard," Kolav said. "I shall cut out your heart and eat it raw."

Cael lunged. His sword sang through the air. Kolav blocked the attack and trapped Cael's sword against the crenellated wall with his own weighty blade. A sledgelike fist sent the elf sprawling back dangerously near the parapet's edge. His sword flew from his hand, slid a few feet over the rain-slick stone, then toppled over the edge. The clang of steel against stone below sounded the death knell.

Cael struggled to his feet. He drew the throwing dagger from his belt, the one he'd stolen from Oros's desk. The minotaur advanced upon him, relentless as the sea's tide.

In a flash of lightning, Cael saw a hunched figure on the

parapet behind Kolav. It held something in its hand, something raised to throw. Cael's eyes widened in surprise, and seeing his reaction, Kolav half-turned to confront the new threat.

It was too late. With a fierce cry of "Nevermind!" the figure launched its weapon. A smooth metallic cube it appeared to be, but as it flew, it unfolded in the air. Kolav threw up his hands in defense, to no avail.

The minotaur staggered back, clutching at the hideous steel spider affixed to his horned head. He bellowed in agony as, with a sickening rending noise, his flesh and sinew struggled against springs of steel and levers of tempered iron. One black horn tore free from his skull, firmly gripped in the metal spider's jaws. Kolav screamed as blood gushed over his face.

With a flick of the wrist, Cael sent his dagger winging to lodge in the beast's throat. Kolav staggered, clutched at the dagger, then toppled backward over the parapet wall. Thirty feet below there was a dull crunch as the minotaur landed in the muddy trench. Slowly he sank, the black mud sucking him down, as he clawed weakly at the wall. In moments, he was gone.

Cael reeled, exhausted, and fell into the waiting arms of his rescuer. A stench more vile than any he had ever encountered greeted him.

"Gimzig!" he cried. "How can it be? You are alive?"

"Of course I am alive, no thanks to the gully dwarves who found me, I nearly died under their gentle ministrations," the gnome answered. "You've grown a beard, it looks superb on you, I never could abide those abominable, youthfully smooth cheeks, nothing like a proper beard to give you a certain nobility. . . ."

"But how, Gimzig? Alynthia saw you dragged away by a sewer monster! How did you survive?" Cael asked as he clutched his small friend.

"I'll tell you, but first let's get down from here, I do enjoy the view, but this is no place for the telling of tales, just follow me, I have a self-extending ladder just over . . . oh dear!"

The tower door slowly swung open. A gray-robed figure

The Thieves' Guild

strode out onto the lightning-lit battlements, a long straight sword in its fist. Cael gasped, recognizing it as his own sword.

"Thank you for returning the staff, Cael Ironstaff," the Thorn Knight laughed. "It makes a truly marvelous sword. I shall enjoy exploring its powers." He tossed the sword playfully into the air.

Cael pushed the Reliquary into the gnome's grimy hands. "Stow this safely in your pack, Gimzig," he whispered.

The gnome nodded. "Let me handle this chap," he muttered as he slid his pack to the ground and opened it. He reached inside, removing another of his folded spiders.

"No," the elf said, shaking his head. "This is between Arach Jannon and me."

"Now we shall finally discover who is the better man," the Thorn Knight said calmly.

"You have the advantage of me, however," Cael said.

"Ah, yes. You lack a sword. Never fear. I am an honorable man."

Sir Arach drew a short stabbing sword from its hip sheath and slid it across the battlement to the elf. Cael stooped and lifted it, testing its weight and feel in his left hand.

"Not much of a match against that," Cael commented, pointing at his own sword.

"No, I suppose not," the Thorn Knight answered. He swung the blade, whistling, through the air. "It is wonderfully balanced, sharp as a witch's tongue. Too good for the likes of you, I'm afraid."

"We shall see," Cael said as he advanced slowly across the battlement, the short sword held before him.

"Yes, we shall," Sir Arach said with a laugh as he charged. He lifted the sword over his head and brought it crashing down. Cael deflected it, then used his injured shoulder to press the Thorn Knight against the wall. They struggled there for a moment, growling, spitting curses at one another, before Cael leaped away.

Sir Arach spun to attack again, then caught sight of the weapon in his hand. It was his own short sword! Returned to his hand as though by magic. The elf's sword, once firmly in his grasp . . . ? He looked up, stunned, to find it back in Cael's hand. The Thorn Knight backed away, a spell forming on his lips, but in a lunge too quick for the eye to follow, Cael's blade split him from shoulder to hip. The short sword fell from nerveless fingers, the spell died on his lips. Sir Arach fell in a heap at Cael's feet, a look of surprise frozen on his face.

Gimzig rushed to the elf's side and helped him to stand. Cael collapsed against the wall. He clutched his bloody sword to his chest.

The gnome lifted the Thorn Knight's body onto his stout shoulders and shoved it over the battlement. Arach Jannon's corpse landed in an awkward sprawl atop the deep mud between the city walls. Slowly, the mud devoured him.

* * * * *

As the new day dawned, Palanthas came out to inspect the damage caused by the storm. Here and there in the Bay of Branchala a ship or galley listed to one side. Their crews were busy pumping seawater from their holds and mending the damages to their rigging and hulls. The cobblestones of Bayside Street were littered with flotsam, seaweed, and puddled foam. Tiny white-and-blue crabs scuttled underfoot, trying to find their way back to the safety of the water, while gulls chased after them, occasionally dueling each other over some particularly choice bit of the bounty of the sea.

Two figures strode wearily along the waterfront. One figure leaned heavily on a tall black staff. His much shorter companion limped along beside him, his misshapen back bent. The tall one spoke in hushed tones, the other chattered volubly in response to his companion's questions.

"Well, as a matter of fact the sewer monster did bite off my foot in the first attack," the gnome said in response to an earlier question. "She took me down for a death roll, but my bones weren't strong enough, my foot came off in her mouth and she swam away, as you can imagine I was in a terrible fix as I had all those heavy metallic devices in my pack dragging me to the bottom of the sewer, and my foot down the gullet of the beast, when what do you know . . . she came back to finish me off!"

The gnome paused for a breath. "She attacked me from behind again, I tell you it was like being rammed in the backside by a minotaur pirate galley, but this time she clamped down on my pack instead of me, lucky thing too, well, you know the delicate nature of the things back there, crikey, but there was a tremendous poing, and then a sharp tug brought me up short, blood, guts, and I don't know what else flowed around me, and what did I see but my own foot go floating by my own nose. I tried to catch it but . . .; here we are, this is where you said *Dark Horizon* was moored." They mounted the steps as Gimzig continued.

"As I was saying I tried to grab it, but it was already out of my reach, and something was holding me firmly in the water, I looked back over my shoulder, and what do you think had happened?"

Cael would have ventured a guess, if the gnome hadn't talked on unabated. "The self-extending ladder, or laddapult as I call it, extended right through the sides of the pack inside the monster's mouth and ripped her clean in half like a loaf of bread. One side was pinned to one wall of the sewer and the other side pinned to the other and, crikey, but I was in an even worse spot than before. Let me tell you I nearly drowned before I was able to wriggle free of my pack.

"I nearly died anyway under the indelicate care of the gully dwarves who found me, a pox on all aghar and their fumbling ministrations, it is a wonder I survived them. I think I might have fared better in the belly of the beast!"

"But you lost your foot."

"Mechanical one," the gnome grinned through the mat of his beard. He wiggled his booted foot for the elf to see. It creaked. "This one needs oil but it's better than the original in many ways and I have several ideas for further improvement, detachable toes for one thing, and . . ."

Cael smiled and looked up, but his smile quickly faded. Gimzig followed his gaze, his voice trailing away.

Dark Horizon was gone.

Cael stared at the empty mooring for a long while, his face grim. The gnome shook his head in dismay.

"Gimzig," Cael said at last. "Can you get me back into Thieves' House?"

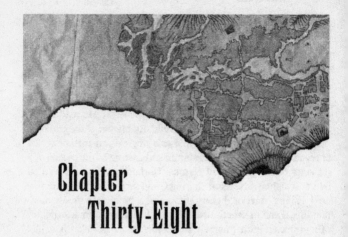

Chapter Thirty-Eight

Alynthia stood before them, her head sagging against her chest, tears of frustration streaming down her face. A tight gag muted her sobs, and her arms were bound cruelly behind her back. Her seven fellow Guild captains glared silently at her across the dimly lit room. The pale-eyed captain from Sancrist wore a grin of triumph, while sadness etched the features of the raven-tressed Abanasinian captain.

Alynthia cared little what the others thought. What broke her heart most was the man sitting directly before her.

"Shall we begin?" Oros uth Jakar asked.

They stood in the same high vaulted room where Cael had been judged and doomed. Captain Oros sat upon his thronelike seat, his back rigid, hands tightly gripping the arms of the chair. To his immediate right stood an empty chair that had once belonged to Alynthia, to his left was the dark alcove where shadows brooded. Alynthia glanced up into that black niche, feeling the customary presence, a pair of unseen eyes that burned her with their gaze. Or did she see something else? She blinked, wondering if a shift in the deep shadows of the alcove were not a trick of the dim light.

"What are the charges?" asked a voice from the alcove. She shuddered involuntarily.

Slowly and with a show of reluctance, Oros removed a roll of parchment from his breast pocket and opened it. He read aloud, "Disobeying a direct order of the Guild. Endangering the Guild by needlessly risking capture while carrying out an unsanctioned entry into the dungeons of Palanthas. Assisting in the escape of a prisoner of the Knights of Neraka. Harboring a fugitive wanted by the Knights of Neraka. Sharing Guild secrets with the uninitiated. Failing to report her activities and location in a timely manner. Illegal and unsanctioned entry, theft, and wanton destruction of a protected entity, namely the Lord's Palace of Palanthas. Illegal and unsanctioned entry of a Guild property on two occasions, namely my own abode, as well as the ship *Dark Horizon*. And the most serious charge of all—aiding and assisting in the escape of a freelance thief under interdict by the Guild."

He rolled up the parchment and slipped it back into his pocket.

"These are indeed serious charges," Mulciber intoned from the shadowy alcove. "We have been sorely disappointed in the actions of Captain Alynthia Krath-Mal. She knew full well our temper concerning this elf, and bore with her the price of his doom should she allow him to escape. That she aided in his escape and that her action indirectly cost us the life of one of our most beloved members, the minotaur Kolav Ru-Marn, pains us. She has forsaken her duty to us, and we cannot forgive her."

There followed a long grave silence.

Mulciber continued, "Since she has been found guilty of these crimes, she is not allowed to speak in her own defense. Will no one now rise and say a word in her favor, before I pronounce her doom?"

No one budged. Alynthia looked into the faces of her fellow captains and saw each turn quickly away. They know, she thought. They know and they say nothing. They are afraid.

Her gaze settled on her husband. She wanted to be looking

into his eyes when Mulciber pronounced her sentence.

"Very well. It is the command of the Eighth Circle that Alynthia Krath-Mal should die," said the voice from the alcove.

Alynthia tried to break free and rush at her husband, screaming unintelligible curses through her gag. Her guards easily caught her and dragged her back.

She'd seen his lips move. As she had gazed intently at her husband and listened to her sentence, she had seen his lips move ever so slightly, forming the words that Mulciber spoke!

Oros rose from his chair, and said with a voice choked with grief, "Take her away."

Mulciber spoke again from the alcove, halting the guards before they'd reached the door with their prisoner. The cracking, ambiguous voice seemed changed somehow, less old and weary, less like stone grating against stone.

"As master of the Guild I exercise my right to commute the sentence of this woman."

All but the captain from Sancrist leaped up in delight at these words. Oros spun and faced the alcove, his eyes narrow slits of alarmed suspicion. "What trick is this?" he growled.

A figure stepped from the shadowed alcove. A gasp went up from the gathered thieves. Not one of them had ever actually seen their dread leader. But he appeared exactly as they had always imagined him—ebon robed and heavily cowled, leaning on a staff as black and mysterious as himself. The hand that gripped the staff was pale and long fingered but looked young and strong. As one, the Guild captains fell groveling on the floor. Alynthia's guards released her and joined their leaders in prostrating themselves. Only Oros remained standing, Alynthia behind him, dumbfounded.

"What is more," Mulciber said from his hood. "I accuse you, Sir Oros uth Jakar, disgraced Knight of the Rose, of betrayal, subterfuge, and obfuscation."

"Get up, you lot of fools!" Oros shouted at the others. "This isn't Mulciber. This is an impostor. It has to be!"

"Why must I be an impostor?" Mulciber asked. "He will not tell you, so I must." The Guild master drew back the cowl of his robe, revealing the pale red-bearded face of Cael Ironstaff.

"Because there is no Mulciber," the elf said.

With a scream of rage, Oros drew a dagger from his belt and rushed him. Cael easily parried the blow with his staff and sent Oros staggering backward.

The other Guild captains had regrouped. Half seemed indecisive, the others looked ready to attack the elf. Alynthia's guards scrambled up, hands nervously gripping their weapons but taking no further action, awaiting orders.

"It was you who betrayed the Guild to the Knights of Takhisis. Alynthia and I discovered Oros last night in league with the Lord Knight of the City and Arach Jannon," Cael said.

Angry mutterings sounded from the gathered Guild captains. Alynthia's guards shifted uncomfortably.

Oros, half recovered from his knock on the head, said thickly, "I was only acting under the orders of Mulciber."

"There is no Mulciber!" Cael shouted. "If Mulciber were real, would he allow me to impersonate him? Wasn't he just here pronouncing Captain Alynthia's doom, and didn't I just step from his alcove? Shouldn't he be striking me dead with his magic for my effrontery?" The elf turned dramatically to the dark alcove.

"Oh mighty Mulciber, if you are indeed real, strike me dead now," he said, bowing. Nothing happened.

The Guild captain from Abanasinia strode forward and pressed a dagger against Oros's throat.

"Captain Wolfheart, what are you doing?" Oros cried.

"You would have slain your own wife to protect yourself," she snarled. "Release that woman!" she barked at the guards.

Alynthia found herself free. The guards left the room in silence.

When they had gone, the swarthy captain from Tarsis said, "I still don't understand. Who, then, is Mulciber?"

"A creation," Cael said. "A fiction perpetrated on you by this man. He used Mulciber to lead the Guild while pretending to be one of the Guildmaster's trusted servants. That way he risked nothing but gained all the benefits of being the leader of the Guild."

"How did this come to pass?" the Tarsian asked.

Alynthia spoke up. "Who besides my husband survived the Night of Black Hammers?"

"Petrovius, and 'He we do not name,' " Captain Wolfheart said.

"Petrovius, bless him, wouldn't doubt you if you told him I was queen of the sea. He couldn't tell you what he ate for breakfast," Alynthia said. "He lives in the distant past, and his mind is sound there, but he would repeat anything Oros told him as truth. Why would he have reason to doubt him? Oros saved his life by hiding him in the dwarven ruins. And why? Because Petrovius knew all the Guild treasures.

"And as for 'He we do not name,'" Alynthia continued. "I doubt Davvyd Nelgaard survived the Night of Black Hammers."

"Apparently my husband has a long history of betrayal," she said coldly as she turned to the man who had been her childhood hero, who had shared her marital bed, who had come within a hair's breadth of becoming her executioner. "He was cast from the Knights of Solamnia for betrayal. He abandoned the crew of the *Mary Eileen* to save himself. He betrayed the old Guild in exchange for treasures he coveted. When he learned what Solamnic relics the Guild possessed, he plotted to steal them, as well as to gain control of the Guild and reshape it to his own designs."

"Lies, all lies!" Oros cried. "I cannot believe—"

Captain Wolfheart's dagger pressed deeper into his throat, starting a trickle of blood and silencing his protests.

"What proof have you?" the captain from Sancrist asked.

"Only this," Cael said as he pulled aside his cloak. Beneath it, couched in the cradle of his arm, lay the cat-sized silver dragon Reliquary.

"Beyond our grasp," Alynthia said. "Because it was my husband who had it all along. We found it aboard *Dark Horizon* last night."

She took the Reliquary from the elf and handed to her fellow thieves, holding it out so that each might approach and reverently touch it. Oros squirmed under the threat of Captain Wolfheart's dagger, glaring at the elf.

"You threw it all away," the disgraced captain whispered to
Cael. "You and I could have done much together."

"I think not," Cael said. "You were more right about me
than you know."

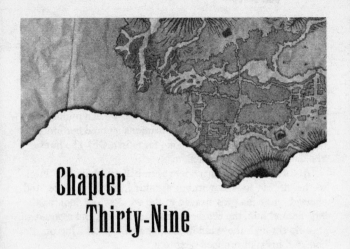

Chapter
Thirty-Nine

"Supper is ready!" Claret shouted from the kitchen. She backed through the door, balancing a heavy crockery tureen on a thick pad while carrying a loaf of bread under each arm. Cael followed her with bowls, plates, knives and spoons piled in the crook of his good arm. The other was wrapped in a clean white sling.

Alynthia slid into one of the chairs and tucked a napkin into the collar of her loose silk blouse. "Smells delicious," she commented as Claret eased the soup tureen to the table.

"It should be. It's an original elven recipe," the girl said.

"Elves!" Alynthia scowled. "I'll bet its full of leaves and twigs."

Claret took the bowls and plates from Cael and stacked them beside the soup. "Sit down," she ordered. "I'm serving." The elf gratefully sank into a chair.

"As a matter of fact, elves don't eat leaves and twigs," Claret continued. "It has clams and lobster and fresh grouper, eel, squid, and octopus. The tomatoes were difficult to find, but I managed it."

"Indeed!" Alynthia said. "Tomatoes this late in the year! You are a marvel."

"That's what I tell everyone, but no one believes me. Gimzig says I'll make someone a wonderful wife someday." (This was for Cael.) "Or a first rate thief." (This was for Alynthia.)

She sighed when both her companions ignored her hints. "I hope I don't have to wait too long for either. Oh! The butter!" She dashed back to the kitchen.

Alynthia tore one of the loaves in half and handed a hunk to the elf. He took it without speaking, bit off a piece, and chewed while his eyes strayed to the window overlooking the bay. Behind him, the bedroom door stood open, and moonlight shining through the window illuminated a pack lying on the bed, and his staff propped next to it.

"You haven't changed your mind, have you?" Alynthia asked softly.

"No," he said. He looked at her, his sea-green eyes distant. "No, the Knights of Neraka are still hunting me," he continued. "Even though they think Arach Jannon and the minotaur fought and killed each other atop the city wall, I am still under the court's death sentence. Then there's Mistress Jenna."

"The Guild could protect you," she said, reaching a hand across the table to cover his. "I could protect you."

"Not forever," he said. "Remember, I am an elf. I will out-live you by several centuries. The Guild will not always be friendly to me." He thoughtfully stroked his bushy red beard, which reminded him of his dwarven friend, Kharzog Hammer-fell.

"There will always be a place within the Eighth Circle for you, as long as I am its master," Alynthia said.

"I have . . . questions, which need answering," Cael continued. "There are people I have not seen for many years. And I have hurt enough people here." He gazed at the kitchen door. They heard Claret banging among the pots and dishes. As though prompted by a terrible thought, he rose suddenly from his chair.

"In fact, I should go now," he said. He strode quickly to the bedroom and gathered his things.

"But . . . what about supper? Claret will be so disappointed," Alynthia whispered. "Please stay and eat, stay just a little longer, and then you can say goodbye."

"I can't say goodbye, not after what I cost her," Cael said. He hurried to the door. Alynthia followed and caught him before he could leave.

"You can't even say goodbye to me?" she asked.

"No," he said. "Please don't ask me to."

"Very well," she whispered huskily. "Will you return?"

"Some day," he said. "You'll take care of her in the meantime?"

Alynthia nodded. He pressed her hand for a moment, then turned and strode away. Alynthia watched him go. As he approached the end of the street, a squat figure appeared from the shadows and joined the elf. The figure turned and waved to Alynthia. She lifted her hand limply in farewell, but the elf never looked back. She closed the door and leaned against it.

Claret entered from the kitchen with a bowl of butter, glasses, and a jug of wine. She paused, seeing Alynthia at the door.

"He's already gone, isn't he?" she asked.

"Yes," Alynthia whispered.

"He'll be back," the girl said with perfect assurance. She set the butter and the glasses on the table.

"A wise woman once told me, 'Never trust the love of an elf. We grow old, while they remain forever young.'" Alynthia returned to the table and poured herself a glass of wine from the jug.

"Yes, but then again Cael is not of pure elven blood," Claret said.

Alynthia pondered this for a moment, then swallowed a sip of her wine. She smiled. "That soup smells delicious. Let's eat before it gets cold!"

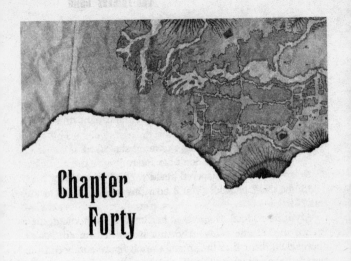

Chapter Forty

Mistress Jenna stepped down from the carriage, accepting the assistance of a black-armored Knight of Neraka. The road on which they had stopped was outside the city proper, high in the mountains west of Palanthas. The night was clear and crisp as the new-fallen snow that blanketed the cemetery beside the road. Nearby, a simple hut leaned beneath a tall out-cropping of rock, a warm glow in its only window proclaiming the occupant to be awake, despite the early hour.

The elder sorceress wore a fine pair of boots on her slender feet, boots enchanted to keep the wearer's feet warm in even the coldest weather. She also wore her heaviest winter robe, red velvet lined with snow-white ermine. Her companion wore the black armor of a Knight of the Lily, a black cloak lined with fox thrown over his broad shoulders. As they exited the carriage, the horses stomped and blew, their breath coming in great clouds that hung in the night air.

Across the way, the door of the hut opened, and a man exited, already cringing and fawning, a lantern dangling from his scrawny fist. As he drew near, there was a smell about him that made even the Dark Knight's nose wrinkle in disgust. The man reeked of his job, even though the ground had been frozen for two months and he hadn't buried a soul since the first day of the month of Darkember.

"Are we all here now?" the gravedigger fawned. "This way, m'lord and lady, this way. Hurry, we must. The sun is near to rising. A fine Yule morn, it'll be. You'll see it with the new light of the day." The Dark Knight waved the man on, dropping in behind him. Mistress Jenna walked at his side.

"This had better not be a fool's errand, Kinsaid," she whispered.

The Lord Knight of Palanthas merely scowled and continued on his way. Their path led among the gravestones. Though the gravedigger had his lamp, the starlight reflecting on the snow provided plenty of light to see by. The gravedigger stopped beside a headstone not unlike the thirty or so others around it.

"This is the dwarf section," the gravedigger whispered. "Many dwarves buried here, many generations of bones. Shhh, the sun! She comes!"

As though the thought of Nature's orb frightened the man who bought his bread with the coins of the dead, he slunk behind the headstone, trembling.

"Found it, I did," he hissed. "Yester morn. Even up here, we get news from the city, though few enough come this way, and those as do ain't likely to return." He cackled, much amused by his own cleverness. Jenna's dark glance put a damper on his mirth. He continued, "So I knowed it was important, knowed who to call."

Jenna turned to face the rising sun. The eastern sky had begun to gray. Far away across the deep bowl-shaped valley in which Palanthas lay, the sun crawled up behind the snow-capped Vingaard Mountains. She waited patiently, thankful for her boots, and wondered when was the last time she had watched a sunrise. She looked at the Dark Knight, and by his eternal scowl, she wondered if Sir Kinsaid ever had.

Finally, the sun appeared between two distant peaks, a watery orange globe promising little warmth. At its appearance, all eyes turned to the tall gravestone. Even in this light, they could see in inscription carved in the granite, though only Jenna could interpret the Dwarvish runes. They read:

Kharzog Hammerfell
Last of the Hammerfells of Palanthas
Faithful Friend
Slain in Battle
23 Fluergreen, 38 S.C.

Above this, in Elvish script that looked newly carved, were the words:

Even thirty generations is not too long to wait, old friend.

Set into the solid granite between the Elvish and the Dwarvish script was an oval stone as large as a goose's egg. Even in the dim light, its beauty was unmistakable. Translucent as the finest porcelain, gleaming with rainbows of color more glorious than mother of pearl, it was an opal beyond dreams of dwarven avarice.

The first rays of the newly risen sun struck the Founderstone, and a glowing, pinkish light welled forth. With a brilliant flash, a light like a star erupted from the stone. Shimmering cascades of sparks fell about the waterchers' feet and spilled across the snow. A gasp of awe and wonder escaped the three visitors, spellbound by the sight. A quiet music filled the air, like water leaping over stones.

"We thought the Founderstone beyond the reach of any thief," Sir Kinsaid whispered as he gazed at it. "When it disappeared three days ago, we believed it was gone forever—only to find it here, decorating the grave of some forgotten dwarf."

"Not just any dwarf," Jenna said, an unwanted smile on her face. "Obviously not forgotten."

"Thorn Knights tried to remove it yesterday, after we were alerted to its discovery," Sir Kinsaid continued.

"A fine reward it should fetch!" the gravedigger interjected hopefully.

"As you can see, they failed. They say it is affixed with sovereign glue. We hoped you might be able to free it," the Dark Knight said. "There would be a reward."

Jenna thoughtfully fingered the items and belongings in her pockets, eyeing the beautiful stone as its light flowed about her feet. In one pocket, her hand closed around a vial of universal solvent, the only known counteragent to magical sovereign glue.

Thinking it over, she shook her head. "It is beyond my power," Mistress Jenna said with a shrug. Sir Kinsaid turned away. Without a word of thanks, he stalked away, his cloak brushing the snow from the top of a nearby tombstone.

Jenna watched him go, then returned her gaze to the Founderstone. "I can think of no better place for it, *l'phae Tanthalas lu'ro*," she whispered.

The War of Souls

THE NEW EPIC SAGA FROM
MARGARET WEIS & TRACY HICKMAN

**The New York Times bestseller
—now available in paperback!**

Dragons of a Fallen Sun
The War of Souls • Volume I

Out of the tumult of a destructive
magical storm appears a mysterious
young woman, proclaiming the
coming of the One True God.
Her words and deeds erupt into
a war that will transform
the fate of Krynn.

Dragons of a Lost Star
THE WAR OF SOULS • VOLUME II

The war rages on…
A triumphant army of evil Knights
sweeps across Krynn and marches
against Silvanesti. Against the dark
tide stands a strange group of heroes:
a tortured Knight, an agonized mage,
an aging woman, and a small,
lighthearted kender in whose hands
rests the fate of all the world.

April 2001

New characters,
strange magic,
wondrous creatures.

ADVENTURE THROUGH THE HISTORY OF KRYNN
WITH THESE THREE NEW SERIES!

THE BARBARIANS
PAUL THOMPSON & TONYA CARTER COOK
Follow a divided brother and sister as they lead rival tribes of plainsmen
amidst the wonders and dangers of ancient Krynn.

Volume One: *Children of the Plains*
Volume Two: *Brother of the Dragon*
August 2001

THE ICEWALL TRILOGY
DOUGLAS NILES
Journey with an exiled elf to the harsh, legendary land known as Icereach,
where human tribes battle for life and ogres search to reclaim lost glories

Volume One: *The Messenger*
February 2001

THE KINGPRIEST TRILOGY
CHRIS PIERSON
Discover for the first time the dynastic history of the Kingpriest and how his
religious-political rule of Istar influenced the world of Dragonlance
for generations to come.

Volume One: *Chosen of the Gods*
November 2001

THE DHAMON SAGA
Jean Rabe

THE EXCITING BEGINNING TO THE DHAMON SAGA

— NOW AVAILABLE IN PAPERBACK!

Volume One: *Downfall*

HOW FAR CAN A HERO FALL? FAR ENOUGH TO LOSE HIS SOUL?

Dhamon Grimwulf, once a Hero of the Heart, has sunk into a bitter life of crime and squalor. Now, as the great dragon overlords of the Fifth Age coldly plot to strengthen their rule and destroy their enemies, he must somehow find the will to redeem himself.

Volume Two: *Betrayal*

All Dhamon Grimwulf wants is a cure for the painful dragon scale embedded in his leg. To find a cure, he must venture into the treacherous realm of a great black dragon. Along the way, Dhamon discovers some horrible truths: betrayal is worse than death, and there is something more terrifying on Krynn than even a dragon overlord.

June 2001

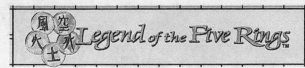

The Phoenix
Stephen D. Sullivan

The five Elemental Masters—
the greatest magic-wielders of
Rokugan—seek to turn back the
demons of the Shadowlands.
To do so, they must harness the
power of the Black Scrolls, and
perhaps become demons
themselves.

March 2001

The Dragon
Ree Soesbee

The most mysterious of all the clans of
Rokugan, the Dragon had long stayed
elusive in their mountain stronghold.
When at last they emerge into the Clan
War, they unleash a power that could
well save the empire . . . or doom it.

September 2001

The Crab
Stan Brown

For a thousand years, the Crab have
guarded the Emerald Empire against
demon hordes—but when the
greatest threat comes from within, the
Crab must ally with their fiendish foes
and march to take the
capital city.

June 2001

The Lion
Stephen D. Sullivan

Since the Scorpion Coup, the Clans of
Rokugan have made war upon each
other. Now, in the face of Fu Leng
and his endless armies of demons,
the Seven Thunders must band
together to battle their immortal
foe...or die!

November 2001